CHANDA'S AWAKENING

DAVE CREEK

Hydra
Publications

ISBN: 978-1-942212-87-4

Hydra Publications
Goshen, Kentucky 40026
www.hydrapublications.com

To Lee Pennington, who led the way.

CHAPTER 1

Both shuttles with the wounded highlanders on board were coming in hot. Triage teams rushed toward the landing pad next to the earthen windbreak against one side of the Human embassy to the planet Splendor.

Earth Unity Ambassador Chanda Kasmira's breath frosted in the cold as she raised her voice over the whine of the shuttles' gravitics, telling her visitor, "I'd hoped something like this would never happen."

Unity Senator Gabriel Galt was a small-framed man in his early sixties. He stood in his thick coat, his hood raised casually over his gray hair, as if he didn't feel the chill. "I imagine you feel like the Unity itself is looking over your shoulder," he said. "But right now we have one job."

"Agreed," Chanda said as she and Galt moved in right behind the triage teams.

The shuttles' rear hatches opened and a line of smart-gurneys, each bearing an injured highlander, rolled down a ramp, then switched to walking mode to make their way across the rough ground. A couple of Unity Marine medics accompanied each patient.

Chanda, Senator Galt, and one member of the triage team, Dr. Phillip McEwan, bore down on the nearest gurney as it halted in front of them. The highlander was strapped down, blood matting his heavily furred body on his chest and arms. He wasn't moving, and his eyes within their recessed sockets remained closed.

"It's Roraten," Chanda said as they walked alongside the gurney which was moving gingerly across the frozen ground toward the embassy entrance.

Senator Galt asked, "You know him?"

"He used to be one of Indirogar's tribemates." Indirogar was the Elder of his tribe, one of the first Splendorians Humans had contacted twelve years earlier when they first learned the planet was in danger. "I rescued him from some slavers a few months ago."

Dr. McEwan checked the lifesign readout on the side of the gurney. "He's in bad shape, but still alive."

As they entered the embassy, Roraten stirred, his eyes focused on Chanda, and he raised his hand to her arm. His grip was weak, tentative. "I did the best I could," Roraten said, his words translated through Chanda's datalink, which was implanted behind her left ear.

"I know you did," Chanda told him.

"But you have to bring the rest of us home."

"I will," Chanda promised as she stopped and let the gurney and Dr. McEwan go ahead into the embassy. She looked back toward the shuttles as the Marine medics who had come down from from the orbiting starcraft *Nivara 2* played traffic cop as best they could, advising the embassy doctors on which patients needed immediate treatment and which could wait.

Chanda took a close look at more of the highlanders — some were trying to move around on their gurneys, clearly in pain. Others, less seriously hurt, seemed more resigned to their situation. Altogether, the two shuttles had brought twenty-one highlanders from the planet Socrates, where they were supposed to settle down and create new lives for themselves.

The attempt had failed, violently, in a sudden battle between two highlander tribes. The *Nivara* 2 had rushed the survivors back here to Splendor for more advanced medical treatment than they could receive on Socrates.

Galt told Chanda, "I'm former military. If there's any way I can help out . . . "

Chanda said, "Let's see what the doctors and Marines need," and led the way into the embassy and down a corridor to the infirmary.

What they needed was help guiding gurneys into position as triage continued, and keeping an eye on medical readouts and the injured highlanders themselves in case anyone suddenly took a turn for the worse.

Chanda also caught glimpses of just how efficiently the doctors worked. She watched as they treated one highlander after another, using tissue menders to repair damage to internal organs as well as flesh, then injecting nanodocs into their systems to perform more detailed repairs and fight infection.

Sometimes the low-tech solutions worked. She got to see Dr. McEwan pull a broken arm back into position manually, and only then did the nanodoc injection follow to hurry along the process of the bone knitting itself.

Dr. McEwan, knowing Chanda was especially concerned about Roraten, came to her when he finished his treatment. "He's doing much better," McEwan said. "Once we got him stabilized, things turned around right away. He's going right into recovery."

"Can I talk to him again?"

"Maybe later. He's asleep now."

"How are the others?"

"Twenty-one highlanders with injuries came back from Socrates. Four died. Seven are missing limbs. We've been working on the tech to regenerate Splendorian limbs and organs. Maybe in a few more years we can do it as easily as we can a Human's."

Galt asked, "And the rest?"

"They'll be OK. They're stable, and they've all got their nanomeds shot into them. That'll take care of everything from damage to major organs to stab wounds to infections."

"I'm grateful for that, Doctor," Chanda said.

Galt said, "Now comes the tough part. Making sure their descendants stay safe, too."

Chanda didn't realize how quickly she'd become accustomed to the sights and smells of the infirmary until she stepped into the corridor and found sudden relief from battered bodies, the moaning of victims, blood everywhere, sharp medicinal smells mixed with that of shit and bodily fluids, all beneath harsh, institutional lighting.

Waiting for her and Galt in the corridor was a burly man sporting a thick dark beard — Captain Trenton Bram, Chanda's Earth Unity Military Liaison and commander of *Nivara* 2, the spacefaring successor to the first *Nivara*, which he had also commanded. Chanda had directed Bram to land that starcraft on the Splendorian surface so she could declare it the Unity's embassy. It was a move that deflected a likely attack on the planet by a warlike Galactic species, the Sobrenians. They had been using Splendor as a target to test some of their weapons, reasoning that since the planet was doomed anyway, the fact that it was still inhabited wasn't important.

Establishing that embassy was all part of the Unity's commitment to saving the lives of future generations on Splendor. In just over eight decades, the gas nebula from a star near Splendor would render the planet uninhabitable. The highlanders were one of three intelligent species that had arisen on Splendor — and recent archeological digs in the northern hemisphere had suggested perhaps a fourth species, most likely now extinct, had once developed there. The Earth Unity had committed itself to evacuating two of those surviving species. Chanda had devoted herself to that mission for the past four years.

After introducing Bram and Galt to one another, Chanda asked Bram, "So what's going on out at Socrates?"

"This was my decision, Ambassador, to bring these highlanders back. I've got a bunch of others still in orbit who aren't injured."

Galt said, "Run the situation for me."

"I was in the first shuttle to land on Socrates. We had six transports right behind us. Pretty standard stuff. We were coming in between two highlander settlements. But no sooner did we start disembarking, than we found ourselves in the middle of a full-fledged battle."

"Between highlanders?"

"Hundreds of them going at it. Lots of bodies, lots of blood. Huts torn apart or burning."

"A war, is what you're telling me."

"I didn't want to believe it, either," Bram said. "Suddenly our disembarking operation became a recovery mission — we got everyone from our party, from all the transports, back on board, most of them not even wounded."

Galt said, "It sounds like a good call, Captain."

Bram gave Galt a nod and said, "We went back into orbit, rendezvoused with *Nivara 2*."

Chanda said, "The polite term for this is a 'cluster event.'"

"I'm sorry, Ambassador."

"I've got to put all the evac missions to Socrates on hold."

Bram said, "*Black Tortoise* just started on its latest run. I can call it back."

"Do that. And go ahead and get the rest of the highlanders from your ship back down here. Then I'm going to request that you and *Nivara 2* head back to Socrates. Send down several squads with as much protection and as many weapons as they need and find out what the hell's going on." Officially, Chanda couldn't command the Unity starcraft or its Marines to do anything, but she usually got her way in such instances.

"If you don't mind," Bram said, "I'll get back upstairs and get ready to boost."

Chanda squeezed his arm. "You did well, Captain. It's everything I expect from you."

Bram flashed a grim smile. "It's just tougher than we thought, isn't it?"

"Yeah," Chanda said, aware of Galt's presence and what it implied. "We just have to keep pushing ahead, a day at a time."

Bram left. Chanda turned to Galt. "I know. Let's talk in my quarters."

Chanda led Galt to her quarters in the embassy and gestured towards a comfortable chair. She offered him a drink and he declined. Chanda made herself a cup of hot tea and settled into another comfortable chair across from Galt. He told her, "You look tired. Probably about as tired as I feel."

"It was rough, I admit," Chanda said. "I feel like a pufferfish who's lost all her air."

"Ah, yes, the animal analogies."

Chanda stopped with her teacup halfway to her lips. "Excuse me?"

"Oh. Sorry. I've been studying up on the situation here — and on you. People have commented on that habit. 'Stuck like hamsters in a tube,' 'like a snake trying to swallow a camel,' 'like a lion eyeing a gazelle — '"

"I get the point. What does it have to do with anything?"

"I'm not just here to look at the situation on Splendor, Ambassador. I'm here to look at you."

Chanda narrowed her gaze. "Did the Unity really send you here?"

"Indeed they did. I checked on any friends or family who might be concerned about you, too."

"And what did you find?"

"I found," Galt said, "that everyone in your close family is dead, and your friends haven't heard from you in, oh, a couple decades or so. Oh, and no hobbies, and not much in the way of romance."

Chanda took a slow sip of her drink.

Galt asked, "You're not going to elaborate? Just sip your tea?"

"I hate when it starts to get cold."

Galt's voice took on a harsh tone. "Don't patronize me, Ambassador. You're dealing with four intelligent species here — the highlanders, valley dwellers, and sweepers from right here on Splendor, and the Buruden, who seem to have settled down here." The arrival of the Galactic species known as the Buruden was another legacy of the warlike Sobrenians. A starcraft filled with many Buruden had been fleeing the Sobrenians when it crash-landed on Splendor.

"Actually," Chanda said, "it's five species."

"Five?"

"You forgot Humanity — perhaps the most difficult species to deal with of all."

"Nice smart answer, Ambassador. But you saw what just happened here. Those highlanders were supposed to be making a new life on Socrates. It isn't working."

"I don't need you to tell me that. And the highlanders aren't our only problem by any means. Many of the valley dwellers aren't doing well on Kardashev." That was the planet where the valley dwellers, the other Splendorian species to be evacuated were supposed to make new lives. Try as it might, Humanity had never found another planet where both the highlanders and valley dwellers could live in their accustomed habitats. Resettling them separately had seemed the only reasonable alternative.

Galt said, "I know about their problems — a lot of suicides?"

"Yes," Chanda said. "Many of them still consider the highlanders as being, if not gods, at least close to them. It's been difficult for them to live on their own."

"Difficult enough that Splendor's ambassador to Earth is coming back."

"Yes. Dijirar." She was a valley dweller, the second Splendorian Humans ever contacted. She'd been the planet's representative to Earth for the past four years. Now, given her homeworld's difficulties, Dijirar was returning home.

"I look forward to meeting her, as well as Indirogar."

"Don't think I'm not going to face facts. I intend to go right to Indirogar and let him know all about the problems on Socrates."

"What Indirogar thinks influences other highlander Elders," Galt said. "If this failure to settle highlanders on Socrates causes him to doubt whether the evacuation plan will work . . . "

"I'll deal with this as I have every other problem that's come up on this world."

"You'd better, Ambassador — or we'll find someone else who can. Your brand of frontier diplomacy isn't always appreciated in the halls of the Unity Senate."

Chanda took a final, unsatisfying cold sip of tea and said, "I'll have a shuttle prepped. Let's go see Indirogar right now."

———

Chanda watched with anticipation as pilot Irene Radford eased the shuttle *Bashi* to a landing just outside the stone huts of Indirogar's village. Chanda, Irene, and Galt put on their thick parkas and stepped onto the snowy surface of Splendor. The highlander made his way to the landing site and grasped Chanda in a familiar bone-crushing hug. "It's so good to see you, friend Chanda," Indirogar said. "Your presence strengthens my hearts." He even gave Irene his signature embrace. Given her short, thin frame, Chanda wondered whether Irene could even take a breath.

Chanda, for the first time, noticed streaks of gray shooting through the dark brown fur that covered Indirogar's body. *His respon-*

sibilities have taken a toll on him, she thought. *And he won't let go of them.*

Chanda introduced Senator Galt -- no hug for him. "Word travels quickly on Splendor," Indirogar told Galt. "I hear you are to judge the job Ambassador Kasmira has done for us — and for your own people."

Galt's features didn't betray any reaction as he told Indirogar, "My job is not to judge. I'm simply to report."

"Bah," Indirogar replied, making a waving-away gesture Chanda was sure he'd picked up from Humans. "Yet here you are. Let us talk."

As they proceeded across the frozen landscape toward Indirogar's home, they passed several huts with animal hides hanging outside. The musty smells from within those huts indicated many highlanders hard at work scraping fat and tissue from carcasses and salting hides they didn't intend to tan right away. Irene said quietly to Chanda, "I still can't get used to that."

Chanda said, "Our ancestors lived that way a lot longer than we've been a tech-oriented culture."

Indirogar's stone hut was warmer than it would have been just a few years earlier; Humans had given highlanders a few tips over the years in constructing their living spaces so they retained heat more effectively. Chanda knew, for instance, that Indirogar's home was insulated with a type of wool made from the coat of a mammal without limbs called the burrower. Highlanders could create such dwellings quickly, which was important for a tribe that often had to uproot itself to follow the quicksleep herds that provided much of its food and furs.

For a highlander such as Indirogar, his hut was much more comfortable as a result -- but for Chanda, Irene, and Galt, the relative warmth of the hut wasn't sufficient to remove their parkas. *If trees were more common, he could build a fire*, Chanda thought.

They all sat on wide mats and leaned back against thick stuffed pillows. Several metal spears, the work of valley dwellers at forges in Splendor's volcanically-heated lowlands, hung against one wall. "For so many of my friends to come see me at once," Indirogar said, "something important must be about to happen. Let us speak of it."

Chanda summarized the conflict the *Nivara 2* crewmembers had discovered on Socrates, their hurried retreat from the planet, and the mission she'd given Bram.

Indirogar's shoulders slumped and he hung his head. "This is a terrible development, friend Chanda. For all of us." He looked at Galt. "Does this gladden your hearts, Senator?"

Galt said, "It does not. I want to see the Splendor evacuation plan succeed."

"Yet this makes it more likely that Chanda may be replaced," Indirogar said. He looked at her. "I understand how you feel. You tell me Roraten is among those who returned."

"He is."

Indirogar said, "So we will have to take him back into our fold, and all the others who had desired to leave with him." Indirogar had accepted Roraten into his tribe briefly before Roraten decided to try to make a new life on the planet Socrates. Indirogar continued: "Friend Chanda, so much has changed. I was once our most skillful hunter." Indirogar braced himself against the floor, got his feet beneath him, and stood. He carefully took down one of the spears hanging on the wall. "Now I'm older, and must be content to watch as others leave for the hunt."

Chanda said, "That's to be expected. There are days I wish I could just stay in bed."

Indirogar's fingers ran down the carefully crafted metal of the spear. He said, "Roraten is among many in my tribe who want me to relinquish my post as Elder and assume that of Eldest."

Galt said, "But -- my research told me you'd abolished the position of Eldest."

Chanda emitted a low cough, rearranged her position against her pillow, and told the senator, "That position is filled -- but in a different way than is . . . traditional."

Indirogar looked directly at Galt. "Our Eldest is still Eluharobak.

He resides in the usual position of honor in the caves on the north side of our village."

"Actually," Chanda said, "his mummified remains are there."

"Oh," Galt said.

Indirogar said, "The position is one of honor, but advisory only. I feel I am still vital, despite growing older. I do not wish to relegate myself to the position of Eldest."

Galt cleared his throat as he rearranged himself on his mat. "If I remember my highlander history correctly, though, one of your predecessor Ahtenhurat's own tribemates stabbed him to death when *he* balked at becoming Eldest."

Indirogar examined his weapon's finely crafted spear point. "That is true."

"We wouldn't want anything like that to happen to you."

Indirogar replaced the spear on the wall and sat again. "With Roraten back on Splendor, he will no doubt renew his ambition to become Elder."

"Strong ambition for someone who was once a slave."

Indirogar said, "Yes, that was our shame. Highlanders working forges. Finding our people doing the work our friends the valley dwellers are meant to do." For generations on Splendor, the highlanders had traded furs for the metal tools and weapons the valley dwellers created in the volcanically-heated valleys where they lived. Highlanders considered it demeaning and disrespectful to their gods to forge their own weapons and tools.

Indirogar continued: "But the insult of wanting to take over as Elder came from Roraten himself! I accept him into my tribe, I feed and clothe him and help him build his own hut -- and this is how he repays me."

Chanda asked, "Does he have much support among your people?"

"More than I might have expected. He will no doubt make my village his home again, and he is ambitious. I need your help, Chanda. Support me in remaining Elder."

Chanda felt Galt's eyes on her. She told Indirogar, "You know it doesn't work like that. I can't take sides in highlander politics."

Indirogar folded his hands and stared Chanda down. "And if you could — what stand would you take?"

"I would take the stand that you should consider what's right for your people."

"Hmm. I see. That I should not consider my own desires."

"You don't want your tribe to suffer. And by denying the importance of one of your more cherished rituals — "

"Is that all this is to you? A ritual?" The dismissive hand-wave again. "Humanity has grown beyond such things, is that what I hear?"

Chanda breathed deeply before replying. "Believe me, we have such rituals."

Indirogar looked at Galt and grinned. "I believe you are right, friend Chanda. Perhaps I see one taking place before me!"

Galt said, "I'm here on serious work, Elder Indirogar."

"Just Indirogar."

"Thank you for that — "

Chanda broke in. "He's not telling you to be more familiar. He's telling you it's not a title like, say, 'Senator.'"

"Oh."

Indirogar stood. So did Chanda and Irene and, after a moment's hesitation, Galt. "We will talk again," Indirogar said. "And I will be most eager to hear Captain Bram's report."

Galt said, "It was good to meet you . . . Indirogar."

The highlander strode right up to the Senator and pressed a finger against Galt's chest. "This is a good woman — a good Human. She has devoted years to my people, and to the valley dwellers whom we revere. Make her leave, and you will find cooperation from the highlanders a rare thing."

Galt's eyes narrowed and he leaned forward. "I respect Chanda and what she's done here. But I make my own decisions. Try to intimidate me, and you will find cooperation from Humanity to be a rare thing."

Indirogar lowered his arm. "We understand one another, then. That is good."

Galt looked toward Chanda, who fought to keep her face impassive. The senator told Indirogar, "Everything begins with understanding, I suppose."

Chanda nodded at Indirogar, then led the way from his hut and toward their waiting shuttle.

CHAPTER 2

Galt didn't speak until Irene had lifted the shuttle *Bashi* away from the outskirts of Indirogar's village and set course toward the Unity embassy. "Is Indirogar always so confrontational?" he asked.

Chanda turned in the co-pilot's seat next to Irene to face Galt, who sat in the rear. "I've never had a problem with him."

"Bullshit, Chanda. He challenged you to support him against his own tribe — something he had to know you couldn't do."

"Which I reminded him of — a decision he respects because he respects me. You notice how his demeanor changed when you stood up to him."

Galt considered that. "I should know better, I guess. I saw the same thing when I was in Starforce."

Irene asked, "Were you a pilot, sir?"

Galt smiled, no doubt eager for the change in topic. "Sure was. Across twenty years, went from 'nugget' to commanding the light cruiser *Sergeant Jelal.*"

"She's a good ship," Chanda said. "It's been here before."

"Her current commander — Davis Hamadi — is a good man.

Anyway, I did that for five years. Then decided I'd had enough of real work and became a politician."

Chanda started to ask, "So why did you — "

The *Bashi* shuddered, its master alarm sounded, and Chanda grasped the back of her seat at the feeling that the floor had dropped from under her. Irene struggled with the controls as the shuttle began to plunge toward Splendor's surface.

"What the hell's happening?" Chanda demanded.

Irene: "Not sure. Gravitics are gone -- this thing's a brick."

Chanda looked across the control panels in front of her. Red lights everywhere — gravitic drive, nav, life support, just about every vital system was cutting in and out. "Can you — "

Galt cut in: "Chanda — she's doing as well as anyone could."

Chanda looked back at Galt, who gave her a confident, confirming nod. *Former pilot*, she thought. *He should know.* She looked forward again. "We're coming up on Skyreach Mountain," she said.

"We're not going to be able to get over it," Irene said. "I'm bringing us down near the Strait of Ancestors." Formed when two oceanic plates spread apart, the strait was less than a kilometer across, but separated two great land masses.

The *Bashi* shuddered again. "Check that," Irene said. "Nav's all bollixed. Can't go that way."

Galt asked, "Where *can* we go?"

Irene's fingers ran arpeggios across the control panel. "West — near the edge of the Great Sea." As Irene turned the shuttle westward, many of the red lights on the control panels went out. From behind them, Galt asked, "You're getting some systems back. How's that happening?"

Irene said, "I don't know. Lemme see if I can get us back to altitude, and back on course." But as Irene tried to coerce the shuttle to regain altitude, the red indicators returned.

Galt said, "Something — or someone — wants us to head toward the Great Sea."

"I'm not going to argue," Irene said. "I'm headed that way."

Chanda said, "I think I know who it is. The sweepers."

The *Bashi's* gravitics brought it down to a smooth landing on a snow-covered ridge overlooking the Great Sea. Irene worked the controls to put the shuttle into standby mode in case they needed to lift off again quickly. "That's assuming we're allowed to lift at all," she said.

Galt said, "I don't understand. These giant creatures out in the ocean somehow affected our shuttle's systems?"

Chanda got out of the co-pilot's chair and started putting on her parka. "That's just a theory. The sweepers can mimic just about any kind of energy field they're exposed to."

Galt gave Chanda a skeptical look. "Even those of advanced Human tech?"

"Well, they've never managed a gravitic field, if that's what you're wondering about. But I wouldn't be surprised if they were able to generate enough of an energy pulse to interfere with our systems."

"But how — "

"Senator, please. It's all just speculation. Let's get outside and try to gather some facts." Chanda led the way out of the shuttle, with Galt and Irene right behind.

Chanda looked all around. Back east, the way they'd come, she could just make out the top of Skyreach Mountain — its base was beneath the horizon, all but its summit shrouded by clouds.

Westward, the ridge Chanda stood on was crusted with snow, but as it sloped toward the water, the surface gave way to mud, then a narrow, pebbled beach that led to the ocean. Gentle waves lapped the shoreline beneath bright blue skies streaked with wispy clouds.

Irene pointed out toward the ocean. "Look at that!"

"I see it!" Chanda said.

Galt shielded his eyes with one hand. "What is it?"

It was Chanda's turn to point. "Out there — not a quarter-K out. A dark spot in the ocean, kilometers wide."

"I see it now — and it's growing — getting closer!"

Irene said, "It *is* a sweeper! Look at all the messenger fish swimming next to it." Chanda saw dozens, hundreds of tiny fish with red and white stripes accompanying the sweeper.

A sudden gust of wind rushed from the ocean and up the ridge. Senator Galt grabbed his hood's drawstrings and pulled them tighter. "I still don't want to believe that such a creature could've nearly caused this shuttle to crash."

Chanda told him, "You'll find a lot of things about Splendor hard to believe at first. Eventually you just accept them."

"With all respect, Ambassador, we'll see how that works out for you eventually."

Chanda sensed a presence, something insubstantial, around her she couldn't quantify. She asked, "Feel that?"

Galt said, "It's as if the air's filled with static electricity."

An ear-splitting scream sounded over Chanda's datalink. Instinctively, she put her hands against her ears, but to no effect. "Back into the shuttle," she said, barely able to hear her own voice. "Maybe that'll block it out."

Before Chanda could take more than a couple of steps, though, the noise stopped.

Irene asked, "You think that sweeper was trying to communicate?"

Galt looked across the Great Sea's waters. "If so, it wasn't very effective."

Chanda said, "It got our attention. And the sweepers have been working with the Buruden to develop their abilities to access Human datalinks." She started making her way down the muddy slope.

Galt asked, "What do you expect to do down there?"

Chanda raised her hands in mock exasperation. "I don't know — maybe say, 'Howdy!'"

As she continued down the slope, Chanda heard Galt ask Irene, "Is she always this exasperating?"

Irene replied, "Some of us think of her as exhilarating."

Chanda found herself grinning as she reached the bottom of the ridge, strode across the dry pebbles of the beach, and stopped where the gentle waves of the Great Sea lapped against the shore. She stood there, taking a good deep breath of salty air.

Galt and Irene came up to either side of her. Galt looked out toward the vast stretch of ocean where the sweeper was floating. He said, "I read about them, but even seeing this for myself, I can still barely believe it — a single creature that stretches for kilometers!"

"I have to admit," Chanda said, "with all the frustrations this planet and its inhabitants give me, Splendor sometimes still amazes me. I can't think of another world that has three intelligent species living on it."

"This sweeper is smart enough to have manipulated the shuttle's systems to make us land here?"

Chanda shrugged. "Well, someone forced us down here. Gimme another explanation."

"How about something that doesn't require pseudo-scientific mumbo-jumbo?"

"Look," Irene said. "It's a whole school of messenger fish."

A mass of the red and white striped fish was splitting off from the sweeper, which could only come so close to shore. The fish managed to remain station-keeping even against the force of the waves that rolled toward the beach. Galt asked, "And what do they — "

Another sharp screeching sound over Chanda's datalink interrupted the senator, and she feared they were in for another deafening attempt to communicate. But the sound faded just as suddenly — *It's like it's tuning into our frequency*, Chanda thought — and in its place she heard, "We are angry. . . . "

Galt looked at Chanda, eyes wide. "Did you hear — "

"Yes I did — and it has to be — "

"This is the sweeper who lies before you."

"It can't be — " Galt said.

Chanda said, "It is! It's talking through the messenger fish — they must help it focus the transmission."

"Again, this is the sweeper before you. I speak for all the other sweepers on this world."

Chanda asked, "What is it you want? Why are you angry?"

"Your presence floats constantly near the highlanders and valley dwellers. The sweepers remain in plain sight, yet go unnoticed."

"What do you want that we haven't given you?"

"We do not wish to be left to die on Splendor after the high-landers and valley dwellers leave."

"We don't want that, either. But we can't take you with us. You're too large."

"Your ways seem like magic to us. You should be able to do anything."

"We can't," Galt said. "We're as limited as anyone."

"*Senator*," Chanda said. "Please. Let me handle this."

Galt fell into sullen silence as Chanda continued: "We've discussed this. We hope to protect the sweepers when the gas nebula overtakes Splendor."

The sweeper remained a dark presence out in the ocean. The messenger fish continued station-keeping, still pointed toward shore. "All life in the oceans will die," the sweeper said.

"Not everything. Lifeforms that dive deep enough as the gas nebula passes should survive."

"*Should?*"

"I have to admit — we can't be certain. But — the Buruden were planning to store genetic samples of all Splendorian life within the sweepers' genetic structure."

"They are already in the process of doing so."

Chanda said, "They were also supposed to help you adapt your-selves to survive the gas nebula."

"That process has also begun. It has not been successful."

Chanda spread her arms as if in supplication. "The Buruden haven't told me any of this."

Silence, then, for a moment, and Chanda could've sworn she sensed the sweeper's thoughts as it considered her words. Finally the sweeper said, "How can you help save us?"

Chanda smiled. *Splendor still amazes me.* "You can keep talking to us like this. The more we know about you, the more we can help you."

"Chanda," Irene said. "The shuttle's systems — "

Chanda said, "I ask you not to interfere with the flight systems of our shuttlecraft, or any other Human craft."

"It was only our way of getting attention."

"I understand your communications can only go so far. What if we place a relay transmitter here to send any of your signals on to us?"

"We can speak with you whenever we like?"

"I would ask that it would only be when it is of utmost importance. I have two other Splendorian species and the Buruden to concern myself with, after all."

"And Humanity," Galt reminded her.

The sweeper said, "We agree to this. We will speak to you again, soon."

As one, the hundreds of messenger fish turned and darted off toward the sweeper, which was already backing away, its dark presence giving way to clear blue waters.

"Well, Senator," Chanda said as she started back up the ridge toward the shuttle, "want to discuss a little more 'pseudo-scientific mumbo-jumbo' as we go visit the Buruden?"

Another flight, this time past the Skyreach Mountains and onward toward the barren plain where the Buruden had created a small settlement. Its main building, which was spread across a quarter-kilometer, consisted of two stories, but stood just under five meters tall.

Its exterior was decorated with broad strokes of yellow, maroon, and gold. A Buruden shuttlecraft, which was a long cylinder sporting similar markings, stood next to it.

The Buruden's arrival on Splendor four years earlier had been a dramatic one, after one of their hospital ships had survived an encounter with a Sobrenian warcraft only to crash into Splendor's Great Sea. Chanda had gotten onto that Buruden ship and led the rescue of both the Buruden and Sobrenians aboard it, along the way getting into some firefights and having to escape within a particularly cramped Buruden lifepod not built to Human dimensions.

Splendor, as it turned out, was strategically placed between the current Buruden homeworld (they hadn't actually arisen there, but they didn't know where their real homeworld was) and that of the Sobrenians.

Even as the *Bashi*'s gravitics eased the craft down to another smooth landing, dozens of Buruden began to swarm from the main building.

As usual, Chanda led the way out of the shuttle. Behind her, Galt took a good look at the mass of beings converging on them and asked, "Are we safe?"

Buruden were quadrupeds, with white, symmetrical, meter-wide bodies, who stood about half a meter tall. To most Humans, they resembled large, mobile starfish. A wide skull on top of the body protected the brain. Four eyes were spaced equidistantly around the sides of their bodies.

It was a sight Chanda was accustomed to. "We're fine. If they wanted to hurt us, we'd already be dead."

"I don't find that reassuring."

As the Buruden drew closer, individuals touched "joiners," sucker-like organs on each of their spiny legs, to one another. "I've heard of this," Galt said. "They're a partially collective species. The more of them join together, the more intelligent a particular group is."

"Exactly right," Chanda said. "And with luck, several of them can form their ambassador. He had to come here from the Buruden homeworld, but he needs to be accompanied by enough other Buruden to be able to communicate."

"That is a truth, Ambassador Kasmira," came a voice in her datalink.

"A truth I acknowledge as well," Chanda said.

Galt said, "I don't hear anything over my datalink."

Irene said, "They use a system that's normally closed to other species. You have to let them touch your link before you can talk with them."

"Am I allowed to make that connection?"

"Certainly," Chanda said. "Lean down so one of the Buruden can touch behind your ear." To the Buruden ambassador, she said, "Senator Galt wishes to take part in the linking touch."

"Very well," the Buruden said, and extended one of his spiny limbs toward Galt.

At the touch, Galt yelped and stood up quickly. "That hurt like hell!"

Chanda suppressed a grin as she watched Galt rub behind his neck. Irene didn't even try to withhold her laughter: "That's why I've never had the damn thing done to me," she said.

Galt gave a harsh glance toward Irene. "I'm glad to be the butt of your joke — especially right here in front of a representative of another species."

The Buruden ambassador, still linked to other Buruden on three sides, said, "Do not take offense, Senator. It is a likely truth that I and the rest of the Buruden are playful and enjoy witnessing Humans as they experience our linking touch."

"He means," Chanda said, "that they have a sense of humor."

Galt said, "I'll consider it a rite of passage."

"We have serious matters to consider," Chanda said to the Buruden. "One of the sweepers just forced our shuttle to land near the Great Sea. It spoke on behalf of the other sweepers, saying they're upset that you haven't made more progress in adapting them to survive the gas nebula."

"That upsets us, as well," the Buruden said. "But our knowledge advances at its own rate. A truth."

Galt asked, "They're much too big to lift away from the planet. What will happen if you can't save them?"

"It is truth that they are in great danger," the Buruden said. "A likely truth is that they will die. A potential truth is that we will yet find a way to save them. That we might consider halting our efforts is an untruth."

Picking up on Galt's confused look, Chanda said, "That means they don't know."

"Damn wordy folks," Galt muttered. The mass of Buruden stared at him impassively.

"Given their physiology, Buruden logic is based on four alternatives. Just as we tend to think of questions as having 'either-or' or 'yes-no' answers."

Galt addressed the Buruden ambassador again. "Do you still fear a Sobrenian incursion toward Splendor?"

"This is likely true," the Buruden said. "That concern has distracted us from our efforts to protect the sweepers."

Chanda said, "The Sobrenians haven't acted up in some time."

"Which could just as easily mean," Galt said, "that they've been marshaling their forces for an attack — either here on Splendor or on the Buruden homeworld."

The Buruden ambassador said, "We monitor the Sobrenians carefully. We've seen no such evidence of a military buildup."

Galt said, "How do you — "

"We do not speak of it."

"But if you — "

Chanda interrupted: "When you hear a straight-forward, single-alternative statement like that from the Buruden, you're not going to get any more information out of them."

Galt looked out over the mass of Buruden before them. "Fair enough. So what do we do next?"

"I don't know about you, but I'm ready to head home. It's been a long day." To the Buruden ambassador, she said, "Let us know if you make a breakthrough regarding the sweepers."

"We will," the Buruden ambassador said. He unlatched his joiners from the other Buruden around him, spun about, and Chanda watched as the mass of Buruden scampered back into their main building.

―――――

Irene guided the *Bashi* to a smooth landing next to the Unity embassy. Chanda was first out, leaving Irene to power down the small craft and make sure its systems were secure.

Galt was right behind Chanda and as they entered the embassy, he told her, "We need to talk again."

Chanda didn't try to hide her resentment. "Very well. My quarters again."

Within moments, Chanda's door slid shut behind Galt as she turned to face him: "Don't sit down. I don't intend for you to stay long. Listen — you have every right to look into my conduct as an ambassador. You have no right at all to examine my personal life."

"Or lack of it, from what I see."

"Remember the part about the five species?"

"I know you're busy, Ambassador."

"I was talking about the most difficult one to work with."

"Sarcasm doesn't become you, Chanda."

"I haven't worried about what 'becomes' me for a long time."

"I know you've had a hard life — your times in stasis, the senseless deaths of your parents, your failed marriage."

"I still think of my parents with love and affection, if you must know."

Chanda's parents, Gregor and Karamojong Kasmira, had been farmers turned Galactic explorers. Get wind of some fascinating discovery in previously uncharted realms, and off they'd go to discover a star that captured a gas giant only centuries earlier. Or they may pass through several multiple-star systems, hoping to come up with a new theory of their formation.

But what to do with little Chanda during those explorations, which were too dangerous for a little girl, who would be a major inconvenience anyway?

The answer was in Calcutta, a city her parents loved for its extensive parks and wide, uncrowded pedestrian walkways. It was also a place where any pleasure you desired, transcendent or paranoid, legal and moral or secretive and forbidden, could be yours. Her parents' pleasure was to place Chanda into stasis while they went exploring.

"You think of them that way despite what they did to you?" Galt asked.

"I set all that aside long ago."

"Did you, Chanda? I see what you call your 'homespace' right over here." Before Chanda could speak, Galt stepped toward a small corner table which held three decorative baskets, seemingly made of bamboo, roots, reeds, grasses, and bark. Designs of stylized stars and planets adorned them.

Galt held out a hand toward one of the baskets. "May I?" he asked.

Chanda feigned nonchalance. "Go ahead. They're replicated. Break it, I'll make another one."

Chanda had to admit that he lifted the basket with respect, perhaps even reverence.

"It's just a container," Chanda said. "One of the others is just like it."

"And the third one's a flour strainer."

Chanda found suspicion creeping into her voice. "That's right."

"Your mother made the originals. She used dyes from soil, and bark — other natural sources."

Chanda started to speak. Found she had to clear her throat. She said, "I told you I still think of my parents with love and affection. I've made peace with my past."

"Then what about the present? Do you have close Human friends? Have you had lovers? Do you take part in recreation or games?"

"None of that's any of your goddam business."

"It may become my business soon, depending on what I find here."

"Then let me offer up another animal analogy. Even a blind pig finds a truffle every once in a while."

Galt handed Chanda the basket and moved toward the door. "I can see I'm not getting anywhere here. But we'll speak again soon." He left, the door sliding closed behind him.

Chanda stood staring at the door, the basket still in her hands. After a moment, she placed it back on the table.

CHAPTER 3

I't's not too often you get to welcome home the first ambassador from an entire Galactic species, Chanda thought a couple of days later. She, Irene, and Galt stood next to the shuttle *Bashi* outside Dijirar's home village and watched the cloudless sky for another shuttle which was due to arrive any minute now.

Dozens of valley dwellers were gathered there awaiting Dijirar's arrival -- most were female, but Chanda could also make out a number of the smaller valley dweller males. Whatever their size, their bodies were slightly reptilian in appearance, though they were actually more akin to mammals. Their greenish skin was lightly scaled, their faces were wide, and their strong legs each had four sharp-clawed toes and webbed feet — they seldom wore shoes. A thick tail helped balance their bodies as they walked.

Most of the village's forges and bellows stood idle. Only a few of Dijirar's fellow villagers went about their work lifting pottery vessels from a furnace or pounding cakes of red-hot iron into tools or spears. The lava flow from a nearby volcano that provided the heat for their manufacturing processes eased past the outskirts of the village.

Chanda was grateful to be able to wear lighter clothing for a change. The high valley walls kept much of the heat of the lava trapped within itself, so they didn't need their parkas. And they'd found activating their lifesuits for casual jaunts outdoors alienated many natives from them.

Galt asked Chanda, "What do you think Dijirar's return will mean for these valley dwellers?"

Chanda said, "She's concerned about her people on Kardashev. She'll want to talk about that right away."

"Will she try to rally her people around herself?

"You mean to protest the evacuation effort or something?"

"Exactly that. This is the same situation as Indirogar and the highlanders. If we can't keep her support . . . "

"I trust Dijirar as much as these valley dwellers do. If we have reason to worry, she'll let us know right away."

Irene pointed almost directly upward. "There it is!" Chanda shielded her eyes and found the tiny form of the shuttle against the glare from Splendor's sun, Pinpoint. It was the shuttle *Dorothy*, from the Unity personnel transport craft *Erasmus*. Irene said, "Must be Akira Kuroda piloting, as usual. She's coming in pretty steep and fast."

"'Hot-dogging,' right?"

"I believe I've heard it called that."

"Jealous?" Chanda asked.

"Not at all . . . well, maybe not much."

"Thought so."

Dorothy dumped speed so quickly and leveled off at such an angle that Chanda knew its passengers had to be grateful for its internal gravitics. *More than a Human -- or valley dweller -- body could stand*, she thought.

But Akira's skills were intact -- the shuttle eased onto the harsh, lava-strewn landscape about fifty meters from the village with a touch as light as its approach had been flashy.

As the whine of the gravitics eased, Chanda and Irene approached the shuttle. Its outer airlock opened, and Dijirar stepped down onto her homeworld's surface for the first time in over two and a half Splendorian years -- about four and a half Earth years.

Dijirar took Chanda into a strong embrace, though it was nothing like Indirogar's. The valley dweller's head came about even to the Human's shoulders. "Welcome back," Chanda said. "We have so much to talk about. First, you should meet Irene Radford, my pilot and aide."

The valley dweller reached up and took Irene's right hand in both of hers, and shook with an ease Chanda realized must have come from countless diplomatic receptions back on Earth. *My friend is a different person*, Chanda realized. *I wonder what other changes I'll see in her. And which ones she might see in me.*

"And this is Senator Gabriel Galt," Chanda said. "He's gathering information for a report on the evacuation effort."

Dijirar shook his hand as well, telling the senator, "I believed we've glimpsed one another at certain receptions back on Earth, but I've never had the pleasure of meeting you."

"It's my loss, Ambassador Dijirar," Galt said.

Dijirar looked around at the villagers gathered to greet her and at the glowing lava flows, the white-topped mountain peaks to the north, and a vast icy plain to the west. "I'd forgotten how it feels to stand on a world that is truly home. You have many lovely mountains on Earth, Chanda, many far taller than here on Splendor. But none so lovely." Dijirar drew in a breath. "And the air smells *right* here, and the gravity is strong -- on Earth sometimes I felt I would float away." Splendor's gravity was about one-third stronger than Earth's.

Chanda said, "I've been here so long, Splendor probably feels more like home to me than Earth would."

"I must disagree. Take yourself home sometime, and you'll see I am right. But we have much to discuss. First, let me greet my own people." As Dijirar took her first steps toward her village, the female valley dwellers, in particular, rushed her in a way Chanda found almost frightening. They lifted Dijirar onto their shoulders and carried her away, some of the small males in tow.

Irene said, "You'd think she won the World Series."

"It's her party," Chanda said. "We'll catch up to her in a minute."

"Chanda, do you mind? I'd like to spend some time with Akira."

Chanda looked back toward the shuttle *Dorothy*. Akira, a tall and lanky woman, was standing there, and gave a big wave. Chanda waved back, and told Irene, "Go right ahead. I'm sure the two of you have some lies to tell each other about your latest adventures."

"Something like that," Irene said and made her way across the hard ground toward the shuttle.

Chanda and Galt followed Dijirar and the teeming crowd among the valley dwellers thatched huts. She told Galt, "I can only hope what I have to tell her isn't about to ruin her homecoming."

Chanda could only smile when they reached Dijirar's hut and the valley dweller had to implore her tribemates to leave her in peace awhile. "I have important business with my Human friends," Dijirar told them, and within a few minutes the final well-wishers returned to their daily routine. *I'm glad to see her so happy*, Chanda thought. *It's great to see her back among her own people.*

Dijirar gestured for Chanda and Galt to follow her into her hut. The valley dweller clapped her hands with joy when she saw two of the short males of her species standing in a corner. They chattered among one another too quickly for Chanda's datalink to translate, and even hopped up and down in excitement a couple of times.

Dijirar indicated wicker chairs. "Would you like some root tea?" she asked.

"I would," Chanda said, and Galt accepted as well. Once it was served, Dijirar sat across from her Human friends, lifted one thick-muscled leg, and waved one of the males forward. Arms wide, it grasped Dijirar's hips and began to sex with her.

Chanda felt herself flush. A glance at Galt found him gap-jawed, and Chanda bit her bottom lip to keep from laughing.

Within seconds, the first male was done and backed away with a liquid sound. "Ah, the familiar warmth," Dijirar said. "One of these gave my friend Adoranon her daughter, Rial, last year. They're excellent breeding stock, so they travel back and forth on your starcraft to service as many of us as possible. I'd requested that they be here the moment I arrived."

Chanda asked, "Are you hoping to conceive a daughter?"

Dijirar beckoned the other male to her, and it went to work as enthusiastically as the first. "What female doesn't?" she asked.

Either of the males who succeeded in fertilizing Dijirar's eggs would receive them back into their own bodies for gestation -- females were not nearly as common among valley dwellers and were greatly prized, while males, though small and frail, were plentiful. With the male carrying a child to term, many children could be conceived without risking a female's life.

"It's thinking of those future generations," Dijirar continued, "that makes me wish the gods would bless me with a daughter." The other male withdrew and joined the other in the corner again.

"How different things are now," Chanda told Dijirar, eager to get a conversation, *any* conversation going. "Splendor's been my home for four Earth years, while you've been living on my homeworld."

Dijirar gripped her teacup gingerly, clearly mindful of the sharp claws of her thumb and three fingers. "And I have learned many things."

"Such as?"

"That Humans are a marvelous people who have learned to make devices that create food seemingly from air, buildings made of stone and glass that will not break, and starcraft that can take us virtually anywhere we want."

Chanda lifted her teacup in salute. "Congratulations. I now certify you as a fully trained ambassador. But it's me, remember? You can dispense with the bullshit."

"Ah, yes, 'bullshit.' A word I learned to recognize even without the translation."

Galt broke in: "It *does* have a fine diplomatic legacy."

Chanda asked, "So what did you really learn?"

"Among other things, how to tell when a Human is trying not to speak of something."

Chanda placed her half-empty teacup on the table, aware of Galt's silence, of the fact that he would be processing her every word. "Not everything is going well with the evacuation effort," she said.

Dijirar said, "I'd heard such rumors before I left Earth. Valley dwellers on Kardashev who cannot bear living without our holy places."

"Those rumors are true."

"Is it also true that some have committed suicide?"

"Yes. I'm sorry." The valley dwellers believed in gods that lived within the giant ice cliffs and glaciers surrounding their warm valleys. The presence of Humanity and an increased knowledge — and awareness — of the scientific method had eroded those feelings among some valley dwellers, but not all of them. The decorations of the weapons they forged for the highlanders were usually tributes to those gods.

Dijirar said, "My niece Utarna is there on Kardashev, with Adoranon taking care of her."

"I've been checking on them. They're all right. But some of their leaders on Kardashev are making noises about coming back to Splendor."

Galt pointed out, "Just as the highlanders may well have to return from Socrates."

Chanda said, "They know their descendants will die here if they do."

But Dijirar said, "That is a time many years away, Chanda. We are no different from Humans in this. We look at our own lives and maybe our children's. Beyond that seems a faraway dream."

"It gets worse," Galt said. "We've had to provide the highlanders on Socrates with spears and tools. Even here on Splendor, a tribe tried to enslave other highlanders rather than forge what they needed themselves."

Dijirar placed her teacup on the table with a smooth, precise movement. "What does Indirogar think?"

Chanda said, "The same as I do. He wants to know more. I've got Captain Bram headed back to Socrates aboard *Nivara* 2. He should be reporting back in a few days. And *Black Tortoise* should be arriving here in a day or so with a shipload of highlanders. Once it delivers them back here, I'm sending it to Kardashev to see how things are going there."

"Then I will wait for those reports." Dijirar beckoned for the males to return to her. "These are difficult times. We have much to decide."

Chanda stood as the first male approached Dijirar again, and Galt quickly followed her lead. "We'll leave you to your, ah . . . task, then."

"Feel free to stay," Dijirar said as the male struggled to climb her leg. "I'm sure we'll have quite a feast later."

Chanda made her way toward the door. "I'm expected back at the embassy," she said. "We'll make it another time, when things aren't so hectic for you." She eased herself through the doorway.

Dijirar said, "Come back anytime. I have so many of my experiences on Earth I want to share with you."

"Thanks," Chanda said as her smart strides led Galt rapidly away from Dijirar's hut.

As Irene lifted the shuttle away from Dijirar's village, Chanda said, "That was an odd moment."

"What's that?" Galt asked.

"'What's that?' Like I could be talking about anything else?"

"Oh." Galt's face broke into a mischievous smile. "You mean Dijirar . . . I guess you'd have to say, mating . . . right in front of us."

"Yeah."

"It's a natural function. And obviously not one with emotions as complicated as they are for Humans."

"Yeah." Chanda kept quiet the rest of the trip back to the embassy, as did Galt and Irene.

As the shuttle settled down onto the snow-covered surface of Splendor, Irene asked Chanda, "Could I have a little help with the post-flight check?"

"Sure," Chanda said.

Galt got up, put on his parka, and started for the airlock. "I'm headed in." He peered out the airlock window. "Looks like the wind's whipping up pretty good. Chanda, we'll talk later."

"Certainly," Chanda said, thinking, *Not if I can help it.* Once he was gone, she told Irene, "So spill it."

"Spill what?"

"You didn't really want help with the post-flight."

"Oh. Yeah." Irene fumbled with the shuttle's controls as she began the post-flight sequence." It's just . . . Akira's staying over another night before she goes back up to *Dorothy*. And we haven't had a chance to be together in some time."

"Oh! You mean, you two -- ?"

"Yeah."

"No problem," Chanda said. "I don't have anything for you tonight."

"Thanks."

Chanda helped Irene finish the post-flight checks. "Damn. That actually starts me thinking."

Irene asked, "Is this where I'm supposed to ask, 'About what?'"

"Might as well."

"Uh, huh."

"So?" Chanda prompted.

"*Oh* -- I get it — about what?"

"Well -- it's been a long time for me."

"Oh. You mean since. . . . "

"Since I last had any kind of . . . romance."

"You don't just mean sex?" Irene asked.

"Well, that too. I've been a little busy the past few years. Saving a planet, and all that. It's been tough even thinking of finding the right partner. Speaking of which . . . no, I shouldn't ask."

"What is it?" Irene asked. "I won't mind."

"Is she the right one for you?"

Irene said, "Not . . . anything permanent. Especially since . . . no, I shouldn't say."

"Is there someone else?"

"Not . . . not really."

"But what you have with Akira is good?"

"*Oh*, yeah. Makes my toes curl."

"Damn," Chanda said. "I'm not sure I've *ever* had that."

"You're missing out. You need a vacation."

"I need a way to avoid Galt the rest of the day." Chanda rose and put on her parka. She headed for the airlock, Irene right behind her, and they trudged through the snow, leaning forward against the growing winds.

———

Chanda tried to avoid Galt, at least for awhile, by avoiding her own quarters and office, instead checking in at the command center that was once the bridge of the starcraft *Nivara*. Several technicians within the circular room nodded greetings as she entered. Her assistant, Ken Westbrook, was examining a readout at a scientific console. He glanced up at her and gave a little wave. Her distracted gesture in return let him know she didn't want to be bothered right now.

Opposite the main entrance stood a large viewscreen that at one time would have displayed the view of a planet the *Nivara* was orbiting, or graphics indicating the layout of a star system or the makeup of a Sobrenian fleet. Now it showed a silent view of the arctic landscape around the grounded starcraft-turned-embassy.

Even without sound, Chanda could tell the wind gusts were strengthening considerably; the tops of snowdrifts were being sheared off, it was becoming difficult to see the familiar string of mountains in the distance, and a couple people were rushing to get inside the embassy.

She heard the door to the main entrance slide open behind her, and a too-familiar voice said, "Looks like everyone got inside just in time."

Senator Gabriel Galt.

Chanda asked, "Come for the view?"

"Actually, Ambassador, I came looking for you. Of course, I could've just called you on your datalink anytime, but. . . . "

"You wanted the challenge."

"And a chance to take the tour of your embassy. I *did* command a starcraft not dissimilar to this one, once. It's interesting to see it adapted to a land-based, civilian purpose."

"And your own purpose in looking for me?"

Galt stood with his arms straight at his side. "Let's not spar, Chanda. Especially not in public."

Chanda spun on one heel and headed for the door, saying, "Let's take it into the hallway, then."

As Galt followed her, he asked, "Couldn't we just talk in your quarters again?"

Chanda faced Galt as the door to the command center closed behind him. "The first time I invited you there you made light of my 'animal analogies.' The second time, you psychoanalyzed me based on my homespace artifacts. I don't want to hear what you'd come up with this time."

"I'm only trying to help, Chanda."

"You're hovering over me like a dog wondering if I've got a treat in my hand — dammit! Now you've got me noticing them!"

Galt put his hand over his mouth and snorted.

Chanda told him, "That isn't helping, you know."

Galt lowered his hand and adopted a serious expression. "I know. I apologize."

"So what do you want from me?"

Galt stared at the floor as if hoping to see his next words there. Then he looked straight at Chanda. "We want results, Ambassador."

"Meaning?"

"Look at what's happening with the evac effort — the highlanders on Socrates are at war, the valley dwellers on Kardashev are so distraught they're killing themselves. You haven't found a way to save the sweepers, and who the hell even knows what the Buruden are doing?"

Chanda's anger flared so fiercely she couldn't allow herself to speak. *The next words from my mouth would have Galt shooting me back to Earth on the next available starcraft*, she thought.

The door to the command center slid open and Ken Westbrook came through the doorway. He had to change his trajectory suddenly to avoid barreling into Galt. "Excuse me," Ken said, flashing Chanda a meaningful look as he passed. *Something's up*, Chanda thought.

The desire to focus on whatever problem had just arisen doused Chanda's anger. *I've got to get away from Galt*, she thought. "Very well," she told the man. "I have to wait for *Nivara 2* to come back from Socrates and Kardashev, then we'll have something to work with."

"And if neither the valley dwellers nor the highlanders can survive on those worlds?"

"Then it's the same as we've always done. Adapt as needed."

Galt rubbed his chin. "I see. Well, you've got until then. So, I guess you'd better go see your assistant. Whatever he was itching to tell you, he didn't want me around when he did it."

Chanda said, "Ken does an excellent job."

"You mean he protects you. That's as it should be. Go ahead. If it's that important, I'll find out about it soon enough."

Chanda headed down the corridor, trying not to feel as if she'd just allowed Galt to dismiss her inside her own embassy.

———

Once she was out of Galt's earshot, Chanda touched behind her left ear to activate her datalink. "Ken — where are you?"

"Your office."

"I'll be there in half a minute."

When Chanda entered her office, she immediately noted Ken's look of concern. "What is it?"

"The Buruden. Sat photos make it look as if they're building a starcraft."

"How the hell can they do that?" Galt's words from just moments earlier echoed through her mind: *Who the hell knows what the Buruden are doing?*

Ken went to Chanda's desk and waved a hand over it to call up a holo. The image from Splendorian orbit showed the dismal plain that was home to the Buruden, the quarter-kilometer long stretch of their main building, and the smaller ones around it, and their small shuttle.

Next to the shuttle stood another craft, still under construction. "I was just there," Chanda said, "and I didn't see anything like that."

Ken said, "Apparently they work fast."

"They had a starcraft in orbit at one time, but it left. I wonder why they're building a new one instead of just calling one back from their homeworld."

"I'd guess you can't wait to go ask them."

"You're right. Get hold of Irene, tell her we're headed right back out."

Ken regarded her beneath raised eyebrows. "And Galt?"

"If you talk to him, you don't know nothin'. I'd like to make one trip without a chaperone."

CHAPTER 4

Chanda had Irene make a wide circuit of the craft the Buruden were building as their shuttle approached the settlement. Chanda said, "It looks like a starcraft all right. Look — you can see the four engine nacelles sticking out from the underside. That's their usual pattern."

Irene pointed to the rear of the craft, which hadn't had all of its outer skin applied yet. She pointed at the interior of the craft. "Those look like new-space generators there. That would seem to confirm a stardrive." Such a drive created "new-space" behind the starcraft while destroying already existing, "natural" space, or "old-space" in front, propelling the starcraft beyond lightspeed without relativistic effects. Irene continued: "This thing already stretches nearly half a kilometer. Just how big is this ship going to be?"

"Buruden ships can be that large," Chanda said. "If all of them are leaving, it's got to hold a thousand or more of them."

"That shouldn't be a problem, then. Should I go ahead and land?"

"Yeah. Let's see what we can find out."

Even after Irene landed the *Bashi*, and she and Chanda got their parkas on and found themselves standing outside the shuttle, there was still no response from the Buruden. Hundreds of them were visible scurrying about on the skeletal form of the starcraft they were constructing, with dozens more making frequent runs between the craft and their settlement's main structure.

"I don't expect a brass band every time we come around," Chanda said. "But a simple acknowledgement would be nice."

"Maybe they're all working on the starcraft," Irene said, her breath visible with every syllable.

"Well, I'm tired of waiting. Let's go see what we can find out." Chanda stuck her gloved hands into her pockets and trudged forward across the bare, uneven ground.

As they approached the work site, the complexity of the Buruden's job became more apparent. The craft stood twice as tall as the main building's five meters, but packed several more levels within that space than a Human starcraft could, given that the Buruden themselves only stood half a meter tall.

"It's a good thing we're not here on an inspection tour," Chanda said. "We'd never fit into there."

A long line of Buruden workers rushed past Chanda and Irene, headed for toward one of the four massive struts that held the starcraft off the ground. Each Buruden was attached to those ahead and behind by the joiners on their legs. None of them turned any of their four eyes toward the Humans as they passed. Chanda watched as they ran up the steep ramp formed by the nearest strut, which was a little over two meters wide, and four tall, then separated into individuals who fanned out across the interior of the ship.

"They're pretty efficient," Irene said.

Chanda looked around the work site in frustration. "Which means that if they really wanted to talk to us, they'd find a way to do it."

"Think we can get their attention somehow?"

Chanda allowed herself a small grin. "Let's try to make that inspection tour."

Irene indicated the strut nearest them. "There's no way we can shimmy up that thing — or fit inside the ship if we did."

Chanda started toward a group of Buruden off to one side working on what appeared to be a large equipment module. "We'll go right over here and make ourselves into pests."

The module was as large as the *Bashi*, and covered with instrumentation that Chanda could make no sense of. The Buruden workers were wielding several different tools in working on the large device. One resembled a spear, which a Buruden appeared to be using to probe the side of the module — to what end, Chanda had no idea. Half a dozen other Buruden were hanging off the side of the module or walking around on top of it.

Irene asked, "What do you intend to do, Chanda? These Buruden are singletons. They're working by instinct — they don't have enough intelligence by themselves to react to us."

"Maybe the direct approach," Chanda said, and went over to the Buruden with the spear-like device and tapped it on its broad skull. "Hello!"

The Buruden kept working.

Chanda sighed. "I've never had this problem before."

"If they leave, without even a word — what's going to happen to the sweepers?"

"That's the first question I'm going to ask — if I can find someone to answer it."

"I hate to say it," Irene said, "but all these Buruden look alike to me. This one right in front of us could be the ambassador and I wouldn't recognize him."

"Doesn't matter. Without being attached to enough other Buruden to become part of a sentient being, he really *isn't* the ambassador." Chanda saw another line of Buruden leaving their main building and rushing toward the same strut as the earlier stream of workers. "I've got an idea, though. Stay right here." Chanda trotted toward the bottom of that strut.

From behind her, Irene shouted, "Chanda, be careful! You don't know that they'll stop for you."

I've never known the Buruden to harm someone if they could help it, Chanda thought.

I have to hope this won't be the first instance.

She reached the strut only seconds before the line of Buruden did, the trotting of their linked legs making the ground rumble. *Will I even have a chance to throw myself aside if it looks like they're not going to stop?*

They stopped, preventing themselves from piling into one another by curling into an "S" shape. The rumbling faded, the ground stilled.

The lead Buruden stared at Chanda with its front and side eyes, all three blinking at once. Then they blinked independently.

Behind her, Chanda heard Irene say, "Looks like a standoff to me."

"Here come another set from the building. Maybe that's a hopeful sign — add a few more and they'll have enough intelligence to carry on a reasonable conversation."

Sure enough, the additional Buruden came up to those already present and joined together. One of them eased forward, attached to others on three sides, and Chanda heard over her datalink, "Why do you disturb us, Human?"

Not the usual Buruden politeness, Chanda thought. *Either they're peeved or just don't have enough of themselves connected here to hold a more polite conversation.* Chanda said, "We're concerned that you're apparently getting ready to leave Splendor, and you haven't said anything to us about it."

"You are not our responsibility," the Buruden said.

Though Chanda was struck by the directness of the statement, without any of the usual business of "likely" or "potential" truths, she recognized that manner of speech even through the datalink translation. "Well, hello, Ambassador. I must ask you, then — what about the sweepers?"

"They were a responsibility we took upon ourselves. And one we may divest ourselves of at any moment."

"Why now?"

The Buruden ambassador said, "A likely truth is that the Sobrenians are about to be a danger to our world."

"But you said just the other day — "

"Things change, Chanda. You know that as well as anyone. The Sobrenians tried to intimidate us several years ago, but did not succeed." One result of that conflict had been a clash between a Sobrenian warcraft and a Buruden hospital ship. The Sobrenians had been humiliated when the hospital ship's crew had destroyed the warcraft, though the hospital ship had been forced to crash-land on Splendor. The ambassador and all the other Buruden on Splendor were crewmembers of that hospital ship.

"If that's true, the Unity needs to know about it. What do you suspect the Sobrenians of doing?"

"They have tried — unsuccessfully — to intercept several of our starcraft as they pass near their homeworld."

Chanda asked, "How near?"

"A relative truth. Not as near as other craft we send into the Sobrenian system itself."

Irene blurted out, "What are you doing that for?"

Chanda shot Irene a studiously patient look as the Buruden ambassador replied: "We are curious. A truth. Yet the Sobrenians accuse us of spying, and have ranged farther out from their homeworld seeking to harass our craft."

"Is Splendor in any danger?" Chanda asked.

"That is a potential truth. Keeping your eyes upon them would be prudent."

"What can we do to help you and your homeworld?"

"If we decide upon a truth or likely truth, Chanda, we will let you know. Now please, stand aside. The only truth we care about now is preparing to go home."

Chanda stood aside as the line of Buruden formed again and

headed up the strut into the still-forming starcraft. Chanda wanted to say something more to the Buruden ambassador, but the individuals making him up had separated from one another and, therefore, wouldn't possess the intelligence to understand her words and respond.

"Let's get back to the shuttle," Chanda told Irene.

Irene said, "I only heard your half of the conversation. What's going on?"

"You *have* to undergo the linking touch sometime. Turns out the Sobrenians may be acting up — some kind of threat against the Buruden homeworld."

"Damn. That's the last thing we need."

"And the last thing I want to report to Senator Galt. But the Sobrenians can be unpredictable. Galt's our direct contact with the Unity right now. We have to decide what to do next."

Once back at the embassy, Chanda called a meeting in the command center with Galt. The two of them sat before the main viewscreen, which showed a live image of Splendor from orbit. It was a world with most of its land area covered with ice and snow, and only a narrow band at the equator revealing green, forested areas that provided Splendor with its breathable atmosphere. Dotting the landscape were volcanos, glowing red. They provided the pools of molten metal the valley dwellers used to create the tools and weapons they used themselves and traded to the high-landers.

From that vantage point, the Great Sea which covered much of the western hemisphere was also visible. Oceanic streams warmed by underwater volcanos came into contact with Arctic-temperature currents to influence the environment on land.

It's important just to take a good look every once in a while at what's at stake here, Chanda thought. *This world is home to three indigenous, intelligent species, plus countless animal species such as burrowers, quicksleep, flamebirds, stinger-stars . . .*

And in just about eighty years, it could all be gone.

Chanda asked Galt, "If the Sobrenians are threatening the Buruden homeworld again, what does that mean for Splendor?"

Galt said, "They've tested weapons here before. They may try again."

"That was before the Earth Unity established a permanent military presence here."

"With all respect, Ambassador, the *Nivara 2*, *Azure Dragon*, *Black Tortoise*, *Erasmus*, and the *George Allenby* are all we have here. *Dragon* and *Tortoise* are often tied up on runs to Kardashev or Socrates, and *Erasmus* and *Allenby* don't have anything other than the most basic defensive weapons. They couldn't stand up to a Sobrenian fleet."

Chanda said, "Reinforcements could arrive here pretty quickly, though."

"Only if there's the political will," Galt said. "And I'm sure the Unity wouldn't be willing to risk all-out war with the Sobrenians over Splendor."

"Thus wasting twelve years of commitment to this planet."

"Which world do you think the Unity will consider to be more important, Chanda? Splendor, or Earth?"

"It's a false choice. We can protect both."

"I admit there could be a middle ground. I can recommend more starcraft here, something less than a full-fledged fleet. Maybe the Sobrenians can be persuaded not to take on the Buruden and the Unity at the same time."

Chanda said, "You mean we'd take Splendor off the table by getting the Sobrenians to focus only on the Buruden?"

"There's another choice — which world do you think the Unity will consider more important — the Buruden homeworld, or Splendor?"

Chanda looked at the image of Splendor before them. As usual, she was struck by this world's harsh beauty — the blinding glint of its sun, Pinpoint, against ice fields where the highlanders lived, the red veins of lava crisscrossing the valley dwellers' homelands. *If the Sobrenians are out to spark a war, this won't be the last hard choice I'll have to make.*

Chanda said, "Let's make the call to the Unity. Ask for whatever forces they can spare."

Galt said, "You realize, Chanda, that if the Sobrenians do turn their attention to Splendor in sufficient force, we may not be able to stand against them."

"We'd cut and run, in other words." Galt started to protest, but Chanda quickly said, "I'm sorry. That's unfair. Come right down to it, I'd embrace the same hierarchy you have — Earth, then Splendor, then the Buruden homeworld."

Galt said, "I didn't expect anything less, Ambassador. I'll get the message sent to the Unity."

The door to the main entrance to the command center slid open and Ken Westbrook came in. "More trouble, Chanda," he said.

Chanda asked Ken, "How much more trouble can we possibly get ourselves into?

"Plenty enough. We just got a message over the relay transmitter. The sweepers are acting up again."

Once again to the ridge overlooking the Great Sea. Soon Chanda, Galt, and Irene were standing by the short, barrel-like relay transmitter. As before, the sweeper was a dark underwater presence that stretched nearly from one horizon to the other, as the messenger fish hovered close to shore.

Over her datalink, Chanda heard the voice of the sweeper who had spoken to them before: "First Humanity all but ignores us. Now the Buruden desert us."

Chanda said, "I understand your concerns. But the Buruden have to worry about their homeworld first."

"And who worries about the sweepers?"

"We all do. But we can only do so much for you right now."

"Then we declare Splendor's oceans to be free of Human technology. None of it will work on or over them, until you find a way to evacuate us."

Galt said, "Now wait just a minute — you can't threaten us like that. We're here to help you!"

Chanda said, "If we can't explore beneath Splendor's oceans or fly over them, that severely limits what we can do."

"That is not our concern."

Galt reached behind his left ear to deactivate his datalink. Seeing that, so did Chanda and Irene. Galt told Chanda, "This is unacceptable. To have most of Splendor's surface area declared off-limits — "

Irene said, "We actually don't fly over the oceans that much. There's only have one submersible on the planet, and no surface ships. And the sweepers' powers don't extend more than a few thousand meters into the air."

Galt turned to confront Irene: "Are you making excuses for these beings?"

"Absolutely not. I'm just saying these restrictions won't have much of a practical effect on what we do."

"You cannot let these beings dictate to us! Chanda, you know them better than anyone here. What do you intend to do?"

Chanda reached to switch her link back on, as did the others. She spread her arms out toward the Great Sea and the dark presence there. "We will not challenge this for now." Out of the corner of her eye, she saw Galt's expression turn to disbelief, then anger. "But if the time comes that the Sobrenians attack Splendor, how will you respond?"

The sweeper didn't answer at first, and Chanda imagined her words being transferred through the messenger fish, to the single sweeper before them, and in turn to all the other sweepers beneath

Splendor's oceans. Finally the response arrived: "We would stand with you against the Sobrenians."

"Thank you," Chanda said. "I didn't expect anything less." She glanced at Galt, saw his irritated expression at her parroting his words from earlier.

"We do not detect a Human presence beneath our oceans. Three of your shuttles are flying over them right now and we will allow them to finish their transit. But let it be known — the oceans belong to the sweepers."

Chanda wanted to say more, but the hundreds of messenger fish were turning as one away from the shore and heading out to sea. As for the sweeper, she could see it slowly backing away.

Galt said, "I cannot believe this. A Unity ambassador bowing to the wishes of a primitive species."

"Just because they live underwater doesn't mean they're primitive. Not having physical tech doesn't mean they're primitive. Dolphins and Saturn floaters and the Aquatiles on Welkin are just as intelligent as we are. Turns out, so are the sweepers."

"Well, they've certainly outwitted us this time. There had to be a way we could've persuaded them not to interfere with our tech."

"Well, you stand here on this hill and keep looking for one. I'm heading back to the embassy."

As Chanda started toward the *Bashi*, with Irene right on her heels, Galt said, "You can't talk to me that way!"

"I just did."

Galt caught up to Chanda, but she didn't slow down. Galt picked up his own pace and asked, "What do you have against me?"

"Humanity has been here on Splendor for twelve years. We still have eight decades before the gas nebula strikes. But you come in here and want overnight solutions."

Galt spoke as Chanda and Irene went ahead of him into the shuttle. "I want solutions that *work*, Chanda."

Chanda sat in the *Bashi*'s co-pilot's position as Irene sat in the pilot's chair. Galt settled in behind them. "You should've been here the last four years or so. We have a disaster a week. We cope with them, and keep going."

"I've haven't even been here a week, and so far I've seen high-landers who've been cut to shreds fighting other highlanders. I've seen the evacuation process halted. And now most of the planet's a no-fly zone."

Chanda glanced at Irene, who was carefully maintaining a quiet, professional demeanor as she prepped the shuttle for takeoff. Chanda told Galt, "Give me a good alternative. What would you do differently?"

"Well, I'd get some considerable forces onto Socrates to keep the highlanders from fighting."

"So Humans could end up fighting the very people we sent to a new planet to save?"

"If that's what it takes, yes."

Irene lifted the *Bashi* and piloted a course for the Unity embassy. Chanda said, "And the sweepers — would you threaten them, too? Perhaps carpet-bomb an ocean full of intelligent beings?"

"Of course not, Ambassador, and I think you know better than that."

"You're right, but show me an alternative that doesn't require using physical force against the very beings we're trying to save, and I'll consider it."

Galt was quiet for a time. Then he said, "There has to be something, Ambassador. I'll keep thinking."

You do that, Chanda thought, as the *Bashi* continued through cold Splendorian skies.

CHAPTER 5

A couple of days later, Chanda was in the command center with Dijirar, who sat in a special chair that accommodated her thick tail. A similar chair stood next to the valley dweller.

They were both positioned in front of the main viewscreen, which once again displayed the orbital image of Splendor. Chanda heard the main doorway open and turned. It was Galt. "Com'on in," she said.

Galt took in the scene before him and asked, "What's the occasion?"

Chanda said, "First of all, I've received a reply from the Unity about the idea of bringing more forces here. Brussels says to forget it."

"That sounds familiar enough. What else?"

"*Nivara 2* and *Black Tortoise* have returned. Captain Bram has given me a preliminary report. Quite honestly, there's hardly a bit of it that's positive. But he's on his way down to give us all the details. And he'll have a special guest."

"I don't particularly appreciate your sense of drama."

"We're here so he can report to all of us at once. I invited

Indirogar, but it looks as if Roraten's acting up again and he can't be spared. So, Senator, have a seat."

Galt eased himself into a chair. Folded his arms. Aimed a very official smile at Dijirar. Took a deep breath. Let it out in a silent sigh.

All of which amused Chanda to no end. *Though I wish Bram would hurry up and get here*, she thought.

As if her wish were magically fulfilled, the main entrance door slid aside again, and Captain Bram entered, carrying a highlander's spear. Chanda immediately noticed that about a third of its length was stained with blood.

Coming in beside him was another valley dweller female. Dijirar stood up in surprise and rushed toward her. "Adoranon!" The two embraced.

Adoranon was a bit taller than Dijirar, about 1.6 meters; her scales were a lighter green, edging slightly toward white at their tips. Galt said, "This is our special guest, I assume?"

Chanda said, "Senator Galt, this is Adoranon. She's the guardian of Dijirar's niece, Utarna. She also has a daughter, Rial. Adoranon moved to Kardashev about three years ago."

Galt stood, but didn't approach Adoranon, who remained standing next to Bram. Chanda continued: "When the *Black Tortoise* arrived at Kardashev, Adoranon insisted upon coming back to Splendor."

Adoranon said, "I wanted to explain what's happening on our new home."

"Please," Chanda said. "Everyone sit down."

Adoranon looked uncertain, but Bram nodded to the valley dweller and indicated the chair next to Dijirar. Adoranon sat, and Bram settled into a chair next to her. After a moment's hesitation, Adoranon began to speak: "The climate where we've settled suits us well enough that we don't need the furs we are accustomed to receiving from the highlanders. But we still miss them."

Galt said, "I understand most of your people still believe the highlanders are related to the gods."

Adoranon said, "That is true. And we all miss our holy places here on Splendor."

Chanda asked, "Kardashev's not about to break out into a war, is it?"

"No, but we've seen suicides, especially among our older people. We valley dwellers aren't many in sheer numbers yet, but as a percentage of population, it's quite a rise."

Chanda spoke for Galt's sake when she pointed out, "And this is at a time when both species — the valley dwellers on Kardashev and the highlanders on Socrates — will need as large a population as possible while still starting out."

Adoranon fidgeted in her seat. "I believe it is only fair you know this, Chanda. I recommend to Dijirar that no more valley dwellers travel to Kardashev."

Chanda said, "I've already suspended the evacuations."

"You must not start them up again. And those already on Kardashev should come back to Splendor."

Galt said to Adoranon, "Tell us why."

"You know how we valley dwellers have traditionally revered the highlanders."

Galt nodded and said, "I do," and Chanda was impressed by his demeanor. *I thought he'd be dismissive of their beliefs, even without meaning to be, in his expression or tone of voice. But he's taking her seriously.*

Adoranon went on: "I've been uncertain for some time about the highlanders' nature. Are they gods, to be able to live in these frozen wastes? Those I've gotten to know well seem to be of nature, as I am, and Humans assure us they are, despite the wonders they're capable of."

Chanda said, gently, "You're far from the first valley dweller to have such doubts."

"I know. And after much consideration, I realized I could live with those doubts. Part of me still wants to revere the highlanders, but another part embraces the reality of them I've witnessed through the years."

Bram said, "Adoranon tells me, though, that other valley dwellers haven't come to the same conclusion she has."

The tip of Adoranon's tail flipped nervously. "That's correct," she said. "Many of us cannot bear the highlanders' absence. And although Kardashev has places as cold as the highlanders' dwelling places, they are too far away for us to travel to easily."

Chanda told Galt, "Kardashev has plenty of hot springs, volcanos, and the like. But it's much warmer than Splendor, and even Earth. Even its polar caps are pretty small by comparison."

Adoranon said, "None of that has stopped many valley dwellers from wanting to travel to those places."

Galt asked, "To the poles?"

"Yes. Some believe they'll find highlanders there. They need them to trade with, to give their lives meaning."

Chanda said, "We've tried to explain this to them — that Kardashev is a different world, with different kinds of life, that there are no highlanders."

"I understand and accept that," Adoranon said. "But not all valley dwellers have spoken to Humans as much as I have, or as Dijirar has. Many of them begin to despair. They . . . "

"Insist upon believing superstitions," Dijirar said.

She said what I couldn't, Chanda thought.

Galt leaned forward. "Adoranon. Do you think we could educate the valley dwellers about the highlanders? Get them to understand their true nature?"

Adoranon exchanged looks with Dijirar, and they both emitted the hissing sound that was valley dweller laughter.

Galt faced Chanda. "Wha'd I say?"

Chanda shook her head. "Would you try to convince a Christian Jesus wasn't divine? A Muslim that Muhammad wasn't a messenger of God?"

"Well . . . I suppose not."

"It's a matter of faith. You have it or you don't. And it's presumptuous at best to try to damage that faith."

Galt asked, "So we should just give up? Bring the valley dwellers home?"

Chanda ran a hand through her hair. "I don't consider it giving up. But I think the valley dwellers' reaction is one reason the evacuation effort should be scrapped entirely."

Bram stood up, holding his highlander spear out in front of him. "I have another reason right here. I took this spear from the dead hand of a highlander. They're in full-scale war on Socrates."

Galt asked, "You went down there?"

"I did. Took a dozen Marines with me, full armor, full complement of very visible weapons. We found some highlander leaders, first on one side, then the other, who were willing to talk."

"So what's causing the conflict?"

"The lack of valley dwellers on the planet. No one to provide them with the tools and weapons they need."

Chanda said, "We trained them how to do all that themselves."

"Which they consider disrespectful to their gods. You know how that led to slavery right here on Splendor. There, without the valley dwellers, there's no one to serve as a calming influence on their culture."

Chanda thought of Roraten, the former slave who was challenging Indirogar for the position of Elder. "Yeah. I guess we know that all too well."

A series of shouts came over Chanda's datalink and she winced. She touched behind her left ear. "Who is this?"

"Indirogar — Chanda, help me! I need you."

It's as if the thought conjured up the person, Chanda thought. "What's the problem?" she asked, as the others around her listened.

"It's Roraten. He and a mob may be about to attack my home! Please come help." The transmission cut off.

Another touch behind the ear, and Chanda said, "Irene — ready the *Bashi*. We're headed to Indirogar's camp."

No response for an instant. Then Irene's voice, out of breath, came back: "Will do. We'll be ready to lift in ten minutes."

Chanda stood. "Indirogar's in trouble. I'm headed to his village. Captain Bram, can I recruit you in case there's trouble?"

"Certainly, Ambassador," Bram said.

"Senator Galt — how'd you like to be issued a stunner and go along, as well? I understand if you'd rather —"

"I wouldn't be anywhere else, Ambassador. I'll meet you at the *Bashi*."

"We're pretty constrained in what we can do. No matter how much we like Indirogar, we can't take sides in a dispute between highlanders."

Dijirar touched Chanda on the arm. "Adoranon and I are also ready to help however we can."

"Indirogar's lucky to have such friends. I'll let you know what we find out." Chanda left the command center and headed for the *Bashi*.

As the *Bashi* came in over Indirogar's village, Chanda saw a large crowd of highlanders outside his hut. Many of them were waving spears and appeared to be banging the sides of metal bowls, a cacophony that went unheard from the shuttle. "Indirogar told me Roraten had more support than he'd expected — but I think he underestimated it! They've got him holed up in his hut," Chanda said. "Look — there's Roraten right at Indirogar's door."

Galt said, "Indirogar would be foolish to try to face that crowd by himself."

Bram said, "Roraten would be just as foolish to go into that hut."

"Is this a dispute we should become involved in?" Galt asked. "This seems like internal highlander politics to me."

"I've had that very concern," Chanda said. "But my intention is to save lives."

"All right. Given that, would you take some advice from me?"

"Of course. You're the military man."

"I'd suggest a decisive entrance on our part — Irene brings the *Bashi* down just on the other side of Indirogar's hut, then the rest of us jump out with stunners at the ready. We either get the crowd to disperse or do a snatch-and-grab with Indirogar."

It's enlightening to see Galt in his element, Chanda thought. "That sounds like a great plan." She touched behind her ear. "Indirogar — we're coming in. Get ready to move."

Chanda heard the highlander over her datalink: "Please do everything you can not to hurt my people."

"Don't worry, my friend. This is a 'stunners-only' mission." To Irene, she said, "Take us down."

Irene brought the *Bashi*'s nose down sharply enough that the village seemed to leap up at them. Galt was already opening the inner airlock door. "I should go out first, Senator," Chanda said. "These people know me."

Galt, to Chanda's surprise, stood aside without argument. *Though maybe he's thinking I can hang myself all the more effectively if I'm first out.*

The shuttle leveled out mere meters from the ground, and Chanda could tell that Irene was "gunning" its gravitics to make a much louder entrance than usual. Many of the highlanders gathered in front of Indirogar's hut fell back, a few of them tripping over one another in their haste. Others stood their ground, and Chanda couldn't help but notice that most of them were armed with the ubiquitous spears of valley dweller manufacture.

The shuttle was still settling to the ground as Chanda leaped through the outer airlock door and moved toward the highlanders in front of Indirogar's hut, her stunner raised over her head. Galt and Bram were right behind her, their weapons also clearly visible.

Chanda picked out Roraten, who was brandishing a spear at the front of the mob. "What's going on here?" she demanded.

Roraten held his spear close to his body. "Ambassador Kasmira —

you must be here to help your friend Indirogar. I thought the Unity couldn't take sides."

Chanda lowered her stunner. "I'm here to make sure no one gets killed."

"Yes, just as your people graciously tried to save me and some of my fellows by sending us to Kardashev. I bear the scars of that decision. But I'm fortunate. Many of those who went there with me never returned."

"I'm sorry about that. But — "

"If I'm to live back here on our homeworld, it will not be under Indirogar. Take him away if you wish. We have no objection to him living out his life with his Human friends."

A voice from behind Chanda — Indirogar! "As much as I love those Human friends, I'll live out my life here — with my own people." Indirogar stood in the doorway to his hut, gripping his spear with both hands.

At that sight, Roraten raised his spear above his head. Chanda's grip tightened on her stunner. She saw Galt taking a step forward, and she held out a hand for him to stop. He did, but his hard features told her he was more than ready to act if the situation escalated.

But after a moment, Roraten lowered his spear, saying, "Highlanders decide their own future. And a future in which you blindly follow what Earth wants is not your own."

Indirogar strode past Chanda. "My decisions *are* my own. I am no one's puppet — either Humanity's or yours."

Roraten's voice grew quiet. "I know you don't want to become Eldest."

Indirogar hesitated, then admitted, "I've learned too well how Ahtenhurat felt those many years ago."

"And you remember how his tribe suffered for it. No Eldest, and an Elder who began to lose support among his own people."

Indirogar's voice growled in anger: "Ahtenhurat loved his people, and sacrificed his own happiness countless times."

"But he made one mistake -- hanging onto power too long. You're about to make that same mistake. You become Eldest, and your power and influence decline, it is true. If you cannot make yourself become Eldest, then at least make yourself a better example to your tribe than you've been in recent times." Roraten indicated Chanda. "Stand up to Humanity. Their representative to Splendor is right here. Tell her you're making the decision that's right for your people."

Indirogar looked out across the mass of highlanders before him. "My decision is the same as it has always been. I am your Elder, and will remain so."

The crowd began to murmur, then several highlanders began lifting their spears into the air and chanting: "Eldest! Eldest!" Others started banging rhythmically on metal bowls.

As the chanting grew louder, Roraten handed his spear to another highlander and approached Indirogar with his hands in plain sight. "Indirogar. It's time."

Chanda thought, *Roraten, for all his audacity, has a charisma that Indirogar can't summon anymore.*

Indirogar looked at Chanda. "You cannot help me in this, can you?"

"I'm here to keep people from being killed, if I can. How highlanders rule themselves isn't my concern."

Indirogar raised his spear and Chanda tensed. But Indirogar stabbed the spear into the ground and declared, "I accept the position of Eldest."

The highlanders' chanting ceased and they began thumping their own spears against the ground in celebration. After a time, Indirogar raised his hands and everyone fell silent. "It's my responsibility to name your Elder. It's a decision that can lead to some surprising choices." Indirogar glanced at Chanda with a mischievous grin.

Chanda's face flushed as she recalled how the late Ahtenhurat had chosen Indirogar's rival Eluharobak to succeed him as Elder twelve years earlier. Ahtenhurat was dying, and wanted to make sure that after his own death Eluharobak would quickly ascend to the position of Eldest, the more prestigious but less influential position.

That had cleared the way for Indirogar to become Elder, as Ahtenhurat had wished. But even after Eluharobak's sudden and unexpected death, Indirogar had resisted ascending to the position of Eldest, employing the fiction of Eluharobak's mummified remains retaining the power of the office.

And what the hell is that grin about as he's looking at me? Chanda wondered. *No, he can't be considering* that. *A Human can't become Eldest.*

Indirogar's grin faded and he faced Roraten. He pulled his spear from the ground and thrust it down again right in front of Roraten. "I name you Elder of our tribe," he said.

The tribe responded with renewed shouts and foot stomping and spear waving. Indirogar turned his back on Roraten and went back into his hut.

Galt told Chanda, "Go see Indirogar. Bram and I will keep an eye out."

"He's not in danger now," Chanda said. "He's just become the most revered highlander in his tribe."

"Still — he's your friend."

Chanda paused in the doorway. "I won't be long." She entered the stone hut.

It took a moment for Chanda's eyes to adapt to the relative darkness, and she heard Indirogar before she saw him, still holding his spear: "So it ends. Roraten has taken my place — just as he wished."

Indirogar's rough fingers ran down the smooth surface of his spear, which had been lovingly forged within the valley dwellers' lands. The end of his tail flipped absentmindedly against the floor. "I've depended upon you for so much. I suppose I'd hoped you could rescue me from Roraten today."

Chanda felt tension building in her shoulders and neck. "You know I couldn't."

"Which you have made clear many times. Humans act as they must. As do my own people. And if those people want Roraten, they may have him. I do not wish to rule over the unwilling."

"The evacuation effort is going to end. All the highlanders on Socrates, all the valley dwellers on Kardashev — they'll be returning home soon."

Indirogar placed the spear back on the wall next to its fellows. "I suppose that gladdens my hearts."

"It makes my single heart sad. Because I don't know how to save your future generations."

"Does Galt not have his own plan?"

"None that he's told me about."

"Then he is useless."

"He's the one figured out how we should confront Roraten just now."

Indirogar said, "Then — I may owe him my life."

"As much as I hate to admit it, you may."

"That makes me dislike him all the more."

Chanda laughed. "You and I need each other. I'll especially need your wisdom as much as I ever did, perhaps more."

"How may the Eldest serve you?"

"If the evacuation effort is cancelled, I have to decide what role I play here on Splendor."

"Perhaps the Unity will assign you to a different . . . world. It is still a difficult concept for me, that there are so many worlds, so many stars."

"Difficult, perhaps. But wonderful. You should see those worlds and stars, Indirogar. Callippus system, a star that collapsed in on itself. A ring of debris spins around it. Giant jets of gas shoot out from its poles."

"It sounds frightening."

"It is," Chanda said. "Wonderfully so. And Dijirar can tell you of all there is to see on Earth. Imagine *deserts*, for instance."

"Failure to translate."

"Great plains of sand as vast as snowfields here on Splendor."

"Why would I want to go to such a place? It sounds as if it would be difficult to survive there."

"The difficulty can be part of the wonder. It's the same for Humans here on Splendor."

"It would be . . . unusual. For the Eldest to take such a journey."

Which means you'd consider it. Good. If I can get you to think about the future . . .

Indirogar continued: "But I cannot consider such things now. I wish to spend one final day among my own people before I ascend into the cave to take my place as the new Eldest."

"Well . . . at least you still have a job."

Indirogar took Chanda by the arm. "Come, my friend. We'll go feast with the rest of the tribe. I'll even find it within me to congratulate Roraten on ascending to Elder. Then we can come back here and talk of planets and stars while drinking too much wine."

"I don't know that I should, Indirogar."

"Someone who says she doesn't have a job has no excuse not to play."

Chanda's every instinct was to put forth a dozen reasons she shouldn't accept Indirogar's invitation. *The same reasons I've had in all the months and years since coming here to Splendor. But everything's changed. And I may not even get to remain here much longer.*

The hell with it. "That sounds great, Indirogar. Let's see if the other Humans would like to join us."

When Chanda and Indirogar stepped outside Indirogar's hut and put the idea to the others, Galt looked at her quizzically but said, "It sounds like a great opportunity to get to know Indirogar and Roraten better."

Bram stood straight and said, "Sounds like a great idea to me, too."

Chanda turned to Irene. "So?"

"I think you owe it to yourself."

"I'm not doing it for — "

Irene grabbed Chanda's shoulders. "Ambassador — *Chanda* — it's OK if you do something for yourself once in a while."

"Yeah. Maybe."

"You never look out for yourself. And I can always tell when you're doing that — when you do that deadpan 'yeah.'"

"Ye — I mean . . . I do?"

Galt said, "It's up there with the animal analogies, Chanda."

Indirogar said, "But I have learned of the most interesting Earth creatures from her sayings."

Chanda let herself grin. "I'm sorry I'm so predictable. And don't have more ready-made material to amuse you."

Irene indicated the center of the village, where most of its population was already gathered. "The feast will get started any minute, Chanda. Let's go."

Chanda put her arms around Irene's shoulders, and gathered Indirogar closely as well. "You're right. I've seldom had a chance just to have some fun these past few years. I'd better take advantage of it while I can."

While I'm still here, Chanda thought, barely realizing the decision she'd made for herself.

CHAPTER 6

The day after the feast in Indirogar's village, Chanda awoke, sat up, held her head in her hands for a long minute, then got up and told her symptoms to the nanodoc in her bathroom. She swallowed the pill it created for her, and within a couple of minutes the pain eased.

She touched behind her ear. "Irene."

No answer for a moment, then she heard muted laughter, and Irene going, "Shush!" Then: "I'm sorry, Ambassador. What can I do for you?"

"If this is a bad time —"

"No, not at all." Chanda could still hear muted laughter in the background, though.

"Please come to my quarters. I've got a little project for you. Now that I think of it, bring Akira, too."

Sudden silence in the background now. Irene said, "Yes, Ambassador. We'll be right there."

It wasn't three minutes later that the two women arrived at Chanda's door. "Com'on in," she told them. "Sit down."

Irene and Akira traded puzzled glances. Didn't sit. Chanda told them. "Don't stand there like I've called you to a Captain's Mast. For one thing, I don't have the authority. For another, you haven't done anything wrong."

"Thank you, Ma'am," Akira said.

"Stop with the 'Ma'am.' 'Ambassador' if you must, but I'd prefer 'Chanda.'"

"Yes, M — Yes, Ambassador."

"Either of you like a drink?"

Another shared glance. "No thanks, Chanda," Irene said.

Chanda indicated Irene to Akira. "See? I've brought her around. There's hope for you yet, Akira."

"Yes, Ambassador."

"All right, both of you — *sit*."

They sat. Chanda sat across from them. "I have a project the two of you can help me with. It entails replicating some equipment, installing it, and testing it."

Irene asked, "What is it?"

Chanda told them.

Akira's response: "Chanda! You can't do that to us!"

Chanda grinned. "I *knew* I'd bring you around. The answer is, I can and will do this. I've devoted myself to the evacuation effort for the past four years, and it's all going to shit. I'm out of ideas. I want to walk away on my own rather than wait for Galt to get the Unity Senate to toss me out."

Irene sat back in her chair and crossed her arms. "You're abandoning us."

That made Chanda think a moment. But she said, "No. I'm not. But I'm beginning to doubt myself — doubt how much more I can really do here."

"That's because of Galt," Irene said. "He's been trying to undermine you since he came here."

Akira said, "He's trying to play on your doubts."

"If they weren't already there," Chanda said, "he wouldn't be able to play upon them."

Irene asked, "When do you want this set up?"

"As soon as possible. I've already made the request for Akira to be attached to my staff for now."

Irene and Akira traded delighted smiles. Chanda asked, "I assume the two of you can handle most of the engineering?"

"I'll need to consult with someone on the medical parts."

"I'd suggest Dr. McEwan — Phillip. He knows his stuff, and he can keep quiet."

Akira asked, "And if Galt catches wind of what we're doing?"

"I don't doubt myself *that* much. I can keep him distracted."

———

Days later, the word came in from the Buruden: they were ready to depart from Splendor and they wished to speak to Chanda before they left. Galt didn't challenge Chanda when she told him, as casually as she could, that she'd given Irene some time off and they'd pilot themselves to the Buruden's encampment.

Soon Chanda stood with Galt before the Buruden starcraft. It stood ten meters tall and was half a kilometer long. Four engine nacelles were slung beneath it, and the entire Buruden community on Splendor, about a thousand, stood next to it.

Galt raised a hand to shield his eyes against the rays of the rising sun. "I can't believe they finished this so quickly. And that they're launching from a planetary surface."

"They could teach us something about stardrive construction," Chanda said. "Maybe just something as simple as being able to jump closer to a planet's grav field. But I've never been able to convince them to."

Galt indicated a mass of Buruden that was detaching itself from the larger group and approaching them. "Well, here's your last chance to say whatever you wish."

The Buruden ambassador, joined on three sides with other Buruden, spoke: "Ambassador Kasmira, we are leaving. It is a truth that the

Sobrenians will await us as we near our home planet. It is a likely truth that my people will enter a fight with the Sobrenians. It is a potential truth that many of us will die. It is an untruth that my people will ever surrender to them."

Chanda said, "I can only wish you the best. If there's anything I can ever do for you, let me know." *Oops*, Chanda immediately thought. *Shouldn't have promised that. I won't even be here.*

"The Buruden thank you. But you should know one last truth before we leave. We tried to convince the sweepers to discontinue their 'no-fly zone,' as you refer to it. But we failed."

"What did you tell them?"

"We informed them of a single truth — that if we Buruden survive our likely conflict with the Sobrenians, we will return to continue our work to find a way for them to survive the coming of the gas nebula."

Galt said, "That's very gracious of you!"

"Consider, Senator, Ambassador — if our species survives, it will be little trouble to return here, especially since the gas nebula does not arrive for several decades. If we do not survive, both Splendorians of all species and Humanity will have much more immediate problems."

Chanda couldn't find words for a moment. She had to keep her voice from choking when she finally said, "Thank you for that warning. I'll be sure to pass it on to the Unity. I'm sure Senator Galt will, as well."

"The sweepers would not deviate from their decision on the no-fly zone. We considered it quite . . . single-minded." Chanda knew that simple phrase implied a level of stubbornness that the Buruden mentality, with their four-level way of thinking, found perplexing.

Without another word, the mass of Buruden turned and retreated toward the larger group. All thousand or so Buruden stood quietly for a few moments, then they split up into groups ranging from hundreds to a couple dozen, and ran full-bore up the four struts supporting their starcraft.

Galt told Chanda, "I don't know that you should've told them that."

"What? That we'd both let the Unity know what they said about the Sobrenians?"

"We're not in a position to speak for the Buruden."

"Then who else is?" Chanda asked. "I'm the ambassador to Splendor and you're on a fact-finding mission for the Senate. I didn't promise we'd be their advocates — just that we'd pass on what they said."

The Buruden starcraft's inertials started up, a much quieter process than for any Human craft.

Galt said, "It could look as if we're taking the Buruden's side in any conflict that comes up."

"Well — shouldn't we?"

The Buruden craft started to rise, ponderously at first, then seemingly with more confidence. Chanda raised a hand against the sun's radiance, then lowered it as the rising starcraft eclipsed it.

Galt said, "These Buruden have some very impressive technical abilities. But so do the Sobrenians."

"Who, you may remember, have already attacked Splendor once. They could do it again."

The sun popped out from behind the Buruden starcraft, which had already achieved an impressive acceleration — straight up into clear, cold Splendorian skies, not bothering to flatten out its trajectory at all.

Galt told Chanda, "You've been an ambassador long enough to understand *realpolitik*. I don't like the Sobrenians any more than you do. But we may have to deal with them."

"With Splendor as one pawn among many."

Galt spoke quietly: "You need to go back home awhile, Ambassador. Splendor's a beautiful place, and I'm impressed with many of the locals I've met so far. But Earth is beautiful, too, and anyone who's Human has ties to the homeworld that pull us back, no matter how far we travel or how long it takes us to come home."

"Do we?" Chanda asked. "Or is that just a subtle way of telling me I should voluntarily return to Earth instead of being relieved?"

"Ambassador, I wouldn't presume. . . . "

Chanda gave Galt a sour look. "You've seen my records. You know how many times I've dealt with the Sobrenians here. I've saved Splendor from being attacked by them twice."

Four years earlier, the Sobrenians began using Splendor as a site to test weapons to see their effects upon an inhabited world — those tests ended when Chanda ordered the *Nivara* grounded to become the Unity's embassy. Later that year, she'd helped rescue the crew of the Buruden starcraft that crashed into Splendor's Great Sea — a starcraft the Sobrenians had tried, unsuccessfully, to take over.

The year after, Chanda had repelled another Sobrenian attack by organizing a coalition of highlanders, valley dwellers, and sweepers, along with the Buruden who had decided to stay on Splendor. That attack had been assisted by a Human named Lewis Tiernan, a former Unity Marine who'd turned against his own people, trying to get Humanity to end its voyaging through space and devote itself to its homeworld.

Galt folded his arms and tried to stare Chanda down. "Those were all great things you did, but they *were* several years ago. We haven't seen a lot of movement lately on the evacuation effort. You have to understand how everything appears back on Earth, Ambassador, and we feel we have a little more objective view of things, more of a view of the big picture."

"Except this isn't always about the big picture, Senator. There are a thousand things here on the ground that can trip you up. You have to have seen that just in the little time you've been here."

"This trip has been enlightening," Galt said, "in ways I never expected."

"I know you want to be scrupulous about this. Though I wonder who would take my place."

Galt said, "I don't want your job. I have grandchildren I'm eager to get back home and spoil."

"But you'd take my place if asked."

"Again, I'm former military. I know what it is to be given an assignment, and to carry it out, whether I want to or not."

Chanda lifted her gaze. The Buruden starcraft was a tiny dot. Then it faded into blue skies. *It may have already broken orbit by now*, she thought.

And maybe they're taking the right path. Toward home. Maybe Galt's right. Maybe that's where I should go, as well.

"Ambassador? Chanda?"

"Hmm?"

"You looked . . . I don't know . . . pensive."

"Oh. Just trying to catch a last glimpse of the Buruden. But there's nothing left to see, is there?"

Once back at the Unity embassy, Chanda managed to ditch Galt and head for the former starcraft's engineering section. A touch to the main doorway, and it opened for her; the only others it would respond to were Irene and Akira.

This room had once contained *Nivara's* Alcubierre stardrive modules. Once Humans had harnessed unfathomable energies here: new-space regulators, phase transition modules, mass-energy resonators, all operating in sync to create the localized distortion in space-time that allowed a starcraft to outpace light itself.

All that equipment was gone now, and Chanda still wasn't accustomed to the way her footsteps echoed off bare walls. Now, in the middle of the room, stood an oval, waist-high pedestal three meters long and two wide, which was surrounded by medical equipment — sensors, monitors, nanomed generators, countless other devices. Chanda knew that embedded into the pedestal itself was other vital equipment that would have to work perfectly to sustain her on her long journey.

Irene and Akira were lost in concentration as they leaned over the pedestal, Irene holding a hand sensor, Akira reaching into the Human-shaped indentation within the pedestal itself.

Chanda watched them work a moment, then asked, "How are things going?"

Akira looked up from her work and beamed at Chanda. "Looks like we're all set."

Irene's expression was dour. "Whenever you're ready to go."

Chanda said, "I don't do this lightly."

Irene looked away from Chanda. "I know."

"Well — you should both take a break. Get something to eat."

"Good idea," Irene said. She turned to Akira. "Coming?"

Akira was leaning over the pedestal again. "Just one more thing I forgot to check out. You go ahead, I'll be right there."

"I will too," Chanda said. She looked into the shell's interior, which featured a recessed section the approximate shape of her own body. She recognized some of the instrumentation — energy conduits, life-support modules, temperature regulators — but had no idea how to operate or maintain any of it. She envied Akira's obvious ease with the tech.

When the doors slid shut behind Irene, Akira looked up from her work and told Chanda, "She's going to miss you terribly, you know."

"She'll be OK," Chanda said. "They'll have another ambassador in here soon enough, someone she can be as loyal to as she is to me. Maybe someone with a much better idea of how to save everyone."

Akira looked up at Chanda. "Yeah. I'm sure you're right."

"Com'on," Chanda said. "Let's catch up to Irene and grab some lunch."

"Sounds great." They headed for the doorway, their footsteps echoing across the former engineering section which was now occupied only by the newly constructed stasis shell.

A week later, Chanda was ready for her "departure." She decided upon a time of nine the next morning, and requested several people to meet with her. She went to her room and would not answer her door or datalink.

Ten minutes before nine, she stood before the stasis shell, alone. *Early in my life when I would climb into one of these things, it's as if I was a time traveler*, she thought. *But I could only go into the future, and just a few years at a time.*

It had been that way as far back as 58 years earlier, in 2092, when she was 15 years old objectively, but only eight subjectively.

Her best friends in Calcutta had been Markus Kesler and Keely Rashid. She and her parents saw them at an outdoor cafe on a clear day after her fourth awakening. Each seemed surprised to see her, and especially surprised that she was still eight years old when they were fifteen.

Markus's voice seemed oddly deep and he looked down at Chanda from a height she never thought she would attain. As for Keely, her newly acquired (or so it seemed to Chanda) breasts and the roundness at her hips appeared to be appendages, not truly a part of the young woman she'd become.

After initial pleasantries, both of them flashed smiles that were at once forced and dismissive, and they resumed their private conversation. She never saw them again.

This will be a much longer journey. Once gone, there's no coming back.

Am I doing the right thing?

Either way, I'll have to live with it.

The doors to the main entrance slid open and Irene and Akira arrived, with the highlander Indirogar and the valley dweller Dijirar. "My friends," Chanda said. "I'm glad you could be here."

Indirogar went to Chanda and held both her hands in his. "Friend Chanda. I don't quite understand what I've been told. You are somehow leaving, yet you will remain?"

"In a sense," Chanda said. "I'll explain everything as soon as the others arrive."

Which didn't take long. Chanda's assistant Ken Westbrook arrived next, then Dr. Phillip McEwan, whose expertise would be needed in the procedure to come. Last to arrive were her Military Liaison Trenton Bram — and Senator Galt.

"Ambassador Kasmira," Galt began, "I demand to know why you haven't — "

"With all due respect, Senator, please shut the hell up!"

"You can't — "

"Senator, *please*. This isn't your show."

Galt shut up. Stood, arms folded. Took in his surroundings, and appeared puzzled by the stasis shell.

Chanda said, "Senator Galt is all too aware of the difficulties we've had trying to save everyone on Splendor. I've had to cancel the evacuation effort. The sweepers have grown hostile toward the Human presence here. Humanity has to come up with another idea about how to save everyone on the planet."

Irene said, "There are plenty of other possibilities." She spoke in plaintive tones that touched Chanda's heart: "Building an orbital habitat. Finding a way to disrupt the gas nebula."

"Technical solutions that don't require my presence."

Galt spoke in a quieter voice than before. "Chanda . . . you should consider my suggestion — go back to Earth. Your home. You have friends, family."

"Actually, I don't. No one I care to see, anyway." *Or who cares to see me*, Chanda thought. She told Galt, "In the past four years, Splendor has become my home."

Dijirar said, "But such wonders I saw on Earth! So many cultures!"

"I'm already from two cultures -- Ugandan and Russian. And I've traveled my homeworld enough to have seen plenty others."

"You could have children -- it doesn't seem to me that there are that many differences between Human males and females -- "

"Hah!" Chanda exclaimed, as the rest of the Humans laughed.

"You just canceled out several millennia of Human relationships, literature, and psychology."

"You know what I mean. At least your males are intelligent."

"Many of them, anyway. Perhaps a few more if you assign sentience to a penis."

"I don't think that was a failure to translate. But how could a -- "

"Never mind. Just try to understand that I think Splendor has become my child."

"Ah. A metaphor. But difficult for a valley dweller to identify with. Child raising is pure biology for us. The . . . genetic link, I believe you would call it . . . is all-powerful."

"It is for a great many Humans, as well," Chanda said. "But I don't think I'm one of them."

"I grieve for you, then," Dijirar said.

"Please don't. Allow me my own way of coping with such matters." She took a moment to gather her thoughts. "My friends — if Splendor is indeed my child, I want to live to see it grow up. To see how it might flourish once the threat of the gas nebula is removed."

Trenton Bram said, "Chanda, I've worked with you a long time. Are you sure this is what you want to do?"

Chanda placed a hand on the side of the stasis shell. "Yes, it is. I'm leaving instructions to wake me in about 2228 if the gas nebula is still a danger and other evacuation efforts haven't been successful. That's about ten years before it's expected to reach here. Maybe there's some insight I can deliver then."

Galt asked, "What if Splendor's population isn't in danger?"

"Then I want to wake up about a century after that, when any re-terraforming effort will have had a chance to take effect."

Irene spoke up: "Please don't leave us, Chanda. Don't you realize — this comes directly from how you were raised. But you hated being placed in stasis then."

"I wasn't making the decision then. I am now."

"Are you sure you're not reaching back to your childhood — doing something that's a comfort to you?"

"I appreciate your loyalty, Irene, if not the cheap psychology. I can only ask you to accept my decision."

Irene wouldn't look at Chanda. "I guess I have to."

She went to each of them one by one. Trenton Bram's embrace was warm, and he held it longer than she expected. "All the usual phrases don't apply," he said. "I can't tell you I expect to see you soon."

"I'll be right here," Chanda pointed out.

"Won't see you *awake*, how's that? You won't be reporting back in my lifetime."

Ken Westbrook said, "How about we just wish you a safe journey?" He went to Chanda, gave her a long hug. When they stepped back from one other, he was wiping away tears.

Chanda told Phillip McEwan, "I suppose I should say a special goodbye to you. I'll be counting on you to look after me."

McEwan said, "Not for most of the time you'll be here. Aren't you afraid you'll be forgotten, or. . . . "

"Or people will just quit caring whether I'm here?"

"I didn't want to put it like that."

"Believe me, if I never wake up, I won't take it personally."

Dijirar was next as Chanda leaned over to embrace her. The valley dweller said, "I've seen the wonders of your world. I wish I might see the wonders of my own that you will experience so many years from now."

"To me," Chanda said, "it'll seem like just a few minutes."

"I will make sure my people remember you."

Then she went to Indirogar, and Chanda braced against the high-lander's usual embrace. This one nearly squeezed the breath out of her. "My dear friend," she told him. Leaning close to his ear, she said quietly, "You're perhaps the one I've become closest to in my time here."

Indirogar said, "Your departure will create an absence in my hearts."

Chanda placed her hand on Indirogar's furred cheek. "I'll think of you when I wake again."

To Akira, she said, "Thanks for all you've done. You've risked your life for me. And be sure to take care of Irene." She embraced Akira.

Then Chanda stood in front of Irene, whose lower lip was quivering and whose face was lined with streams of tears.

It was Irene who moved first, taking Chanda into a hug that rivaled Indirogar's. *She's shaking*, Chanda realized. *I don't deserve someone this loyal.*

Chanda kissed Irene on the cheek. "Take care of yourself. And of Akira."

Irene took Chanda's hands in hers. "I'll never forget you."

Chanda smiled. "Well, I hope *someone* remembers about me. Otherwise I may never have a chance to wake up." She went to the stasis shell and took a step up onto its platform. Akira and Phillip stood on either side, ready to work its controls, Akira concerning herself with the engineering while Phillip tended to the medical side.

Chanda swung her legs over into the recessed portion of the pedestal and sat within it. "I wish I had some deep final message for you, my friends. But I don't. Only that I wish the best for all of you — and for the future of this planet." She nodded to Akira and Phillip and settled down within the stasis shell.

A hard, clear dome rose from the sides of the shell, encasing her. Immediately, Chanda flashed back to those times from her childhood when her parents would coax her into such a device — once, what was supposed to be a gap of a couple years became eight. Chanda saw wisps of gray in her mother's hair — she'd been 49 years old when Chanda went into stasis, and when she came out her mother was 57. Her father had been 47, and had turned 55, with deepening lines at the edges of his mouth and the corners of his eyes.

Chanda pleaded with them never to put her into stasis again, never to leave her again.

But they did, one last time. Nine years later, hundreds of thousands of light-years out from Earth, an unmanned Arol probe ship discovered their ship, the *Wanderer*. The eventual report concluded that a catastrophic failure of the ship's life-support had doomed her parents. No mysteries, no conspiracies, no attacks by "unknown aliens," just an accident.

If only they'd died making some grand discovery, or diverting to rescue someone in trouble, Chanda thought. *Just like the heroes in some cube drama.*

That's enough of those thoughts, Chanda decided. *I'm taking this thing I once hated and turning it around, making it a positive. Now I've got what I hope is a brighter future ahead. Even if I can't contribute to saving Splendor, I can at least see how it all turns out.*

Who knows what I might awaken to? If all goes well, and it's a century after the passing of the gas nebula, I might see a Splendor much the same as now, with highlanders and valley dwellers and sweepers living as they wish, but without the threat of the gas nebula.

Or the Splendorians might have embraced Human tech, allowing the valley dwellers and highlanders to stay longer in each others' realms.

Some of them might even become spacers! Certainly each species is intelligent enough, and by then several generations would've been exposed to the idea.

What's that? Oh, everyone's staring at me. Seems a little rude. But at least they care enough to have that last look.

'Course, they could come down and sneak a peek anytime they like in the next few decades. Maybe I'll be part of a tour.

Mind's wandering now. Enough of spinning fantasies. As usual, the truth will be completely unexpected. What's the phrase . . . not only stranger than we imagine, but stranger than we can imagine.

Can't keep eyes open. Ready for sleep. And when I wake. . . .

CHAPTER 7

No fantasies now, only swirling memories, as if my life is flashing before my eyes — am I dying?

As a young woman of sixteen subjective years, forty objective, I rose at five to fetch water from the well in New Lancaster Habitat, often craning my neck to see others my age performing similar chores 1.2 K overhead.

In and out of the stasis shell so many times. My parents dying. My grandparents the Ssalis raising me in the "purposely primitive" New Lancaster Habitat, only the Bible and Shakespeare to read, rising at five in the morning to fetch water from the well.

My first lover at age 17 subjective, 41 objective, — Henry Adair, our furtive, desperate coupling in a barn, thin stalks of straw like needles against my back, the hurried warmth we'd generated borne away into the cold air.

My brief marriage to a sexless Arol, tender but without passion, doomed from the beginning, my betrayal of it sexual, its own purely emotional.

My arrival on Splendor, age 45 subjective, 69 objective, and only now, nearly four years later, do I realize I'm a vessel as empty as my *beloved homespace baskets. So many that I've loved are dead, whether literally or emotionally, and I need my work to be filled up, to be whole.*

"Chanda — wake up."

Can't keep my eyes open. Still want to sleep. It can't be time to wake!

"Ambassador!"

Chanda opened her eyes. The dome of the stasis shell stood open and Irene stared down at her. Chanda said, "Not 'Ambassador' any longer. I don't . . . Irene, why are you here? Did you take the cold sleep, too?"

"No, Chanda. It's. . . . "

"You're not even any older. How long?"

"It's only been two weeks, Chanda."

"What the hell?" Chanda tried to raise herself up. Mistake. Her head swam and she lowered herself again.

Another voice: Dr. McEwan. "You'll be OK in a minute, Chanda. Your vitals are good. In a minute you can sit up and we'll get a good, hot meal into you."

"Never mind that. What the hell happened? I was supposed to sleep for decades!"

Another voice from behind McEwan: "We need you, Chanda." Gabriel Galt stepped up to the stasis shell. "You may be the only person who can prevent a war between the Sobrenians and Buruden."

"But I'm not an ambassador. I quit."

"The Unity reinstated you."

Chanda raised herself up again, and this time her head behaved. "So I have them to thank for this."

"Thank the Sobrenians and Buruden," Galt said. "*They* requested you."

Chanda assumed they would head toward the embassy's commons, but as it turned out, she and Senator Galt, along with Irene and Akira, who would serve as her aides, were soon aboard a shuttle that lifted them toward the Earth Unity light cruiser *Sergeant Jelal*, Senator Galt's former command.

Soon she and Galt were sitting down in the *Jelal*'s mess hall and Chanda was eating that good, hot meal (a vegetable stir-fry, washed down with iced tea).

The starcraft quickly boosted toward the Sobrenian homeworld where they would begin negotiations with the Sobrenian and Buruden delegations. Sometime later talks would move to the Buruden homeworld, then conclude on Splendor, which was considered neutral ground.

As Chanda and the others were still chowing down, the *Jelal*'s captain, Davis Hamadi, came into the commons. "It's a pleasure to see you again, Ambassador," he said as Chanda hastily wiped her mouth, stood, and shook his hand. Hamadi was a sandy-haired man of medium height. Chanda had worked with him briefly about three years ago when the *Jelal* had delivered Chanda's embassy staff after the grounding of the first *Nivara*, then taken Dijirar to Earth to be Splendor's ambassador there.

"I understand you were given this mission at the last minute," Chanda said.

"We were close by, and quite happy to help out our former commander Senator Galt. I understand you're going to be busy during this trip. It should take about four days. I'm here to serve you, as is the rest of my crew."

Chanda said, "I appreciate that, Captain."

Galt explained, "Brussels suggested that some minimal military presence might be important to make an impression on the Sobrenians."

Captain Hamadi's expression turned sober. "I have to warn you, Ambassador. We don't know what to expect inside Sobrenian space."

Chanda said, "I'm sure your crew can handle any task we ask of it. In fact, I have one I like to request of you."

"Name it."

"If I remember correctly, the gas nebula heading toward Splendor will be close to the path we'd take to the Sobrenian homeworld."

"It is," Hamadi said.

"I'd like to go there."

"To go there — you mean, just to have a look at it? There's not much to see, quite honestly."

"Indulge me, Captain."

"Well, certainly. We can get away from Splendor a bit — that'll take more time than the rest of the trip. We program a short jump — it's about as far away as Saturn is from our own sun. We'll be there in a few hours."

"Thanks, Captain."

"Thank you for your confidence," Hamadi said. "I'll leave you to your work. Let me know if you need anything."

"Will do," Chanda said. Then, with only a quick glance at Galt, she kept her knife and fork busy for several minutes. "You gotta excuse me," she told Galt between bites. "I'm always hungry coming out of the stasis shell." Eventually she swallowed a bite of her food and paused for a moment. She asked, "So why are we headed to the Sobrenian homeworld first?"

"They insisted," Galt said. "Some kind of implied insult if they weren't first in line."

"I'm sure they made some sort of condescending remark about 'pre-sentient' species."

"That looks like what they consider the Buruden to be."

Chanda's tongue pushed a glob of food to one side of her mouth. "That's what they consider everyone who isn't Sobrenian to be."

"Humanity included?"

"You wouldn't believe how many times I've had to hear that."

"Fortunately, the Buruden don't seem to have as much ego. They readily agreed to go second."

"Tell me more about how what's been going on."

"It started when the Sobrenians began making threats against the Buruden."

"Weren't they already?"

"It's become more serious. The Buruden keep flitting manned probes into the outer edges of the Sobrenian system. They say they're just curious."

"Which they are. Especially in small groups, they're like little children, distracted by anything shiny."

Galt said, "The Sobrenians don't see it that way. They consider it spying."

Chanda finished a long gulp of tea and leaned back in her chair. "How do we know this?"

"We have our own probes -- just *outside* the Sobrenian system, mind you. But they're heavily shrouded and rely only on passive sensors — and never try to enter the system itself."

"Have the Sobrenians ever been able to intercept any of the Buruden probes?"

"No."

"That's what driving them crazy, then. What have they done to retaliate?"

"They've been intercepting other Buruden starcraft — ones with crews — that pass nearby their system. They've even tried to board them, but you've seen their ships — parts of them are so small Humans certainly can't fit into them, and even though most Sobrenians are smaller, it's a tight fit for them, too."

Chanda asked, "They haven't tried to take any Buruden back to the Sobrenian homeworld?"

"Keep in mind this whole conflict between them is because the Buruden are lurking at the edge of the Sobrenian system, looking in on them. They seem . . . *spooked* is the best word I've come up with about the Sobrenians' attitudes toward the Buruden. I get the impression the Sobrenians' dislike of them is more than political. It's somehow visceral."

"I'm sure a lot of that goes back to this 'pre-sentient' business. The Sobrenians can't stand when another species gets the better of them."

Galt said, "It'll be interesting to see how they react to the Buruden delegation when it lands on their homeworld, then."

Chanda leaned forward again. "So why wake me up for this?"

"Don't you want to try to keep a war from starting?"

"That's not how I meant it. Why *me*? I was out of everyone's way, which was my intention. I didn't feel very wanted. Now two Galactic species can't negotiate a peace without me?"

Galt rubbed his hand over his face, and Chanda realized the man seemed quite tired. *What's his role been in all this?* she wondered, then said, "I'm sorry. I didn't mean to sound bitter."

"It's all right, Chanda," Galt said. "So much is at stake here."

"I'm glad you understand that. And I'm sure you realize if I'm going to do this, I'm the one in charge."

"I haven't thought of it any other way, Ambassador."

"No reluctance? No second thoughts?"

"Ambassador, you know my background. I know how to take an order."

"And do so in silence if you have to."

"Yes."

"Don't. If you see a problem, with me or anyone else, let me know right away. Your knowledge and experience complement mine."

"I appreciate that, Ambassador."

"It's the only way I know how to do business. And we have people on three worlds — four if you count Earth — depending on us."

Galt asked, "We should start prepping for these negotiations. When would you like to start?"

"I've had a long day — and I've got a lot to think about. I need to get some sleep — yes, I know that sounds odd, since I just finished sleeping for two weeks."

"I know the process takes it out of you, Ambassador. We have a few days — let me know when you're ready."

Moments later, Chanda pressed her palm against the door to her quarters and it slid open. Irene and Akira looked up simultaneously; they were sitting next to each other on a couch to the right of the doorway. Irene quickly stood, as did Akira, an instant later. "We unpacked most of your things," Irene said. "Wanted to make sure everything was in good shape. Hope you don't mind."

"Not at all, believe me. I'm much happier having the two of you here." Chanda took a look around and nodded. "Pretty standard quarters. None too big, but bigger than anyone but the captain's, I'd guess."

"Certainly bigger than ours," Akira said in a near-whisper. Irene nudged her in the ribs.

Chanda said, "That chair looks good. I'm sitting down." Irene and Akira exchanged looks, then sat across from her.

After a moment, Irene asked, "Are you all right, Chanda?"

Chanda leaned against one chair arm and covered her face with one hand. "It's just . . . I expected to wake up a century or more from now. All of Splendor's problems . . . if not solved, at least ended, one way or another. I was prepared for the entire evacuation project to be a failure. I wasn't ready to be thrown right back into this, with everything worse than ever."

Irene said, "You'll cope, Chanda. You always have."

Chanda lifted her head. "Don't you get it? I *wasn't* coping. I was running away. I was going to sleep my problems away. The very thing I hated my parents doing to me, I did to myself. I thought I was making some great sacrifice, turning this hated thing into something positive. But I was fooling myself."

Irene went to Chanda and leaned over and embraced her. Chanda surprised herself at how desperately she accepted that embrace. She closed her eyes tightly and let herself sob.

After a couple of minutes, Chanda's chest quit heaving and her breathing slowed. She released Irene from her embrace. Irene seemed to let her go only reluctantly, but moved back to sit on the couch next to Akira. "I came in to look at you there in the stasis shell almost every day. I'm . . . glad you're back with us."

Chanda wiped her eyes and cleared her throat. She thought Akira looked vaguely uncomfortable. "Sorry," Chanda told her and Irene.

Akira smiled, though it looked forced. "Absolutely nothing to be sorry about, Ambassador."

"Please — it's — "

"Chanda, I know. I'll make sure to remember from now on."

"Thanks. After all, it's just a name. I've had to remember who I really am. And make sure I act in a way that lives up to it."

Chanda didn't say anything for a moment. A time passed when she wasn't aware of anything. When she opened her eyes again, it was nine hours later, she had a massive crick in her neck from falling asleep in her chair, and Irene and Akira were obviously long gone. *It's as if I can still feel their presence, though,* Chanda thought. *Good thing. I get the feeling I'm going to be leaning on them a lot during this trip.*

It was only moments later that Hamadi called Chanda to the ship's briefing room. The *Jelal* had arrived at the gas nebula for the "viewing."

Captain Hamadi was the only person present in the briefing room, which was just large enough to accommodate about a dozen people. Blast shields covered one wall. The room had no furniture, not even any chairs. Chanda blinked as she looked around.

Hamadi's face featured a bemused smile. "I like short meetings," he said. Let people sit down, maybe with a drink sitting in front of them, they settle in, get too comfortable. I like them to stay focused."

"I like that idea so much I might have to steal it," Chanda said. "What about bathroom breaks?"

"Allowed, but not encouraged."

"Thank you for indulging me."

"I understand the impulse. Nature itself appears to be against you — an unsatisfying enemy."

Chanda said, "That's perhaps a high-flown way of putting it."

"You must excuse me, then. Perhaps the gas nebula is only a physical thing to you, with no emotional component."

"I've spent the better part of four years on Splendor, working toward the day this thing hits the planet. So maybe it means more to me than I've considered."

"We're actually past it, looking back toward Splendor. You realize this thing is so diffuse you really can't see anything under the normal display. But there's a control panel by the wall to view false colors and sensor readouts."

"I'll take advantage of that. Although just being here may be enough. Go ahead and make plans for your next stardrive jump, make it whenever you're ready. I'll be fine."

"As you wish, Ambassador," Hamadi said, and left.

Chanda touched the control that raised the blast shields. They lifted silently, uncovering the broad viewscreen of the briefing room, revealing the starfield beyond, which was dominated by the system's primary, called Pinpoint. Otherwise it teemed with suns beyond counting. As Captain Hamadi had promised, Splendor itself, just over four billion kilometers distant, hovered in the middle of the view, barely more than a star itself, but illuminated with reflected light that revealed hues of blue and green and brown that Chanda perceived as signs of life.

As Hamadi had indicated, the gas nebula itself wasn't visible, though it was the better part of a light-year across. It was, however, made of high-energy particles that would sterilize Splendor in just over eight decades though it was not nearly as dense as, say, Earth's atmosphere.

A star Humans eventually called Aeolus went supernova back in 7918 B.C. It was 16 light-years away from Splendor, but the nebula of hot gas expanded at thousands of kilometers a second. When it finally struck Splendor, those high-energy particles would kill most life on the planet and bring a soaring mutation rate among any survivors. Those survivors might not last long enough to breed successive generations, though, if enough food sources died that they never had a chance to reproduce.

Chanda went to the control panel and switched the viewscreen over to false color images — from wisps of red indicating carbon through strings of green showing oxygen, to threads of violet revealing nitrogen, and a dozen other shades representing as many other elements.

The ambient temperature was nearly eight thousand degrees Celsius. Without the protective shields of the *Sergeant Jelal*, Chanda and the entire starcraft's crew would die within seconds in this environment.

Just a list of facts, Chanda thought. *They don't explain Indirogar's pride in his tribe or Dijirar being so eager to return back home or the sweepers' indignant reaction to Humanity being unable to find a way to save them.*

They don't explain what the Splendorians really mean to me.

The gas nebula's speed was slow by Human standards, since it would take nearly eight decades more before it enveloped Splendor. *And still time is running out*, Chanda thought. *With the evacuation project failing, we have to find some other way to save everyone on the planet — three sentient species — imagine if that fourth one the archeologists are talking about survived.*

Maybe constructing a habitat, even a series of habitats orbiting Splendor would work — evacuate everyone into an ecology that replicated Splendor's own, only in orbit. That way the highlanders and valley dwellers can continue to live together.

It's the sweepers that's tough — how in space do we even get them on board some type of craft to boost them into orbit?

Chanda's mind rebelled then, and she couldn't make herself consider such matters any longer. She switched the viewscreen back to the real-color view, considered not the statistics but the beauty of Splendor and the surrounding starfield until, as promised, the *Sergeant Jelal* jumped into stardrive, the swirling colors of the creation of new-space sweeping from her mind the image of the gas nebula inexorably bearing down on the planet Splendor.

CHAPTER 8

As Captain Hamadi promised, four days later Chanda and Senator Galt were standing on the *Sergeant Jelal's* bridge as the craft fell out of stardrive into the Sobrenian system.

The nav officer, sitting in front of Hamadi, reported, "Course as expected, Captain."

Chanda was entertained by Galt's reactions as he watched the routine process of Captain Hamadi taking in information that the starcraft was secure following the jump. *He wants to jump in there and guide the ship in himself,* Chanda thought. *Hamadi could the greatest starship captain ever, superhuman, even, and Galt would think he could do a better job.*

The sensor officer next to nav said, "Four Sobrenian warcraft closing in." Galt widened his stance and his shoulders lifted, as if he were preparing for a fight. Captain Hamadi asked, "What's their status?"

"Shields down, no weapons armed."

Apparently Galt couldn't stand it any longer. "They're several light-minutes out. They could have those weapons armed by now and we wouldn't know it —"

"I understand, Senator," Hamadi said in a carefully neutral voice. "Thanks." Galt took the hint and relaxed his stance and kept his mouth shut.

Within those ten minutes, those four Sobrenian warcraft, each a dark green, each the shape of a water drop, closed in. One made challenge, audio only: "Starcraft of pre-sentients, identify yourself," came the impersonal translated voice over the bridge's comm.

Chanda and Galt stood on either side of Captain Hamadi's commander's chair at the center of the bridge. Hamadi said, "An odd way to start out even for the Sobrenians. They have to know 'pre-sentient' is an insult to us."

"They do," Chanda said. "That's why they said it. Let me respond."

Hamadi said, "Channel's open."

Chanda looked toward the main bridge viewscreen — the left side showed the four Sobrenian craft, the right was dark where the visual of the Sobrenian addressing them would normally be. "Unidentified Sobrenian craft. This is the Earth Unity starcraft *Sergeant Jelal*, Ambassador Chanda Kasmira speaking. We are here at the request of your government. Is this how you receive guests — by referring to them as pre-sentients?"

No response for a long moment, and Chanda was determined not to fill that silence — it was the Sobrenian's turn to speak. Finally, the blank side of the viewscreen came to life, revealing the commander of one of the Sobrenian craft before them.

The Sobrenian stared out from the viewscreen, looking down his blunt, rough-skinned snout. After a moment staring directly at Chanda with both eyes, the left one began to swing independently in its socket, a move Chanda always found disconcerting. The Sobrenian was clearly taking in details of the *Jelal*'s bridge.

The Sobrenian said, "I am Captain Remkina of the Sobrenian warcraft *Mendassa*. We have been expecting you."

Remkina's many-layered robes were blue, with faint red lines running through them. *So he's of fairly low rank*, Chanda thought.

Otherwise he'd have more colors on those robes. "We expected someone . . . higher placed . . . in your government or military to greet us," Chanda said. "Was no one else available?"

Now both eyes stared at Chanda again. "I am carrying out the orders I've been given. As are you."

"Then let's both continue carrying out our orders and continue to your homeworld. And as I have done before in dealing with Sobrenians, I would remind you that however you regard us, Humanity does not consider itself pre-sentient, and will continue to act as if we do, indeed, possess sentience."

The Sobrenian's image disappeared from the viewscreen. Seconds later, all four warcraft spun slowly around and boosted in the direction of the inner system. Captain Hamadi said, "We're receiving instructions on when to make a short stardrive jump to take us closer into the system, then we can take the in-system drive the rest of the way in."

"Very well, Captain. Do what they say. The Sobrenians are very straightforward in these practical matters. You can trust them."

"Very well, Ambassador." To his bridge crew he said, "Monitor those instructions and follow them precisely unless I say otherwise." He punched a control on the arm of his chair. "All crew — prepare for stardrive jump."

Senator Galt told Chanda, "You handled that well. I see why the Unity wanted you here."

"You should've known *that* before we ever left Splendor."

Galt lowered his voice. "I didn't mean it that way, Ambassador."

Chanda considered that. "I'll take you at your word, Senator."

Within a couple of hours, the *Jelal* fell into orbit around the Sobrenian homeworld. From the starcraft's bridge, standing next to Captain Hamadi once again, Chanda saw a world shrouded beneath thick cloud cover, with only narrow strips of ocean and land visible.

Both of the planet's moons, the closer one called Kimli and the more distant one, Aldera, each about half the size of Luna, were visible as thin crescents.

Many of the land areas she could make out consisted of rough terrain, scarred with craters, the result of a comet strike that happened 288 years earlier. Entire cities, even nations, had been destroyed, and many Sobrenians found themselves in a war among themselves for the planet's remaining resources.

Captain Hamadi said, "It's amazing that you can still see the effects of the comet, even from orbit."

"It's affected the entire outlook of their species, even generations later," Chanda said. "The comet nearly wiped them out. Mass casualties. Much of their infrastructure, their tech, destroyed. They believe only the strongest of them survived."

"Is that where this business of calling other species 'pre-sentients' came from?"

"Most likely. If nothing else, I'm hoping we can discover a little more about them."

Hamadi rose from his chair and shook Chanda's hand. "The best of luck. May God walk with you. Yes, I know, you don't believe. I will therefore take the responsibility of prayer upon myself."

Chanda said, "I certainly appreciate the sentiment. I'll keep you updated on what's happening down there."

———

Half an hour later, Chanda sat in one of the rear seats of the shuttle *Rico*, Senator Galt next to her, Akira and Irene in front as pilot and co-pilot. Chanda was impressed all over again not only by their skills, but by the fact that their reputations must have preceded them — it was unusual for a starcraft commander like Hamadi to allow someone not one of his own crewmembers to pilot one of "his" shuttles.

Rico descended through the cloud cover, accompanied by a

Sobrenian fighter craft on either side, toward the Sobrenian capitol city, which was called Piroveka. Apparently it had made quite a successful recovery from the comet strike, as it sprawled along both sides of a wide river for about fifty kilometers, and extended back from that river for about twenty K on either side.

The areas closest to the river saw the tallest structures, but apparently the Sobrenians' theories of architecture didn't aspire skyward as much as Humanity's — there were no equivalents of the 1600-meter Sao Paulo Tower, for instance. Most of the buildings in the downtown area barely topped out at what would be about thirty stories on Earth.

As well, those buildings tended not to be the boxy structures Humans seemed to favor — many were gently sloping pyramids, others circular structures topped with ornate domes. Most seemed constructed of various forms of concrete and steel, although a few seemed as if they'd been woven of some sort of filament. Dominant colors of those buildings were green and gold.

The wide streets appeared to be designed for pedestrians only, though high-speed trains emerged from underground in several places and crossed the river only to make a quick descent on the opposite side. Chanda also saw several aircraft crisscrossing the skies.

Akira guided the *Rico* toward a landing pad on top of one of Piroveka's taller buildings. To one side, Chanda saw a Buruden landing craft, one much larger than the Human shuttle. It was a long cylinder with four engine nacelles beneath, a smaller version of the craft she'd watched leaving Splendor, the usual bold strokes of yellow, maroon, and gold signaling its origin.

Galt said, "That's quite an impressive shuttle."

Chanda explained, "The Buruden have to travel around with three or four dozen individuals to be able to function properly."

"I get it. Too few, and they don't have enough intelligence to cope."

"That's it, exactly."

Seven Sobrenians were already standing near the pad. Chanda

saw that most of them were armed with pulse rifles. "I hope that's an honor guard," she said.

Irene said, "You don't think they'd have us come all this way just to kill us?"

"Not really. But the Sobrenians are nothing if not unpredictable sometimes."

"With all respect, Chanda — that's not very reassuring."

Senator Galt said, "I can't tell what the function of this building is — whether it's their seat of government, or something else."

"The cultural cues are all wrong," Chanda said. "You go through much of North America, you see a facade of limestone or marble in a Greek or Roman revival style, and it's likely to be a governmental building. But we don't know what the equivalent of that is here."

"Or even, I suppose, if there is an equivalent."

"Exactly."

Akira eased the *Rico* down onto the pad. She and Irene began going through the post-flight checklist. The two Sobrenian fighter craft made a final pass overhead, then shot nearly straight up and were gone in an instant. The seven Sobrenians marched toward the shuttle.

"The one in the lead isn't armed," Chanda said. "I hope that's a good sign."

"Powering down," Akira said. "Get ready for planetary grav."

The sound of the shuttle's systems, which had hummed along beneath awareness for the most part, faded.

Chanda instantly felt lighter — the inertials that maintained a single Earth gravity and protected them from accelerations that would crush a Human body faded. Now the Sobrenian homeworld asserted its own grav, which was just over four-fifths that of Earth, and a definite relief from Splendor's 1.3 G which they had left behind just days before.

The Sobrenians halted before the *Rico*'s airlock, the six who were armed forming a semi-circle facing it. The seventh one, the only female, apparently unarmed, stood expectantly just in front of the lock. "Everyone grab a couple ration bars and put them in your pockets," Chanda said. "That's just in case the Sobrenian concept of Human food misfires. Remember, no weapons. No exceptions, even stunners. We'll leave our bags here for the time being. So -- time to meet our fate." She moved to the inner airlock door and opened it, then operated the controls that equalized the shuttle's internal pressure with the outside air.

"Smells kind of sweet," Irene said.

Chanda opened the outer lock and stepped down onto the building's roof. *The first Human, as far as we know, to step onto Sobrenian soil.*

Galt, Irene, and Akira stepped down right behind her. The lead Sobrenian stepped forward — she was slightly shorter than the rest, just coming up to Chanda's shoulders. As well, her shoulders weren't as broad as the others, and even her snout was shorter. Her blue robes had lines of red and gold running through them.

Thank goodness she's looking at me with both eyes facing the same way, Chanda thought.

The Sobrenian held out her hand. Chanda, surprised, took it and shook.

"I am Govanek, Ambassador Kasmira," the Sobrenian said. Chanda's datalink translated her words. "I'll be your guide here on our homeworld. You seem surprised I shook your hand. I was selected for this job due to my familiarity with Humans."

"Very good! I'm Earth Unity Ambassador Chanda Kasmira. Here we have Senator Gabriel Galt, and my aides Irene Radford and Akira Kuroda."

"A pleasure to meet all of you," Govanek said. "I will escort you to the quarters we've prepared for each of you. Please let us know if anything is unpleasing to Human sensibilities."

"I'm sure everything will be fine."

Govanek turned and walked toward the semi-circle of armed Sobrenians, three of whom spun on their heels and preceded her toward a cargo lift at one corner of the roof. As Chanda followed

Govanek, she glanced back and saw the other three Sobrenians fall into place behind Galt, Irene, and Akira. *I'm not sure who's being protected from whom*, Chanda thought.

Everyone filed into the lift, and without anyone pressing a button or making a voice command, its doors slid closed and it began to descend. No one engaged in small talk. *I suspect silence in lifts or elevators is universal among Galactic intelligences*, Chanda thought.

I can't tell how quickly we're dropping. For all I know, we could be end up halfway down the building, or in an underground chamber.

The lift slowed, and Chanda thought, *What will be revealed on the other side of these doors? Could be a mundane, even disappointing, corridor. Or they could open right upon our spacious, luxurious suite.*

The lift eased to a halt, and the doors parted silently, revealing:

Cacophony, harsh lights sweeping across a darkened room from a dozen directions, an assault of smells.

The source of the cacophony — Sobrenian troops ranged through a windowless circular room 30 meters across, brandishing their pulse rifles and barking orders.

The source of the harsh lights — they were mounted on top of those rifles, were the only illumination in the room, and revealed various groupings of Buruden rushing about, seemingly without a specific destination. Chanda saw the same linked masses of a dozen or so Buruden pass by two or three times, each time in a different direction.

She couldn't place the source of the smells. *Plenty of time for that*, Chanda thought as she turned to Govanek: "What the hell is going on here?"

"It seems," the Sobrenian said, "that we're having a little difficulty with the Buruden ambassadors."

Chanda winced as the light from one of the pulse rifles flashed into her eyes. "I don't think all this running around with weapons is helping anything."

Govanek kept one eye on the chaos around them even as the other looked up toward Chanda. "It's what my people do, Ambassador. But your people seem to have an affinity for the Buruden. Perhaps you can help."

"Can we get some lights on in here?"

"I don't know why they've failed. I'll try to find out." She headed toward several Sobrenians who seemed above the fray, standing to one side.

Chanda raised her voice: "Is a Buruden ambassador available to speak to me?"

No response — until Chanda opened her mouth to speak again, and stopped cold when she saw a group of about a dozen Buruden approaching her, all linked together. They halted before her, and Chanda heard over her datalink, "You are Ambassador Kasmira. This is a truth?"

"I am. Have we spoken before?"

"You have spoken to some elements of me. My current configuration recalls those times."

"Very good. What's the problem here? Is it anything I can help you with?"

"We are becoming quite ill. It is a likely truth that many of us will be incapacitated within the next few hours. It is a potential truth that most of us will be."

Chanda took a sharp intake of breath. "Is it something the Sobrenians are doing? Some kind of bio-attack or something?"

"No. It's this planet's gravity. It's too weak for us. We need to be in quarters where it is controlled."

"Of course!" Chanda said. "Your people went through the same problem when you first came to Splendor — and the grav's even lighter here. But why didn't you bio-engineer individuals for conditions here, like you did on Splendor?"

"These negotiations were planned at the last minute. We had no opportunity to pre-breed individuals. It is now too late to do so."

Galt asked, "Have you tried to ask the Sobrenians for help?"

"We did, much as that assaults our sensibilities. None will endure the linking touch. So we tried to access their systems ourselves."

Chanda thought, *I've got to catch Govanek's eye.* To her chagrin, that's exactly what she did — the Sobrenian only had the left one aimed at her when she waved. That was enough to summon their guide, though.

"We need more than the lights," Chanda told Govanek. "The Buruden are from a high-grav world. They become ill if the gravity's too light for them."

"That must explain why they tried to access the room's systems — violently."

"They said no one would 'endure the linking touch,' as they put it."

"Most Sobrenians would not want to risk alien tech being placed within their bodies."

Galt said, "We've never been harmed by it, and we've all done it."

"Not all of us," Chanda said, looking at Irene.

"Wait a minute," Irene said, putting up her hands. "Getting me to do this won't help the Buruden."

Chanda put her hand across Irene's shoulders and guided her toward the group of Buruden. "Of course it will — if you demonstrate that the process isn't harmful."

"I don't even like trips to the dentist — or giving blood."

Galt said, "But those are painless procedures."

"My point exactly," Irene said. "This *isn't*. Why don't you just translate?"

"We don't need the extra job," Chanda said. She pressed down gently on Irene's shoulders. "Just lean over. It'll be done in an instant."

The lead Buruden extended one of its spiny limbs toward Irene's neck. Irene squeezed her eyes shut. "Tell me when it's about to — OW!"

The Buruden said, "It's over."

Irene rubbed her neck. "*Thanks.*"

Chanda squeezed her lips together to keep from smiling.

The Buruden ambassador said, "Thank you for enduring the brief pain."

Irene told the Buruden, "Oh, but that's great! I can understand you now."

Chanda turned to Govanek. "You've seen how it works. And that Irene is unharmed."

Govanek cast two doubtful eyes upon Irene. "It didn't seem to be a pleasant experience for her."

"Diplomacy often requires sacrifices."

Irene rubbed her neck again.

"Very well," Govanek said. She went to the lead Buruden. She didn't have to lean down as far as Irene.

The Buruden's limb thrust again. Govanek winced.

The Buruden said, "I hope you understand me now."

"I do," Govanek said. "Let me take you to our technical staff. We'll see how to adapt your portion of this room to your needs."

"Wait a minute," Chanda said. "This portion?"

"Yes," the Sobrenian said. "All of the off-world ambassadors are staying in this room." Govanek hurried off to another group of Buruden, presumably the above-mentioned technical staff, with the Buruden in tow.

Irene said, "These aren't exactly the accommodations we expected."

"Just remember," Chanda told her. "Diplomacy. Sacrifices."

CHAPTER 9

Within minutes, the lights came back on, and Chanda told Galt, Irene, and Akira, "Wait here." She pushed her way through the crowd of Buruden and Sobrenian security forces to find Govanek. She turned out to be addressing a group of Buruden. Next to them was a stack of nondescript boxes. *Their equivalent of luggage?* Chanda wondered.

When Govanek saw Chanda, she said, "Ah, Ambassador Kasmira. It's good you're here, too. We need to address certain matters. Watch out!"

With the next step Chanda took, a force pulled at her leg, her ankle turned, and she stumbled and fell to the floor, cracking her knee hard against its unyielding surface. She caught her upper body with both hands, then slid herself backwards. "Well, it looks like you got the grav fixed for the Buruden." That grav, Chanda knew, was 2.3 times that of Earth, and a full G beyond the Splendorian gravity she'd become accustomed to over the past four years.

Chanda got to her feet as Govanek said, "I apologize, Ambassador. The Buruden and I were just discussing how to mark the high-gravity areas of the ambassadorial facilities."

Footsteps sounded behind Chanda, growing louder by the instant. She looked back — Irene was there, asking her, "Are you all right, Chanda — I mean, Ambassador?"

"I'm fine, don't worry about me." Looking past Irene, Chanda saw Galt and Akira approaching as well. *Damn, people, I'm not some sort of wilting flower.*

She turned back toward Govanek. "So, about these facilities — do you really intend for all of us to live in this one room? I mean, it's quite large, but — "

Govanek said, "These are the facilities my superiors have mandated."

"But I don't see beds . . . or a place to eat, or . . . bathroom facilities."

"Failure to translate on that last part — but I believe I heard the actual Human word enough to understand its meaning. Facilities not just for bathing, but for other matters of hygiene."

"Yes," Chanda said. "Other matters."

"Give us the specifications, and they will be provided."

"No one had thought of this before now?"

"My superiors — " Chanda wondered whether Govanek was using that term as a way of saying none of this was her idea. " — insisted upon waiting for the arrival of both Humans and Buruden before working on the details of your quarters. We seldom accept visitors on our homeworld, and many of us are . . . uncomfortable with the idea. We wished to consult with you on your needs rather than make assumptions."

Chanda said, "Irene and Akira will speak with you about the actual engineering for the Human areas."

"That would be excellent," Govanek said, and took the two women aside, apparently to consult with some of the Buruden, as well. Chanda was also gratified to see that the Sobrenian security personnel were leaving.

Who knew, Chanda thought, *that our first challenge would be designing a place to stay?*

Galt said, "This is completely unacceptable. These Sobrenians are testing us — seeing how much humiliation we'll accept. We're barely here a few minutes, and all of our ambassadors and staff are dealing with — architecture! We're supposed to be preventing a war here!"

Chanda said, "I understand that this seems ludicrous at first glance. But these are the circumstances we find ourselves in — we've got to deal with them."

"You're the ambassador — Ambassador. But I don't have to like this."

"I never do," Chanda said. "Now, while Irene and Akira are taking care of practicalities, let's go talk to the Buruden about the actual negotiations."

"Now you're talking, Ambassador."

Chanda headed across the wide room again and made her way toward the largest gathering of Buruden she saw — about a dozen of them. "Let's see what we can find out," she told Galt.

"How forthcoming do you think they'll be?"

"I guess that's what we're here to find out."

As Chanda got nearer to the group of Buruden, she took her last few steps slowly and gingerly, the tip of her foot probing for the change in grav. Eventually her right foot stamped to the floor involuntarily. "I guess that's as close as we can comfortably get." To the massed Buruden, she said, "Can I speak to your ambassador?"

The group of about a dozen linked Buruden skittered around until one of them faced Chanda. "This is the ambassador." *I never know whether it's that individual talking or the group,* Chanda thought. *And if it's the group, I suspect it's a slightly different group each time.*

And I have no idea whether that makes a difference.

Chanda asked, "Do you know what the Sobrenians intend to do with us here? And why we're being grouped together like this?"

The Buruden said, "The Sobrenians do not trust 'out-worlders.'"

"That," Chanda said, "is a truth."

"In particular, they do not trust Buruden. We are uncertain why that might be. We consider ourselves to be a pleasant and curious species."

"Do you mean 'curious' as in the Sobrenians find you to be curious, or meaning you possess a curious nature?"

"We believe both would be at least a potential truth, perhaps a likely one."

Galt said, "But then there's the 'pleasant' part. The Sobrenians seem to disagree with you there."

"We consider that their loss," the Buruden said. "Then we have the Sobrenians themselves. Are you aware of the origin of their violent culture?"

"Somewhat," Chanda said. "I know that even though the comet strike was nearly three centuries ago, it affected the way the Sobrenians think of themselves — their obsession with weapons, their bluster when speaking to other Galactic species."

"That whole 'pre-sentient' business," Galt said.

The Buruden said, "Part of them believes carrying a firearm will protect them against anything — even their own insecurities."

"Should you speak so freely?" Chanda asked. "The Sobrenians may have surveillance devices in here."

"We typically speak freely about them during our infrequent contacts. It is another thing about us that irritates them."

"Have they given you some sort of schedule? Do we know when and where negotiations will start?"

Our Sobrenian guide, Govanek, told us negotiations are to begin as soon as possible."

Galt made a low chuckle. "That means whenever the hell they want — tomorrow or the day after or next month."

"Another likely truth. As to where — it seems the Sobrenians do not intend to let us leave this room until this first round of negotiations is complete."

"Not leave this room!" Galt said. "*That* should be the first point of negotiation — to keep from being locked up like this!"

Chanda told him, "Maybe we should go with Captain Hamadi's idea -- not give anyone anything to eat or drink, or anything to sit on —"

"That last requirement would be no impediment to us," the Buruden said, squatting on all four of its spiny legs.

"I suppose not. But we'd also not allow bathroom breaks —"

"Perhaps, then, you should *require* consumption of drinks, to make the process even faster."

"That's not a bad thought."

Galt said, "I can't believe you're both joking at a time like this."

"The point," Chanda said, "is that the Sobrenians already have us discussing our accommodations and working to improve them instead of addressing the negotiations between them and the Buruden. It's a classic tactic if you want to delay substantive talks."

A heavy sigh from Galt. "So what do we do next?"

"Unfortunately, we deal with our accommodations. Otherwise no work gets done, anyway."

The Buruden ambassador said, "A truth — this is why such tactics are effective."

"Tell me about it," Chanda said. "I could really use a place to pee right about now."

―――――――

Hours later, Irene and Akira, working with Govanek and a group of Buruden separate from the ambassador, were constructing rudimentary quarters for each species. "I'm allowing for three bedrooms," Irene said as she walked Chanda and Galt through the makeshift facility, "and a common area that includes a small kitchen." Each room was barely large enough for the four Humans to fit into at the same time. The walls were a pale green, without any decoration.

"I'm glad you finished the bathroom first," Chanda said. "I was afraid I'd have to ask to go back to the shuttle."

"Believe me, Ambassador, I was being selfish. My eyes were turning yellow. And I'm pretty grateful you suggested bringing those ration bars along."

Akira said, "One thing I give these Sobrenians — they know their engineering. And their construction nanotech works fast."

"One thing I'd like to know," Chanda said. "Who came up with the baby poop green for the walls?"

Galt said, "*That's* the color! I was trying to place it."

"The Sobrenians picked the settings," Irene said. "I can try to — "

Chanda held up her hand. "No, no — not a serious concern. Listen, it's been a long day. Let's try out our great new rooms and get some sleep and in the morning try to come up with a plan to jump-start these negotiations."

Galt said, "You mean until the Sobrenians come up with another way to delay them."

"Which is likely. But we've coped with this first delay pretty quickly. We'll have to see what they throw at us next."

Akira said, "I hope it's a good meal."

"Keep your expectations low. One Galactic intelligence preparing food for another — especially for the first time — has led to some horrific scenes."

Akira shrugged. "Oh, well!" She took Irene's arm in her own. "Let's head to our room and work up an appetite anyway." Irene aimed a what-can-you-do expression at Chanda and Galt, then let herself be led away.

Galt said, "I'm not looking forward to dealing with these Sobrenians."

"They do get on your nerves," Chanda said. "But we don't have a better alternative."

"Good night, Ambassador — *Chanda*. At least I know not to fill my head with dreams of a luxurious breakfast."

"I've been through enough of these kind of meals — the tough part is smiling rather than grimacing as you force yourself not to spit out that first bite."

Chanda made her way toward her quarters. She stepped through the doorway, careful not to bang her knee on the bed, and undressed. She discovered either that the light control was broken or that Sobrenians weren't willing to let her sleep in complete darkness — she couldn't get rid of a dim glow that seemed to permeate the room from the very walls. Certainly there were no obvious light fixtures. *Have to ask Irene and Akira about that in the morning*, she thought as she crawled into bed.

For now, though . . . I can't keep my eyes open. I'm ready to get some good sleep. And when I wake. . . .

———

A voice from a far distance was telling Chanda to wake up, and once again she believed she was about to awaken a century or more after her time on Splendor, and before she opened her eyes she spent a moment anticipating the wonders to be revealed before her. . . .

. . . and realized it was Irene's voice waking her — again.

Chanda forced down her disappointment before opening her eyes and telling Irene, "I'm awake. What's that I smell?"

"Breakfast. Looks like bacon and eggs. We've also got fruit and some kind of cereal."

"The bacon part smells good."

"It *is* good. There's a sort of buffet outside our quarters, and I stole a slice on the way."

Chanda rose from bed and began to dress. "Count your blessings. I've been on a couple diplomatic missions where your first breath after you wake up has you gagging."

"It seems you can thank Govanek. Apparently she's somehow familiar with Human tastes."

As Chanda stepped out of their makeshift living area into the round room, the smell of the bacon became even stronger, and she went right for the buffet. She had to lean over just a bit, given that Sobrenians were generally shorter than Humans. She grabbed a small plate and took samples of bacon, what appeared to be a biscuit, and a couple of pieces of native fruit. She also grabbed a plastic bulb containing a reddish liquid.

Akira and Galt were already chowing down, standing to one side of the buffet table balancing their drinking bulbs on their plates. Chanda took a bite of the bacon, then of the biscuit. "It all seems good."

"Wait until you try that fruit," Irene said. "It's great, and so's the drink."

"No chairs?" Chanda asked.

Galt tilted his head toward the mass of Buruden that took up most of the space of the large room, many of them squatting on their locked legs. They'd not constructed any sort of quarters for their stay. "My guess is, the Sobrenians' theory is that if the Buruden don't need chairs, then we don't either."

Chanda said, "No buffet for them?"

"They ate earlier," Irene said. "Something that was alive and squirming and made some pretty loud squealing."

Akira said, "Until one of them would hunker down over it, then sit. Just for a moment."

Irene hugged herself. "It was pretty disgusting."

"You walked over there to check it out!"

"All right," Chanda said. "That's enough. We need to get some work done. And there's Govanek, coming in right as we need her."

The Sobrenian approached the Humans first, saying, "Greetings. I hope the food has been of decent quality."

"It was quite good," Chanda said. "How'd your people learn so much about Human food?"

"I was the geological specialist aboard our starcraft *Meradeus* when it traveled to the Moruteb system."

"Oh! Very impressive." About a year and a half earlier, the Moruteb system had been disrupted when a rogue star, Neska, and its two remaining planets passed through it. Two planets were pulled into another and vaporized, another was ripped away from its home star to be captured by the rogue — it was a scientist's dream. "Quite a journey, then," Chanda said. "So you know our friend Mike Christopher." His starcraft, the *Asaph Hall*, was one of the exploratory ships that traveled to Moruteb to study the disaster, along with the *Meradeus* and Cetronen and Drodusarel starcraft. On an earlier voyage to Splendor, he'd come up with the evacuation plan that Chanda had tried, and failed, to implement.

"I know Mike quite well," Govanek said. "I've told him I'm determined to make an exploratory voyage with him sometime."

Chanda said, "Right now, we're concerned about beginning negotiations. Are they to be held in this room?"

"That had been our intention. However, my superiors — " *There's that phrase again*, Chanda thought. " — have decided that to understand our position in these negotiations, you should understand our relationship to our planet, and something of our culture."

"What does that mean?" Galt asked.

"It means," Govanek said, "that we are taking a trip."

It was only minutes later that the Sobrenian security guards emerged from the lift, as usual brandishing their pulse rifles. Chanda watched as the Sobrenians made their way toward the Buruden first, apparently trying to herd them toward the lift. But the Buruden wouldn't budge at first, as they moved around to align themselves into a new configuration. Individual Buruden detached their spiny legs from current companions and skittered around to attach themselves to other individuals.

The Sobrenians grew impatient, and began barking orders, too many for Chanda's datalink to translate at once. They gestured with their rifles, indicating the direction they wanted the Buruden to go.

"That's not going to work," Chanda said. "The Buruden will take as much time to reconfigure as they want."

"What is it they're doing?" Galt asked.

"Anytime they take on a new task, even something as simple as heading out on a trip, they rearrange themselves, each group focusing its intelligence only on one mission. One group will be in charge of navigating, so to speak — which direction are we headed in, that kind of thing. Another will pay attention to security — any sort of threat from predators if they're in the wild, for instance."

"Or from Sobrenian security right here," Irene said.

"In this case, that's exactly what it looks like. Either way, until the Buruden arrange themselves, they aren't going anywhere."

Akira said, "Govanek's stepping in. Maybe she'll calm things down."

"Or not," Chanda said, rushing toward the growing crowd of Buruden and Sobrenians at the lift.

Galt was right behind her. "What's going on?"

"The Buruden look like they're going to go into swarm mode."

"What's that — ?" Galt began, but Chanda had no time to answer. She headed toward the largest mass of Buruden even as it left their high-grav part of the room and began to surround several of the armed Sobrenians, some of whom pointed their pulse rifles at the Buruden.

Govanek waved her arms around, trying to get the attention of the other Sobrenians: "Do not shoot! We must remain calm!"

Chanda said, "Is the Buruden ambassador present? Can you form him if he's not?"

The swarm of Buruden paused, even as most of the Sobrenians froze in position, yielding to Govanek's pleas. Then about a dozen of the Buruden moved away from the Sobrenians and reconfigured themselves. "We are the ambassador," Chanda heard over her datalink.

"I know how upsetting it is for you to be herded around like this, but these are your hosts. They want to show us some of their culture."

Three of the ambassador Buruden's four eyes, spaced equidistantly around its head, looked toward Govanek. "So far all we are seeing of the nature of Sobrenians are weapons and rudeness."

That's actually a nice summation of their culture, Chanda thought. "Govanek," she said, "can't we move around without weapons being brandished all the time?"

"Ambassador, this is for your own protection."

"There's no one here to protect us from! And you've been pointing those weapons at *us*."

"My superiors insist upon this, Ambassador."

Good, Chanda thought. *I've distracted her from the Buruden for now.* "I insist upon seeing these superiors, Govanek. We're supposed to begin negotiations as soon as possible."

Govanek stood as tall as she could, though the top of her head only came up to Chanda's shoulders. "I intend to follow my lawful orders," she said. "I have respect for your people, Ambassador Kasmira. But I do not serve them. I serve my own."

Chanda held out her hands. "I don't expect anything less. But you have to understand that diplomats can't be treated like prisoners."

"If you were being treated like prisoners," Govanek said, "you would not have such luxuries as we've provided. No soft beds. No meals designed for your metabolism. The weapons would be aimed at you constantly."

"That almost sounds like a threat."

Govanek folded her hands in front of her. "It is not. It is . . . a description."

Chanda glanced toward the Buruden. They'd reorganized themselves into four groups of about a dozen apiece and stood apart from the Sobrenians. *Thank goodness my stalling for time worked*, Chanda thought. *If they'd kept swarming like that, and the Sobrenians responded — this whole mission could've been over in an instant.*

"Perhaps," Chanda said, "it would be best if we started over."

Govanek said, "That must have been a failure to translate."

"It means let us set aside how the morning as gone so far, and make a new beginning."

"I see." Govanek's right eye looked toward the Buruden as her left eye remained focused on Chanda. "I am agreeable. If the Buruden are willing to do so, as well."

"We are," the Buruden said.

"Then let us proceed," Govanek said, and led the way into the lift.

As she, Galt, Irene, Akira, and about a dozen of the Buruden filed into the lift, Chanda realized that for the first time since awakening from her brief hibernation, she felt satisfied. *I'm where I should be, doing what I need to do*, she thought.

CHAPTER 10

The lift's doors slid back, and Chanda, Galt, Irene, and Akira were back on the building's roof. The first thing Chanda noticed as they left the lift was the addition of a Sobrenian shuttlecraft between the Human and Buruden ones. Like larger Sobrenian craft, it was shaped much like a water drop turned on its side, round at the stern and narrowing to a tip at the bow. What would have been the water drop's smooth surface, however, was marred by the Sobrenian craft's inevitable array of weaponry.

The Sobrenian security guards were letting the Buruden head toward their large shuttle, but wouldn't let Chanda or her colleagues approach the *Rico*. Instead, they indicated with their pulse rifles that they should move toward the Sobrenian ship.

Now it's our turn to be herded, Chanda thought. "I don't like this," she said.

"Absolutely right," Galt said. "I don't begrudge the Buruden getting to take their ship, but we should be allowed to take ours as well."

Govanek said, "Ambassador — Senator — you underestimate the negotiating I had to do with my own people to allow even one non-

Sobrenian shuttle to travel within our airspace. The Buruden have unique physical needs, as we saw last night. By boarding their own shuttle, they can maintain the gravity they need."

"What about when we arrive?"

"Only a few will venture outside their shuttle at any particular stop. Once those return, they will share their experiences with those who remained aboard."

One of the Sobrenian security guards came up to Chanda, ignoring Govanek, and gestured with his pulse weapon for Chanda to move on. Chanda turned back to Govanek and said, "You know, these guys can speak, and we'll understand them. They don't have to go around waving those rifles at us."

"Their orders say otherwise," Govanek said.

"Why are they not allowed to interact with us? Is your government afraid of what they might hear?"

"They have their orders, Ambassador."

The Sobrenian guard drew closer and extended a hand toward Chanda.

"Govanek, if that guard touches me, these negotiations will never take place."

Govanek whirled toward the guard and let loose a string of invective that Chanda's datalink couldn't keep up with. The guard backed off.

"Thank you," Chanda said. "If you'll excuse us, my colleagues and I would like to board your shuttle at our own pace."

Both of Govanek's eyes stared directly at Chanda, and she had the sense that the unusually easygoing Sobrenian had finally discovered her anger. But with a rustle of her robes, Govanek extended her arm as if to present the shuttle for the Humans' pleasure and stood aside as they walked casually toward it.

Chanda entered the Sobrenian shuttle's passenger cabin and the first thing she realized was that the craft had no windows. She squeezed into a seat clearly designed for slimmer Sobrenian bottoms. Irene sat next to her, flashing a smile that Chanda thought might be covering nervousness. Akira ended up behind them seated next to Senator Galt.

The Sobrenian guards took seats all around them, sitting with backs straight and pulse rifles at their sides. Govanek took a seat directly in front of Chanda.

Galt leaned forward in his seat to tell Chanda with a grin, "Normally you'd have a window seat."

Chanda said, "What can you do? An ambassador can't have all the perks all the time, I guess. But we don't even have a way of telling whether we've lifted off or not." She leaned forward to ask Govanek, "Have we lifted off? How long will this trip take?"

Govanek didn't turn in her seat, and spoke in a low voice. "You should remain calm. The trip will take as long as it requires."

"Which is it, Govanek? You won't tell us, or you don't know?"

"I've not been informed of the trip's expected duration. With all respect, Ambassador, perhaps you should take this time to meditate or sleep."

"Sorry — most Humans can't just slow our metabolism on demand the way Sobrenians can."

"Unfortunate. Perhaps it's a skill you should develop."

"Listen, I'm sorry about that little dustup back there — " Chanda hesitated, expecting the world "dustup" to elicit the "failure to translate" comment from Govanek. But the Sobrenian's eyes were closed and, whether she was actually in a meditative state or feigning it, she didn't respond.

Chanda leaned back in her cramped seat. Irene told her, "Time to just sit back and enjoy the ride, huh?"

"Yeah. No windows, no sense of movement, no idea of how long we'll be sitting here, surrounded by guys with guns. Pretty enjoyable."

After a few minutes of inconsequential thought, Chanda placed her hands in her lap, settled back on the headrest (which was low enough that her head tilted back fairly sharply but not uncomfortably), and gave herself up to her thoughts. Exhausted as she had been the previous night from her journey here to the Sobrenian homeworld and the necessity of negotiating for and helping construct suitable quarters, she'd fallen right asleep, her usual routine for settling her thoughts as she gave herself up to sleep having been disrupted.

So take advantage of this moment, she thought. *What have we learned, and what's our next goal?*

First of all, we've learned the Sobrenians know very little about diplomatic niceties. Plus, I've gotten too used to dealing with people I know — Indirogar, Dijirar, any number of other highlanders and valley dwellers back on Splendor. Even the Buruden ambassador, even though he's made up of different combinations of Buruden sometimes, is fairly familiar to me.

As are Sobrenians. But not here on their homeworld. Govanek isn't typical of them, and I can tell she's protecting us from the worst her superiors can muster.

But where is she taking us? What kind of orders might she have that could override her basic decency and leave us in danger?

I'm willing to risk myself, and Galt is former military — he knows these kinds of risks. But Irene and Akira are explorers — and my friends. I don't want to risk them . . . don't want . . .

Chanda awoke with a start when a hand came down on her shoulder. "What? What is it?"

"We're here," Irene said.

Chanda cleared her throat and sat up in her seat. "Where's here?"

"I guess we'll find out as soon as they open the hatch."

Govanek stood by the exit, motioning for the security guard to remain seated, then waved Chanda, Galt, Irene, and Akira toward her. Chanda led the way, telling Govanek, "Very nice, not having the guards hurry us along — we like this much better."

"I understand the Human need for courtesy. It's something we practice among ourselves, but not as much among other Galactic species."

"We're all here to learn, Govanek. I'm sure I'll have to ask you for patience with us at some point."

Govanek opened the inner airlock hatch. "We realized we have the opportunity to show you something wonderful — but only today, and rather shortly, so we must hurry. The security guards will remain here."

Govanek entered the airlock, opened the outer hatch, and a breath of sea air, damp and sweet, swept in. Chanda saw that the shuttle had landed at the edge of a great cliff, a teeming ocean beyond. A sudden burst of swift winds ruffled her hair and misted her face.

"The Buruden have already landed," Govanek said. "We must catch up to them."

Chanda stepped down the shuttle's ramp and followed Govanek around to the craft's bow. There, she saw a gentle swath of land that eased down into the water. Waves crashed and sprayed.

Beyond stood an island beneath clear blue, cloudless skies, its base of wind-roughened rock giving way to a plain speckled with a smooth carpet of vegetation boasting colors ranging through the rainbow from a vibrant emerald, past an orange-tinged yellow, to fiery red.

In the eastern skies beyond the island, the Sobrenian moons were rising, Kimli in its closer orbit a disk seemingly twice the size of Earth's moon, nearly full in the radiance of the sun shining over Chanda's shoulder. It was a pale globe, its many craters telling the tale of continual meteor strikes across the millennia. The other moon, Aldera, appeared smaller in its more distant orbit, though it was about the same size. It appeared to have weathered the centuries relatively unscathed, its smooth plains shining brightly even in the daylight sky.

The Buruden shuttle stood next to the Sobrenian one, and about a dozen Buruden were making their way down the gentle slope that led to the water. Despite the discomfort they must feel in the planet's .8 grav, they clattered down the path with obvious enthusiasm.

"What is this place?" Chanda asked Govanek.

"It's called The Path of Victory," the Sobrenian said.

Galt said, "Oh, yes, very nice. I was interested in seeing this."

"I haven't heard of it," Chanda said. "But then, I kept my studies on the way here focused on politics and not geography."

Govanek said, "This place means more to us than simple geography. It's where a great astronomer and warrior named Syrilla won a great battle against an enemy of the people."

"How'd he do it?"

Govanek pointed toward the two moons. "They will demonstrate that in just a few moments."

Irene looked skyward. "What do they do?"

Galt laughed, a sound unexpected enough that Chanda found herself grinning at him. "The moons don't do anything themselves," Galt said. "It's the effect they have down here."

Chanda understood now. "Something with the tides?"

Govanek said, "Exactly. This happened centuries ago — "

"Earth year 1403," Galt said.

"Syrilla wanted to attack the island you see before us. It held the fortress of the warlord Turellen."

Akira asked, "Why did Turellen hole up over there?"

"His people were expert sailors," Govanek said, "among the very few on our world then."

Galt said, "Which meant no one could get to him — or at least, had a heck of a battle ahead of them trying to scale that island."

Govanek said, "But once a year Kimli and Aldera align in such a way that it creates a gravitational resonance — see how close in the sky they appear to be? You can see its effects beginning even now!"

Chanda looked down the slope and saw that the amount of water crashing against the main shoreline as well as the island was considerably less than just a few minutes ago. "Imagine," Govanek said, "that we are Syrilla's warriors. They are uneducated, incurious about the sky, ignorant of how tides work. This was long before the comet strike, long before we developed stardrive or even in-system space travel."

The water level between the shoreline and the island visibly receded now; the waves' thunder grew quieter, their spray no longer moistened Chanda's face. "I've never seen a tide go out so quickly," Chanda said.

"Neither had Syrilla's soldiers," Govanek explained. "But Syrilla had performed the proper calculations. He understood what would be the proper time for his attack."

The water continued to drop, revealing that the strip of land that led to the shoreline didn't stop there, but continued straight toward the island. "Imagine Syrilla's warriors charging the island aboard their niroxes," Govanek said.

"Sorry?" Chanda asked. "Failure to translate."

Galt said, "The Sobrenian version of a horse, only with claws at the sides of their hooves and a carnivore's teeth."

"Got it. You don't want to see a whole troupe of them coming right at you."

"You are correct, Ambassador," Govanek said. "Turellen's soldiers were taken by surprise — they believed the sea's movements to be random and had never prepared for a land invasion. Most of their defenses were strung around the rocky base of the island, aimed outward at the sea, not toward land. Their cannons could not be turned to target the land bridge, and they employed few archers."

Galt said, "The few forces at the top of the island were killed or captured quite quickly."

Govanek folded her hands in front of her. "As our Buruden friends would say, that is a truth."

Irene said, "It looks like our Buruden friends are eager to visit the island."

The twelve linked Buruden began to move across the land bridge, which was just over seven meters wide. Vegetation similar to Earthly moss covered much of its surface that wasn't bare rock, and many of the Buruden's steps made squishing sounds as they proceeded.

"Guess we might as well follow," Chanda said. "How long does this bridge last?"

Govanek said, "About an hour. Just enough time to tour the ruins of Turellen's compound and return to our shuttles."

Irene said, "The Buruden are sure to become too ill even to last that long."

Akira took Irene's arm in her own. "Let's make the most of it, then." The two women started down the path toward the land bridge. Chanda, Galt, and Govanek followed.

A harsh breeze whipped up from the south, strong enough to make Chanda stagger. "Be careful," Senator Galt said, grasping her arm. "This pathway's plenty wide enough, but still — "

"Thanks," Chanda said. "It must have been quite a sight to see those Sobrenians riding their — what were they?"

"Niroxes," Galt said.

"Yeah. Hooves with claws. Carnivore teeth. Quite a sight, I guess, to see them riding across this unexpected bridge."

"This piece of Sobrenian history is something I just happened to come across in my studies before we came here. I couldn't have imagined we'd actually get to see this."

"You didn't know the alignment of the moons was due today?"

"Not at all. I never thought there was a chance we'd get to see it."

Chanda couldn't help but look past the island toward the Sobrenian moons. *Something tells me the tides they're generating aren't the only unseen forces we're dealing with here.*

Once on the island, Govanek pointed out some of the highlights of the remnants of Turellen's compound, which consisted mostly of rubble collapsed into foundations, with the occasional wall or support still standing. The ruins gave little sense of their long-gone inhabitants or their ambitions. Govanek pointed out buildings that had been quarters for Turellen's troops, along with structures devoted to preparing food and manufacturing weapons ranging from cannons to spears to knives with elaborately carved handles of bone that reminded her of the valley dweller craftspeople back on Splendor.

The Buruden split apart and scattered across the extent of the island, each of them no doubt taking in impressions as individuals that would be shared with the others when they reunited — impressions that would, in turn, be passed on to the rest of the Buruden when they rejoined them aboard their shuttle.

Govanek led Chanda and her colleagues to the island's largest structure, Turellen's home. "This," the Sobrenian said, "is where the warlord lived in comparative luxury and planned his conquests. He was secure, he believed, in the knowledge that no one could touch him on this island. But he was wrong. His ambitions were shattered in an instant."

The Buruden were coming together again, each joining with another and another until the entire dozen were making a quick retreat back across the land bridge, no doubt before they became ill in the light Sobrenian grav.

"Poor guys," Irene said. "They can't even enjoy this for very long."

"Remember, we cannot either," Govanek said. "We should get back across before the tide turns." She led the way toward the land bridge and the Humans followed.

"Be honest with me, Govanek," Chanda said as they walked. "This all seems just a little too coincidental."

"What do you mean?" the Sobrenian asked.

"Just yesterday we were going to be sequestered in those makeshift quarters. But today, you decide that we'll see some of your planet's sights, and it just happens to be the day of the alignment of these moons, and the appearance of the land bridge?"

Govanek said, "It does appear somewhat fortuitous, doesn't it? But perhaps our intent here was to dispel a myth about us."

"That myth being?"

"That Sobrenians use only brute force in military situations. That we are not capable of guile or a subtle grasp of tactics." Govanek continued toward the mainland as Chanda and her colleagues paused on the middle of the bridge.

Chanda said, "This is just more delay. Playing with our minds. Every minute we're here oohing and ahhing over the wonders we're seeing is a minute we're not making significant progress on an agreement the Sobrenians likely do not want."

Galt asked, "So why bring us to their homeworld to begin with?"

"You have no idea how many times in my career I've asked myself that at the start of negotiations."

"And how often does it turn out well?"

"You don't want to know," Chanda said. She and the others started up the slope overlooking the island. At the top, Chanda paused and turned toward the sea.

Govanek was standing next to the Sobrenian shuttle. "We are ready to leave, Ambassador," she said.

"I'm not," Chanda said without turning. "I'm going to watch the tide come back in." Which is just what she and the others did, as the waves came smashing back, pounding the sides of the land bridge, overflowing and concealing it again. Thunder, salt smell, moisture on Chanda's face.

CHAPTER 11

Chanda spent the shuttle ride back to the city of Piroveka mostly in silence; the unchanging environment of the Sobrenian shuttle, with no outside view or sense of movement, gave her the feeling of being in detention for an unspecified offense. *It's like we're just sitting in the same place, and stage sets are being moved around us,* she thought. *Perhaps our offense is simply that of being here.*

Eventually, Govanek rose and addressed them. "We have arrived back at the site of your quarters. And we are ready to begin preliminary negotiations."

That got Chanda's attention. "Really? I'd hoped we'd have some time to prepare before the initial session."

"You have been eager to begin, Ambassador. We'd assumed you had already prepared."

Galt said, "Of course we have. Let's get started."

Chanda threw him a withering look, but didn't care to contradict the Senator out loud. On her way off the shuttle, across the landing pad, where the Buruden shuttle had already arrived, and into the lift, Chanda forced herself to ignore Govanek and the inevitable security detachment, even her colleagues, to keep her breathing even, to focus on what she knew about these two Galactic species and how she might manage to keep them from starting an inter-system war.

The trip down in the lift was mercifully as silent as the shuttle flight, and as the doors slid aside, Chanda felt as confident as she'd ever been in the moments before potentially life-saving negotiations. When she saw a long table standing between the Human and Buruden living areas, and — finally! — chairs at the table, she knew the negotiations were actually about to begin.

When she saw the person standing in the center of the large circular room, however, all that confidence, every bit of information she'd hoped to draw on during these negotiations, was swept away.

Chanda's legs locked up — she didn't move, *couldn't* move. It was Govanek who took her arm gently and guided her out of the lift, with Galt, Irene, Akira, and the Sobrenian guards following. As the lift's doors closed behind her, Chanda heard Galt say, quietly, "What the hell?"

Was this person Human? *Maybe*, Chanda thought, and his features were somehow familiar. But those features had taken on a Sobrenian cast — his skin wasn't smooth like that of Human flesh, but rough like a Sobrenian's. His nose was wider and longer than a Human's, as if mimicking that of a Sobrenian snout. He wore blue Sobrenian robes, with lines of red and green running through them. But he also wore boots, whereas most Sobrenians went barefoot, as their feet were as dexterous as their hands.

But this person was too tall for a Sobrenian, just a bit taller than Chanda — most Sobrenians, like Govanek, only came up to her shoulders.

And then the person spoke —

"A pleasure to see you again, Ambassador Kasmira."

— And memories tumbled together and Chanda focused on that voice and the recognizably Human features of the man and did a sharp intake of breath and clenched her fists to keep them from shaking. "Lewis Tiernan," she said.

"Oh, my God," Irene said. "It *is* him."

"Goddam bastard," Akira said.

Galt said, "I've heard of him — but this can't be Tiernan!"

Tiernan held his arms wide, as if to embrace them all. "But it *is*, my friends? How do you like my new look?"

Chanda said, "You have to admit, it's unusual for a Humanity First activist."

"We all learn and grow in our own ways, Ambassador. As I first helped the Sobrenians gain insight into Human ways —"

"To help them try to take over Splendor!"

" — and fulfill their species' most basic aims —"

"By killing innocent beings of three intelligent species!"

"Really, Ambassador, it's rude to interrupt."

Chanda folded her arms. "Why are you here?"

"I thought you'd be more interested in my appearance."

Galt said, "You're the same traitor to Humanity no matter what you look like."

Tiernan said, "I'm here as part of the Sobrenian diplomatic team."

"They trust you that much?"

Tiernan indicated his face. "As you can see, I'm *becoming* one of them."

"How the hell did you get back here among the Sobrenians?"

"The Unity didn't know what to do with me once you sent me to Earth, Ambassador. I was born on Goldsmith's Planet, you know — that was the first time I'd even been to Earth. And I found I'd been advocating for a world that didn't deserve it."

Galt asked, "What do you mean?"

"I found it overrated — its so-called beauty mundane, its people lazy or devoted only to virts and drink and sex. I wanted out, and the Unity didn't object."

And never bothered to let me or anyone else on Splendor know that they'd cut him loose, Chanda thought.

Tiernan continued: "The Sobrenians were more than happy to take me in. I've abandoned my original ideas about Humanity's relationship to the rest of the universe. I see it as entirely appropriate now to give up my Humanity, to embrace a better way. The Sobrenians find Humanity in some ways as "chaotic" as the Buruden, because Human society is still diverse, not a monoculture the way many other Galactic intelligences have become."

"All right," Chanda said. "Enough of this. When do negotiations begin?"

"How about right now?" Tiernan asked, as the doors to the lift opened again and another Sobrenian came into the room.

This new Sobrenian was clothed in robes of blue, red, and green that featured lines of gold, gray, and orange running through them. *Finally, someone high-ranking*, Chanda thought. But she looked on in frustration as she realized the Sobrenian was accompanied by a Garotethan, a Galactic species the Sobrenians mistreated without mercy.

The Garotethan stood barely a third of a meter tall, his skinny brown body covered in Sobrenian-style robes of a deep green which had no other adornment. His head was smooth and hairless, and were wide at the forehead while narrowing toward the chin. He had slit-like eyes, a wide and flat nose, and a mouth that was only a thin slash.

The Garotethan followed about a step and a half behind his Sobrenian "client," and Chanda, through past experience, knew the Garotethan had to be ready to perform his Sobrenian master's bidding, whether that might be fetching a drink, eavesdropping on conversations in his client's absence, or merely listening to his boasting of his many magnificent (or dubious) accomplishments.

"This is Nysar," Govanek said. "He is chief negotiator. Lewis Tiernan will assist."

No Garotethan for Tiernan, Chanda realized. *At least not yet. Perhaps he doesn't rate one. Too bad for him.*

Nysar made no greetings, didn't even look at Chanda or anyone else, but sat at the table closer to the Human side of the room. His Garotethan stood to the right and slightly behind him, a constant but mostly unnoticed presence. Tiernan made his way over to the table —

noticeably limping — and sat at the far end. Govanek stood to one side.

The Buruden remained on their side of the room, linked together, away from the table.

Govanek indicated the other table and told Chanda, "Won't you sit?"

Chanda looked around. "What about the Buruden?"

"They require no seating, of course. They will remain in their gravity-controlled area of this room."

"But these negotiations are supposed to be between you and the Buruden."

"That is true. But these are the seating arrangements we have decided upon here. When we continue on the Buruden homeworld, they can make other arrangements."

Chanda turned toward the Buruden. "What do you think of these arrangements?"

"The Sobrenians discussed them with us," the Buruden ambassador said. "We must agree. When they come to our world, we will make the arrangements."

I hear some potential for mischief in that, Chanda thought. *But that's something to worry about later.*

"Very well, then," Chanda said, and sat, conscious she was squeezing her butt into her chair much as she had aboard the Sobrenian shuttle. *Not the most graceful descent,* she thought, *but at least I achieved a soft landing.* Her legs barely fit beneath the Sobrenian-sized table. *I feel like I'm an adult sitting at the children's table,* she thought.

Senator Galt sat next to her. Irene and Akira went off to stand to one side, ready to attend to either of them if needed. *I wish they'd sit down,* Chanda thought. *They remind me a little too much of the Garotethans, standing there like that.*

Chanda was about to address Nysar, but the Sobrenian spoke first. "We demand that these . . . creatures . . . cease their violations of Sobrenian space."

And so it begins, Chanda thought. "Perhaps it would be better if we referred to one another in more respectful terms."

"Already you take the creatures' side."

Galt said, "That's not fair. It's just that — "

Nysar said, "A Sobrenian is speaking," and Galt fell silent, but Chanda could see in his clenched jaw and stern gaze the anger he was suppressing. Nysar continued: "Look at Tiernan — he sits here in total deference to me, as he should. This is our world, and you and the other pre-sentient species will, in turn, defer to us."

Which was just the kind of remark Chanda needed to hear to allow herself to reacquire the self-confidence and focus Tiernan's presence had stolen from her. "With all respect, Nysar, your government requested my presence. I assume it was because you value it."

"The Human will — "

"The Human will speak as long as she wishes! Or negotiations will end immediately." Chanda sat back in her chair and her body stiffened in a moment of panic when her chair threatened to overbalance and tip backwards.

Nysar stared at her with both eyes, as if he were wondering what sort of being he was regarding.

I hope Nysar isn't accustomed to reading a Human's face, Chanda thought. *I might've revealed too much for an instant.*

And was this chair designed that way on purpose? I wouldn't put it past the Sobrenians, though it would be one of the odder psychological strategies I've encountered.

Chanda waited just another moment, still quite aware of Nysar's eyes staring at her, and leaned forward again ever so slightly until her chair was stable again. She was determined not to speak until Nysar did. *Another universality among Galactic species*, Chanda thought. *Maintain silence, and the other person has to fill it.*

Unless you're in an elevator.

"So," Nysar said. "It is as Captain Remkina of the *Mendassa* warned us. You do, indeed, insist upon acting as if you are sentient."

Chanda held up her hands in a what-can-you-do gesture. "It's our way," she said. "Might I suggest that to save time, we all pretend Humans are sentient? It will help you anticipate our behavior more efficiently."

Nysar looked at Tiernan. "Speak to me."

"I told you they are quite clever. Not to be underestimated."

"But it is so difficult. My child, I confess that sometimes I even look at you as. . . ."

"As somehow pre-sentient? I know. But that's due to my nature. As I resemble the true race more, you'll perceive me as truly one of you."

My child? Chanda thought.

Tiernan looked at her. "I know this must seem odd to you."

Damn unsettling, is what it seems like. "I wonder what relevance it has to the negotiations before us."

Nysar kept one eye on Tiernan as the other swiveled toward Chanda. "You should know that even Humans can take a better path, can move closer to true sentience."

Chanda placed her hands flat on the table. "Are we going to address the issues we came here to negotiate?"

Nysar's other eye turned toward Chanda. "Perhaps not right now. We're just starting to learn about one another. Tiernan and I already have much to discuss." Nysar stood, as did Tiernan. Chanda and Galt rose, as well. "You have much more of our world's beauty and culture to witness. Gain more insight about us, and we will speak again."

Nysar turned and started toward the lift, the guards falling into lockstep around him. Tiernan lingered a moment and looked deeply into Chanda's eyes, as if searching for something within her. Despite herself, Chanda felt a chill run down her body. Then the spell was broken as Tiernan turned and, still limping, followed Nysar into the lift. Govanek nodded toward Galt, then Chanda, and was the last in. The lift's doors closed.

Galt asked, "Are most negotiations with other Galactic intelligences like that, Ambassador?"

Chanda said, "I can't say that 'most' of them follow a common pattern. But that one was certainly farther off the usual path than most."

Irene said, "We could be here forever if this is how things proceed."

"Now, *that* part isn't unusual. Every negotiation I've ever been a part of takes longer than you expected."

Akira asked, "Even when you start anticipating it taking longer?"

"Maybe *especially* then." Chanda turned toward the Buruden. "What are your thoughts on these negotiations?"

The Buruden ambassador said, "A truth is that they are taking longer than we anticipated. A likely truth is that they will not be fruitful. A potential truth is that they will. That we would abandon them now is an untruth."

"So that's it," Chanda said. "We keep going."

Just before she went to bed a knock came at the door to Chanda's cramped quarters. "C'mon in," she said.

Galt entered. "A word, Ambassador? I'm hope I'm not disturbing you."

"Not at all," Chanda said, curious as to what brought the Senator to her. "Sorry I can't offer you a drink. And I can barely offer you a place to sit."

"I spent years aboard military starcraft. They can get kinda cramped — but this is ridiculous."

"You're concerned about something. Tell me."

"This Tiernan fellow —"

"Yeah."

"He tried to help the Sobrenians take over Splendor, once. He's a traitor to Humanity."

"Apparently the Unity disagreed."

"*Politics*," Galt said. "The man is dangerous. And he disgusts me."

"This whole business of becoming a Sobrenian?"

"That makes him doubly a traitor as far as I'm concerned."

"I don't hear a bit of racism there, do I?"

Galt stiffened. "You don't. I don't care *what* he's becoming. It's *who* he's becoming."

"Then I apologize. Tiernan's changed his attitudes, that's for sure. *He* was the one prejudiced against non-Humans. Hated the Buruden treated his injuries after that battle on Splendor, for instance."

Galt said, "I'm here to support you any way I can, Ambassador. Just wanted to make that clear."

"I never doubted it."

"I'll watch your back when Tiernan's around."

"It sounds as if you're aching for a reason to take him out."

"It won't be the first time I've had to clean up a mess the Unity left me."

"Do me a favor, will you?"

"Whatever you need, Ambassador."

"Talk to Captain Hamadi up at *Sergeant Jelal*. See if he can get a coded message out to the Unity. I want to know exactly how Tiernan got away from Earth."

"Will do."

"It looks like we're taking another trip tomorrow. I guess we'll just see what cluster event that brings," Chanda said. Galt nodded, and left. Chanda crawled into bed and fell into a restless sleep.

The next day, Chanda and the others entered the Sobrenian shuttle again and saw that both Govanek and Tiernan had arrived ahead of them. Tiernan stared at Chanda as she sat in an aisle across from him. *Thank goodness his eyes can't look in two directions at the same time,* she thought. *At least not yet.*

"I'm sure you're wondering why I'm here," Tiernan said.

Chanda said, "I'm sure you're eager to tell me."

"Today I show you what it was like to take part in a ritual normally reserved for Sobrenians about to become an adult. I believe it was the will of the Shaper."

"So you're embracing Sobrenian religion, as well."

"The Shaper appeals to me for its power and ability to gain respect. It can accomplish many things."

Galt, who was sitting just behind Chanda, said, "The way you've been talking to us, I'd have thought the other Sobrenian god would appeal to you more."

"The Giver? Too moralistic — I don't want a god or anyone telling me what I *should* do. Besides — " Tiernan leaned close to Chanda and lowered his voice. " — its followers are often hypocrites. They say they respect its teachings, but set those teachings aside when it's convenient."

The shuttle lifted, providing another ride that featured no scenery and no sense of movement. About fifteen minutes later, Chanda, Galt, Irene, and Akira stepped out of the shuttle and found themselves at the entrance to a valley nearly two kilometers wide.

Once again, the Sobrenian security forces remained within the shuttle, though Govanek and a limping Tiernan came outside. The Buruden sent out their usual group of a dozen individuals, presumably different ones than those who had witnessed the receding tides on their previous trip.

Sheer, rocky cliffs stood to either side of the valley, which was filled with dense vegetation that featured the same bright greens, reds, and yellows they'd seen around Turellen's island compound.

Chanda caught a whiff of a combination of scents — a sweetness much like Earthly honey, the sour smell of spoiled meat, a pungent odor of burnt fur.

Deep within the valley, Chanda noticed tall plants that resembled slender trees, but whose limbs seemed to move independently of the wind — those limbs also swayed and bent in a manner closer to tentacles than any type of wood.

Someone — or some*thing* — was running among them, uncaring

whether it was seen or heard, making many of the "trees" sway even more violently back and forth. A series of high-pitched screeches burst forth, sounds worthy of an efficient predator. "Damn," Chanda said. "That doesn't sound friendly."

Galt said, "And it sounds big."

Govanek came up to them and said, "It is not, as you say, 'friendly.' It is a predator, the adrono, native here to the Sharaith Valley. It is often a vital part of the ritual you are about to witness."

Galt asked, "We're about to see the end of the *koraht*, aren't we?"

"Yes. I wish you could witness a more intimate look as it plays out, but that could make you, unfortunately, a participant. It would be too dangerous."

Chanda said, "Now, this I've heard a little something about, though I don't know the details. It's a survival ritual, isn't it?"

"Much more than that," Govanek said. "It is a rite of passage for our young people, and has a deep spiritual component. It is also when they are finally considered fully adult and sentient."

Interesting, Chanda thought. *Even their own children aren't thought to be sentient until they reach a certain age.*

Galt shook his head. "These young people have to make their way through a wilderness area with nothing but a sword and the clothes on their backs. They try to build shelters against the heat or cold, depending upon the time of year, and search for anything safe to eat. This is always in an area with a great many poisonous plants and fruits. Those who survive those dangers often fall prey to the adrono."

Chanda said, "But that's — "

"Don't say it!"

Barbaric.

Govanek gave them both a questioning stare, but didn't press the issue. Instead, she told them, "We should see the first of the survivors coming out of the valley soon."

Tiernan looked intently toward the edge of the tree line, took a couple of steps forward. "Here they come," he said, his voice quiet with awe.

Chanda watched in growing horror as one young Sobrenian after another came out from the valley — here was one using his bent sword as a makeshift cane, keeping his bloody right leg off the ground. Another, immediately behind, was bleeding profusely from his head, his blood darker than a Human's. More followed, many with wounds clearly revealing the parallel slashes of an animal's claws, no doubt from an adrono attack.

Chanda started forward, but Galt grabbed her shoulders from behind and held on tight. "No."

"But if we can help —"

"You can't. Remember, you're an ambassador."

And shouldn't interfere. "You're right."

The sound of a gravitic drive came from overhead, and another Sobrenian shuttle, larger than the one that had brought them from Piroveka, settled down next to them. About a dozen Sobrenians rushed out of that shuttle, gurneys and medical equipment at the ready.

"Thank goodness," Chanda said, as she saw that another dozen or so injured Sobrenians were leaving the valley. Some could barely place one foot before the other, and a few were crawling — one, having suffered a severed arm, was dragging himself by his remaining arm, but was clearly losing blood — and strength — quickly. "But — the medical teams aren't heading toward the injured."

Tiernan said, "The injured must make it to them."

As Chanda watched, several of the young, injured Sobrenians were doing just that — they stopped in front of the medical teams, who placed those with the worst injuries onto gurneys and led those who could still walk into the shuttle.

Chanda's heart raced and her breathing turned ragged. It took all her will not to rush forward to help the most severely injured Sobrenians, who were still struggling to reach medical care. She turned to Govanek: "What lesson are we to take from witnessing this? Especially when yesterday you were trying to demonstrate that there's more to your culture than brute force?"

Govanek stared into the distance, into skies beyond the struggling Sobrenians. "You believe we are too harsh toward our own people?"

"I'm not about to make such a judgement." *I'm lying*, Chanda thought. "I just want to know how this relates to our negotiations."

"You and the Buruden are here to understand us better." Govanek still didn't look toward the struggling individuals, a number of whom were groaning in agony as they tried to advance the final few meters to safety and medical care. "This is part of who we are."

Chanda stepped closer to Govanek to look more intently into her face. Govanek's left eye swiveled to stare back at her, the right eye continuing to look skyward. "May I ask a personal question?" Chanda asked.

Govanek turned her head toward Chanda and both eyes focused on her. "I'm here to serve however I might."

"How did you perform during this ritual?"

"I . . . prefer not to answer."

Tiernan said, "Really, Ambassador — you should know better than to ask such a thing."

"I'm here to learn," Chanda said.

"Not at the cost of our dignity," Tiernan said.

Which makes me wonder all the more what happened, Chanda thought.

Tiernan told Chanda, "You should ask, instead, how *I* performed. I'm newly Sobrenian in outlook, even though my physical transformation is still in progress. It was an honor for Nysar to insist I take part."

Again the connection with Nysar, Chanda thought.

Tiernan continued: "Actually, I did quite well. I'm still healing a bit — you may have noticed my limp — I'd made it through the most hazardous areas, although it took me longer than I'd expected. An adrono came out of nowhere and slashed me on the leg. But I didn't let that stop me. A couple well-placed knife slashes, and the adrono was dead."

Galt said, "But you'd been a Unity Marine, trained to a professional level. That had to give you an advantage."

"Yet it took me longer than I thought it would to finish, and an adrono nearly killed me. I think that everything considered, it was a fair matchup."

Chanda took another look at what was now a long line of injured Sobrenians trying, and is many cases, failing, to reach medical help. *I don't even want to think of how many others are lying in that thick forest, dead or unable to move.* She told Govanek, "Do we have to stay here any longer? I think we understand this ritual now."

Govanek started to speak, but Tiernan interrupted: "Don't have the stomach to keep watching, do you, Chanda? How very Human of you."

Chanda began walking toward the Sobrenian shuttle, purposely not saying anything more to Tiernan. *Let him think what he wants.*

Chanda heard movement to her left and saw that the Buruden were gathering themselves together and heading back into their own shuttle. *I wonder if that's due to the higher grav or if they just can't stand to watch this display any more than I can.*

Either way, I can't blame them.

Behind her, Tiernan said, "So you make a move, and your Buruden lackeys do as well."

Chanda started up the shuttle's ramp. Tiernan was on her heels, with Galt, Irene, and Akira right behind him. "The Buruden do what they want," Chanda said. "I don't control them."

The final Buruden cleared the entrance to their shuttle; those who'd stayed aboard must have been keeping the craft on standby, because it instantly lifted off and headed back toward Piroveka.

A hand grasped Chanda's arm. Tiernan. She tried to pull away, but he held tight. "Just a word, Ambassador — " Chanda turned toward Tiernan just as Galt came up behind him and pulled the Human-turned-Sobrenian away from her.

Even as Galt raised his fists, though, Tiernan took a step back and spread his arms wide. "I apologize, Senator Galt. And especially to you, Ambassador Kasmira. I was in the wrong to touch you. I just wanted to thank you for agreeing to witness our ritual, at least for a few moments."

Chanda caught Galt's eye and said, "Let's just go."

Galt lowered his fists, but didn't try to hide his disappointment at not being able to engage Tiernan. As Chanda went inside the Sobrenian shuttle, she couldn't help thinking, *How am I supposed to keep the Sobrenians and Buruden from getting into a war with one another when I can barely keep a brawl from breaking out right in front of me?*

CHAPTER 12

Later that day, Nysar called another for round of negotiations. *Or what passes for them,* Chanda thought. All the players gathered again — she and Galt faced Nysar and Tiernan across the negotiation table, with the Buruden once again banished into their high-grav side of the room. Govanek stood to one side, with Irene and Akira opposite.

Nysar looked at Chanda and tilted his head to one side, as if he were trying to perceive something about her and coming up short. After a moment, he said to her, "I believe you saw an example of Sobrenian culture and tradition today."

"I did. A little violent for my own taste. But I'm not here to judge."

"Yet that very statement implies you are judging, even as it fails to say why you are really here."

"I'm here to try to help you and the Buruden find a way short of war to settle your disputes."

"Yes," Nysar said. "Our disputes. We dislike their incursions into our space. We dislike their spying upon us."

"With all respect, the Buruden representatives are right here. You can speak directly to them."

Nysar kept one eye on Chanda as the other eye glanced toward Tiernan. Nysar said, "We wish not to speak directly to . . . these beings. We wish for you to mediate between us."

"I'm not here just to be a messenger girl. The two species have to interact at some point."

"We will interact with you, only."

Tiernan said, "Nysar is already making a concession speaking to *you*. Accept it."

Chanda said, "Is this more of that 'pre-sentient' business?"

Now it was Tiernan's turn to glance toward Nysar. Chanda couldn't tell that anything more than a glance went between them, but Tiernan said, "In part. But of the two species, we prefer to speak to Humanity. The Buruden . . . disturb us."

"How so?"

Now, for the first time, Nysar glanced toward the Buruden's side of the room, where they stood, linked and silent. Chanda thought, *I can't believe the Buruden just sit there and let all these insults against themselves go unheeded.*

Nysar said, "We would prefer to speak of them without their presence."

"So — you'll criticize them behind their backs, but not to their —" *Dammit, they don't have faces*, Chanda thought. *Or backs, for that matter.*" — you'll criticize them when they can't hear you. Is this Sobrenian courage?"

From behind her, the Buruden ambassador said, "Let the Sobrenians speak as they may. Their words cannot insult us."

Nysar still stared at Chanda. Then he said, "Sobrenian courage lets us speak as we wish, then."

Chanda couldn't help but notice that Nysar was pointedly responding to the last thing she'd said, not to the Buruden's words. "And that courage says?"

"These beings make stardrive incursions into our system with their probes. They spy upon us. We believe that eventually they will come closer to our homeworld, and that they will attempt to invade it."

Chanda asked, "What proof do you have of this?"

Nysar actually indicated the Buruden with a wave of his hand, though he still didn't look in their direction. "You need only examine their behavior! They can inundate a landscape with hundreds or thousands of individuals, all scurrying around in different directions, in apparently random patterns."

"Every Galactic species explores its surroundings in different ways. If you look at — "

"Explores? Overwhelms, you mean. They are even more chaotic than yourselves, *Human*. And their mindlessness in small groups makes them a danger — how can you reason with something which is only as intelligent as an adrono?"

"How can the Buruden expect to reason with beings who won't even see them as sentient, let alone equals?"

"*Equals?* We Sobrenians have a grand and complex culture, filled with great literature and artwork and weaponry. We do not run aimlessly through fields as animals do, gathering vague impressions of our surroundings as perceived through a limited intelligence."

Chanda turned and asked the Buruden, "Do you have any response to this? You should take up for yourselves."

Chanda heard over her datalink, "We must allow the Sobrenians their opinions. As they must allow ours."

They're biding their time, Chanda thought. *Maybe they have a surprise in store for the Sobrenians when negotiations move to their own homeworld.*

Nysar actually let one of his eyes glance toward the Buruden's area of the room. "You see how they refuse to defend themselves? This is how we will prove ourselves the better species."

Chanda said, "I didn't know that was the goal here."

"Humanity may interpret these negotiations as it wishes. We Sobrenians know our goals, and intend to achieve them."

"Let's speak some more of any evidence you may have of Buruden intentions toward your system — "

"Let's not. These negotiations are ended for the day. We must decide whether they will continue at all, and whether military options might be more fruitful."

Chanda felt as if an electrical shock passed through her body. *Military options? How did we jump to that conclusion so quickly?* "Nysar, I think that's premature. Plus, we have to be able to work at this for more than just a few minutes at a time."

"We will convene again when all parties agree to," Nysar said. He rose, as did Tiernan, and they started for the lift with Govanek close behind. Chanda stood and watched as the lift doors opened, the three of them entered, and the lift doors closed.

Galt asked, "I know I keep asking this. Do these things always take this long to get started?"

"I've been through worse. But not much. You have to understand, the Sobrenians tend toward bluster. They talk a good fight, but sometimes that's all it is. In the meantime, they delay and then delay some more."

"You realize they could be using this time to get ready for a real war."

"Of course I do. And sometimes they work their way past the bluster and actually take the shot. I've been there when it's happened."

Galt leaned in close. "The Buruden aren't helping."

"I know. I'm going to have a glass of hot tea and gather my thoughts and come back out here and try to figure them out."

———

A few minutes later, Chanda approached the Buruden side of the room. She stopped just short of the point where their 2.3 grav would take over and addressed the two closest individuals to her. "I'd like to speak to the ambassador, please, if you can form him."

Those two Buruden joined their legs together as a couple more rushed in from nearby and several more emerged from their living quarters. Within fifteen seconds, Chanda heard, "I am the ambassador."

"Very well — Ambassador, with all respect to you, do you have a plan for these negotiations?"

"You see our plan in action. We listen to the Sobrenians."

"You need to be more forceful. They're leading us along, taking advantage of being on their home turf."

"Part of that was a failure to translate," the Buruden ambassador said. "But we understand most of it. We are waiting to assert ourselves after we return to our homeworld. That is a truth."

"That's it?" Chanda asked. "No likely or potential truths, or untruths?"

"We are united in this."

That's a rarity, Chanda thought. "Then I can only continue as I have — trying to get the Sobrenians to talk more, to make demands that you can respond to."

"That we are happy with your efforts is a likely truth and a potential truth for most of us."

Not the most overwhelming show of support I've ever had, Chanda though. "And if that changes, or if you want to become more assertive during negotiations, you'll let me know, correct?"

"That is also a truth."

About the most I can hope for, I guess. Chanda walked away from the Buruden and headed toward her quarters.

That night, Chanda was in her cramped bedroom, ready to change clothes and go to bed when she heard the faint rumbling of the lift's doors as they opened. She stood still a moment, listening. *Maybe it's just a late delivery, or a routine message about what we're doing tomorrow*, she thought.

A knock at her door. When she opened it, there stood Govanek. "We request your presence at a religious ritual," she said.

"Now?"

"Typically, it takes place late at night. And it is happening in this building."

Chanda put aside thoughts of sleep. "Can Senator Galt accompany us?"

"Certainly. A dozen Buruden are attending. But that is only because . . . "

"Because otherwise they won't be intelligent enough to make sense of what they're seeing."

"Yes."

"We'll be ready in a moment."

"I will wait at the lift."

Chanda went to Galt's quarters, knocked, and he opened his door just a crack. "What is it?" he asked.

"A religious ritual."

"A *Sobrenian* religious ritual?"

"What other kind would there be here?"

"Sorry. Still waking up. Lemme get dressed."

The next knock was at Irene and Akira's quarters. She heard muffled sounds from behind the door, received no response, knocked louder. An abrupt quiet then, and a high-pitched "Just a minute!" and then Irene was opening the door. "Oh!" she said. "What is it?"

Chanda explained. "I just wanted to let you know Galt and I are going to a Sobrenian religious thing. Hold down the fort. I don't know how long we'll be."

Akira's voice from behind Irene: "Have fun, Chanda!"

Chanda couldn't help grinning. "Oh, I expect it to be plenty of fun."

Chanda and Galt met Govanek at the lift. To Chanda's surprise, it began to descend. *I'd already imagined ourselves as being banished to some otherwise forgotten basement area*, Chanda thought. *Or that perhaps this ritual would be performed on the roof, beneath the stars.*

Within moments, the lift settled to a stop and its doors slid open. Chanda and Galt followed Govanek into a dimly lit room, another round one like their quarters, only smaller. It contained no pews, no altar, and no decorations other than wall-sized murals, one to the left, a different one to the right. A couple of dozen Sobrenians stood with their backs to the lift. *The congregants, I suppose,* Chanda thought. *If that's the proper word.*

Immediately beyond the lift stood the dozen Buruden. *I wonder why they always seem to arrive before we do,* Chanda wondered. To either side and directly behind them stood several Sobrenian security guards, pulse rifles at the ready.

Galt leaned close to Chanda and whispered, "Do you think those rifles are a regular part of their religious services?"

"The Sobrenians love their guns. About as much as they seem to hate the Buruden. For now, I'm trying to figure out this imagery." Chanda pointed out the mural to their left. It appeared to extoll the virtues of hard work, portraying Sobrenians pushing large boulders across rough ground, operating heavy machinery against the backdrop of an entire city under construction, and floating in spacesuits outside an unfinished orbital habitat, all of that performed against a backdrop resembling a starfield.

To the right, the other mural showed what appeared to be a Sobrenian hospital, with doctors treating youngsters, and a group of adults sitting and listening, apparently enthralled, to a clearly elderly Sobrenian. Here the background was a wilderness landscape, all desert sands and rough mountain peaks.

"It's just a guess," Chanda said, "but I'd imagine the mural on the left represents the Shaper — the practical god."

Galt said, "Which makes the one on the right the Giver — the moral god."

A voice from the darkness to their left: "Excellent! I commend you on your insight."

Tiernan. *He must've come from a hidden doorway,* Chanda thought. He approached Chanda and Galt with a measured gait that was clearly imitating the way most Sobrenians walked, but which seemed out of place for the longer-legged Human.

"Wasn't that hard to figure out," Chanda said.

"Yes, but how far into the Sobrenian mind does your insight lead you?" Tiernan indicated the mural devoted to the Shaper. "You see the progression indicated here — we advance from digging in the dirt to creating great cities to colonizing the skies." Tiernan turned his attention to the Giver's mural. "Over here, we depict healing technologies being used in a hospital, but also the wisdom of our elders."

"We?" Galt said. "Our?"

Tiernan placed a rough-skinned hand on his chest. "I'm Sobrenian where it counts — in here." He moved that hand to his forehead. "And most importantly, in here."

Chanda said, "This isn't why I came here."

Tiernan tilted his head slightly and raised one hairless brow. "My journey of enlightenment doesn't fascinate you?"

"I'm more enthralled by the idea of sleep."

"For a diplomat, you don't spare anyone's feelings."

"Your idea of diplomacy must come from bad cube dramas. You're getting a good taste of the behind-the-scenes stuff. Besides, I'm just conforming to what appears to be the basic Sobrenian style of diplomacy."

"That's right," Galt said. "Force shields up, all weapons primed and ready."

Chanda shot Galt a *don't-push-it* look.

A low tone, more felt than heard, sounded. Tiernan said, "The ritual is about to begin. We'll stay here in the back so I can explain what's going on. I'm sure I can trust you to maintain the proper decorum."

"Of course," Chanda said. "We're your guests, after all."

A light came from above, dim at first, then brighter and brighter until it was almost blinding. Chanda found herself squinting as movement caught her eye where the two murals met. A Sobrenian she hadn't noticed before stood there. *Another hidden doorway, I imagine.*

This Sobrenian was wearing robes more elaborate than any

Chanda had seen before, many-layered, with fabrics of green, blue, and gold, and each layer of fabric featuring multiple lines of additional colors running through them. "I've never seen such clothing even on high-ranking political leaders," Chanda whispered to Tiernan. "She's certainly higher in your society than I would've anticipated."

"That's because you're still learning about our society," Tiernan said.

"Is she a priest, or any other kind of prelate?"

"The Sobrenian word translates best to 'guide.'"

The rumbling faded away. The Sobrenians gathered together stood facing the guide, who raised her arms toward the bright light and began to speak.

Chanda's datalink didn't provide a translation. A glance at Galt, and his expression confirmed he wasn't hearing anything, either. As much as she hated the idea of touching Tiernan, she nudged him on the arm and pointed behind her left ear, where the datalink was implanted.

Tiernan explained, "She's speaking an ancient tongue — not commonly used, much like Latin on Earth."

"So this is the sermon?"

"More like advice — those who follow the Shaper should devote themselves to building things, making scientific discoveries — practical stuff. Those following the Giver should perform good deeds for others."

"I'd have thought the two factions would have separate services."

"Each hears what's expected of the other so they're fully informed about one another. It's a matter of respect, and an acknowledgement that some of us follow both gods."

The guide's exhortation went on for several more minutes, with the Sobrenians standing attentively throughout. Then the guide lowered her arms. She spoke more softly now, and Chanda unconsciously strained to hear her words even though she couldn't understand them.

Tiernan said, "She's telling us that no matter which God we follow, religion is not separate from the rest of life — it imbues everything."

"That's not something I've come across much in my dealings with Sobrenians."

"That's because we take it for granted. Our self-worth is also wrapped up in religious thought. We believe our culture is the highest that exists and that we are the pinnacle of creation. Our entire world is sacred ground, and all other worlds are unclean by comparison."

Chanda caught a glimpse of Galt's face and saw it was contorted in anger and frustration. "So far," Chanda said, "I haven't seen a lot that's much different from many Human religions."

"Oh, we have one big difference, Ambassador. Just wait."

The guide fell silent. She lowered her head, as if in prayer. So did the other Sobrenians, Tiernan included. That went on long enough that Chanda found herself suppressing a bored sigh. *How much longer will this go on?* she wondered.

Without warning, a high-pitched tone filled the room, so loud it seemed to pierce Chanda's skull — she covered her ears, but couldn't block out the wrenching sound, or the pain. She looked toward Galt, who'd fallen to the floor and was covering his head and moaning. Next to him sat Tiernan, his combined Human-Sobrenian features etched with pain, but who somehow was managing to *smile*, as well. She forced herself to look around, and saw a similar expression on most of the Sobrenians. As for the Buruden, they stood impassively, by all accounts unaffected.

The tone shifted, and so did the pain — it centered in her gut now, as if her insides were on fire — she bent double and clutched her stomach, but nothing helped. Every nerve ending in her body was firing more painfully than she'd felt in her life.

The sound ceased. Chanda collapsed to the floor, exhausted. She couldn't make herself open her eyes at first, and was aware only of the low moans of those around her, both Human and Sobrenian. The first voice she made out was Galt's: "Ambassador — Chanda — are you all right?"

She opened her eyes. Senator Gabriel Galt was kneeling next to her. His face looked as if all the blood had drained from it, and every line on that face stood out in sharper contrast than before. "Are you OK?" she asked him.

Galt stood up, then helped Chanda to her feet. He said, "I feel like I got into a fistfight in a dark alley — and lost."

"What the hell happened? Some sort of malfunction? Or attack?"

Tiernan came up to them. "Neither. That was part of the ritual."

"You could've warned us," Chanda said. "And why were we even included?"

"One reason was technical — we can't isolate parts of the room to receive that blessing."

Galt muttered, "Hell of a blessing."

"And the other reason?" Chanda asked.

"We felt it would be a meaningful experience for you to undergo. An opportunity to understand us better."

Galt rubbed the back of his head. "We understand you better, all right. I consider what just happened to be an attack on Earth Unity personnel. I'd like to — "

"You'd like to calm down and let me handle this," Chanda said. Galt wound down, but stood there fuming. "Tiernan, what's the meaning of that ritual?"

"It's a sample of what Sobrenians believe they will feel in the afterlife."

"With all respect to our hosts' religious sensitivities, they have a funny idea of what heaven must be like."

"That's the point, Ambassador. Sobrenian religious concepts don't include heaven. Only what Humanity would think of as hell."

Chanda drew in a deep breath and placed a hand on her chest. Her heart was still racing. "Doesn't sound like they're much concerned with repentance or, what do people say? Going to their reward, that's it!"

"It's a motivator for *this* world. Doing well is its own reward in life."

Galt said, "Sounds like a tough sell."

"To most Humans, it might seem fatalistic. But the Sobrenians accept their fate, and work harder to find satisfaction day to day."

The Sobrenians attending the service were filing out of the room, using several exits Chanda hadn't seen earlier — no doubt how Tiernan and the guide had entered.

"That's it?" Galt asked. "No 'God be with you,' or anything?"

"Our gods' work is already done," Tiernan said. "What happens to us now is our own responsibility."

Chanda caught Galt's eye and tilted her head toward the lift. "I'm ready to get some sleep."

She started to walk away from Tiernan, but paused when he spoke again: "A good idea, Ambassador. We're taking another trip tomorrow."

"Shouldn't we continue negotiations? This is serious business, here."

"All in good time, Ambassador. And what you'll be seeing tomorrow is as serious as it gets for us Sobrenians."

Galt said, "I knew it. I'm surprised we haven't already made this trip — we're going to the site of the comet strike, aren't we?"

Tiernan said, "Yes, the one place, the one event as meaningful to us as our relationships with the Shaper and the Giver."

Despite herself, Chanda was intrigued. *It's perhaps the one place on this planet I wanted to make sure to see,* she thought. *Perhaps it's Human nature — we're drawn to the site of big events, particularly disasters. Not something to be proud of, but after all, we're a naturally curious species.*

CHAPTER 13

In the Earth year 1862, even as Confederate forces retreated from Shiloh and Union forces found themselves too exhausted to pursue them, a comet 100 meters wide made of ice and dust, traveling 25 kilometers per second, pierced the atmosphere of the Sobrenian homeworld and exploded 15 kilometers above the planet's surface.

A shock wave and fireball equal to 200 Hiroshima bombs struck just to the southeast of the city of Daturak, a major Sobrenian population center and trading seaport and spaceport.

Destruction was total for an area five kilometers beyond the blast site, the blast vaporizing manufacturing facilities, docks, and countless homes in an instant — along with over 100,000 Sobrenians — metal workers, ritual combat instructors, spacecraft pilots, followers devoted to the Sobrenian gods known as the Giver and the Shaper, doctors, mothers and fathers, sons and daughters.

Minutes later, Sobrenians a thousand kilometers away turned their heads at a sudden loud, sustained sound that seemed to fade only grudgingly. That night, they watched in wonder as a bright glow from beyond the horizon filled half the sky.

Seismographic sensors hundreds of kilometers away detected the landscape's shuddering against the impact, and Sobrenian scientists were baffled at first, as no known fault lines existed there.

With most police, fire, medical, and communications facilities in Daturak destroyed, much of the survivors' suffering went unrelieved for hours, days, even weeks, as rescuers struggled to make their way into a city whose roads were mostly demolished or blocked by debris. The story was the same for many smaller cities also ravaged by the comet strike.

Aerial rescuers were the first to see a crater unlike anything they expected. Since the comet didn't strike the ground intact, rather than leaving the classic round and deep crater rimmed with debris, it left one that was long and shallow instead, one 500 meters long, 50 deep, and with no ring of debris.

The comet strike itself was only the beginning of the Sobrenians' problems. The entire planet's ecology was affected for years afterwards, with clouds of dust and debris circling the world for years, reducing the average temperature and playing hell with the planet's lifeforms, including many food sources.

---

288 Earth years later, Chanda and Galt stood beside Tiernan, Govanek, and a dozen Buruden on an overlook above the carefully preserved city of Daturak. In the middle distance, a half-kilometer of so away from the site of the comet strike, Chanda saw skeletal outlines of factories and docking facilities that had been directly beneath the shockwave — with its energies coming straight down upon them, they managed to stand even against the full force of the blast.

The area closest to them was a wide, debris-filled plain, largely scoured of any structures. To either side, in the far distance, Chanda saw portions of buildings that survived the blast, some of them industrial, others clearly residences.

In the time since the comet strike, the Sobrenian government had forbidden any reconstruction or resettlement in Daturak. Over the years, its scientists had carefully devised combinations of energy fields and nanotech protocols that prevented Daturak's structures from rusting or corroding, kept plant life from growing among the debris, and barred animals from making new homes there.

"This is hard to believe," Chanda said. "The entire city, maintained exactly as it was immediately after the comet strike."

The air was quiet and still in a way that implied more than a natural calm. *It doesn't even seem as if my voice carries more than a few meters*, Chanda thought.

Tiernan said, "After a catastrophe like this, you can see how it mobilized the Sobrenian people to join together for a single cause — its own survival."

That's not how it was, Chanda thought, and was about to say so when Galt beat her to it.

"You seem to be forgetting about all the world war that began just days after the comet hit the planet."

Tiernan turned his head toward Galt and once again Chanda was grateful that Tiernan's eyes didn't yet work independently. "There was some . . . reassignment of resources," Tiernan said.

Galt said, "Daturak was a key port — both sea and space — and industrial center. Its loss created a vacuum which others were only too glad to fill. So many resources — or at least easy access to them — were lost that wars started over them."

"You exaggerate the importance of those conflicts."

"More Sobrenians," Galt said, "died in those wars than from the comet strike."

"A Human view of history, which I once believed. Now I've been taught the real story."

You've been taught the sanitized version, Chanda thought. She touched Galt's arm to get his attention. "You needn't bother," she told him.

Tiernan pointed toward the Buruden. "Ask *them* what they did after the comet strike. They aren't as benign as you seem to think they are."

I never knew the Buruden had anything to do with the Sobrenians then, Chanda thought. She turned toward the mass of Buruden. "Is the ambassador with us?"

The Buruden separated their joiners, jumbled their positions, then linked up again. "The ambassador is here," Chanda heard over her datalink.

"Tiernan is making what sounds like a serious charge against your people. Do you have a response?"

Galt cut in: "Ambassador, do you really think this is the time — "

"Of course it's the time." Chanda turned her attention back to the Buruden.

The ambassador said, "Our stardrive technology was much more primitive back then, of course. We'd not made contact with the Sobrenians yet. But we sent emissaries to see if we could help with their recovery effort."

Tiernan said, "They sent spies to see if we were ripe to exploit."

"Really?" Galt asked. "'We?' Your ancestors weren't on this planet. They were probably fighting in the American Civil War."

Tiernan looked down his nose turned burgeoning snout. "I owe my allegiance to new ancestors now."

Chanda said, "Please, let's let the Buruden ambassador speak."

The Buruden said, "That our people came here to exploit the Sobrenians is not a truth. That we wondered whether they might be a threat to us is a potential truth. Determining how their military capabilities had been affected is a likely truth. Desiring to mitigate the suffering of a population in jeopardy is a truth."

Tiernan said, "You hear how they talk. You can't make a bit of sense of them."

"You don't go to the trouble," Chanda said. "You don't want to consider another way of thinking."

Tiernan held up his rough-skinned hands, ran them down his face and elongated nose. "Does this look like someone unwilling to look at ways of thought different from Humanity? Does this look like someone who hasn't kept an open mind about how to conduct his life?"

Galt chuckled. "He's got you there, Ambassador."

"*Fine*," Chanda said. She looked out toward the vast wasted landscape. "Certainly I can understand that something like the comet strike — and what happened afterwards — changes a people." She turned toward Tiernan. "What they became seems to have a great appeal for you."

Tiernan said, "They became a better people than Humans. They *strive*. They *fight*. Almost three hundred years later, and sometimes it's as if the comet landed yesterday."

"I'm not sure that's a good way to think of it. And I'm mystified as to why a natural disaster made the Sobrenians so militant."

Galt said, "I am, too. After all, Earth was struck on purpose by asteroids during the Great Human War and didn't react that way. That was just 47 years ago. I've been to the ruins of Florence."

Tiernan said, "And it seems Humanity has learned nothing from that experience. My original race has grown soft, fit only to explore."

The Buruden ambassador spoke up: "It is difficult for us to understand such linear thought. Humans and Sobrenians share this — to send ideas down a single path, or perhaps two, instead of considering the natural foursome of ideas."

Tiernan cast the group of Buruden a hateful look. "Don't lump my people's way of thinking in with Humanity's. We're nothing alike."

Chanda said, "You realize, of course, that this isn't the best way to find common ground during negotiations."

"My job isn't to negotiate. It's to show you our culture."

Galt said, "You mean to show us what you think is the superiority of your culture."

As Tiernan smiled, Chanda fought not to grimace; such a Human expression laid over partially-Sobrenian features wasn't pleasant to view. "What do you think my response will be to that, Senator Galt?"

"I should've realized," Galt said. "Your response — 'same thing.'"

"Precisely."

Chanda said, "Let's get back on track here. Tiernan, you say the Sobrenians can still feel as if the comet strike happened yesterday. Shouldn't they want to keep their culture intact?"

"Yes, *we* should."

"Very well — *you*. Having rebuilt their society over nearly three centuries, I'd think it would be inexcusable to let a conflict with another Galactic intelligence strike a different kind of blow to it."

"That will not happen," Tiernan said. "We are too strong."

"Even so, the destructiveness of a war — "

Tiernan pointed at the joined Buruden. "Look at them! Do they seem a threat? Standing there, as if they could take on a squad of Sobrenians armed with the most efficient pulse rifles of any Galactic species we're aware of?"

Chanda glanced at the Buruden, hoping they'd respond. But they did not. *Which makes me wonder if Tiernan isn't right*, she thought. "That isn't for me to say," was all she told Tiernan.

The Human-turned-Sobrenian made as if he were suppressing a yawn. "I believe it's time for us to go." He indicated the barren plain before them that once was a thriving city. "If you haven't learned the lesson we intended here, then it serves no purpose to remain."

The Buruden broke up their group of a dozen and skittered back to their shuttle. Tiernan continued: "You see, they can't wait to run away! It will be interesting to witness tomorrow's negotiation session." He turned his back on Chanda and Galt and headed back toward the Sobrenian shuttle.

Chanda didn't say anything more as she followed Tiernan and Galt. As she climbed the ramp into the Sobrenian shuttle, she paused a moment for a last look back at the carefully preserved landscape of destruction. *This was a natural disaster*, Chanda thought. *But Tier-*

nan's clearly saying the Sobrenians are willing to risk a series of such catastrophes to get what they want from the Buruden.

In that moment, she couldn't contemplate all those deaths, and the millions more who died in the subsequent war. *I wasn't thinking clearly just now*, she thought. *Tiernan, for one, isn't just willing to risk a war. He seems to embrace the idea, just as the Sobrenians embrace this place where so many of their own died.*

Could this be a planet of martyrs?

Chanda, barely aware of her own actions, entered the Sobrenian shuttle and settled into a seat as far away from anyone else as she could, as she contemplated that idea during the trip back to the city of Piroveka.

Chanda called her colleagues into her cramped room that night. She stood in the doorway to her bathroom as Galt found a spot by the entrance and Irene and Akira sat on the edge of her bed.

"The attitude of the Sobrenians worries me," she told them. "I realize I've used the word 'bluster' to describe their actions at times, but keep in mind I've also pointed out sometimes they actually take the shot. I'm starting to worry we may be near one of those times."

Galt said, "Before you take that thought much further, Ambassador, I should let you know what I've heard from Captain Hamadi aboard the *Jelal*."

"Please do."

"It seems the Unity was just as surprised to hear about Tiernan being here as we were to find him here. Turns out he'd made a deal with the Unity when he arrived back on Earth from Splendor. He agreed to provide inside information about the Sobrenians, since he'd worked more closely with them than any other Human."

Chanda said, "And in return he kept his freedom."

"Exactly," Galt said.

Irene asked, "So how'd he get back here?"

Galt said, "Captain Hamadi could only find out what amounts to rumors and speculation. Tiernan supposedly was going to become a double agent. His cover story was that the Unity had agreed to send him back here to the Sobrenians in exchange for them considering closer diplomatic ties with Earth."

Chanda frowned. "Is there any chance that actually happened?"

"That's where Hamadi's sources dry up. *Somehow* he got back here. Whether the Unity sneaked him into the system somehow, I don't know."

"The main question is, why's he here? Does he hate his own species so much?"

"I don't care," Galt said. "I consider Tiernan a traitor to Humanity. And this business of making himself into a Sobrenian I find disgusting. But he's only important in how he affects Sobrenian actions."

Akira spoke up. "So far he seems like Nysar's lap dog."

"Don't underestimate either of them," Chanda said. "Tiernan may be disgusting, but he's crafty. And Nysar is typical of a great many other Sobrenians I've dealt with. We're still in the bluster stage, and part of that's showmanship — which is part of diplomacy, too. I'm as guilty of it as anyone."

Galt said, "Govanek seems sympathetic toward us."

"I think she is. Apparently the time she spent working with Mike Christopher impressed her."

Irene said, "You're not thinking of trying to turn her against her own people?"

"I don't get a sense that we'd be able to. But she might be a good source of information that we're not going to get out of Tiernan, for instance."

Galt's face bore a quizzical look. "So what happens next? Tiernan said we're supposed to have another negotiation session tomorrow."

"We keep our eyes and ears open," Chanda said. "And see if there's any hope of actually getting the Sobrenians and Buruden to interact."

"I know one thing I'm going to do," Galt said. "I have a few more chips I think I can call in. I don't like how Hamadi was told only so much about Tiernan. I think I can dig up some more dirt on him."

"I have no argument with that. I'll see all of you in the morning."

Galt, Irene, and Akira left. As Chanda shut the door after them, she thought, *If I have no expectations, I guess I can't be disappointed.*

CHAPTER 14

The next morning, Chanda woke up, dressed, and wandered out to the usual breakfast buffet. *Thank goodness for Govanek*, she thought. She skipped the meat and biscuits and grabbed a plate of fruit and a plastic bulb filled with the usual red liquid.

A few minutes later, a bleary-eyed Galt entered. Chanda couldn't help but favor him with a smile and say, "I hope you don't feel like you look."

Galt cast a fake scowl back at her. "Good morning to you, too."

"I've had my share of rough nights here. Mostly due to worry."

"Yeah. Same for me. Listen, I'm sorry if I seemed too pessimistic last night."

"You didn't say anything I haven't thought." Chanda peered through the partially open doorway down the hall of their habitation. "Have you seen Irene or Akira?"

"They're another reason I didn't get a lot of sleep. Didn't you hear them?"

"Rough nights aside, I usually have that diplomat's skill of being able to sleep anywhere and in any position. But I admit, last night must've been a good one."

Galt said, "I don't mind it, actually. Reminds me of . . . well."

"You don't have to —"

"That's all right. I don't even mean the sex. It reminds me of being young. Oh — there they are."

Chanda couldn't help grinning at the sight of Irene, who looked even more bleary-eyed than Galt, but was trying to put up a good front. She went right to the food and drink without a word. Akira appeared slightly more hearty, and managed a grin that was almost a leer along with a small down-by-the-waist wave.

Galt wasn't grinning, though, and asked Chanda quietly, "You think they'd be in good enough shape to pilot the shuttle if we had to make a quick getaway?"

"One quick stim shot from the shuttle's medkit and they could stay awake and alert for the next three days," Chanda said. "Besides, they're tired, not drunk." She watched them pile their plates with meat and biscuits. "I've seen both of them easily shake off 'tired' and be ready to go."

"I'm sure you know your people, Ambassador."

"It's my ass, too, Senator. If I wasn't confident in them, they wouldn't be here. But why might we have to -- "

The door to the lift opened and Nysar, Tiernan, Govanek, and the usual phalanx of Sobrenian guards exited. "Uh oh," Chanda said. "They're early."

Akira caught sight of the entourage and put down her plate and its uneaten food. Irene stood with her back to the lift and was still filling her plate when Akira poked her in the arm. Her annoyed expression changed to surprise when Akira pointed out the Sobrenians plus Tiernan. Irene put her plate down as well, and she and Akira took their accustomed positions at one end of the negotiation table.

Nysar had already made it to his usual chair even as Chanda started toward the table, Galt right behind her. Tiernan settled in next to Nysar, with Govanek standing at the other end of the table from Irene and Akira.

As she sat, Chanda glanced back toward the Buruden. About a dozen of them had gathered together and stood there, linked.

With everyone in position, Chanda turned her attention to Nysar. *I'm not about to be the first one to speak,* she thought. *He wants to play this game, he can make the first serve.*

Both of Nysar's eyes stared at Chanda. She thought, *Reading Sobrenian facial expressions is hit-and-miss even if you're familiar with them. But at least he's giving me his full attention.*

Nysar said, "Tiernan tells me your trip to the site of the comet strike may have been less than enlightening."

Chanda looked at Tiernan, whose lack of expression rivaled Nysar's. "With all respect, I'd say perhaps it was Tiernan who wasn't enlightened."

Tiernan's face betrayed him now, as his newly-wide nostrils flared and Chanda could make out a pinkish flush beneath his rough skin. *He's bursting to speak,* Chanda thought, *but doesn't dare take precedence over Nysar.*

One of Nysar's eyes swiveled toward Tiernan, then back toward Chanda. "Tiernan's enlightenment is not your concern. We believe Humanity may be incapable of understanding Sobrenian culture, and how the comet strike affected it — ultimately for the better."

Galt said, "Hell of a way to improve the species."

"That aside," Chanda said, "What does our understanding of your society have to do with these negotiations?"

Nysar said, "We believe anyone who wishes to deal with us fairly must possess that understanding."

"Do you wish to have a similar understanding of the Buruden?"

Nysar, as usual, did not even glance toward the Buruden's side of the room. "We do not require that."

"There are at least two parties to any negotiation. Certainly each should have sufficient understanding of the other to — "

"We do not wish to understand these chaotic vermin!"

That final word was followed by a tense silence which Chanda was determined not to be the first to break. She heard movement behind her, turned in her chair, and saw the dozen Buruden unlinking, standing next to one another as individuals rather than the linked ambassador.

Chanda turned back toward Nysar, who sat impassively before her. Tiernan's expression was no more forthcoming.

More sounds from behind her, and Chanda turned again to see the Buruden walking in a straight line toward the lift. She said to Nysar and Tiernan, "Pardon me a moment, please," and went to the Buruden. "Is there any way we can convince you to continue these negotiations? I understand your reaction, but — " Chanda let her voice tail off as she realized none of these Buruden was linked, that collectively they didn't possess the ability to respond to her.

"Would you form the ambassador, please?" she asked, but the Buruden stood waiting for the lift's door to open.

At a gesture from Nysar, one of the guards opened the lift doors and the Buruden filed in. The doors slid shut and they were gone.

Her mind racing, drawing on all her experience to come up with a solution, Chanda headed back toward the negotiation table. Galt caught her eye with a questioning look as she approached, but she had no response for him as she sat across from Nysar and Tiernan again.

She sat up straight, folded her hands before her, and gazed at Nysar. *What in space could I say to him that might salvage these negotiations? He's not going to apologize. I have nothing left to bargain with.*

Unless . . .

"Why did you request my presence here at these negotiations?"

One of Nysar's eyes swiveled toward Tiernan while the other looked at Chanda. "Failure to translate," Nysar said.

"I believe that response is . . . less than forthcoming. The Sobrenian government asked for my presence — as did the Buruden. Why did you want me here?"

Tiernan said, "Nysar doesn't have to defend himself to you."

"Which means," Chanda said, "there *is* something to defend against." She glared at Nysar. "That was the first time you explicitly acknowledged the presence of the Buruden — but it was with an insult. Why?"

Nysar stood. "These negotiations are over."

Chanda stood, as well, with Galt right behind her. "These negotiations barely had a chance to begin. That's even though your government went out of its way to request them, and had me awakened from stasis to head them up."

Nysar headed toward the lift, with Tiernan, Govanek, and the guards following. *I'll be damned if I want to chase after him*, Chanda thought. *But I don't want to yell at his back like we're kids on a schoolyard, either.* A few quick steps, and she caught up to Nysar and Tiernan just as they made it to the lift. *It's not back from taking the Buruden yet*, she thought. *I've got a few more seconds.*

As Chanda was about to take those final couple of steps to approach Nysar, though, Tiernan stepped in front of her, hand raised, not quite touching her. "Nysar doesn't need to speak with you anymore."

"Maybe he does," Chanda said. She indicated Nysar's multicolored robes with their multiple lines of color running through them. "You're the highest-ranking Sobrenian I've ever encountered. Yet you seem to be acting in direct conflict with your government's wishes."

Tiernan said, "You don't know our government's wishes."

"I know it by its actions. The joint request with the Buruden to start these negotiations — having me awakened — allowing Humans and Buruden to set foot on your soil for the first time — none of that was done lightly."

"This is not your concern," Tiernan said as he continued to block her way.

Chanda, feeling silly even as she did, feinted to the right, then made a quick two-step to the left, faking Tiernan out sufficiently that she was able to confront Nysar directly. "You're the only Sobrenian official we've met during these negotiations. But you've never given us a title, even something as simple as 'ambassador.' What exactly is your title, anyway?"

Nysar stared at the lift doors, and Chanda felt she could feel the impatience emanating from him. "I think you were a compromise pick — your government was conflicted and said, fine, we'll take part in these negotiations, but the person running them won't be in favor of them."

The lift doors opened and Nysar stepped forward. Tiernan managed to place himself between Nysar and Chanda, who stopped at the edge of the lift entrance. Nysar remained facing the back of the lift, but Tiernan turned toward Chanda. "You and your people should get ready to leave this planet," he said.

Chanda was aware of Galt's presence as he came up behind her, and grateful for the moral support. She told Tiernan, "We're not leaving until these negotiations are rescheduled."

"They will not be," Tiernan said. "You have been our guests, but all guests must eventually leave."

"And if we refuse?"

Nysar took this opportunity to face Chanda. "You will be removed."

Chanda asked, "Do you really want to do that? Do you know what it would mean to forcibly remove four Human diplomats? How do you think the Unity would react to that?"

"The Unity would react as we demanded it react."

"Nysar, I can't believe how often I have to remind Sobrenians that Humans act as if we are sentient — which surely ought to shape how you react to us."

"And if it does not?"

"Then you have a diplomatic incident on your hands. Add that to the mess you've made of relations with the Buruden. . . . " Chanda trailed off, hoping Nysar would bring himself to the conclusion she wished for.

Nysar stared at Chanda. *I can withstand his staring*, she thought, *as long as both his eyes are pointed in the same direction.* Finally, he said, "You will remain here. You will hear a decision from us soon."

Tiernan looked at Nysar in clear amazement as the lift's doors closed.

Chanda faced Galt, Irene, and Akira. "Well, I suppose we'll soon find out whether this play has another act."

Galt told Chanda, "I commend your performance there — but are you so sure of your theory?"

"I'm a diplomat, not a scientist," Chanda said. "Theories that depend upon someone's behavior are notoriously shaky. But maybe you noticed the lack of bluster right there at the end."

"What I noticed," Akira said with a grin, "was Tiernan about to pass out when Nysar said we'd be hearing from him."

Chanda said, "What I'd like to imagine is Nysar sending Tiernan running after the Buruden shuttle, trying to get them to come back."

Irene asked, "So what's next?"

"Senator Galt knows this from his military days, I'd guess — hurry up and wait."

Irene started toward the breakfast buffet. "In that case, I'm headed back to the food."

———

Hurry up and wait it was — Chanda hung around the area of the lift for a while, just in case the Sobrenians came right back with the Buruden in tow — not likely, she believed, but she wanted to be there to lord it over Nysar and Tiernan (if only in her mind) if it happened.

After a while, it was clear their return, if it happened at all, would not be swift. She and Galt discussed possible scenarios to come, ranging from a complete abandonment of the negotiations to a renewal of them that might seem endless.

At one point, Chanda wandered over to the former Buruden side of the common room and stretched her arm out past its unmarked border. She was grateful for that arm to be pulled downward under the Buruden's accustomed 2.3 G. *Maybe the Sobrenians assume the Buruden are coming back,* she thought. *Or it could just be no one's remembered to switch it off.*

Hours passed. Another meal arrived, delivered by several Garotethan servants who wouldn't respond to anyone's questions. *Most likely,* Chanda thought, *they don't even have the datalinks that would let them understand us.*

More hours passed, and Chanda sat with Galt, each of them snacking at what was once the negotiation table. "So," Galt asked, "do you think they're coming back?"

Chanda favored him with a feigned frown. "How many times have you asked that?"

"You've given me an answer each time."

"And each time it's been, 'In just a few minutes,' which hasn't turned out to be right. Or I've said, 'Maybe in a couple days,' which — we don't know yet."

Galt popped some kind of fruit that resembled a cherry into his mouth. "At least they're not trying to starve us out."

"There you've done it — given them the idea."

"You assume they're listening to us."

"Of course they are. That's why I haven't been 'sparing anyone's feelings,' as you say. If a Sobrenian knows how you feel in private is different from what you say to their faces — or snouts — they consider you a hypocrite."

"What about that 'snout' comment? They might consider that insulting."

Chanda said, "Any less insulting than calling the Buruden 'vermin' and referring to them and Humanity as 'pre-sentients?' Say, have you seen Irene and Akira?"

"I think they went to take a nap. At least, that's what they said it was . . . they were . . . doing."

"I envy them their energy," Chanda said. "But I don't share it. I'm ready to sack out."

The lift doors parted.

Tiernan walked through the doorway.

He looks pissed, Chanda thought. *At least as much as I can tell looking at those blended Human-Sobrenian features.*

Tiernan came up to Chanda and Galt, standing nearly at attention before them. "Negotiations will continue," he said.

Chanda stood up. "I appreciate that. When will Nysar — "

"Nysar will not be attending."

"Oh! Then — "

"And negotiations will not continue here. Instead, they will continue on the Buruden homeworld, as previously agreed to."

"Really?" Galt said. "Did the Buruden — "

"What the Buruden did is of no importance. Please get ready to leave. These accommodations will be shut down within the hour." With that, Tiernan spun on one heel and returned to the lift. The doors closed and he was gone.

Chanda said, "He's really come a long way in mastering those Sobrenian-style interruptions, hasn't he?"

"Which isn't even the most irritating thing about him," Galt said. "But what do you make of this business of moving to the Buruden homeworld?"

"It was the plan from the beginning — maybe the Buruden demanded that as a concession."

"I don't exactly see the Sobrenians going to them and begging. Hell, Nysar would barely acknowledge their existence."

"But it seems he's out," Chanda said. "I wonder who'll take his place."

"Whoever it is, they can't be worse — wait a minute, what am I saying? Of course they can."

Chanda headed toward their quarters. "Let's let Irene and Akira know what's going on."

Galt, following her, said, "You're not going to get all nostalgic over leaving your wonderful Sobrenian home?"

"My goal," Chanda said, "is never to see it again."

It took less than an hour for Chanda, Galt, Irene, and Akira to pack their bags, make their way up the lift one final time, and come out onto the roof of the building where the shuttle *Rico* awaited them. The only Sobrenians to see them off were the inevitable set of guards, who stood impassively, pulse rifles at the ready.

Chanda was walking right behind Galt, who seemed suddenly pensive as they drew near the shuttle. *It's as if he expects something to happen right here as we leave*, Chanda thought. *An assassination attempt? The Sobrenians usually like to kill you face-to-face.*

Galt went up the ramp into the shuttle first. As Chanda approached the small craft, she paused and took what she assumed would be a last look at the city of Piroveka, and its sloping pyramids and domed structures on either side of the wide river.

Irene came up next to Chanda and stood next to her, as Akira said, "I'll go and start the pre-flight."

"Great," Irene said. "I'll be right there."

As Chanda and Irene took in the sight of the high-speed trains dashing across the river and of pedestrians in the broad streets far below, she couldn't help but wonder what the average Sobrenian, if such a being even existed, would think of the stop-and-start negotiations she was trying to keep on track.

Do any of them even have an idea of what's at stake? Sobrenian society isn't exactly known for its openness. Will a Sobrenian family be going about its business one morning, headed for work or school, when suddenly their industries become the targets of energy bolts or their city centers blossom in atomic fire?

A hand clapped against her shoulder. Irene. "You don't have to look so down on yourself," she said. Her face sported a broad smile. "You'll make this work."

"My gosh, look at you," Chanda said. "I don't think anyone could live up to that of confidence you have in me."

"Don't fight it, Chanda — use it!" Irene moved toward the shuttle. Chanda followed her, shaking her head in wonder.

———

As the *Rico* approached the cruiser *Sergeant Jelal*, Chanda received a message over her datalink. It was Captain Hamadi: "Ambassador, I'd appreciate it if you and Senator Galt would come see me in my quarters after you dock."

"Will do, Captain," Chanda said. She told Irene, who was piloting, "The senator and I are meeting Captain Hamadi. Can you and Akira take care of the post-flight and getting our bags to our quarters?"

"Of course, Ambassador," Irene said. "Do you think it's something serious?"

"Well, hell," Galt said, "how can it be anything but?"

Irene made a knowing nod as she aimed the *Rico* toward the *Jelal*'s hangar bay.

Minutes later, Captain Hamadi received them in the small living area of his quarters. Chanda and Galt settled next to each other on a small couch while Hamadi poured himself a cup of tea. "Can I offer you anything?"

"We're fine," Chanda said. "The one thing the Sobrenians did well was feed us. So what do you have for us?"

Hamadi sat in a chair across from Chanda and Galt. "A Buruden craft of some sort has been destroyed at the edge of this system."

"What the hell? Was it manned?"

"We believe so."

"How could that happen without either the Sobrenians or the Buruden mentioning it?"

Galt said, "Maybe that's why the Buruden left when they did."

"What were the circumstances?" Chanda asked.

"We're not terribly sure," Hamadi said. "It was one of our own probes, of course, farther out, that perceived the incident. A

Sobrenian warship is supposed to have intercepted and destroyed the Buruden probe when it tried to go farther into the Sobrenian system."

"You'd think the Sobrenians would want to brag about that."

"Maybe not," Galt said. "Nysar hardly wanted to acknowledge the Buruden's presence those during negotiations, such as they were."

Chanda said, "And the Buruden hardly said word one."

Hamadi told them, "I made the decision not to pass this on to you while you were still on the planet. This wasn't like when I told you about Tiernan — you'd asked for that. I got the word about the probe being destroyed just after negotiations broke down, and I knew I'd be seeing you in person soon. We consider our comm pretty secure, but I didn't want to take the chance of the message being intercepted."

"Fine work," Galt said. "The Sobrenians and Buruden probably have no idea we know any of this. That could play to our advantage."

"Depending upon who the new negotiator is on the Sobrenian side," Chanda said.

Hamadi asked, "You don't think they'll advance Tiernan to head negotiator, do you?"

"I don't think so. I think he's pretty trusted, but more useful to them as a source of information and some kind of weird showpiece — a Human who not only defected to the Sobrenians but is *becoming* a Sobrenian."

Galt said, "I wanted to thank you for the quick turnaround on Tiernan's background earlier."

"Background you should have received long before," Hamadi said. "Sometimes I think we're most efficient at keeping secrets from ourselves."

Galt said, "His ideas are spookier than his appearance. He appears to have given up on Humanity."

Hamadi took a sip of tea. "Yes, something we cannot allow ourselves to do. We must remain confident, my friends. This situation seems quite dire — but I have faith that we can find our way to a peaceful conclusion."

Chanda said, "I envy you your faith."

"I trust in God, my family, my friends, and my colleagues, in that order. I have faith aplenty, Ambassador. I'd gladly loan some of it to you if I could."

"I'll keep that in mind, Captain, if we find a way to make that happen. But the Sobrenians, in particular, seem to have faith only in themselves. That makes our task harder."

Galt said, "One of their aides, Govanek, seems to have gone the opposite direction of Tiernan. She's the only Sobrenian I've ever met who's had an engaging personality."

"Well . . . at least you'll be dealing more with the Buruden during this next phase of negotiations. They're generally more likable, aren't they?"

Chanda said, "That's not a generalization, Captain. I'd consider that a verifiable fact. And it's why I assume everything has to go better this next time around."

A couple days later, with Splendor situated between the Sobrenian and Buruden homeworlds, Chanda asked Captain Hamadi to make a quick jaunt into the Splendorian system to find out how things were going there. The *Sergeant Jelal* jumped just close enough to the planet to allow for live subspace comm — a closer approach would require using the much slower inertial drive, which would take too long.

Once in-system, Chanda gathered Galt, Irene, and Akira in her quarters and made contact with her Earth Unity Military Liaison Trenton Bram. When his holographic image appeared before them, Chanda was struck by how tired he looked, and how grim his expression was. *He usually hides his emotions pretty well behind that beard of his*, Chanda thought. *Things must be rough down there.*

"Hello, Chanda," Bram said. "I'm not going to ask how things are going for you. I received your coded reports the other day."

"I understand. But how are things going on your end?"

"About as well as could be expected."

"You know me too well, Trenton. You have to realize the next question is how much you're expecting."

"Well, not a helluva lot, as it turns out. We've had some successes. Nearly all the highlanders who were on Socrates are back here on Splendor. Same for the valley dwellers on Kardashev. But that's causing its own problems."

Galt asked, "Are their home villages having trouble taking them back in?"

"That's part of the problem. But in some cases, entire villages were evacuated — now we're having to re-establish them from scratch."

"I understand the difficulty," Chanda said. "I hope we can get these negotiations settled as soon as possible so we can get back there to help you."

"I really need you here, Chanda," Bram said. "I admit that. We're getting a lot of resentment, especially from the highlanders about being bounced back and forth like this. It's not helping Humanity's credibility any."

Irene asked, "What about the sweepers?"

"They don't feel too kindly toward us, either. Just the opposite problem from the valley dwellers and highlanders — they still want off the planet and don't believe we can help them."

"They may be right," Chanda said.

Akira spoke up: "I think Irene and I could tackle that problem once we get back — there has to be a solution to it."

Chanda told them, "One problem at a time, please — though I appreciate the offer." To the holo of Bram, she said, "All right, thanks for the update."

"Sorry I couldn't give you better news," Bram said.

Chanda's features twisted in a wry grin. "That's all right — it's getting so I wouldn't have it any other way. After all, what's life without challenges?"

CHAPTER 15

Once again, the shuttle *Rico* glided out of *Sergeant Jelal*'s hangar bay, Irene and Akira piloting, Chanda and Galt sitting behind them. The Sobrenians' starcraft had arrived in-system before them, and Chanda wondered how the dynamics between them and the Buruden would be different here on the current Buruden homeworld.

Enough time to worry about that once we land, Chanda thought as Irene eased them out of orbit. Chanda looked down at the planet, which was mostly shrouded beneath thick clouds. "You can tell there's a more intense greenhouse effect," she said. "It almost looks like Venus."

The planet was about as dense as the Earth, but twice its diameter and eight times the mass. That provided a thicker atmosphere, but thanks to its primary being cooler than Sol, the world maintained temperatures comparable to Earth's.

The *Rico* sank into the thick, unchanging clouds. After a few minutes, Chanda mused, "Are we still descending? It looks like we're sitting inside one big cloud."

"Don't worry," Irene said with a grin. "We're getting there."

Finally the *Rico* burst out of the cloud cover, and Chanda saw a Buruden city — in fact, the only Buruden city — spread out beneath them. It wasn't nearly as large as the Sobrenian city of Piroveka — while it was situated along a river, it extended only about five kilometers along it, and two on either side of it. The city was laid out on a grid as precise as geography allowed, with roads running directly north-to-south and east-to-west. It primarily served as a focus of food production, communications, and transportation. The majority of Buruden industry and agriculture, not to mention population, was spread throughout the planet in much smaller communities.

Akira said, "The Buruden sure don't like to build very tall, do they? None of the buildings in this city is over what would be three stories in a Human building — and they're all round."

"Round and short and squat," Irene said. "Like the Buruden themselves."

"Architecture can reveal a lot about a society," Chanda said.

Galt asked, "You're not going to go into limestone or marble facades, again, are you?"

"I thought I was being quite informative before."

Galt shrugged. "That's one way to think of it."

"Look at those wide streets! And what are those vehicles down there — buses or trolleys of some sort? They're six meters wide, and all of them are round."

"Coming up on landing," Irene said as she guided the shuttle toward a landing pad at a small spaceport on the outskirts of the city. Several small Buruden spacecraft sat in tight rows at one corner of the port next to a control tower that was the tallest structure they'd seen so far — the equivalent, perhaps, of five stories.

"All right," Chanda told the others. "Brace yourselves for when the grav goes off." The Buruden homeworld's gravity was two and a half times that of Earth. *I'm not looking forward to this*, Chanda thought as the *Rico* settled down onto the landing pad.

Galt said, "At least we don't have a bunch of soldiers here to meet us."

"There's *no one* here to meet us," Chanda said.

Irene told them, "Here comes the grav." She powered down the shuttle's intertials.

Chanda groaned as her weight more than doubled. She felt as if she could barely lift her hands from her lap. *I'd swear I can feel the skin tightening over my face,* she thought, *and my internal organs rearranging.*

"Here comes one of those round vehicles," Irene said. She pointed toward a car decorated with the typical strokes of yellow, maroon, and gold. A Buruden perched in a transparent dome on top guided the vehicle. As Chanda had guessed during their descent, the car was about six meters around, large enough to hold several dozen Buruden. *It'll be a tight squeeze for us,* Chanda thought. *That roof is pretty low.*

Chanda retrieved her kit and was first to the inner airlock door. "Lifesuits on, folks — we can't breathe that stuff out there." The extreme pressure of the air meant oxygen could burn a Human's lungs and nitrogen narcosis and acute carbon dioxide acidosis were dangers.

Chanda touched her left middle finger to her palm and her lifesuit activated — the nanotech implanted throughout her body formed a spacesuit which topped itself off with a bubble helmet. After activating his own lifesuit, Galt hefted a backpack over one shoulder. It contained plenty of medical nanotech devices and other supplies.

"Everyone ready?" Chanda asked.

Galt said, "I wonder whether we should keep someone aboard the shuttle."

"One of the few things the Buruden indicated to me ahead of time was that we'd be away from the 'port, and without transportation back and forth. I'd hate to coop someone up in the shuttle for a couple weeks or more."

Irene asked, "How about operating it remotely to come and get us if we need it?"

"Not allowed," Chanda said. "And it was presented just as 'a truth,' without all the rule-of-four stuff."

"That's settled, then."

"I know we'll be taking a chance. But it's worth it. Everyone ready to cycle through?"

The others indicated they were, and they crowded into the small airlock.

Chanda opened the outer lock and stepped down gingerly in the high grav onto the landing pad's paved surface. *Another first for Humanity,* she thought. *And I didn't have a phrase fraught with meaning ready. No 'one small step' or any of that.*

Then the side of the vehicle opened up and suddenly Buruden individuals were skittering around everywhere. Chanda watched as their quadrupedal bodies, having no sense of backward or forward, left or right, switched direction almost more quickly than the Human eye could perceive it.

Several Buruden positioned themselves around their own vehicle, with others approaching the assembled Humans, all of them running around in circles to no apparent purpose.

Oh, my gosh, Chanda thought. *It never occurred to me that we'd see the Buruden in their purest form, and that their behavior might be even more manic than we've ever realized.*

The Buruden gathered around the car settled down first. Those in front of Chanda and the others took a few more seconds to slow down, but eventually attached joiners to one another and formed a group of about a dozen, all of whom stood before the assembled Humans and looked up at them expectantly.

"Is the ambassador among you?" Chanda asked.

"He is not," came the reply over her datalink. She couldn't tell which individual Buruden made the response, or even if all of them did.

"Will he be coming here, or are you about to take us to him?"

"We are here to take you to your housing. We believe you will find it suitable."

"Let's go then," Chanda said, and walked with a leaden stride to the waiting car. *I was right about the tight squeeze,* she thought as she ducked down to keep from cracking her head on the top of the wide but low doorway. The Buruden, averaging only about half a meter tall, no doubt considered the vehicle pretty roomy.

Once inside, Chanda realized the next challenge. "No seats," she told the others as they came in behind her.

"The Buruden don't need them," Irene said, flinching as the top of her head brushed the low ceiling.

Chanda started toward the opposite end of the vehicle, keeping her head down as she went. "Back here we can at least sit and lean against the rear wall. Who knows what kind of ride we're in for." She put down her bag and sat on the floor, grateful for that little bit of relief in the 2.3 grav. Irene sat next to her, with Akira and Galt settling in next.

The Buruden piled in immediately in front of the Humans, unlocked their joiners, hunkered down, and locked their legs. The front doorway closed and the car started moving.

Its initial acceleration was low, and Chanda thought, *Maybe we'll have a nice leisurely ride into the city and we can see some sights.*

That hope disappeared abruptly when the car shot forward, pressing Chanda's back against the side of the vehicle. Then it changed direction just as abruptly, but without turning — the car was simply moving to the left now, without having turned itself. Rather than sitting in "the back" of the vehicle, Chanda now felt as if she were sitting on one side. "We should've known," she said, "that it would turn just like a Buruden does."

Galt said, "That explains the driver being on top — it doesn't matter which way he's facing."

Another abrupt turn, this time to the right, and it felt once again as if they were in the rear of the car. The next turn sent Chanda careening into Irene, who braced herself against the floor. "Sorry," Chanda said.

"Don't worry about it," Irene said. "Our lifesuits protect us in more ways than one, I guess. I think we're all going to be piled up against one another before this trip ends."

"Too bad this thing isn't big enough to have gravitics," Galt said.

The car quickly left the spaceport and headed toward the city center. Now Chanda and her colleagues had a chance to get a closer glimpse into life on the Buruden homeworld. All the streets were wide enough to accommodate three of these cars across. Adjoining sidewalks were also wide, apparently to provide enough room for any linked mass of Buruden that might walk down them.

Irene said, "All the buildings are round — which I guess makes sense given their physiology."

Their car barely slowed down even once it made its way into the middle of the city, even though traffic grew thicker by the moment. Chanda said, "I'd bet these cars are controlled by some central system. Which is good, given we can't be going much slower than 100 kph."

"But look at the Buruden drivers," Galt said. "They all look like they're hard at work guiding each car."

Irene craned her neck to look ahead of them. "I don't see any pedestrian crosswalks. How do the Buruden — especially when they're all bunched together, get across the street without getting squished?"

"Look there," Chanda said. "A tunnel entrance — headed right under the street. No one has to wait or slow down for anyone else, whether you're walking or riding."

Galt said, "Slowing down does seem to be against the grain for them."

Akira indicated the Buruden driver in the bubble above them. "I feel odd talking about them like they're not here."

Chanda said, "They might as well not be here. They're not linked together. Individually, they can only act on instinct."

"I know that," Akira said, "but it's hard to see how they function sometimes."

"If there was some sort of emergency, different individuals would link together, depending on what it was, and tackle it. That's why there are so many on board. Otherwise, we're left waiting."

Galt said, "It looks like we're slowing down."

The round vehicle made a much less violent turn toward one of the ubiquitous round buildings. A wide oval doorway irised open, admitting the car into the darkness beyond.

After a few moments, the car halted. Chanda stared out into the darkness, trying to make out the nature of their surroundings. Before she could perceive anything, several of the Buruden started linking together. Chanda heard over her datalink, "Please follow us."

Chanda picked up her bag and, hunched over once again beneath the low ceiling, followed the mass of Buruden out of the vehicle.

Only to hit her helmeted head on the ceiling when she tried to straighten up. "Watch out, everyone," she said. "Still not a lot of headroom."

"We apologize," the Buruden said. "For us, of course, this area is quite spacious."

"At least it's getting brighter," Galt said.

Chanda addressed the closest group of linked Buruden. "You seem to have a gift for the dramatic."

"This area is previously unused. Its systems are only now coming online."

The light increased, finally revealing — a blank wall.

"I don't get it," Chanda said.

"These are your quarters," the Buruden said, and as if their words commanded it, a door-shaped seam tall enough for a Human to walk through appeared in the wall and slid aside, revealing the outer door of an airlock large enough to accommodate the four of them.

Chanda took a tentative step forward, but paused as the Buruden spoke again. "We will leave you to inspect your quarters and determine whether you find them acceptable. Negotiations will begin in the morning."

"Thanks," Chanda said, and watched as the Buruden mass split apart and boarded the car again. It went out the way it had come, the wide door to the street rolling open, then closed again.

"Let's see what they've done for us," Chanda said, and entered the airlock. That first step was unexpectedly light-footed, and Chanda's face broke out in a wide grin. "They got the grav right," she said as the others eased in beside her.

Akira indicated a control panel next to the lock's inner door that featured a single button. She gave Chanda a sideways look. "Seems simple enough to operate, I guess."

"Go ahead, then," Chanda said.

Akira pressed the button and Chanda felt the rush of air even through her lifesuit, as the atmosphere within the lock rushed out and was, presumably, replaced with air a Human could breathe.

The inner door slid open without a sound. Chanda took the first steps in and placed her bag just beyond the doorway. The main room was round, of course, about twelve meters wide. The ceiling was low — Chanda could touch it without even extending her arm completely. The walls were an unadorned pale green. Placed in random positions throughout were what appeared to be crude representations of a couch and several chairs.

Chanda raised her left arm and checked the sensor readouts on her lifesuit. "Everything seems proper," she said. "The grav's one G, atmosphere is the proper mixture, and just as importantly, the proper pressure."

All the same, when Galt deactivated his lifesuit without warning them, Chanda reached out in concern. "Why'd you do that?"

"Because otherwise *you* would've. And we can't do without you, Ambassador."

"Much as I appreciate the sentiment, there's not a one of us I consider expendable."

"Not the point, Chanda. Just that someone had to go first."

Chanda and the others deactivated their own lifesuits. Chanda wrinkled her nose. "Smells a little bit like a barn or a stable," she said.

Galt said, "The air *is* kind of rich. Otherwise, they've done a great job with the grav and the rest of the environmentals."

"I thought they would. You may have heard about them crashing that hospital ship into the Great Sea four years ago."

"I did."

"By the time we got a submersible down to it and forced our way in, they'd adapted its environment to our physiology. We didn't even know it at the time. Turns out they can withstand a lot of variation in atmosphere and pressure — it's grav that they can't adapt to very easily."

Irene said, "Why don't we check out the rest of the place?"

Akira went to one of the chairs, which looked as if it was crudely carved out of wood — its seat was hard and flat and just high enough that Akira had to back onto it on tiptoes. The chair's back stood perfectly perpendicular to the seat. It had no arms, and Akira folded her hands in her lap. "At least it gives you good posture," she said.

Galt spoke from around a corner, his voice echoing slightly: "Looks like we've got a bedroom here. Could be one little problem."

"What's that?" Chanda asked as she headed that way. "Oh, wait, I see."

Only one bed stood in the middle of the room. It was round, of course, quite big, made in the same crude manner as the furniture in the main room, and had no bedding.

Irene whispered something to Akira and both women began to giggle. Irene clasped a hand against her chest and fought for breath.

Chanda felt the infectious pull of that laughter and pressed her lips together a moment to fight it. She said, "All right, ladies. Anything you'd care to share with the rest of the class?"

Irene coughed, pounded her chest a couple of times, composed herself reasonably well, and said, "No, Chanda — uh, Ambassador."

Galt, pointedly ignoring Irene and Akira, went toward another room, but paused in the doorway. "Oh, boy," he said. "Another, bigger problem."

Chanda said, "Oh, com'on, we can put up with anything. Oh, wait — is that what I think -- "

"Yeah. It is."

"Yeah. The bathroom."

CHAPTER 16

Chanda managed to cope with the intricacies of the bathroom as she got ready for bed. When she was done, she changed into bedclothes and relinquished the bathroom for Irene and Akira. She went into the bedroom, where Galt stood with his hands on his hips regarding the Buruden's concept of a bed for Humans.

"At least it's big," Galt said.

"We're all adults here," Chanda said. "We'll make do."

When Irene and Akira emerged from the bathroom, Chanda asked them, "So, how was it?"

"Not as hellish as I'd feared," Irene said. "But we gotta get some things changed."

Galt said, "I expected that inter-species diplomacy might involve danger, fear, or disappointment — but not downright humiliation."

"All right," Chanda said as patted one side of the bed. "Here's the girl's side." She pointed to the farther side. "And there's the boy's side."

Galt said, "Sounds fair enough to me. I promise to be a perfect gentleman." Once Chanda and Irene and Akira settled in on their side, Galt curled up perpendicular to them on the other side. Chanda was lying on her side with her back to Irene and Akira and was just about to drift off to sleep when muffled chuckling from the other two women brought her fully awake again.

She rolled onto her back. "Is this how it's going to be all night? Didn't your parents ever threaten to turn around and go right back home if you didn't settle down?"

"Sorry, Mommy," Akira said, and the bed shook from her and Irene's suppressed laughter.

"I should've kept insisting on 'Ambassador,'" Chanda told Akira.

The laughter shut off. "Sorry, Ambassador," Akira said.

Irene said, "We'll be good from now on."

"Thank you," Galt said from the opposite side of the bed.

Chanda awoke from a restless night's sleep in a room that had turned chilly overnight. *We've got to get some kind of bedding in here*, she thought. *We should've realized beings who squat to sit and sleep wherever they find themselves wouldn't understand much about Human habits and customs.*

Soon after everyone made their trips to the Stygian concept of a Human bathroom, a group of Buruden called on them, cycling quickly through the airlock.

The Buruden linked together. "The negotiations are about to begin," they said.

"Excellent," Chanda told them. "Where do we go?"

"For your convenience, we have created a pathway directly to the negotiation site." One of the Buruden individuals unlatched from the mass of them and went to an empty part of the main room. One leg reached out and pressed itself against a seemingly blank part of the wall.

A seam appeared in the wall, just like the one that had revealed the doorway to their quarters the day before. The Buruden led the way through the doorway, and Chanda, Galt, Irene, and Akira followed down a short hall into another round room, one much larger than their quarters.

Once they were in, the seam closed and the wall appeared utterly smooth again.

The first thing Chanda noticed was an exact duplicate of the negotiation table they'd used back on the Sobrenian homeworld. *Sort of nice to see something familiar,* Chanda thought. *Though a little more legroom would've been an improvement.*

Why couldn't they have duplicated our quarters, as well?

The linked Buruden turned toward them as one and Chanda heard the voice of their ambassador, who said, "As we did during the previous attempt at negotiations on . . . the other world . . . we will stand in a higher-gravity area."

Don't tell me the Buruden are going to start this business of not referring to the other species, Chanda thought. *I hope these negotiations don't become a mirror image of the earlier ones.*

The Buruden turned their attention to another part of the room, and a new seam appeared. The newly-formed doorway wasn't as tall as the one Chanda and the others had walked through, since Sobrenians were mostly shorter than Humans. First came a small group of Buruden, then the Sobrenian delegation entered, led by someone Chanda didn't recognize, a female this time. *Nysar's replacement, no doubt,* Chanda thought. *And there's Govanek — I'm actually glad to see her. Not so glad to see the inevitable Garotethan servants.*

And — right beside Govanek —

Chanda traded amazed looks with Senator Galt. "Goddam," he muttered.

It was Lewis Tiernan — but he'd changed even more. No Human nose for him anymore, it was definitely a snout. His shoulders were broader, his arms more heavily muscled, and his feet were bigger.

And he's shorter! Chanda realized. *He used to be a bit taller than I am, and now the top of his head just barely comes up past my shoulder.* Tiernan's blue Sobrenian robes, with their lines of red and green running through them, had been altered to fit his new stature.

How the hell did they do that? Chanda wondered. She suppressed a grin at the thought of a shin-ectomy.

Tiernan approached Chanda and said, "From the way you're looking at me, you must be impressed by my improved appearance."

"Well . . . impressed would certainly be a way to describe it."

"Ambassador Chanda Kasmira — let me introduce Sedra, our new chief negotiator."

So, this one has a title, Chanda thought. *Though you'd never get the Sobrenians to admit I influenced that.*

To Chanda's surprise, Sedra extended her hand to Chanda, who took it and shook. *Govanek's given this one some lessons,* Chanda thought. *I wonder if she tried with Nysar and they didn't take.* "Pleased to meet you," Chanda told Sedra.

"Shall we sit and begin our negotiations?"

"Certainly. But I'd like to suggest a different seating arrangement, if I may."

Sedra said, "I suppose you'd like to be able to easily see the Buruden negotiators as well as me and my colleagues."

"Exactly what I was going to say." Chanda looked toward the Buruden. "I imagine you don't have any objection."

The Buruden ambassador said, "Arrange yourselves as you see fit."

Chanda stood aside as Sedra and Tiernan sat at the table facing the Buruden, with the Garotethan kneeling next to Sedra and Govanek standing at one end of the table.

Irene and Akira went to the other end of the table, where Chanda sat as she indicated Galt should sit next to her. *This is still like I'm sitting at the children's table,* Chanda thought. She said. "Shall we begin with — "

Sedra said, "Please pardon me, but I must insist upon making one point — actually several, about our accommodations."

"Chief Negotiator," Chanda said, "Perhaps another time would —
"

"No, this is the time. I believe our Buruden counterparts are deliberately being disrespectful to us. Without mutual respect, negotiations cannot proceed."

I can't believe this, Chanda said. *I've always heard of such tactics — forced debates over the shape of a table or the quality of food, but I've never seen them in action.*

Sedra continued: "Our quarters smell bad — "

Check, Chanda thought.

"— we were provided only one bed for the three of us — "

Also check, Chanda thought. *And typical that she didn't even count the Garotethan, although I bet they made her — or him, I can't even tell — sleep on the floor.*

The Buruden ambassador spoke up: "It is a truth that we miscalculated the needs of both the Sobrenians — "

They referred to the Sobrenians! Yea! Chanda thought.

" — and the Humans. But this is easily solved."

"Then we must solve it immediately," Sedra said.

The Buruden continued: "It is a likely truth that these adjustments will take a little time."

Sedra stared at the mass of Buruden with her eyes spread slightly apart to take them all in. "Immediately, we say!"

"It is a potential truth — "

Chanda thought, *Sedra needs to realize that whenever the Buruden start in on their four-is-everything logic, you can't divert them.*

" — that the success of our negotiations would be best served by continuing them as the adjustments continue. That the best outcome would be for us to suspend negotiations is an untruth."

Chanda tried to break in: "May I suggest — "

"The Human may *not* suggest anything," Sedra said.

Chanda stood up, wishing the table were tall enough for her to place her hands flat upon it without leaning over ridiculously far. She tried not to show a reaction as she caught a glimpse of Galt, who appeared to be palming some sort of device. Instead, she addressed the Sobrenian diplomat: "Chief Negotiator, I'm supposed to be here precisely to suggest things. I was told that both the Sobrenians and the Buruden requested my presence. What, then, do you believe I'm here for?"

Sedra kept one eye on the Buruden while turning another upon her. "You are here to help both our species' representatives in any way you can, including making sure we are all treated with respect."

"How about respect toward three intelligent species on Splendor?"

"We care only about our own homeworld," Tiernan said, as Sedra nodded her approval.

The Buruden said, "Ambassador Kasmira is correct. Our priority should be negotiating toward peace."

Sedra turned both her eyes toward the Buruden. "We believe in the reality of a perpetual state of war. We assume the reality of war, and that negotiations are only respites from it."

Chanda sat down. "Are we talking about interplanetary conflicts? Other than testing your weapons on Splendor — " *And killing countless innocent valley dwellers in the process*, Chanda recalled. " — the Unity isn't aware of any such current conflicts."

"Whatever their nature, they do not concern you, Ambassador," Sedra said.

The Buruden ambassador said, "Our only concern is to avoid a needless war."

"Both sides," Sedra said, "must agree that such a war is needless. Perhaps we Sobrenians have decided it is time to stand up for ourselves."

This is spinning out of control, Chanda thought. "Let's get right to the heart of this issue," she said.

"Failure to translate," she heard in both Sedra and the Buruden's voices. Galt gave Chanda a look of frustration. "Sorry," Chanda said.

"Idiom. Let's look at the primary dispute here — the Buruden probes into Sobrenian space."

"We are curious," the Buruden ambassador said. "It is part of our nature. We would not suppress the Sobrenian enthusiasm for weaponry, as long as they do not use them against us. Neither would we have them suppress our enthusiasm and curiosity."

"You spy on us!" Sedra said. "You fail to leave when we demand it. But let us consider something more important."

Chanda asked, "And what might that be?"

"The issue of our accommodations."

Chanda forced herself not to groan. "Chief Negotiator, we were just beginning to tackle substantive issues here."

"*We* determine what is substantive to the Sobrenian species," Sedra said.

The Buruden ambassador said, "Ambassador Kasmira. We are willing to look into the Sobrenians' objections."

Chanda's hands gripped the edge of the table. *Now I'm stuck,* she thought. *If both sides want to continue this line of bullshit, I've got no place to go.*

She looked at Galt. A frustrated shrug was his only reaction.

Chanda rose again. "Very well, then." She looked toward the Buruden. "I trust you can address the Sobrenian Chief Negotiator's concerns?"

"That we will try is a truth. That we will succeed is, we hope, a likely truth, but may be only a potential truth. That we will achieve perfection is an untruth."

Sedra stood up, and Chanda was surprised and impressed that she looked right at the Buruden and said, "We look forward to your gracious attempts." She started toward the hidden door that led to the Sobrenian quarters, with the Human-Sobrenian hybrid that was Tiernan right behind her. Chanda couldn't help but notice that Govanek cast a long look at her before falling into step as well.

The seam opened, and the two Sobrenians and Tiernan and the Garotethan walked through it, half a dozen of the Buruden following in a mass close behind, others staying in the negotiation room.

The rest of the Buruden approached Chanda and the other Humans. Chanda heard, "We understand that you have issues with your accommodations, as well."

"We do. But I wish we could address something more substantive."

Galt said, "Ambassador, let's face it. Nothing's going to happen today. We might as well play along."

"I agree," Irene said. "And I can't stand the idea of the Sobrenians having comfortable quarters and we don't."

Akira said, "Yeah, there's no reason *everyone* should listen to you snore."

"I don't —"

"*Do.*"

"Fine," Chanda said. "Let's go."

Once they returned to their quarters, Chanda told the six linked Buruden before them, "The first thing we'd like to address is . . . well, a bit of privacy."

"Failure to translate," the Buruden said.

"Uh . . . Humans like to be alone sometimes."

Galt said, "It gives us a chance to gather our thoughts about the day we've just finished and anticipate the day ahead."

The group of Buruden stared at them, each with three of their four eyes staring unblinking, as if trying to process what they were hearing.

"I know," Chanda said. "Failure to translate."

Irene said, "There aren't enough of them to understand what we mean. Some of them stayed behind."

"Is the ambassador among them?" Akira asked. "What if we asked him to bring more of them along?"

Chanda said, "They can only form the ambassador when there's a critical mass — and I'm pretty sure six isn't enough." To the Buruden, she said, "Can you bring the ambassador here? Or anyone else who can try to understand what we need?"

The Buruden said, "We will do that." And they unlinked and skittered separately into the airlock that led them outside.

As the Buruden continued to cycle through the lock, Galt said, "I wonder if the Sobrenians are going through this same frustration."

"Maybe it's payback by the Buruden for the way they were treated on the Sobrenian homeworld."

Akira said, "Can't say as I blame them."

"But it's not helpful," Chanda said. "We're supposed to be here to prevent a war — one that could be fought in Splendorian space." She asked Galt, "Why the hell did they even ask for me if neither species is going to cooperate?"

Galt shook his head. "The Unity didn't explain very much. Just that the Buruden and Sobrenians wanted to talk, and they wanted you to mediate."

Irene said, "I wonder if they wanted someone motivated enough to stick through this." When Chanda looked at her quizzically, Irene continued: "You've dedicated the last few years of your life to Splendor. You're the only person who has both that commitment and the negotiating skills to do this."

"Skills I haven't much displayed so far."

"I disagree," Galt said. "But Irene's right. You've stuck it out — made trips to two planets Humans haven't even set foot upon before. Put up with that bastard Tiernan baiting you every chance he gets. One thing, Ambassador — while we were sitting around the negotiating table, I got a good scan of him."

"I wondered what you were doing. And whether the Sobrenians would call you out on it."

"Not likely! Tiernan's been doing the same thing to us every chance he gets."

"Oh."

"Don't worry, I've been blocking his scans as much as I can."

"And what have you learned about him?"

"I haven't had a chance to look at the results in any great detail. But I'll let you know something soon." Galt ran his hand through his hair. "Changing your species . . . that's commitment above and beyond. For whatever reason he's doing it."

"Either reason makes him a danger," Chanda said.

CHAPTER 17

Only minutes later, the Buruden returned. About two dozen cycled through the airlock, then assembled themselves into a mass before Chanda and her colleagues. "We are here to make your accommodations more pleasing," Chanda heard over her datalink.

"Excellent," Chanda said. "First, we'd — "

"We understand what you require. Those who attended you earlier are here among us. Now we are of sufficient number to interpret your earlier words."

"All right. How can we help?"

"We believe you would be best served by leaving your quarters for a time. May we suggest a tour of our city?"

Chanda recalled the manic ride aboard the Buruden vehicle that brought them from the starport into the city. "That's really not necessary. We'd be more than happy to — "

"We must insist, Ambassador. The Sobrenian quarters are also being revised, and they have accepted our offer."

"What the hell, then," Chanda said. "We might as well learn a little something while we're here."

Irene addressed the Buruden: "Where do you suggest we go?"

"We have little that other species would consider tourist attractions," the Buruden said. "We do not indulge in organized art forms. We have no gods and no religious institutions or rituals."

Chanda asked, "So what do you suggest we see?"

"We believe it to be a truth that this, our only city, should be of some interest to you. A likely truth that the landscape just outside would also be of interest. A potential truth — "

Chanda held up her hand. "You've convinced us," she said. "We'll go on the tour. A truth, indeed."

To her surprise, the Buruden halted their four-way litany. "Very well — a vehicle is awaiting you outside."

"Here we go, then," Chanda said, and activated her lifesuit.

They cycled through the airlock. Chanda groaned under the renewed force of the Buruden homeworld's 2.3 G. Waiting for them was a smaller version of the round vehicle that had brought them from the starport, just large enough for the four of them. A single Buruden, the driver, sat on top of the car. Chanda said, "I suppose we just get in and he knows where to go."

"Let's give it a shot," Galt said, and led the way in, carrying the emergency backpack. By unspoken agreement, each of them sat equidistantly around the inside of the car. Chanda braced herself, but the Buruden driver eased out of the building and toward the street unexpectedly slowly, which made her smile. "Maybe he's gotten the word," Chanda said. "Maybe he knows he's supposed to take it easy on the frail Humans."

The car shot forward. Chanda, who was sitting to the "rear," found herself flattened against the interior of the car. It made a sharp right onto the street and her left shoulder slammed into the car's interior next to Galt, Chanda's lifesuit taking the brunt of the impact. As she looked at everyone else holding on for dear life, she said, "I guess we frail Humans have to look after ourselves."

The car accelerated without hesitation to the 90-100 kph that appeared to be the standard speed for Buruden surface vehicles, even within a crowded city. It took a spot in the middle lane of three, giving Chanda and everyone else another good look at the round buildings on either side of the street and the sidewalks filled with masses of linked Buruden.

"Where's everybody *going*?" Chanda wondered. "And so quickly!"

"What if we see something interesting?" Irene asked. "Do we have a way to ask the driver to stop?"

Galt said, "We hardly have a way to make anything out, we're going by so fast."

Chanda noted, "One of these buildings looks much like the next, anyway. I can't tell which one may be an industrial facility or an agricultural center or a daycare."

Galt stood up and banged on the car's ceiling. "Hey, up there! We'd like to stop and see something!" He stood there looking up at the ceiling as if expecting an answer to appear upon it. After a moment, he sat again. Galt looked at the others and shrugged. "I didn't *expect* it to work . . . but it was worth a shot."

Irene said, "I wonder if we're on some sort of pre-programmed trip."

"Could be," Chanda said. "Despite not having tourist attractions, maybe the Buruden have a specific destination in mind for us."

"I was worrying more about how long the trip might be, and whether there's a bathroom nearby."

"Hey, we're slowing down," Galt said. The car merged into the right lane and pulled into a driveway next to one of the inevitable round buildings and stopped. Its door opened.

"Well," Chanda said, "I guess we've arrived."

"But where?" Akira asked.

Galt said, "Let's get out and find out."

They exited the car, moving carefully in the planet's 2.3 grav. They stood beneath iron skies. *The cloud cover's so thick,* Chanda thought, *it seems I could reach up and touch it.* Chanda's attention was still drawn at first to the traffic around them that swept past at what seemed like unreasonable speeds. *Though it's all mostly silent,* she thought. *Whatever powers these vehicles, it's pretty impressive.*

"Watch out," Galt said, putting out an arm to keep Chanda from stepping into the path of a dozen massed Buruden. They passed by at the speed of a Human sprint racer.

"Thanks," Chanda said. "This whole society seems to move around at full throttle."

Irene asked, "So why are we here? Are we supposed to visit this building?"

Akira said, "I wish we could tell what kind of building this is."

Galt indicated another vehicle pulling in behind their own. "Looks like more tourists. Maybe they know what's going on — uh, oh."

The other vehicle contained Sedra, Tiernan, Govanek, and the Garotethan. "Uh, oh is right," Chanda said. "On the other hand, what other 'tourists' did we expect?"

The Sobrenians (Chanda had come to think of Tiernan as one) left their car. All three, Tiernan included, wore Sobrenian-style spacesuits — the species had never embraced nanotech-based lifesuits.

With both of them in protective suits, Chanda heard Sedra's voice over her datalink: "What a pleasant encounter, Ambassador. I suppose your quarters are also undergoing renovation?"

"They are. I'm sure they'll be much improved by the time we all return."

"We can always hope. Perhaps then we can perform some of the work we came here to do."

As if you haven't been the one holding things up to begin with, Chanda thought. "As you said, we can always hope." *And of course, here comes Tiernan toward me. Anytime we find ourselves in the same place, he has to come sniffing around.*

"Ambassador — what a happy surprise."

"Well," Chanda said, "It *is* a surprise."

"Clever as always." Tiernan looked toward the round building before them. "Any idea of its function?"

Galt said, "We were thinking we might see if we can go inside and find out."

We were? Chanda thought. *Fine, then.* "Great idea. Let's see how far we get." Since it was his idea, Chanda waited for Galt to make the first steps, then fell in behind him with Irene and Akira at her side. They had to pause a couple times to wait for groups of linked Buruden to pass. A glance back, and Sedra and Tiernan apparently had decided not to follow, but Govanek, after a moment's hesitation, began running to catch up to the Humans.

"Good to see you, Govanek," Chanda said. "What do you think of the Buruden homeworld so far? I know you want to be an explorer."

"You must know how unusual that is for a Sobrenian. But I find all of this exhilarating."

Here's our happy surprise, Chanda thought. *Govanek, by all accounts, is the real deal — perhaps the only one of us without an agenda. She could be a valuable resource.*

They arrived at what they assumed to be the front of the building, but were stymied by a solid wall. "It must be like our own building, and our quarters," Chanda said. "Only we don't know how to make the seam appear."

Irene approached the wall and ran her gloved hands over its surface. "Maybe there's a sensor that activates when you approach it."

"It might not respond to a Human in a lifesuit."

Irene lowered her hands. "That's a point."

"Look here," Galt said, pointing behind them. A group of about two dozen linked Buruden was approaching the building, but they were not proceeding as quickly as the majority of Buruden masses they'd seen before; in fact, many of them seemed infirm, with legs that shook as they walked along, eyes that stared unseeing, or bodies that Chanda thought looked — *withered.*

As the Buruden came to within a couple meters of the building, they unlinked as a seam less than a meter tall opened in the building, and they rushed inside.

Galt said, "They looked like an old-time freight train going into a tunnel."

"And the seam's still open," Akira said.

Chanda leaned over to examine what little she could see of the building's interior. "Pretty narrow path."

"We'd have to crawl," Galt said.

"You're not actually thinking about going in there?"

Irene said, "It looks as if they're inviting us."

"Unless the door just malfunctioned," Chanda said.

Govanek spoke up. "If I may suggest, Ambassador, that seems unlikely. The Buruden technology we have seen so far appears to be quite efficient. And we've seen that they don't seem to know the subtleties of interacting with other Galactic species."

"So you believe this is an invitation to enter?"

"I do."

Chanda indicated the doorway. "Go right ahead."

Govanek didn't hesitate. She lowered her head and passed through the entrance to the building. The Sobrenian was just short enough that she could walk through the tube-like entrance simply by bending over.

Chanda said, "Well, I'm not about to be upstaged."

Galt told her, "We'll have to crawl."

"'We?' I don't want you or anyone else blocking my way out." She tilted her head toward Sedra and Tiernan, who remained beside the Buruden vehicle they'd arrived in. "Keep an eye on them — make sure they don't get into any mischief."

"Will do," Galt said.

Chanda let out a long sigh and tried to kneel down enough to walk through the entrance, and realized that was futile. *I guess there's no way to do this with dignity*, she thought, and, gingerly in the 2.3 grav, got down on hands and knees and made her way through the entrance.

The round passageway was a deep black, yet illuminated just enough that she easily saw her way forward. Govanek was well ahead of her, still moving forward, walking bent over but with a determined stride.

A noise from behind her, and Chanda saw that the entryway she'd used had closed up. "Comm check," she said. "Senator Galt — Irene — Akira — do you read me?"

No response, until Govanek spoke up from just ahead of her. "Apparently we are cut off from them, Ambassador. But don't worry. I'm sure we'll be safe in here."

Chanda couldn't help grinning. "Typical explorer mentality," she said. "The usual leap-before-you-look attitude."

"Not all of that translated, Ambassador. I suspect an idiom at work. But I believe I understand. Although that makes me wonder why you followed me."

"Point taken. Do you see anything ahead?"

"I believe we're about to come out into a large room. I can't tell its purpose yet."

Thank goodness, Chanda thought. *My knees are killing me, especially in this higher grav.*

She could see that Govanek had reached the end of the tube and was standing in a much bigger circular space, one that looked to be the size of a large factory or warehouse. *Do the Buruden even have warehouses?* she wondered. *Many species just replicate what they need when and where they need it.*

Chanda stood, her knees a bit shaky as she raised herself to her feet. *What the hell is this place?* she thought. She and Govanek were looking over a vast open space with some sort of processing equipment far below them. Giant vats were filled with fluid being churned by an unseen mechanism. Languid clouds of steam rose toward the ceiling. The pathway they stood upon led downward and past the open top of each vat.

"That fluid looks like it's fermenting," Chanda told Govanek.

"Something tells me we're glad we can't smell the output of these vats."

Govanek split her gaze between the vats below and Chanda. "I fear you are correct, Ambassador. But I cannot decide what the purpose of this place is."

Chanda pointed to a series of pipes that ran outward from the bottom of all the vats. "Each pipe seems to run toward a different destination. I wonder if the vat is separating different components of that fluid and sending them for processing somewhere else."

"That seems likely, Ambassador. "But I have to wonder what happened to those Buruden we followed in here. They seem to have disappeared."

"That's true. And I don't see another pathway they could've taken."

A rumbling came from behind them and Govanek said, "Watch out, Ambassador. Here come more Buruden."

The unlinked group of Buruden, numbering another two dozen, advanced much as the one they'd followed here did — more slowly than most Buruden they'd ever seen, all of them appearing either wounded or damaged in some way.

Or —

"They're *old*," Chanda said as the Buruden filed past them and headed down the ramp toward the vats.

"Ambassador?"

"These Buruden. I wondered what was wrong with them. I'd never seen a group of them before that all had some sort of infirmity. But that's it — they're all old."

Govanek said, "I wonder if they use their older citizens to do certain types of work. Perhaps they employ them to do simple tasks that give them a sense of usefulness in their later years."

The Buruden reached the part of the ramp that ran past the vats — and jumped in.

"What the hell!" Chanda exclaimed as she watched the bodies of the old Buruden sink into the churning liquid and begin to dissolve.

Govanek said, "We've got to save them!" and started down the ramp.

Chanda leaped forward and grabbed Govanek by the shoulders, grateful for the Sobrenians' smaller stature. "Remember what I said about leap-before-you-look? This is another example."

"But — they're dying."

"They're . . . recycling themselves."

"I can't imagine — how horrible!"

Chanda made herself look at the series of vats again, which revealed no sign of the Buruden's remains. "It all adds up. When individual Buruden become too ill to be useful in their society, they sacrifice themselves for the greater good."

Govanek turned away from the vats. "It's disgusting."

"Yes, it is. And I'm sure our societies do many things just as disgusting to the Buruden."

"Such as . . . the *koraht*, I suppose."

"A good candidate," Chanda said.

Govanek said, "I could tell you were disgusted by it, also."

"That's true — so it's probably just as well you never saw Thanksgiving dinner when both sides of my family got together."

"Failure to translate."

"Also just as well — look, another group of Buruden is on the way."

But as this latest mass of Buruden exited the tube from outside, they halted next to Chanda and Govanek and linked together.

Chanda heard over her datalink, "We have been instructed to explain the function of this area."

"I believe we already figured it out," Chanda said. "You recycle your aging bodies here."

"You are correct."

Govanek asked, "How can you do that? Just walk down there and kill yourselves?"

"We are not killing ourselves. We are regenerating."

Chanda said, "You mean — your consciousness somehow survives?"

"Not at all," the Buruden said. "But this consciousness will not survive when we unlink. A truth. We are glad you understand this now." And with that, the Buruden mass unlinked, made their way as individuals down the pathway to the vats below, and hopped in, their bodies dissolving within seconds.

Chanda said, "We've seen enough here," and led the way back through the tube.

Chanda approached the exit to the building on hands and knees and was gratified when the seam opened for her without any fuss. Galt was standing at the exit and helped her onto her feet. Irene and Akira were right next to him. "We were getting pretty worried about you," Galt said. "We kept trying to get through to you — nothing!"

"Govanek and I . . . well, we found out what goes on in this building." She recounted what she and Govanek had witnessed inside.

"Oh, my God," Irene said, and the concern in her voice was such that Chanda looked more closely at her and wondered if she should be concerned about her — Irene's face looked as if all the blood had drained out of it and she was rubbing her gloved hands together as if coping with a deep worry. "How could you stand to witness that?"

"For them, it's a natural function," Chanda said. "Not very pleasing, to be sure. I don't really want to talk about it right now. Let's get back and see how our quarters are coming along."

She turned to Govanek, who still looked shaken, as much as Chanda could tell in a Sobrenian. Sedra and Tiernan hadn't moved from their position next to their vehicle, and didn't look as if they were going to. *They don't seem very concerned about Govanek,* Chanda thought. She told her, "You did a great job in there. Maybe you'll be an explorer yet."

Govanek said, "I believe today I've learned not all exploration is a joyful experience."

"You have a gift for understatement." She indicated Sedra and Tiernan. "I guess you'd better get back to your friends."

Govanek started to say something, then paused, seeming to think better of it. Then she told Chanda, "Thank you for accompanying me." Govanek headed toward the vehicle that had brought her and Sedra and Tiernan and the Garotethan to this place.

She wanted to say something else, Chanda thought. *But knew her friends . . . or maybe I should say colleagues . . . would hear her over the datalink.*

"Let's get the hell out of here," she told her own colleagues, and headed toward the other Buruden vehicle.

CHAPTER 18

Chanda remained quiet the entire trip back to the building that housed their quarters, and barely noticed the usual jostling of her body as the vehicle took its abrupt turns. She was barely aware of her body at all, even given the oppressive gravity of the Buruden homeworld; emotion ruled her entire consciousness, pushing out nearly all sense of rational thought.

Images swirled through her mind, one after another — Buruden plunging into that deadly cauldron, Sedra's obdurate insistence upon respectful accommodations before real negotiations could continue, Tiernan's maddening physical and mental transformation into an enemy of Humanity, all the way back to Unity shuttles landing on Splendor and disgorging wounded or dying highlanders, a symbol of her failed evacuation effort.

Such thoughts receded only when she became aware that their vehicle was coming to a halt. Galt's voice came to her as if from a distant room: "Chanda? Ambassador? We're here."

Chanda's body rebelled at the idea of rising in the strong grav, but she made herself stir and followed the others out of the car, through the airlock, and into their quarters, where they let their lifesuits fold themselves back into their bodies.

It was Akira who broke Chanda's reverie when she exclaimed, "Look at this place! It's so much better!"

Chanda had to admit their quarters were much improved — they were expanded, and separated into three bedrooms, while retaining a common room big enough for all of them to gather. Chanda let herself be amused as she watched Akira make a beeline for the bathroom. "It's not an entrance to the gates of hell anymore," Akira said. "Can I use it first?"

Galt's eyes flicked toward Chanda, who maintained her silence. "Sure," he said. "Go crazy."

Irene went that way, as well. "I'll help," she said, and the two of them slipped into the bathroom together.

Galt stared at Chanda for a long time before he said, "What's wrong, Ambassador? How can I help you?"

It took Chanda a moment to come to grips with the idea of engaging with another Human being. "I don't know that you can, Senator. That anybody can."

"We're counting on you, Ambassador. The Buruden and the Sobrenians both insisted you were the one person they trusted to come up with a negotiated solution here."

"Did they? Or are they each just using me as a way to stall while they build up their own forces?"

"Believe me, Chanda, there's something to be said to that kind of stalling. Every day the fighting doesn't break out is one more day people go on living, one more day that means the fighting might not break out at all."

"And one more day that both sides have more time to prepare, to make the eventual war that much worse."

Galt looked at Chanda as if he were seeing his own hopes turn to ashes: "You can't let what you saw back there color your perceptions."

"That's *not* what I'm doing."

"Bullshit. You were sulking the whole way back here."

"Sulking? How can you say — "

"I can *say* because I've been in combat. What you've been through isn't a tenth of what I've seen."

Chanda voice remained low. "I know that."

Galt gave Chanda a piercing look. "At the same time, you deserve a few moments of peace. You've carrying the heaviest burden here."

"Oh," Chanda said. "I thought — "

"You thought I was going to say you weren't up to the job."

"Well. . . . "

"I've been on your side all along. I just may not show it very well."

Irene and Akira came out of the bathroom, each of their faces beaming. "The Buruden finally got it right!" Irene said. "It's like paradise in there . . . " Irene's voice trailed off as she stared at Chanda's face. "What's wrong?"

Chanda said, "I have to wonder what the Buruden were doing in showing us that facility. There had to be a reason for it, but I don't know what it is."

Akira said, "Irene and I were just talking about that — don't look so surprised, we have serious conversations — and we think it was their way of showing how little individuals mean to them, and how determined they are as a species to survive."

"Interesting theory," Chanda said. "What do you have to back it up?"

"Just this," Irene said. "What's the one thing the Sobrenians seem to be afraid of about the Buruden?"

"Being overrun by them."

Irene continued: "Remember how Nysar described them — *chaotic.* And he feared what he called their mindlessness. Well, what would seem more chaotic and mindless to a Sobrenian than throwing yourself without a fuss into a vat that's going to melt you down to your component elements?"

Galt said, "So the message from the Buruden to the Sobrenians is that you're fighting an entire species — there are no civilians, there are no uncommitted. If you fight them, you have to kill every one of them to win."

Chanda said, "That's a hell of a message — but what if the Sobrenians learn the wrong lesson from it?"

Irene said, "We may be trying to prevent a genocide."

"It does focus your attention, doesn't it? Let's just hope the Buruden and Sobrenians have the same focus tomorrow — now that our problems with accommodations have been addressed."

"Our accommodations are still less than perfect," the Sobrenian chief negotiator Sedra said.

Chanda heard Galt groan. They sat together at the negotiation table, with Sedra and Tiernan and the Garotethan in their accustomed places, all of them across from the massed Buruden. As usual, Irene, Akira, and Govanek stood to one side. Chanda said, "I'd really hoped we were past that."

Sedra addressed Chanda directly, both eyes aimed at her. "Apparently you and your colleagues consider the Human accommodations adequate. We do not feel the same about the Sobrenian side."

"With all respect, Chief Negotiator — "

"Respect is exactly what we demand. Without it, we cannot continue."

A booming voice Chanda barely recognized as coming from the Buruden said, "The Sobrenians believe you must be satisfied personally — a difficult concept for us — before you can proceed as a species. Not a truth. Your delays could prevent us from achieving an agreement to maintain the peace. A potential truth. Without an agreement, a war could begin very soon. A likely truth. That war would bring massive destruction and could mean the end of both our species. A truth!"

A bit long-winded, as usual, Chanda thought. *But a good summing-up.*

Tiernan turned his head toward Sedra. *An unusual move for a supposed Sobrenian,* Chanda thought, then realized: *He still can't turn his eyes independently yet.*

"I hope you'll allow me," Tiernan said, and Sedra gestured acknowledgement. Tiernan spoke directly to the Buruden: "You have no right to threaten war against us! We are the injured party here. Your probes are making incursions into *our* space. We Sobrenians will defend ourselves as we see fit."

The mass of Buruden shifted around, as if the individuals that formed it were rocking on a restless ocean. *I've never seen a group of Buruden so upset,* Chanda thought.

The Buruden said, "We are naturally curious. We harm no one."

"The looking is the harm," Tiernan said. "You have no right to spy upon us."

Chanda raised her arms. Amazingly, Tiernan fell silent and the Buruden didn't try to get some more words in. "I'm impressed that we're making real progress here. Angry words may not seem like 'progress' to you, but they help define the issues we need to look at."

Now the Buruden interrupted. "That the Sobrenians have responded to our curiosity with the threat of war is a truth. That they are harassing many of our starcraft that happen to pass by their system is another truth."

Uh, oh, Chanda thought. *A double "truth" — that means the rest of their foursome of various types of truths also have to be doubled.*

We could be here awhile.

But the Sobrenians weren't having any of that. Sedra, her hands folded calmly before her, spoke quietly but firmly: "I do not care to wait through your purposely irritating rule-of-four constructions. Please answer straightforwardly. Will you cease your incursions into our system?"

"I will provide you the respect of answering in a way that is difficult for our species. We will not cease what you call incursions. A truth."

Very impressive, Chanda thought. *For the Buruden, downright pithy.* She said, "Well, it seems we've identified one of the major points of contention. Now we need to look at possible solutions."

Sedra said, "The only possible solution is for the Buruden to withdraw. Otherwise that threat of war is a very real one. *That* is the only 'truth' you need to concern yourselves with."

Chanda said, "There's another world to be concerned with here, and three more sentient species."

"Ah, yes," Sedra said. "Your precious planet Splendor. I look forward to visiting it, I've heard so much about it, and about the exploits of my people there."

Exploits, she says, was Chanda's first thought. *Testing weapons by firing them at innocent valley dwellers. Attacking a Buruden ship that ended up crashing into the Great Sea.* "Chief Negotiator," Chanda said, "Splendor is the Earth Unity's main concern in these negotiations." *And the power of the Unity is the only stick I have to beat anyone over the head with,* she thought.

Sedra said, "It's so unfortunate that an entire world might become a pawn among interstellar powers."

Galt spoke up. "It's unfortunate that such powers would consider an entire world to be a pawn."

Dammit, Galt, Chanda thought. *There's a time for straight talk, but we weren't there yet.*

Though maybe he can be the "bad cop" to my "good cop." "Let's refrain from name-calling for now," Chanda said. "I'd like to ask the Buruden ambassador — just what is it you want from the Sobrenians?"

The Buruden ambassador said, "We wish to be able to express our natural curiosity. You saw how interested we were at Turellen's fortress, especially as the flood water receded and returned. We witnessed fascinating details involving tides and gravitation, military tactics, Sobrenian sociology and psychology, and many other topics."

Sedra stood and raised his voice: "We do not wish to be a 'topic!' We are a sovereign people, and will not be studied as if we were bugs beneath a microscope."

Chanda tried to interrupt: "Chief Negotiator, perhaps a little calm —"

"This is not a time for Sobrenians to be calm. It is a time to declare that no Buruden will ever step upon our soil again."

The Buruden began, "Our curiosity —"

" — Is not to be abided!"

Chanda said, "Chief Negotiator, perhaps if you were to sit down. . . ."

Tiernan spoke up now: "Ambassador Kasmira, you are not here to give Sobrenians stage directions!"

"That's not my intention, by any means."

"Then please refrain from doing so," Tiernan said.

"What I will do," Chanda said, "is try to keep these negotiations focused on preventing a war."

Sedra kept one eye on the Buruden and the other on Chanda. "Then there is one thing you must do, Ambassador."

"What is that?"

"Have the Buruden continue to modify our accommodations."

Galt started to stand up, but Chanda grabbed his arm and he settled into his seat again. She managed a diplomatic smile that she was actually ashamed of, thinking, *Sedra and Govanek and the Buruden probably don't know any better, but certainly Tiernan can see how insincere it is. I've been out of the trenches too long.* She said, "Apparently this is the time for us to adjourn for the day. Chief Negotiator Sedra, I will speak to our Buruden friends on your behalf."

Sedra stood. "Gracious, as always."

Chanda frowned. *I can't read Sobrenian faces any better than they can read Human ones, but I'd bet Galt's left nut that Sedra's smile is as insincere as mine.*

Sedra headed toward the seam in the wall that led to the Sobrenian quarters, Govanek and the Garotethan right behind. This time, Chanda noted, she didn't risk a look backward at the Humans. Tiernan stepped over to Chanda. *It's disconcerting to have to look down at him,* she thought. Tiernan extended his hand and Chanda shook it. Tiernan said, "Have patience, Ambassador. I'm still educating my colleagues in the ways of Humans." As Tiernan shook Galt's hand, then Irene and Akira's in turn, Chanda thought, *That was as disconcerting as looking down at him.*

As the seal closed behind Tiernan, Chanda spoke to the Buruden: "You heard Sedra's concerns. Will you help them again with their accommodations?"

"We will," came the response from the Buruden. "We intended to all along. Your request was not necessary. A truth."

"Thank you," Chanda said, and watched as the Buruden left through another seam that sealed itself instantly afterward.

Chanda waited for Irene and Akira to join her and Galt and said, "We're being used."

Galt said, "I wanted to jump across that table and grab Sedra by the neck."

"The first few negotiations like this I was a part of, I felt the same way."

"How do you keep from doing it?"

"You visualize what Splendor will look like if the Sobrenians and Buruden fight there as a surrogate for their own homeworlds. Then how pissed off you are won't seem so important."

Irene said, "What's next, Chanda?"

"We go back to our own quarters, I suppose. And try to anticipate the next move from either the Sobrenians or Buruden."

Galt said, "We shouldn't just anticipate, Chanda. We should make a move of our own."

"We're the go-betweens, Senator. We don't have a 'move.'"

"Sorry. Military mentality. I'm used to looking for a way to attack and overwhelm."

"Unfortunately," Chanda said, "diplomacy is more complicated than that. And more frustrating."

They went back to their quarters. Chanda insisted upon a brain-storming session on ways to break the deadlock with the Sobrenians. She poured some hot tea and sat on a much more comfortable couch in their new, smaller common room. Irene and Akira picked juice drinks they'd discovered among the supplies the Buruden had provided. "It's a little like orange juice," Irene said.

Akira added, "It helps that the nearest orange is about 240 light-years away — so there's nothing to compare it with."

Galt didn't have a drink; he sat in a chair across from the couch. "First of all, lemme pass on what I've learned during that scan about Tiernan's . . . transformation."

Chanda said, "I assume it's all biotech based."

"It is. And it's been an accelerated process. It looks like he's been at it less than a month."

Irene said, "That's a hell of a transformation in a pretty short time."

"And," Galt said, "it looks like quite a painful one."

Chanda asked, "How can you tell that?"

"Part of his biotech is geared toward pain control — mostly neural blockers."

"I can't say I feel bad for him. The more he hurts the better, as far as I'm concerned. Anything else?"

"That's about it," Galt said. "Don't know how that helps us with anything, but at least we know more about what he's going through."

"Well, he and the Sobrenians are as frustrating as ever. What do all of you think about these so-called negotiations so far?"

Galt held up his hand and interrupted her. He touched behind his left ear. "Excuse me, Chanda, I'm getting a private message from Captain Hamadi. He . . . says it's important . . . it's narrow beam . . . security."

Chanda waited, eager to know what was important enough that Hamadi couldn't delay in telling them, and had to resort to such a technically challenging link. She watched as Galt listened, his hand still held absently behind his ear. She saw his eyes widen, his breathing quicken. Galt stood up, muttered, "No! Dammit, lost the signal." He sat down again. "Captain, you're back, sorry. Tell me again."

Chanda sat on the edge of her seat, desperate to know what Hamadi was telling Galt. After a few more moments, Galt lowered his hand from his ear; his eyes stared but did not see, his mouth hung slightly open.

Chanda reached her hand out toward him. "Senator Galt — what —"

Galt stood, emitted a low growl, turned and picked up his chair, the growl became a scream, and he slammed the chair against the closest wall. Neither gave; the chair didn't break or even bend, the wall was unscathed. Galt dashed the chair against the wall again — and again! Still no effect.

Galt let the chair slip from his hands; it dropped to the floor with a clatter.

Chanda stood. She went toward Galt with slow, measured steps. He stood there breathing so hard Chanda worried he'd hyperventilate. "Senator Galt," she said, to no response. "*Gabriel.*"

Galt looked up at her, seemed to regain awareness of his surroundings. "It's Tiernan," he said. "He's an even bigger bastard than we realized."

Chanda took Galt by the arm. "Come sit with us," she said. "Tell us what happened." Irene and Akira made room on the couch as Chanda uprighted Galt's chair and sat across from them.

Galt sat leaning forward, hands folded. "I had some chips I could call in," he said. "Any Unity Senator who's worth his salt does. So I found out about Tiernan, but goddam if part of me wishes I hadn't."

"What the hell did he do?" Chanda asked.

"He really was supposed to go to the Sobrenian homeworld and be a double agent. A Unity patrol ship — the *James Rowland* — was supposed to drop him off at a Sobrenian outpost at the edge of their system, then hightail it back to Unity space. Apparently the Unity was pretending it was sending Tiernan back for 'humanitarian' reasons — great description, huh? But he was really supposed to be a double agent."

"But I'm guessing it didn't go that way."

"The *Rowland* made it out of the Sobrenian system, all right. But it was discovered about three light-years away from the Unity outpost where it was supposed to check in. No answer from the ship. A Unity crew finally boarded. Found blood pooled two centimeters deep in some places — everyone on the *Rowland* dead. But most everyone had been stunned first before they died — stunned in their sleep, in fact. The actual killings had been committed up close and personal — strangled, stabbed repeatedly, throat cut, that kind of thing."

It took a moment before Chanda could find her voice. "And . . . no Tiernan, I suppose?"

"One lifepod was gone. Presumably Tiernan was on it."

Akira spoke up. "It would take a helluva cold-blooded son-of-a-bitch — and a damned skilled one — to kill the entire crew of a patrol ship — that's about ten people. And how did he get hold of the stunner?"

"And why would he kill the crew," Chanda asked, "if he was being dropped off here anyway?"

Galt said, "Could be the crew figured out he wasn't sincere — maybe they were going to take him back to the Unity."

"Something else," Chanda said. "If he managed to kill the crew, why didn't he just take the cruiser in? Or if he couldn't fly it by himself, he could've at least destroyed it."

Galt said, "It seems someone on the crew managed to lock out the ship's self-destruct systems and set it for a stardrive jump that would take place whether anyone on it was left alive or not."

Chanda said, "Which means he had to get the hell off that ship — thus, the lifepod escape."

Irene said, "I'm guessing this isn't something we ask Tiernan about."

"No," Chanda said. "We have an advantage if he doesn't realize how much we know about him. Though I'd sure like to bring him to justice."

Galt said, "I want nothing more than to wrap my fingers around his half-Sobrenian neck. But this mission's too important. Too many innocent lives, of six species."

"Six?" Chanda asked. "We had the number at five back on Splendor — highlanders, valley dwellers, sweepers, Buruden, Humans."

Galt looked at the floor. "I'm not a monster, Chanda. I'm including the Sobrenians. They have their own innocents."

Chanda leaned forward and squeezed Galt's shoulder. "I'm glad you feel that way. We'll get through this somehow. But I can't be content anymore just to absorb his punches. Knowing what he's done, I — we — have to punch back."

Galt looked at Chanda. "Govanek?"

"Yes."

Irene asked, "You really want to try to turn her?"

"I was already thinking about it," Chanda said. "But I didn't want to antagonize the Sobrenians."

"Not a factor anymore," Galt said.

"I don't understand," Irene said. "Are we trying *not* to antagonize the Sobrenians by keeping quiet about Tiernan, or trying *to* antagonize them by trying to turn Govanek?"

"That," Chanda said, "is one of the mysteries of diplomacy."

Galt said, "Also known as 'working both sides of the street.'"

"I'm glad I'm a pilot," Irene said. She swept her hand down in a chopping motion. "Just point me in the right direction."

Chanda said, "That's the problem, isn't it? Finding the right vector." She told Galt, "So I guess I was wrong before. Looks like we do have a 'move.'"

CHAPTER 19

Chanda went to bed early that night, but tossed and turned and could think only of Tiernan. Even as sleep finally eased upon her, she anticipated that any dreams or nightmares her mind might generate this night would be of him.

———

Chanda awoke, and her first thought was of Tiernan. She was vaguely aware that she'd dreamt of him, vague images of him hovering over her bed, seeing everything she saw, even hearing her thoughts, perceiving her doubts.

Stop it, Chanda, she thought. *He's a creepy bastard, but not supernatural. One good energy bolt to the heart and he's no one's problem.*

Chanda peered out into the hallway to check on the bathroom, which was still communal, but that was of small consequence, since the seating arrangements and plumbing were no longer something to fear. *A small comfort, perhaps, but a necessary one*, she thought, grateful to see it was unoccupied. Afterward, she dressed and gathered with the others in the common room.

As they awaited the arrival of the Buruden to take them to the latest negotiation session, Galt said, "I know I wasn't the best example yesterday, but we've got to contain our emotional reactions to Tiernan. If he suspects we've learned what he's done, any advantage we have over him is gone." He looked toward Chanda. "That goes double for you, Ambassador. He likes to bait you. If he was still fully Human, I'd almost say he was flirting with you."

"He thinks he's distracting me from my job. He's always been wrong."

"I know."

"But that business with him killing the crew of the *Rowland* disturbs me. It tells me there's more to him than we know."

Galt said, "Just remember Tiernan's not all you have to be concerned about."

"You're right. I've got to be firm with Sedra from the beginning today. No bitching about the accommodations, no more stalling."

Galt said, "She runs so hot and cold, just in her attitude. Trying to be charming one minute — as much as a Sobrenian can be — then hardline the next."

The seam to the corridor leading to the negotiation room opened, and about a dozen Buruden, marching single-file, entered. They linked legs, and when they spoke, Chanda didn't have a sense that she was hearing the Buruden ambassador. "We will not have a negotiation session today."

"What the hell?" Chanda asked.

"The Sobrenians intend to supervise the continued renovation of their living area themselves."

"This is ridiculous," Galt said.

Chanda said, "I'd like to go see Sedra. We have to get these negotiations back on track."

The Buruden said, "Sedra thought you might insist upon that. She refuses."

"The hell? Take me to her anyway."

"We will not."

Galt said, "This is in your own best interest. We're trying to prevent a war that could kill millions of your own people."

"We will not take you to the Sobrenians. Instead, we have another trip for you to take. In fact, one of the Sobrenians wishes to accompany you."

Chanda's eyebrows raised. "Who?"

"Govanek."

Chanda traded looks all around with her colleagues. "Well, then . . . let's go."

Minutes later, Chanda and her colleagues were activating their lifesuits and stepping into the airlock. As it cycled, Galt told Chanda, "At least this might be an opportunity to talk to Govanek alone."

Chanda said, "I'm having second thoughts. Is this really wise, to try to feel out Govanek about helping us?"

"Maybe even defecting?" Irene asked.

"That's just it -- this is too easy. Too convenient. Are we being set up to talk to her? And we'll be in our lifesuits much of the time — anything we say will have to be transmitted among us, and it would be very easy for someone to listen in. And we don't know whether she's sincere or not."

Galt said, "I see what you mean — we're supposed to trust Govanek even as she may be trying to pry secrets out of us? You think her entire attitude toward us is an act?"

"I looked over everything Mike Christopher said about her in his reports about the *Asaph Hall*'s mission to the Moruteb system. He said she was eager to go on another exploratory mission sometime, perhaps even with him. And he thought it was a good idea."

Akira asked, "But doesn't trying to turn her mean we're taking sides, in a sense?"

"Not 'in a sense,'" Galt said. "We'd actually be taking sides."

Chanda said, "Well, Senator, we just have to keep the larger goal in mind."

"I am — I'm imagining what could happen to millions of innocents on Splendor if we don't make something happen."

Chanda said, "Let me be clear about this — if we had a similar opportunity among the Buruden, I'd take it. The Sobrenians are not sympathetic players in this whole mess. But it's the Buruden who started it. They don't seem to understand that their curiosity can lead to war."

The airlock finished its cycle and the outer lock opened. Chanda led the way out, bracing herself against the higher grav.

The usual round Buruden vehicle awaited them. Chanda, Galt, Irene, and Akira boarded the car, ducking beneath its low ceiling as usual. Govanek was already there, with her spacesuit rolled up next to her. *I wonder why she took it off*, Chanda thought. *She had to wear it to get out here, and it's a lot more trouble to take it on and off rather than just deactivating a lifesuit.* Which is what she and the other Humans did as they settled onto the floor.

Govanek said, "It's wonderful to get to explore a new world with Human friends!"

Chanda didn't have to force her smile; Govanek's enthusiasm was infectious. She asked, "Do you know where we're going?"

"Absolutely no idea," Govanek said. "And isn't that the wonderful part? Certainly it will be somewhere no Sobrenian — and no Human — has ever visited."

Govanek's motivations seem so pure, Chanda thought. *They make me want to trust her implicitly.*

Which also makes her potentially dangerous.

The car accelerated swiftly, exiting the building and heading down a crowded street. Similar vehicles sped past in both directions, and what seemed like hordes of Buruden pedestrians, some linked, some unlinked, rushed down the pedestrian walkways. Galt wondered, "Is it always — what did they call it back in the market economy days — 'rush hour' — here?"

"Looks like," Chanda said. "Though I don't know the nature of the Buruden economy."

Govanek tilted one eye toward Chanda and the other toward Galt. "From what little I've been able to gather from our Buruden friends, I'm not certain they even have what we might think of as an economy. When there's work to be done, they do it."

"Makes sense," Galt said. "They almost seem to have a hive mind."

Their vehicle soon left the city behind and took a familiar route to the starport where they'd landed. A Buruden shuttle was awaiting them, a large one similar to the craft the Buruden delegation to the Sobrenian homeworld had traveled in.

The car's airlock fit easily against one of the shuttle's locks, and everyone went across without having to deal with lifesuits or spacesuits.

Chanda told Galt, "This shuttle has a gravitic drive. If we're lucky, the Buruden have anticipated giving us Earth grav."

With that first step into the shuttle's airlock, located just behind the pilot's cabin, Chanda said, "Yes! I guessed it."

"That feels great," Irene said.

Akira pointed out, "There still aren't any seats."

"You can't have everything," Chanda said. "Besides, with gravitics in full force, at least we won't get thrown around like in their cars. And we have windows. We can see where we're going — not like that Sobrenian shuttle, where we might as well have been in a simulator."

Once the Humans and Govanek were aboard, the unseen pilots lifted the shuttle smoothly and effortlessly, rising over a rural area which gave them a closer look at the Buruden homeworld's vegetation. Most of the first plants they glimpsed huddled close to the ground, but spread their broad leaves out over wide areas, many of them in multiple layers. "You'd think we'd see something resembling a tree," Chanda said. "The grav here isn't *that* high."

"Keep patient," Galt told her. "We've been out of the city for all of a couple minutes. Imagine the same impression we'd get of such a small area back on Earth."

"Look at the colors!" Irene said. "All the green plants look like they were imported directly from Earth, but there's so many deep reds, it's an amazing contrast."

Chanda said, "I'm starting to see some different features. Look over there — there's a gap in the vegetation. The landscape's barren."

Irene said, "You're right — then more vegetation, then another gap, and on and on."

Govanek spoke up. "I have studied this. The plants with their wide leaves are aiming themselves straight up, toward their share of sunlight. The fallow areas come about because the diffuse sunlight that comes through the clouds can only support so much vegetation across a particular stretch of landscape."

As the shuttle continued to rise, it entered the low cloud cover and the landscape below faded into whiteness. "Just once," Chanda said, "I'd like an itinerary — where we're going, and how long it'll take to get there."

After about an hour, Chanda spotted an extensive mountain range extending out from the layer of clouds. Individual peaks shone red and gold in the morning light.

"Looks like we're headed toward that one mountain," Chanda said, pointing out the tallest peak of the bunch. "Seems like we're slowing down, anyway."

The shuttle circled that tallest peak, and Chanda saw that it was relatively flat on top. "That looks taylor-made for a shuttle to land," she said.

As the shuttle descended toward the mountain's peak, Irene said, "I'd love to go to the Buruden's real homeworld someday, if we ever knew where it was. What must it be like?"

Govanek said, "Perhaps that is a journey several of us could make together."

"You never know," Chanda said. "Working on Splendor's taken up the last few years of my life."

Govanek turned both eyes toward Chanda. "I've heard much about your sacrifices," she said.

Chanda was caught unawares. "You have?" Out of the corner of her eye, she saw that Galt, Irene, and Akira had suddenly become intensely interested in this conversation.

"I know you've put aside most Human emotional connections. You have little close family left, so you haven't visited Earth in years."

"Well . . . yes, that's true."

"As for sexual relations — "

"Oh, look," Chanda said. "We're coming in for a landing."

Govanek craned her neck to look out the window as Chanda tried not to show that yes, she *did* notice Irene holding her hand over her face to hide the laughter she couldn't quite suppress, Akira's pressed lips serving the same purpose, and that even Galt was allowing himself a wry smile. *So much for ambassadorial dignity,* Chanda thought as the shuttle settled down onto the surface of the mountain.

Irene looked out of the shuttle's wide windows. "It's beautiful," she said as she pointed out several other mountaintops peeking out above the clouds.

Chanda said, "I know it might be easier to see all this from the comfort of the shuttle, but we're here — let's enjoy it close-up." She was about to touch her left middle finger to her palm when Govanek said, "Ambassador, didn't the Buruden tell you?"

"Tell us what?"

"You don't need lifesuits up here." She indicated her rolled-up spacesuit. "I brought mine to get to the ground vehicle, but the pressure is weak enough here that we can breathe freely."

Galt held his left arm up, pulled back his sleeve, and operated the sensor cluster embedded within his arm. "She's right, Chanda. We can breathe the air out there without a problem."

"OK," Chanda said. "A little gift from our Buruden friends, I suppose."

Govanek asked, "They didn't tell you about this?"

"They hardly speak to us."

"Interesting. They spend much time in our quarters. Of course, much of that time they're working on our accommodations. But several of them remain linked together so they can speak with us. Tiernan seems . . . especially irritated with them."

Good, Chanda thought, and remembered the odd seating arrangements the Buruden dealt with during the first round of negotiations back on the Sobrenian homeworld, how they were separated from the Sobrenians and Humans. She remembered the Buruden ambassador explaining, "When they come to our world, we will make the arrangements." *I heard the potential for mischief in those words back then,* Chanda thought. *Maybe this is payback.*

Galt lifted his backpack containing the emergency medical supplies. "Let me go outside first, with this — just in case."

Chanda said, "But you told us the atmosphere was fine."

"We can't risk you. I'll go out."

Irene said, "You have those grandchildren to spoil. I'll go without my lifesuit activated, and Akira takes the backpack."

Galt looked toward Chanda, who nodded. Galt handed the backpack to Akira with obvious reluctance. She and Irene went through the inner airlock doorway, closed it. Chanda and Galt, ducking beneath the low ceiling of the shuttle, then leaned down to look through the inner door's knee-height porthole.

Akira activated her lifesuit and looked toward Irene, who nodded. Akira hit the control that opened the outer lock. Irene tensed as the Buruden homeworld's atmosphere filled the lock. A deep breath, and she turned toward the inner airlock door as a wide smile burst across her face. "It's fine!" she said. "Com'on out!"

"As simple as that, I suppose," Chanda said, and opened the inner lock. She went through it, bracing herself against the increased grav, and followed Irene and Akira outside, Galt and live right behind her.

They stood overlooking an ocean of clouds that was dotted with the blunt peaks of several mountains, part of a chain that ran toward the eastern horizon. Chanda blinked against a brief moment of disorientation as she watched the clouds' languid movement past the tops of those rugged peaks; for an instant it appeared as if the mountains were moving instead.

Chanda smelled a hint of something sweet, and felt something close to a burst of adrenalin rush through her body. A quick exhalation, and she took another breath, and it was as exhilarating as the first one.

Galt said, "I thought it would smell like a Buruden ship. You know, like. . . . "

"A stable or a barn. Yeah. But remember, this isn't their original homeworld."

Govanek said, "This is a rare opportunity for us. I am now the first Sobrenian to breathe air freely while standing upon the surface of — not the original, as you say — but at least the most recent Buruden homeworld. Just as you are the first Humans to do so."

Galt said, "A small distinction in the history of Human exploration, perhaps — but we'll take it."

"It's like they say," Chanda told them. "Some days you get the chicken, some days it's feathers."

Govanek said, "Failure to translate."

"Don't worry about it, Govanek," Galt said. "Sometimes Chanda's animal analogies don't translate for other Humans, either."

Chanda told Govanek, "Perhaps we can go a little bit away from the shuttle and discuss something."

Govanek said, "I'm sure that would be very interesting," and kept one eye on the dark, rough ground ahead of them and the other on Chanda as they walked.

"This is far enough," Chanda said as they drew near a precipice. She could see only about seven meters downward, then the mountain beneath her faded away into whiteness.

Govanek said, "I sense you have something important to talk about."

"I want to make sure no one should be able to hear us, first."

"I don't have my spacesuit. You haven't activated your lifesuit. My datalink, and I assume, yours, are not activated except to translate over the distance between us."

"You assume correctly." Chanda looked out across the mantle of clouds enveloping all she could see of this planet. *I wish I could just enjoy its beauty*, she thought. *Maybe someday.*

"Ambassador?"

"Sorry. Lost in thought. I wondered . . . do you know anything of the circumstances in which Tiernan arrived in your home system?"

Both of Govanek's eyes looked toward Chanda. "I heard Tiernan say something to Nysar at the beginning of negotiations."

"Can you tell me precisely what he said?"

"I don't know if it's appropriate to tell you. Are you hoping I will say something in Humanity's favor about the behind-the-scenes machinations involving these talks?"

"Govanek, I think you've been wanting to tell me something for quite a while."

"And if I speak to you in this way — will there be an advantage in it for me?"

"What do you mean, 'advantage?'"

"I mean, that if I speak out against my superiors, I will in a sense no longer have a homeworld."

Chanda thought a long moment before she said, "You're talking about defecting."

"A harsh word. One I do not know whether I am willing to embrace yet."

"I'll give you what I call my greatest honor. I'll speak to you as bluntly as I do those who work with me. You'd best make up your mind about that word. Embrace it, push it away — but you have to *decide*."

"It's a difficult thing. . . ."

"To betray your people?"

"You *do* speak bluntly," Govanek said. "But I am not the traitor. Sedra and Nysar and their ilk are the traitors."

"Humans who change their loyalties often feel the same way."

"Yes. Tiernan." Chanda could hear the disgust in Govanek's voice even through the datalink translation. "You should hear him, Ambassador. Many Sobrenians are bigoted against Humans. Forgive me, but many consider your species to be weak and gullible. Tiernan's attitude eclipses them all — he has developed a true hatred for his own people."

"He's been cultivating that hatred for some time," Chanda said. *And as honest and straight-forward as you seem, Govanek, I have to wonder whether Tiernan's cultivated you. Are you really here to defect, or are you another of Tiernan's distractions — or worse, are you trying to insinuate yourself into my good graces, then spy upon us?*

Govanek continued: "The way in which Tiernan is having himself transformed into a Sobrenian — many of us find that distasteful."

Chanda said, "With all respect to your own species, Govanek, many of us Humans find it distasteful, as well."

"I do not wish to be a part of a regime that looks for war and embraces one such as Tiernan."

"So just like Tiernan is becoming a Sobrenian — "

"With all respect to Humanity, Ambassador, I have no wish to become Human. I simply wish to live among people who are not so eager to begin an interplanetary war."

Chanda asked, "So what was it Tiernan said?"

"He did not speak to Nysar of specifics — just something that was a great achievement for Sobrenians. And since Sedra has taken over the negotiation sessions — "

" — Such as they are — " Chanda said.

" — he's made no reference to it at all."

"All right — back to your people in general — if they're looking for war, why are they taking part in these negotiations?"

"You see how ineffective they have been, Ambassador. They allow my people a final few moments to build their forces while getting to know their enemies a little better."

"'Enemies,' plural? So Humanity is included?"

"Yes, along with all the species living on Splendor. When the war arrives, it will begin on Splendor."

A stunned silence, as Chanda's heart pounded. "They want to use Splendor as a staging area."

"Exactly. They also believe the Buruden, having seen what the Sobrenians are capable of, will voluntarily relinquish this current homeworld of theirs."

"How many homeworlds have they had?"

"We don't know. Neither do we know the location of their original homeworld."

Chanda said, "They're quite mysterious in many ways."

"And my people have an irrational fear of them. One I do not share, by the way. I find them fascinating."

"You have the explorer's instinct. Perhaps you're making the right decision wanting to defect. But Govanek, I don't know whether I can accept you — at least not yet."

"I understand — these negotiations are complicated enough."

"It would have to be at the last minute, when we're leaving to go back to Splendor. But you have to be certain. I can't take this risk — can't let Irene and Akira and Galt take it — unless I know you're certain."

Govanek looked away from Chanda and stared across the cloudscape. "I . . . can you understand what it means to know you may never be able to go back to your homeworld again?"

"Well . . . I know what it's like to have nothing worth going home to."

Govanek looked toward Chanda again. "I didn't know your life held such tragedy."

"I wish I hadn't even said that much," Chanda said. "After a time, you live the life you have, and don't worry so much about the one you don't."

"You have regrets."

"Who doesn't? But my biggest regret is that I haven't yet made Splendor safe. I don't know whether you're my best opportunity to make sure that happens, or the best way to make sure I fail."

"You must trust me."

"Govanek, I can't tell through the translation whether you were making a plea or just stating a fact."

"Clearly it was both."

Chanda drew in a breath of this world's air. It wasn't nearly as exhilarating as those initial ones she'd taken just off the shuttle. "How can I trust someone who hasn't even given me a clear decision yet?"

Govanek didn't speak for a moment. Then she said, "Then I have much work ahead of me. Can I ask you to be patient?"

"You can ask," Chanda said. "But my answer depends upon a situation that's changing day-to-day — even moment-to-moment."

"So you cannot make me any promises."

"The only promise I can make is that I'll do the best by you that I can. That depends on how much shit is hitting the fan at a particular moment."

"Failure to — "

"I'm sure." Chanda took a final long look at the beauty of the majestically floating clouds, and the mountain peaks that seemed to be taking a journey among them. "We'd better get back down to the city. Down to reality — or what passes for it."

CHAPTER 20

As Chanda approached the shuttle, Galt gave her a questioning look. All she could give back was a faint smile and a shrug. "Let's pile in," Chanda said. She ducked low as she entered the shuttle and settled in on the floor.

Once everyone was aboard, the shuttle lifted from the mountaintop and headed back the way it had come. After a few minutes, it descended into the clouds, the effect inside the shuttle being that of a total whiteout. *Oddly enough,* Chanda thought, *I've never experienced one back on Splendor.*

When the shuttle dipped down beneath the clouds, however, she could tell that the Buruden craft was racing across the landscape much faster than it had been on the trip out. "Where the hell are we going so fast?" Chanda wondered.

Galt said, "As much as I can tell, I think we're headed back the way we came."

Irene pointed ahead of them. "You're right — there's the starport. But we're coming in pretty hot."

The Buruden starport grew in their ports at an alarming rate.

"Thank goodness this thing has inertials," Chanda said. "We'd be paste against the walls otherwise."

The shuttle slowed precipitously in the final moments of its approach. "Uh, oh," Irene said.

"I don't like 'uh, oh,'" Chanda told her. "What is it?"

"Reception committee."

"Uh, oh," Chanda said, looking out the side ports. "Both Sedra and Tiernan. And a bunch of Buruden."

Govanek came up next to Chanda and looked over her shoulder. "Perhaps we shouldn't have talked about — "

"About *nothing*. And certainly we shouldn't talk about it right now."

"You're right," Govanek said, and sat against a wall and didn't move. *It's as if she turned herself off*, Chanda thought. *Emotionally, perhaps she has.*

The shuttle settled onto one of the many landing pads. Chanda told the others, "Let's get this over with."

"Whatever 'this' is," Galt said.

Chanda hesitated at the outer airlock door. *I really don't want to go out into that increased grav*, she thought. *I can't decide if it's more tiresome physically or mentally.*

But I'm making a traffic jam here, so — She activated her lifesuit against the deadly air pressure, braced herself against the 2.3 Earth grav of the current Buruden homeworld, and stepped through the airlock.

Tiernan was right there to greet her, of course. "Always a pleasure, Ambassador," he said, one eye focused on her, the other clearly straining to swivel to one side to look at her companions.

Showing off, are we? Chanda thought. As she regarded him, she had to use all her experience and training not to reveal her feelings about him, had to force away the images of the bloody bodies of the crew of the *James Rowland*, had to suppress her disgust at what he'd done. *That knowledge may be the only power I have over him*, she thought. *I can't squander it.*

A closer look at Tiernan, and Chanda realized his torso had grown even thicker, to about twice that of a typical Human male. His face was utterly dominated now by his Sobrenian snout. *And he's not wearing boots!* Chanda realized. Even Tiernan's feet had been transformed — they'd been sculpted so that they were as wide as typical Sobrenian feet, and their toes had been elongated so that they resembled fingers, and looked as if with a little more work, Tiernan would be able to use his feet with the same dexterity as his hands. *All of which means he's undergoing this transformation even here on the Buruden homeworld,* Chanda thought. *I can't imagine such an effort, especially since it reportedly involves so much pain.*

If I admired Tiernan, I'd appreciate him all the more — as it is, I can't imagine such an effort being wasted on a traitor and warmonger.

Tiernan said to Govanek, "I hope you enjoyed your journey with your Human friends."

Chanda thought, *I can't tell if Tiernan's indulging in subtext there, or not.* Her next thought: *I hope Govanek can keep her composure.* She saw Sedra and her Garotethan standing to one side, a bit away from the group of a dozen Buruden who stood, unlinked, as if waiting for something to happen.

Govanek told Tiernan, "Thank you, I did. We had a pleasant trip."

Tiernan said, "That's wonderful. Always nice that we get to know one another better." He indicated the Buruden. "These Buruden, however, don't seem to subscribe to that same theory. They insisted we come here to the starport, then unlinked and haven't spoken to us."

Chanda said, "They rushed us here from our trip into the mountains."

Tiernan rubbed his eyes. Chanda thought, *Trying to move them independently must be tiring them out. Poor baby.*

Irene asked, "Do you hear that?" She was looking skyward.

Chanda followed Irene's gaze, but didn't see anything. "What do you hear?"

"It sounds like a gravitic drive — but straining."

"A ship in trouble?"

"There it is!" Irene pointed, and Chanda saw a Buruden craft, considerably bigger than the shuttle they'd just exited, approaching the starport from the west.

"That looks large enough to be a passenger ship," Chanda said. "I wonder what happened to it?"

Chanda heard a sound behind her, and turned to see the dozen Buruden linking their legs. When they spoke, she could tell the Buruden ambassador was speaking: "It was . . . attacked. A truth."

Chanda looked toward Tiernan, who looked, in turn, toward Sedra. The Sobrenian Chief Negotiator said, "If this ship was fired upon by Sobrenian forces, you can be sure it was for a good reason."

The Buruden ambassador began to reply: "We believe that assertion to be an untruth. Give us new information, and it may become a potential truth at best. The possibility of being a likely truth — "

Sedra said, "We will not listen to your four-part litany of lies."

"Very well," the Buruden said. "Then we will speak to the Humans."

Chanda said, "This isn't the time to try to settle this kind of disagreement."

"We agree," the Buruden said. "Many lives are at stake."

Chanda asked, "If that ship's in so much trouble, why didn't it rendezvous with an orbital station?"

"Both its gravitic and reaction drives were damaged. It could not perform the precise maneuvers needed to perform a successful rendezvous."

Irene said, "So it came straight in -- aerobraking instead."

"Yes," the Buruden ambassador said. Chanda noticed Sedra approaching quietly as the Buruden continued: "This remains a dangerous maneuver, and many of those aboard may yet die."

Several of the round Buruden vehicles began to congregate to one side of one of the larger landing pads. Chanda told the Buruden, "It looks like some of those vehicles have firefighting equipment —

others I'd guess are some sort of rescue vehicles — ambulances, and the like."

"You are correct," the Buruden ambassador said.

"But there's a third type I don't recognize."

"Those are simple body recovery vehicles."

"Oh. For the — "

"Yes. For the dead. But at least their remains can be easily made part of our whole again."

Chanda said, "You mean — taken to that facility Govanek and I saw?"

Several of the individual Buruden looked directly at Chanda with one or two eyes. "You understand, Ambassador, that we are not overly sentimental about individuals among us. With us, sentience — even simple awareness — is contained within the group. For the individual, it is fleeting at best."

Sedra said, "We Sobrenians believe in the individual above all. As long as the individual adheres to the will of the group."

Galt said, "That sounds exactly like what the Buruden said."

Sedra turned to Tiernan, saying, "We are leaving."

Tiernan pointed to Govanek. "Come with us. Your days of fraternization with Humanity are over."

Govanek, unwisely, gave Chanda a look she knew was too fraught with meaning for her own good. But she went along quietly, following Sedra and Govanek to their Buruden vehicle. *Thank goodness she didn't try to say anything to me,* Chanda thought. *Doubly so that she didn't try to defect here and now.*

The whine of the starcraft's gravitics grew louder, and Chanda shielded her eyes against the sun as she looked up. "It's coming in pretty hot," she said.

The craft began trailing thick black smoke as it came in dangerously low. Then one side of its fuselage seemed to bulge — an instant later, Chanda heard the sound of the explosion. "That thing's going to blow apart if it doesn't get down soon," she said.

Now that the craft was closer, Chanda could see the typical wide strokes of yellow, maroon, and gold across its round body, which resembled nothing more than the flying saucers of Earthly mythology.

Now Chanda made out more detail — the four engine nacelles beneath, the large fin on top, its tip curving forward — and she could see that the crippled craft might barely make it to the starport, if not the specific landing pad it was aiming for.

Chanda stared, every nerve tense, as if by sheer force of will she could convince the craft to stay aloft long enough to make the pad, to save as many lives as possible.

The craft wobbled in its course, and to Chanda it looked as if the planet itself had grown impatient to embrace it as it suddenly slowed and arced rapidly toward the ground.

A final screeching attempt by the gravitics to break that fall, and the starcraft struck the surface of the starport's main field with a sickening grinding sound that it seemed would never end. A couple of the engine nacelles split into pieces, sending sharp shards flying along with various liquids and gases.

The saucer itself began to spin along the ground, rapidly enough that Chanda hoped the craft's gravitics hadn't failed. Its rotation slowed along with its forward motion, and the various Buruden vehicles moved toward the craft as it rocked back and forth and finally came to a halt. Smoke arose from within the craft, then flames shot from inside it.

Chanda said, "I wonder how badly the hull was breached before it hit atmosphere."

The Buruden ambassador said, "Many of its passengers died while the starcraft was still in deep space. We fear many more may have died in this hard landing."

The firefighting vehicles were first on the scene and began spreading a foam that quickly suppressed the flames even as airlocks opened all along the ship and its passengers began coming out. Chanda was struck by the fact that all the Buruden were individuals — none of them was linked together. Those who could walk well enough to get out of the stricken starcraft got well away from it and gathered together silently, waiting.

Chanda turned toward the Buruden mass standing next to her. "Let us help — our lifesuits can protect us, and we're all trained in emergency situations."

"Absolutely not," the Buruden said. "Our people have this well under control. And you're unfamiliar with the layout of our ships and our rescue protocols." They indicated the ambulances and other rescue vehicles which were moving in. Unlinked Buruden rushed through the airlocks and into the craft.

Chanda said, "They don't have protective suits."

The Buruden ambassador said, "The rescue teams have been bred so that their bodies are resistant to being damaged by dangerous fumes or fluids as well as extremes of heat and cold."

"Why aren't some of them linked together? I'd think that would help them cope with an emergency situation."

"Even unlinked, our individuals have sufficient instinct and knowledge to perform such a rescue mission. And they often link with those who are injured, to prevent them from becoming disoriented and to aid them in leaving the damaged craft."

The Buruden rescuers were bringing out some of the injured. Many of them were linked to a line of other Buruden they were guiding outside to stand with the others who had made it out on their own.

The Buruden ambassador continued: "The rescuers' priorities are simple, of course — rescue those who are relatively uninjured, then those whose injuries are severe but can be repaired, then those unlikely to survive, then gather the remains of those who have died."

Galt told the Buruden, "Our priorities as Humans would be somewhat different. We'd go after the most severely injured first, hoping we could save them. Many times someone who appears unlikely to survive can make it after all if that person gets medical treatment in time."

"A momentary link with a distressed Buruden tells a rescuer all that is needed about an individual's chances for survival."

"As you told us," Chanda said, "you're not overly sentimental about individuals."

"No more than you would be of the skin you're utterly unaware of shedding constantly, or of a lock of hair that someone might clip from your body. A truth."

Chanda had to admit the Buruden were quite efficient in their rescue procedures — it appeared all the uninjured Buruden were standing around, unlinked, well away from the crippled starcraft. Those who appeared to be severely injured were being carried, bodily, by groups of linked Buruden rather than on gurneys. They were loaded into waiting ambulances, which were large enough that each one could carry up to a dozen Buruden.

The body recovery vehicles moved in next. As much as Chanda didn't want to, she made herself watch as the Buruden dead were removed. *Unsentimental indeed,* Chanda thought as the Buruden emergency workers carried about two dozen bodies from the wreckage. Some were missing limbs or had been severely burned. Once the recovery vehicles were filled, they started off at the usual breakneck pace and headed toward the city, no doubt to arrive within minutes at the reclamation facility she and Govanek had visited.

The Buruden ambassador said, "Now investigators will examine the inside of the ship for more evidence. But transmissions made at the time of the attack clearly stated that the Sobrenians had attacked this ship."

Chanda said, "My condolences over your losses. But quite honestly, my main concern has to be these negotiations. Do you think they're still worth pursuing?"

"You must speak to the Sobrenians about that. They did not seem to be in a talkative mood."

Chanda said, "A truth, if there ever was one."

CHAPTER 21

Chanda kept quiet the entire way back to the city; it was only when they reached their quarters and deactivated their lifesuits that Chanda said, "Pack up. Get ready to leave."

Irene and Akira whipped their heads around toward her. "What?" they asked simultaneously.

"You heard me. We're leaving, quick as we can."

Galt said, "We're just giving up?"

"We're using the advantage of surprise — getting the hell out of here before the Sobrenians do."

"You think they're about to head out, too?"

"Why would they stay here? They obviously have no intention of taking part in serious negotiations. They clearly know something's up with Govanek."

Irene said, "You're not just going to abandon her?"

"Tell me how to bring her along."

"I — well. . . ."

"Just what I thought." Seeing the hurt in Irene's expression, Chanda said, "Diplomacy's the art of the possible."

Galt spoke up. "That's not quite what Bismarck said — he said it's *politics* that's the art of the possible."

"A great fictional starship captain said it the other way once — and it suits my purposes better."

"Fine," Galt said. "Let's get packed."

"Irene," Chanda said, "I need your help."

Irene's sad-sack expression disappeared. "What can I do?"

"Pack up for me while I let Captain Hamadi know what's going on." She touched behind her ear. "Ambassador Kasmira to Captain Hamadi."

"Hamadi here. What can I do for you, Ambassador?"

"We'll be headed for the starport in just a few minutes. I hope you can expect us within the hour."

"Have negotiations gone that far south already?"

"I'd say about to the south pole."

"Understood. Should I put the ship on alert?"

Here's where it gets tricky, Chanda thought. She was in charge of the mission, but Hamadi commanded the *Jelal*, and she didn't have the authority to order him around. "If I were you, Captain, I wouldn't do anything that sensors would pick up."

"Understood," Hamadi said. "I'll keep shields down. Won't arm anything or perform any kind of active sensor sweeps. But I'll get everybody to stations, just in case. And put a shuttle on standby."

"Well done, Captain. See you soon. Ambassador Kasmira out."

"Ambassador?" Galt's voice was tentative, as if he didn't want to interrupt her thoughts.

She turned toward him, saw that he and Irene and Akira had gathered all their bags, Irene holding both her own and Chanda's, Galt also carrying the backpack containing the emergency medical supplies and other equipment. "I guess we're ready to go," she said.

Galt showed a crooked grin. "We barely got to know the place, once it was made to our liking."

"Here's the tough part. How do we call for our ride? They've always approached us." Chanda activated her datalink. "Ambassador Kasmira to the Buruden ambassador."

No response.

Irene said, "They might not even have the Buruden ambassador formed right now."

"That's true. Ambassador Kasmira to any Buruden representative. Well . . . still nothing."

"So what do we do now?" Akira asked.

"We're not going to just sit here, I'm damned sure of that," Chanda said. She went to Irene and took her bag from her. "Lifesuits on. We'll hoof it if we have to."

Galt didn't try to hide his amazement. "*Walk* all the way to that starport?"

"It's about 10K, if my perceptions are correct. Not all *that* far, even walking in over two gravs. But give me a better idea. The Buruden wouldn't agree to let us operate the shuttle remotely, remember."

Galt looked as frustrated as Irene had looked hurt earlier. "Dammit, Ambassador, you know I don't have a better idea."

"Then let's go. Besides, maybe we can hitch a ride with someone. I'll bet something happens along the way."

"That's just what I'm worried about," Galt said. "What that 'something' might be. But don't worry. I may have a couple tricks up my sleeve."

"What the hell does that mean?"

"Like you said — maybe something will happen along the way. If it does, we'll see what I come up with."

"For now, we'll just let that comment stand," Chanda said. "Let's get going."

Lifesuits on, Chanda led the others through the airlock. She ducked her head as she entered the large, dimly lit room beyond. Galt asked, "Do you think the outer doorway will open for us?"

"If it doesn't," Chanda said, "I guess we go back and just sit after all."

As they drew closer to the unseen exit, however, it outlined its wide oval shape in the sheer wall ahead of them, then irised open. "Thank goodness," Irene said.

As they made their way out onto the adjoining street, Chanda paused a moment to survey the scene. It was just as they'd seen it the previous times they'd come this way, though those views had been from a vehicle. Buruden cars rushed past at over 100 kph, on lanes three across in each direction. On the sidewalks, groups of Buruden, both linked and unlinked, passed by.

"No one seems to be paying us any attention," Chanda said.

Galt said, "That's because no one's told them to."

Chanda looked down the street in the direction of the starport. "All right. Sooner begun, sooner done." They began to trudge down the sidewalk, careful to keep an eye out for groups of Buruden, though they seemed perfectly capable of dodging the Humans in their midst, even traveling at their usual breakneck speed.

Chanda worked to keep up a healthy pace, grateful that her lifesuit helped her body adapt to the constant exertion in the unaccustomed 2.3 grav as it kept air circulating close to her body, provided her a sip of cool water from her helmet tube whenever she wanted, and at a touch of a control, helped support her legs as they grew ever more weary.

Just stop thinking about it, Chanda told herself. *It's not that bad, just a bit uncomfortable.*

Irene said, "How long do you think it'll take to get there?"

Chanda could hear her strained breathing and the doubt in her voice. "It should just be a couple of hours if we estimated the distance properly," she said. She clapped Irene on the shoulder. "I have faith in you. You'll make it."

Irene's relieved look told Chanda she'd said the right thing.

Galt said, "The exertion isn't that bad. It's just a different kind than you're used to."

Chanda said, "And I'll be damned if I'm heading back to cower in our quarters. Forward, always forward." She bore down then, trying to make her steps a little longer, trying to keep up her pace, as an example for the others, if nothing else. *Eyes straight ahead*, she thought. *Focus on the goal.*

She couldn't believe what that gaze straight ahead showed her. "Goddam," she muttered. "Look at that."

About the equivalent of a city block ahead of them strode Sedra, Tiernan, Govanek, and the Garotethan, all of them in their space-suits, also apparently headed toward the starport.

Galt said, "Can you believe that shit?"

Chanda found herself grinning. "I like seeing them walking along as pitiful as we are."

"Except for Govanek," Irene said.

"Yeah. Except for Govanek. Let's hold up a minute." She activated her datalink through her wrist control again. "Ambassador Kasmira to Captain Hamadi."

"Hamadi here."

"I want that shuttle now. It seems the Sobrenians started taking a walk before we did."

"I was just about to contact you — the Sobrenians just launched a shuttle of their own. I'll get the *Dubois* on its way. Of course, that'll light us up in the Sobrenian ship's sensors, too."

"I understand. If they start any mischief, I know you'll do what's best for your ship." *Including leaving us stranded down here if staying becomes too big a risk*, Chanda thought. "Thanks, Captain. Ambassador Kasmira out."

Galt asked, "So now what do we do? Just pace them or try to catch up with them?"

It was Akira who spoke up next - a surprise for Chanda: "Ambassador, if I may — I'd say we catch up to them and take Govanek away from them."

"A fine plan," Chanda said. "Except I don't think it'll be that easy."

Galt said, "Let's at least do the catching up part — I'd hate to be a block behind them only to watch their shuttle take off with Govanek on board."

"You realize that if we steal Govanek from them — "

" — Not steal," Irene said. "We're offering asylum."

"However the Sobrenians perceive it, this means any negotiations are finished."

Galt said, "Do you have any doubt they're finished anyway?"

"I suppose not. Just wanted to make sure."

Galt passed Chanda. "Let's get going, then."

Damn, Chanda thought. *As much as I like the Buruden, I'll be glad when we can lift off this planet.* She quickened her own pace, and soon she could tell they were gaining, little by little, on the Sobrenians. All this time, of course, Buruden pedestrians rushed past in either direction as if they didn't see them, and on the main roadways Buruden vehicles flashed past at their typical speeds of 100-plus K. *That makes every footstep I take seem that much more leaden,* Chanda thought.

Irene said, "I can't believe they haven't looked back and seen us yet."

"And you know they haven't," Chanda said, "or Tiernan would've convinced Sedna to call a halt just so he'd have another chance to throw insults at us."

"One more good insult," Galt said, "and I'm tempted to punch him in the nose . . . sorry, *snout*."

"They're about to go out of sight around that one corner up ahead — oh, look — Govanek looked back and saw us."

Irene asked, "It doesn't look like she said anything to Sedra or Tiernan."

"She's not very good at hiding her reactions, though," Chanda said. "Let's try to catch up — I don't like having them out of our sight."

When Chanda and the others got to the corner, Chanda raised a hand for the others to halt and peered around the curved wall of the building on the corner. "They're still going," Chanda said, "but we're catching up to them."

"I don't think I can go any faster," Irene said. "Even stopping to rest doesn't do any good in this grav."

"I agree," Chanda said, "even though the Sobrenians have to be suffering worse than we are — the grav's about three times what they're used to."

"Except for Tiernan," Galt said.

"But who knows what his new Sobrenian body can take. Let's keep going. We'll see just how close we can get to them."

"Are we really going to try to snatch Govanek from them?"

"We *have* to," Irene said.

Akira interjected before Chanda could reply, "We *don't* have to. I know you call me a 'hot-dogging' pilot, but I know what I'm doing when I'm flying, and I don't take unnecessary risks. We're kinda at a disadvantage down here — twice our normal weight, no weapons, dealing with hostile Sobrenians and . . . whatever Tiernan is."

Chanda said, "I have to say, Akira, I'm impressed. That's as long a speech as I've heard you give."

"Please don't think I'm scared."

Galt, his voice strained with the exertion of their 2.3 grav trek, said, "Please don't think you have to be ashamed if you are."

"If I am, it's for all of you, not myself."

"Listen," Chanda said, "let's not worry about who's scared and who's not. The question is whether it's worth taking the risk to let Govanek defect."

Galt said, "I think if she asks to, we have a moral duty to help her."

"I agree," Chanda said between puffing breaths, "but only so far. Akira has a point. I don't mind risking myself for that goal, but I need to know the rest of you think it's worthwhile."

Irene said, "You already know what I think."

"I'm ready, too," Galt said. "I just *like* her, I want to see her have a better life. Though I have to admit, I'm probably just as motivated by the idea of rubbing this in Tiernan's face."

Chanda looked at Akira. "What do you think?"

Akira said, "I think if we're all this determined, then it's not as much of a risk as I feared."

"Then here we go," Chanda said, and pushed forward that much harder.

CHAPTER 22

Chanda wasn't paying any attention to the Buruden, whether in groups or as individuals, who passed them by, didn't concern herself with the Buruden vehicles that sailed by them at 100 K or faster, couldn't think about the *Sergeant Jelal* shuttle *Dubois* that wouldn't come clear of the usual cloud cover for another twenty minutes or so.

She focused only on those three Sobrenians ahead of her. *And I'm surely thinking of Tiernan as being as much a Sobrenian as Sedra or Govanek,* she thought. *He's gone all the way over now, both physically and in terms of the prevailing attitude of Sobrenians toward Humanity.*

Yet we're hoping to claim Govanek as one of our own. Is that what we're doing here? An eye for an eye? Trading Tiernan for Govanek?

If so, who cares?

Galt said, "Govanek's looking back at us."

"I know," Chanda said. "She's going to — there it is! Sedra and Tiernan see us."

"Keep going?" Irene asked.

"*Hell,* yes."

Govanek was shameless about looking back now — after about the third time she did, Tiernan rewarded her with a cuff to the back of the head.

"Dammit," Chanda said, as she tried to push herself even harder. "I was afraid of this."

Irene asked, "That they'd abuse Govanek right in front of us, just to provoke us?"

"That's right," Galt said. "Which means we have to be careful — set our feelings about Govanek aside."

Chanda said, "The hell with that. I consider my feelings about Govanek a motivator to kick their asses."

"If we're going to do some ass-kicking, we need some tools." Galt handed his backpack to Irene. "Hold that a moment, as we walk, please," Galt said. He asked Chanda, "Walk in front of me so the Sobrenians can't make out what I'm doing."

Galt rummaged around in the pack as the others looked on. Galt pulled out a hand scanner, the energies of his lifesuit wrapping around it when he touched it. Galt broke the device into three pieces in a way a scanner wouldn't normally come apart. He swiped a finger across each piece and they changed shape and became a short cylinder, a handgrip, and a trigger mechanism. Galt quickly clicked them together.

Chanda didn't know whether to be impressed or appalled. "A stunner pistol? How'd you get that through scans?"

"It's smart tech, but not that smart — flies under the radar, you might say."

"But the power source —"

"Is a metal strip along the back of my helmet. Akira, would you do the honors? It peels right off."

Akira reached toward the back of Galt's helmet, peeled off the metal strip, and handed it to Galt.

"Thanks," Galt said, and folded the strip a couple of times and slid it into a thin slot on the side of the stunner. "It's been soaking up solar energy every time we've gone out, staying charged. It's only good for a burst or two, but it should be able to pierce their spacesuits." He stuck the weapon into his belt at the small of his back and retrieved the backpack from Irene. "Thanks," he told her.

Irene said, "It looks like you've got a few other surprises in there."

"Maybe. Keep in mind the Sobrenians may have surprises of their own."

Chanda said, "I know I can trust you to use that stunner judiciously. Let's catch up to them."

With a few more minutes of effort, Chanda and the other Humans came up to within a few meters of the Sobrenians. "The next time Govanek looks back," Chanda said, "I'm going to wave her back toward us."

Govanek looked back a couple of seconds later, and Chanda motioned for her to come to them. After only an instant's hesitation, Govanek turned and approached her Human friends.

Tiernan instantly turned and faced Chanda and the others. Sedra took only a couple more steps before halting and also turning toward them.

Chanda raised a hand and Galt, Irene, and Akira stopped alongside her as Govanek joined them.

Tiernan said, "You can have the traitor. We don't want her."

"I suppose you *would* be able to recognize a traitor," Chanda said.

Tiernan advanced toward them with a gait that Chanda recognized from his days as a Human, but which seemed incongruous duplicated by his shorter Sobrenian legs. "I'm loyal to the people who've nurtured me," he said. "I never found that among Humanity."

Suddenly Chanda had to know the answer to the question that had bothered her since Captain Hamadi had first informed her of the circumstances of Tiernan's arrival in the Sobrenian system. "How'd you kill the entire crew of the *James Rowland*? And more importantly, why?"

Tiernan halted right in front of Chanda. "The *Rowland* was on a diplomatic mission. You know all about those, don't you, Chanda? How effective they are?"

"Some more than others, it seems."

"Yet we insist upon these little performances, don't we? Meeting face-to-face, developing 'relationships,' learning to trust one another. That's what I did, starting the moment I arrived on Earth from Splendor. I spoke 'sincerely' about wanting to change my life, make amends for what I did on Splendor."

Galt asked, "And they believed you?"

"Thanks to some nanotech protocols that let me fool the inevitable truth scan. The Sobrenians are quite advanced with biotech." He took a step back and spread his arms to display his new Sobrenian form. "As you can see. Plus, I never 'broke' — not in public areas, not in quiet moments with individuals during more 'intimate' and 'honest' conversations — *never!*"

Sedra stood impassively, listening to the Human-turned-Sobrenian speak.

"So the *Rowland* crew was told you'd regained the Unity's trust — and they believed that."

"Not all of them, mind you, but enough."

Galt said, "And like the coward that you are, you stunned them in their sleep, then killed them."

"I was quite imaginative about it, actually," Tiernan said. "Even stunned, several fought for that last breath or made glorious sounds as my knife severed their windpipe. I felt . . . relieved. Yes, that's it — relieved of my Humanity."

Groups of Buruden continued passing them by in either direction, ignoring the argument among members of two other Galactic species.

Galt took a step forward and Chanda put out an arm to stop him. "They trusted you enough that you got to steal a stunner from their stores?"

"Not at all, Chanda. I was much cleverer than that. More Sobrenian tech — it was smart tech, you see, but only *so* smart."

At this unconscious parroting of Galt's words, Chanda's face felt as if it were burning. It took all of her conscious will not to turn toward Galt to accuse him of —

Of what? Chanda thought.

Tiernan continued: "The stunner appeared to be a common hand scanner, you see — "

Chanda thought, *And I bet you took it apart —*

" — and I split it apart into three pieces — "

— and it formed a stunner —

" — and I put them back together as a stunner — "

— and inserted a metal strip —

" — then I had several metal strips that were also tiny solar panels that powered the thing. Each one only had a tiny charge, but I had plenty."

And I'm just about ready to set Galt loose and tell him to put his stunner right against one of Tiernan's bulging Sobrenian eyes and fire when ready.

Tiernan continued: "The only other question you have, I suppose, is . . . ?"

"Why?"

"Why kill them? To establish my own credibility with my adopted world. Plus, I didn't *want* Humanity to have diplomatic relations with the Sobrenians. I was *ashamed* of Humanity."

Galt said, "Because we aren't all cowards like you, who kill decent women and men in their sleep?"

"Because the Sobrenians have their priorities straight. They know what's important. Just as I knew my desire to transform myself was more important than the lives of the *Rowland*'s crew."

"You son-of-a-bitch!" Galt muttered.

"You never knew my mother," Tiernan said, calmly. "But if we're going to trade insults, let's try this one — incompetent fool." Tiernan touched a control on the wrist of his spacesuit —

— and Govanek's spacesuit dissolved!

Govanek grasped her throat and slumped to the ground. A group of linked Buruden diverted around her.

Chanda fell upon Govanek — nearly getting the breath knocked out of her in two gravities — and embraced her, Chanda's lifesuit field expanding to envelop the Sobrenian.

Galt pulled the stunner from his belt, pointed it at Tiernan, and fired. Tiernan fell, unconscious.

Govanek, beneath Chanda, still gasped for air, and it was all Chanda could do to hold her down.

Chanda glimpsed a flash of motion — Sedra! She moved more rapidly than Chanda could've imagined, right toward Galt.

Galt pivoted toward Sedra —

— and wasn't fast enough. Sedra rushed *past* him and pushed Irene into the roadway where Buruden vehicles were racing past at 100 kph!

The many round Buruden vehicles swerved frantically, trying to avoid Irene as she fell onto the roadway.

Chanda's first instinct was to get up and rush toward Irene — *But if I do*, she thought, *Govanek will surely die.*

Sedra pivoted, touched a control on her spacesuit's wrist, and pointed at Galt.

His lifesuit faded, and he collapsed just as Govanek had.

Shit! Chanda thought, and started dragging Govanek toward Galt. *I don't know if my lifesuit can sustain all three of us*, she thought.

A quick glance — Irene wasn't getting up.

Chanda saw the Garotethan writhing on the ground, its spacesuit gone. Collateral damage from one of Sedra's murder attempts? Chanda knew she'd never reach it in time to save it.

Akira, without looking, dove into the street. Two of the Buruden vehicles collided, and Akira covered Irene's body with her own. Both cars missed them by mere centimeters.

Galt was crawling, also, but *away* from Chanda. "No," she said, "Stay right there!"

Beneath Chanda, Govanek began going into a seizure. She couldn't drag her any farther.

Galt made it to his backpack. With trembling hands, he opened it and pulled out what looked like some sort of web.

Sedra was leaning over Tiernan, who looked to be coming around.

Akira got up and pulled on Irene's arms to lift her off the roadway.

Galt sat up, pulled the web over his body and touched a control — it activated an energy field Chanda recognized as the same kind a lifesuit generated, one that extended all the way to the ground.

Another set of cars collided — and clipped both Akira and Irene. Their lifesuits hardened into armor at the first hint of impact, but their bodies went flying. The rest of the Buruden vehicles, though, managed to stop short. Traffic was blocked, no doubt a rarity on this world.

Neither Irene nor Akira was moving.

Galt pulled open a pouch attached to the side of the net and reached inside with a hand shaking so badly the contents of the pouch scattered all over the ground.

Sedra managed to get Tiernan to his feet and they started down the street again.

Several individual Buruden stopped beside them, regarded them with two or three eyes at a time, then linked together and approached Chanda.

Movement overhead caught Chanda's eye. *Could it be the* Dubois? Chanda wondered. *No — not this quickly. The laws of physics don't change for our convenience.*

Govanek's seizures began to subside. *Whether she's over them or dying, I don't know,* Chanda thought. She pulled Govanek close to Galt, who was fumbling with a packet of pills. She wished she had a way to help him.

Chanda aimed her left fist at the still forms of Irene and Akira and touched the sensor controls on the top of her arm. *Damn. Irene has a concussion and internal bleeding, and a possible severe neck injury. Akira has a broken arm and leg, and a collapsed lung. Both unconscious. Their lifesuits' biotech is doing as much as it can —*

— But that's only so much. I've got to get them out of here, and Govanek, too. At least Govanek appeared to be breathing somewhat normally. Chanda had no idea how this atmosphere and pressure affected Sobrenians, or whether Human doctors back on the *Jelal* would be able to help her. But she was still stuck here keeping her lifesuit field around him.

Akira stirred, groaning. "Just lie right there," Chanda told her. "We'll get help to you quick as we can." *Though I don't know just how quickly that'll be,* Chanda thought. Akira let herself collapse onto the roadway again.

The linked Buruden said, "Negotiations appear to have taken a new turn. A truth?"

Chanda stared dumbfounded. "You're the ambassador?"

"This is the only place on our world diplomats are required, after all. It was a simple task to find examples of the individuals necessary to form me."

Chanda saw Galt finally managing to open the pill packet. He swallowed a single pill.

First things first. Chanda indicated the injured Humans to the Buruden. "You have to help them."

"We can do better than that. We give permission for your shuttle to land here within our city, so that Humans may treat them."

"The other shuttle approaching —"

"Is Sobrenian. It has no such permission. But we choose not to enforce our restriction. The sooner the Sobrenians leave, the better."

Chanda touched behind her ear as she watched the Sobrenian ship's dark water drop shape descend toward the broad sidewalk. "Ambassador Kasmira to the *Dubois*."

A woman's voice came over Chanda's datalink: "*Dubois* here — Lt. Leyla Mura."

"Lieutenant — the Buruden have given you permission to land at my 'twenty.' Watch out for a Sobrenian ship that may be rising from this same location."

"We spotted it, Ambassador. ETA five minutes."

"Ambassador Kasmira out." She turned to Galt. "How are you doing?"

Galt sat with one hand on his chest and the other against the sidewalk. "Better. The pill — "

"Don't try to talk. I know. It took on the effects of the atmosphere and pressure."

Sedra and an obviously weak Tiernan boarded the Sobrenian shuttle. They didn't spare even a backwards glance for the Garotethan they'd left behind. Their shuttle closed up its entrance and lifted.

Galt indicated Irene and Akira with a tilt of his head. "How . . . they doing?"

"They're both out of it. Plenty of internal injuries and broken bones. The *Dubois* will be here in a minute. You're sure you're better."

"Better. Not good. Glad we're not . . . walking the rest of the way."

"I sort of understand how Tiernan could sabotage Govanek's spacesuit. But how the hell did Sedra make your lifesuit go away?"

"Don't know . . . gotta . . . find out."

Now it was the *Dubois'* turn to glide in for a landing. As it settled onto the sidewalk, the Buruden ambassador said, "We will take your injured Humans to your shuttle. We can do so without harming them."

"Thank you," Chanda said. The linked Buruden rushed off, split into two groups, and surrounded Irene and Akira, lifting them effortlessly and taking them toward the shuttle even as three Humans in lifesuits were exiting.

"It's all right," Chanda told them. "They'll get them aboard safely." One of the Humans, a woman, followed the Buruden back through the shuttle's airlock, while the other two, a man and another woman, approached Chanda and Galt carrying a web similar to Galt's. "I'm

Jira Beshada," the woman said, "and this is Ben Farrington. We're both Assistant Medical Officers from the *Jelal*." Jira threw the web over Chanda and Govanek. "Let's get you out of here, too."

Galt, still encased in his own web, tried to stand, then thought better of it. "Think I need some help."

Jira reached down and pulled Galt to his feet, then gave him a shoulder to lean on. Ben picked up Govanek, keeping the web wrapped around her. *Thank goodness for that*, Chanda thought. *It's enough for me to drag my own ass toward the shuttle in this gravity.*

In fact, stepping through the *Dubois'* airlock and into a single grav was even more of a relief than Chanda imagined. Her first step through the inner lock was tentative, and at the second one her head began to swim. Ben grabbed her arm and started to guide her to a seat. "No, no," she protested, "I've got to see how Irene and Akira and Galt are doing."

"They're in back, Ambassador," Ben said. "The best thing you can do for them right now is let us work on them."

Chanda sank into her seat. The *Dubois* lifted and, looking down on the scene below, Chanda saw that the usual traffic pattern on the roadway was returning to normal — damaged vehicles were being pushed to one side, allowing the normal 100 kph+ flow to be restored. *For all I know*, Chanda thought, *that was the first traffic jam the Buruden have ever experienced.*

She could also see the linked Buruden who had formed the ambassador unlinking and going on their separate ways. *Damn*, she thought, *and I left without saying a farewell or a how-do-ya-do to them.*

Just as well, I suppose. They're not sentimental.

CHAPTER 23

Chanda fidgeted as she sat on an exam table aboard the *Sergeant Jelal* and let Ben Farrington poke and prod at her. "I'm really OK, you know," she said. "The others are the ones in bad shape."

Ben pulled out a hand scanner and ran it over her body. "I've certainly heard that plenty of times before. Mostly from starcraft captains and ambassadors — people who won't let me steer the ship or negotiate a treaty."

Chanda let out a deep breath. "I don't know about steering the ship — but about now I'd let you go after the treaty."

Ben finished his scan. "Sobrenians are tough, huh?"

"The Buruden are about as bad — and I *like* them." She leaned over to try to catch a look at the scanner's readout. "What's it look like?"

Ben glared at her in mock exasperation and turned the scanner away from her. "Well, for an ambassador, you know what you're talking about. Other than a bit of overexertion and stress, you're fine."

"Hmm. Maybe I should ask to steer the ship next."

"Don't overestimate yourself." He pointed a stern finger at her. "You wanna know my prescription?"

"Do doctors still give prescriptions?"

"Only behavioral ones. Get some rest."

"Easier said than done."

Ben said, "So rest isn't a good option for you."

"I have four friends in there — well, two good friends, one sort of friend, and someone I respect professionally — and I have to make sure they're all right."

"Akira was bitching at me and Jira awhile before you got in here. Not anything for herself, but concerned we weren't doing enough for Irene." A satisfied smile. "I can tell she really loves her."

"Really?" Chanda said. "I thought it was supposed to be pretty casual."

Ben held up his hands in a not-going-there gesture. "I just know what I hear. But if I take you in there — afterward, you'll get that rest?"

"I'll be sure to."

Ben held out his hand. "We'll shake on it."

Chanda shook. "See? You negotiated a treaty after all."

"Which still means no one's steering the ship. Com'on, let's get you in to see your friends and sorta-friend and respected professional."

Chanda followed Ben into the next room and was struck by the sight of Irene and Akira lying in adjacent beds — Akira sitting up on the side of hers, legs dangling, staring with a deeply worried look at Irene. Jira Beshada was checking out the string of sensor readouts over Akira's bed, which varied little from normal readings — those over Irene's bed were all over the place. From what little Chanda could tell from those readings, Irene was still in bad shape.

Akira looked up at Chanda and held her arms out. Chanda

walked into that embrace, holding onto Akira for a long, silent moment.

When they broke the hug, Chanda asked, "First of all, how are *you*?"

Akira rubbed her right arm with her left hand. "Mine was pretty easy. Mend the arm and the leg, inflate the lung, and I'm good to go. But I'll be moving at half-speed for awhile."

Chanda touched the edge of Irene's bed. "But she had a bad concussion and a neck injury."

Akira said, "Docs say she'll make it, though."

Chanda turned to Ben and Jira. "What about it, docs?"

"She *should*," Jira said. "It's delicate stuff, though, even for our most advanced nanomeds."

"Damn."

"The best thing we can do for her now," Jira said, "is be quiet and let those little guys work their charm."

Ben touched Chanda on the arm. "We're gonna go check out Senator Galt and Govanek. Chanda — don't stay long. You and Akira remember your prescriptions."

Despite herself, Chanda grinned. "I'll remember."

The docs left. Akira said, "They're doing a good job — but I didn't realize that at first. I let myself go a little crazy."

"I heard about that. Ben — Dr. Farrington — said he could tell you really love Irene."

"Yeah. I guess I do. I only wish . . . " Akira pulled her legs onto the bed and tucked them under the covers.

Chanda sat next to her. "Wish . . . what?"

Akira looked toward Irene. "You really have no idea, do you?"

"About what?"

"Irene."

"What about her? I couldn't ask for more from her — she does a great job, I couldn't ask for anyone to be more loyal."

"It's more than just loyalty, Chanda. She's in love with you."

"With — but I thought -- you and she. . . . "

"We *are* involved. And it's great. But you're the one she loved first, the one who got away. I'm a fun time, but you're the one she wants to take home to meet Momma."

"But she knows I'm not attracted to women."

"Exactly. She can never have you and she knows it. That makes it all the more frustrating for her."

"I don't know what to say."

Akira said, "You shouldn't say anything. She'd be mortified to know you found out." Akira looked toward the floor. "Maybe I shouldn't have told you."

"No, I'm glad you did. I just wish I could do something for her."

"I'm ashamed to tell you — when we thought you were going into the cold sleep forever . . . "

"You'd be around to comfort her. You'd be rid of the competition."

"I don't actually think of it that way. But if that was how it was going to work out . . . "

Chanda put an arm around Akira's shoulders. "Sorry I made things inconvenient."

Akira covered her mouth to hide sudden laughter. "It's better having you back, Chanda." She indicated Irene, whose eyes were still closed, and whose breathing was shallow. "If either one of us were believers," Akira said, "we could pray."

"Either way," Chanda told her, "we can still hope."

"One thing we can hope for is to find a way to stop the Sobrenians from attacking Splendor. I know a lot of my motivation is what they did to Irene, but that world is more important than her, or me, or any of us. Saving Splendor will be the best revenge against them."

"My recommendation to the Unity will be to align ourselves with the Buruden against the Sobrenians."

Akira showed Chanda a humorless grin. "Guess it's hard to continue negotiations with people who tried to kill you."

"Yeah." She embraced Akira again. "That one's for Irene. Let me know the instant you know something new, no matter the time."

As Chanda approached Govanek's bed, she was gratified to see that the Sobrenian was sitting up and actually looking chipper — at least as much as she could tell about a species that had few facial muscles and only limited expression. "Ambassador Kasmira!" she exclaimed. "I'm so glad to see you."

"I'm glad you're looking well. I think our doctors were concerned about having the expertise to treat you properly."

"They have done an excellent job. But I understand Irene is not faring as well."

"She has a bit of a rough road ahead."

"I hope for the best for her. She was quite brave."

Chanda sat on an unoccupied bed next to Govanek's. "So were you — to commit yourself to coming with us. You didn't hesitate."

"I . . . could no longer align myself with Sedra or Tiernan or any of their type. And I fear they have become dominant in our government."

"You were always different, weren't you? Even being an explorer is unusual for your species."

"I was foolish. I thought my position with the diplomatic team was because I had excelled during the Moruteb exploratory mission. I had made some scientific discoveries, landing on an icy world called Risula. I confronted a Cetronen captain about his condescending attitudes toward my people. These things became well-known. So Tiernan requested me. Where some of our superiors distrusted me because of my ties to other species, he saw an opportunity."

"Get close to the Humans — ingratiate yourself among us."

"Learn as much as I could about you — then betray you."

"But you couldn't do it."

"I swear to you, Ambassador Kasmira, my approaching you and the other Humans was sincere."

"I believe you. But we're going to ask for your help, now.

Anything you can tell us about possible Sobrenian tactics, or their goals in attacking Splendor, would be helpful."

"Unfortunately," Govanek said, "I'm not trained in military matters. And it's become clear I don't understand them very well."

Chanda said, "But you know the players involved — Sedra and Tiernan in particular. What is it they want?"

"They want to use Splendor as a base of operations, most likely to launch an attack against the planet the Buruden are inhabiting."

"Are they interested in Splendor's population? Would they want to enslave the valley dwellers or highlanders?"

"I would say not. While the Splendorians are fine people, neither species is technically advanced — there's little they could do to serve Sobrenians without extensive training."

Chanda asked, "But would they leave the Splendorian population alone?"

"If that population did not bother them, I believe so. But you've seen how welcoming the valley dwellers and highlanders have been toward Humanity. I suspect they would be less so toward Sobrenians, especially given what would certainly be a heavy-handed presence."

"I fear you're right," Chanda said. "I'm imagining how my highlander friend Indirogar would react if part of his tribe's property was taken for a Sobrenian base."

Govanek said, "I can tell you that Sedra and Tiernan would not hesitate to take revenge upon an entire village for one person's transgression."

"I believe that."

"They could not hide their true intentions. Once I understood that — I had to leave them."

"And your own people," Chanda said. "You may never be able to go home."

Govanek didn't say anything for a moment, and Chanda saw that she was trying to work up the nerve to say her next words. Finally, she said, "Tiernan often taunted me about how I passed the *koraht*.

Sedra, and before her, Nysar, often joined in at such times, which they found quiet amusing."

"What happened?"

"I am not an efficient fighter, whether of adronos or anything else. The moment I saw one, my second day in the wilderness, I ran. Another student, a friend of mine, saw me and took pity on me. He traveled with me the rest of the way, even though that is forbidden. He . . . roughed me up some and told me I should say an adrono had attacked me. I was ashamed, but I did it."

"So he made everything look good?"

"Except that word got around about that 'favor.' It seems yet another student saw my friend striking me to simulate the adrono attack."

"So you never quite fit in."

"Not the way I did with Humanity during the Moruteb mission. Not the way I feel I do sitting right here."

Chanda stood and touched Govanek's shoulder. "I'm glad you feel that way."

"Please understand me, Ambassador — I don't consider myself a traitor. I think Sedra and Nysar are the ones who should be considered traitors. They even tried to kill me — someone who considered herself a loyal Sobrenian."

"I'm glad they didn't succeed."

"My loyalty now is to Humanity. But I won't do anything to harm my homeworld. I still love it. I still love my people."

"I wouldn't expect anything else. I'm grateful for whatever you can do. Whatever happens between Splendor and your people, we're going to need your help."

———

Chanda headed to the next room down to see Galt, who was sitting up as Ben was finishing a detailed scan. "How you doing?" she asked.

Galt started to speak, but had to stop and clear his throat first.

"Better than I'd feared," he said. "Nitrogen narcosis and acute carbon dioxide acidosis are a bitch."

Ben placed a hand on Galt's shoulder and said, "Those nanites you swallowed did the job, though. Another day, and you won't even know anything had happened to you."

Galt raised his eyebrows at Ben. "Oh, I'll know. That's a memory you might say is seared into my brain."

Ben looked at Chanda. "Starcraft piloting lessons later?"

"Can't make it," Chanda said. "Doctor's orders."

Ben favored Chanda with another wide smile as he left. Chanda felt her eyebrows raise at that, but turned her attention toward Galt.

The senator indicated the doorway to the next room. "How's everyone else?"

Chanda sat down on the bed next to Galt. "Irene's in bad shape, but she's expected to pull through. Akira says she's at about half-speed, but knowing her, she could still probably outrun or outfight about anyone on the ship. Govanek seems about as well off as anybody."

"And yourself?"

"Mostly just tired. But that's a professional hazard."

Galt looked toward the floor. "I'm sorry about the stunner, Ambassador. I saw how you looked at me when you heard Tiernan explain how his weapon worked. But where do you think he got the idea for the gun? Remember, at one time he was a trusted Unity Marine. I never told you about my stunner because I was afraid that if you knew about it — "

"That I'd make you give it up. Maybe you don't know me as well as you think. But you were probably right not to say anything. Being unarmed generally makes me more tactful — a good quality in a diplomat."

"And I can figure out that Tiernan had a protocol set in Govanek's spacesuit ahead of time — that's how he made it disappear. But what the *hell* did Sedra do to mine?"

"I'm going to ask you to try to figure that out as we head back to Splendor."

"And when we get there — what happens then?"

"I wish I had the faintest idea. A lot of it depends on the Sobrenians' next move. Certainly we're done with negotiations. I want to get the Buruden involved in some kind of defense for the planet."

"I don't envy you that, Ambassador . . . Chanda. You might wish you'd taken the cold sleep after all."

"No. None of that. No more sleeping — except for the next few hours."

"Ah, yes," Galt said. "You got the prescription, too." He lowered his voice and leaned toward her. "If you ask me, a better prescription would be to get to know that Dr. Farrington — Ben -- a little better."

Chanda was taken aback. "Really? The Sobrenians could attack at any time, the evacuation project is in shambles, and you think I should be looking for a *date?*"

"I'm not saying you should marry him, Chanda, or even go to bed with him. But he's obviously interested in you, and I think it would be good for you if you had someone to talk to just as . . . a regular person, and not an ambassador."

"Or an enemy to be crushed and humiliated."

"There's that, yes. I've had no reason to mention this to you, but I send a message every night to be delivered through subspace channels to Earth."

"Your grandchildren?"

"You bet. The kids — Sadie's six and Dinah's eight — love getting the messages, but aren't great about sending many back. I don't care — I talk to them, I ramble for its own sake. My daughter claims I've forgotten she exists. She doesn't say it seriously. I think. The important part is that I have this connection to people. So talk to this Ben guy."

"Well, I'll think about it," Chanda said.

"Excuse me," came a voice from behind them, one which Chanda recognized — and she felt herself blushing, of all things!

It was that "Ben guy." *Did he hear anything Galt and I were saying?* she wondered. "Yes, uh . . . Doctor Farrington."

The doctor said, "Captain Hamadi just received a priority message for the two of you from the Unity in Brussels. I can have it sent down here."

"That's fine," Chanda said. "Please do so." *When did I start speaking so formally?* she thought.

"It's audio only," Ben said as he punched commands into a comm unit on the wall. "Just ask the comp to play it whenever you like. I'll give the two of you some privacy."

When Ben was gone, Chanda said, "Computer, play most recent message from the Earth Unity."

The recorded message began: "This is Earth Unity President Liam Marsden. Given the outcome of recent events on the Sobrenian homeworld and, especially on the current Buruden homeworld, I feel we must make a change in leadership."

Uh, oh, Chanda thought. *Here it comes.*

The message continued: "Earth Unity Ambassador to Splendor Chanda Kasmira, I am relieving you of your duties effective immediately. I honor the work you have done over the past several years on Splendor. But recent events tell me we need a fresh start, and fresh ideas. I also believe we need someone with military experience, which Senator Galt has."

Chanda caught a glimpse of Galt looking at her, and was surprised at the sympathy she saw on his face. He shook his head slowly. Almost in a whisper, he said, "That's not fair."

Chanda listened to the rest of the message: "Given the current circumstances, we cannot allow this position to remain vacant. Given his recent experience dealing with the Buruden, along with his past military service, I name Earth Unity Senator Gabriel Galt the Interim Ambassador to Splendor. Senator Galt, please acknowledge your receipt of this message and your acceptance of the position immediately upon receiving it. Good luck. Message ends."

Chanda folded her hands in her lap. Her eyes stared without

seeing. She was aware that Galt was saying something, but her mind couldn't latch onto the words. She felt powerless, as if President Marsden's message had sapped her of energy, left her without a clear path to take next.

Galt spoke again. "Chanda?"

She reacted to Galt only slowly, turning her head toward him with no intention of speaking.

Galt said, "Ambassador?"

"You don't call me that anymore. I call you that."

"Sorry. That habit's going to be tough to break. I didn't know this was going to happen. But you probably don't know how much of a political football Splendor has become back on Earth. It's considered a waste of resources by a lot of people."

"We're saving three intelligent species!"

"I'm not agreeing with them, Chanda, just telling you what the president is dealing with. And people are concerned about the Sobrenians, as well — a violent species that could one day have designs on Earth."

"All the more reason to stop them cold right here at Splendor."

"I understand that, Amb . . . Chanda. But that's a tall order. Believe me, I had no ambitions toward this job."

"I know. You wanted to get back to your grandchildren." Chanda felt she could barely perceive herself speaking; it was as if her own words approached her ears from far away.

"It pisses me off, actually," Galt said. "I know we didn't start off on the right foot when I first came here, but I hope you know I've come to respect you and to respect how difficult this job is — maybe impossible."

"The president made it pretty clear what he wanted."

"I know. Politicians know exactly what they're doing when they appeal to your sense of military duty. But you notice he didn't say anything about what might be next for you."

Chanda started to focus. When she looked at Galt this time, she perceived every line on his face, every bit of determination written there, how he looked at her with utter sincerity as he said his next words. "You're right," Chanda said. "He didn't recall me to Earth."

"And the president's known for his precise use of language. Perhaps politics —"

" — The art of the possible, as you pointed out —"

"That's right. Politics might have made him replace you, but he didn't get rid of you. He knows how much I'll need your help."

Chanda considered that. *If that's the only way I can stay here and have a chance of helping Splendor survive . . . that's a small price. I never cared about the title anyway, only about the work.*

Chanda said, "I'll give you whatever help you need."

CHAPTER 24

D ays later, as the *Sergeant Jelal* fell into orbit around Splendor, Chanda made sure to be on the bridge standing next to Captain Hamadi. She knew the best view of the planet would be on the large viewscreen there. *I want to get a good look at it in a moment of calm before getting back to work. Whatever my work will be, now.*

Splendor was a world mostly of white and blue, with swaths of green concentrated around the equator in dense forests. Most of the rest of Splendor's land area was cold, dry, and windy.

Evolution worked slowly on Splendor — with relatively little land area compared to Earth, weathering happened slowly, less fertilizer fed the life in the oceans, and few plants provided oxygen to fuel the metabolisms of the planet's animal life.

In fact, Splendor had fewer examples of all types of life — plants, animals, insects.

Yet not just one or two, but three sentient species developed here — valley dwellers, highlanders, and sweepers. How did that happen?

I hope this world survives long enough for us to discover more of its mysteries.

Captain Hamadi said, "It's a beautiful world, uh . . . how do I address you now?"

"'Chanda' is just fine. Ambassador Galt referred to me as a free-wheeling diplomat-at-large."

"'Chanda' it is, then.

"So much of the planet has been familiar to me for so long — look down there — " Chanda pointed out a narrow water channel between two major continents. It was filled with countless icebergs and ice floes. "That's the Strait of Ancestors, near Dijirar's village — " Chanda indicated a cloud-topped mountain next to a vast glacier that had flowed downward from it centuries ago. "Just to the east, that's Skyreach Mountain." Her hand indicated a broad mountain range to the north. "Those are the Heavenlock Mountains."

"And it's even farther north of there, isn't it, that the archeologists are working?"

"Sure is. They think they might have found the remains of a *fourth* intelligent Splendorian species. Or maybe an ancestor to one we already know about."

Captain Hamadi said, "I've been to a few other worlds in my day. To me, this seems the most wondrous."

"I can agree with that. But it may also be the most frustrating." Chanda made herself turn away from the planet's beauty. "Speaking of which, I've got to get to work back down on Splendor pretty soon — doing whatever my new job entails."

"Perhaps we'll see each other again soon. Ambassador Galt has called in some favors and I'll be keeping the *Jelal* here at Splendor for awhile."

"That's good to hear, especially since it looks like you'll be taking care of Irene for awhile." She shook Captain Hamadi's hand. "In fact, I'd better make sure to see her before I leave."

———

When Chanda arrived at Irene's room, Akira was there, as she expected, holding Irene's hand, leaning over and speaking to her. Chanda's heart fell when she saw how limp that hand was, how Irene didn't respond to Akira's words. *I hate to take her away from Irene,* Chanda thought. *But I'm going to need her down on the planet.*

Irene's eyes fluttered. Chanda heard Akira gasp. She barely had time to take another breath before both Ben and Jira rushed into the room. "We saw that spike in consciousness," Ben said. He felt Irene's pulse with his left hand and placed his right hand on her forehead while Jira took Akira's arm and guided her back a step, then checked Irene's sensor readouts.

"Things are looking much better," Jira said. "In fact, any minute now — "

Irene's eyelids slid slowly open and she said in the faintest of voices, "What . . . happened? Where am I?"

Akira leaned over to embrace Irene, but Jira grabbed her shoulders. "Keep it gentle for now," she told Akira.

"Absolutely no problem," Akira said, and grasped Irene's hand in both of her own this time. "It's so great having you back, sweetie!"

"Where'd I go?"

"I've just got a little time. Lemme explain it to you."

Chanda said, "I'll give the two of you some time together." As Chanda went out into the corridor, both Ben and Jira followed her. Chanda said, "So she'll be OK?"

"That was the turning point," Jira said. "I think she'll be fine." She gave Ben what looked to Chanda like a too-meaningful look, then said, "I'd better look in on Govanek. She's looking forward to going down to Splendor to work on that archeological site." She headed down the corridor.

That left Chanda and Ben standing next to one another. Ben didn't say anything for an instant, which led Chanda to say, "Thanks for everything you've done to help Irene." Her next thought: *Dammit, Chanda, you fell for the biggest conversational trap in the world — you can't stand the silence, so you speak first to fill the gap.*

Her next thought: *Why am I even thinking that way? This isn't a competition.*

At least, I don't think it is.

Ben said, "Those two — they're quite a couple."

"They have something special, all right — something hard for most of us to find."

Ben smiled confidently at Chanda. "You just have to keep open to the possibility."

"Tough to do on a starship assignment," Chanda said. "Or even a planetary one."

"Being tough to do just makes it all the more satisfying when it happens, don't you think?"

"Yeah. Well. I suppose I'd . . . best get my things ready to go down to the planet. Then, unfortunately, I've got to take Akira away from Irene."

"I know you'll let her get back up here as often as she can," Ben said. "Irene is better off resting awhile, anyway."

"Thanks again for . . . everything, Ben."

"You're certainly welcome. And, uh, Ambassador?"

"It's . . . just Chanda now."

"Chanda, then. I hope to see you again."

The moment Chanda smiled at Ben, she knew it felt forced, but hoped it didn't *look* forced. *I wish I could do better*, she thought. *But all my best thoughts are still focused upon that planet below us.* She made herself work some enthusiasm into her voice as she said, "I hope we'll see each other soon."

Chanda turned and left, wishing she could turn around and see what emotions Ben's face revealed, wishing she knew which emotions she wanted to see.

Chanda, Akira, Galt, and Govanek sat in the rear of the *Sergeant Jelal* shuttle *Rico* as it ferried them down toward Splendor. Akira told Chanda, "Irene and I got to talk about what the Unity's done to you, Chanda. We think it's completely unfair and you should protest." She nodded toward Galt. "No disrespect, uh . . . Ambassador Galt."

"None taken," Galt said. "I agree with you."

"As do I," Govanek said. "I've been as impressed with Chanda as I was with my friend Mike Christopher."

Great, Chanda thought. *The architect of the evacuation project. The one who got us all into this in the first place.*

That's not fair, though. I accepted the plan. I fought more than anyone to try to make it work.

Govanek continued: "I am also impressed with Senator and Ambassador Galt. I believe you will do what's best for Splendor."

Galt said, "I do the job I'm assigned."

"And he's exactly right to do that," Chanda said. "In fact, I think not being the ambassador might give me a little more freedom than I had before."

Galt feigned covering his ears with his hands. "Maybe I shouldn't hear this."

"Don't worry. I'm not going to try to take over the planet or start some sort of rebellion. But I will speak a little more freely and perhaps suggest some courses of action that politicians like some people — " She indicated Galt. " — might not be able to put forward."

Galt said, "Chanda, it isn't enough that I'm being kept away from my grandkids longer than I expected, and have the responsibility to save an entire planet. You have to insult me by calling me a politician."

"Sorry," Chanda said. "I didn't mean to — " She stopped cold when she looked at Akira and saw the tears running down her face. Chanda leaned over and embraced her. "I know. Don't worry. Irene's going to be fine."

"I know that," Akira said. "I just . . . miss her already."

Chanda cupped Akira's face in her hand. "We'll get you back up there soon as we can."

Akira said, "Whatever we can do to keep those Sobrenian bastards off this planet, we'll do it. Right?"

"That's exactly it," Galt said. "Whatever we can do."

Akira straightened up in her seat, sniffed once, and folded her hands in her lap. "Then I'm satisfied."

As the *Rico* approached the former starcraft *Nivara*, now the Unity's embassy on Splendor, Chanda couldn't help thinking, *I'm glad Akira's satisfied. I just wish I was certain we could come through for her — and everyone on the planet.*

Chanda, Akira, and Galt entered the embassy as the *Rico* lifted off to rendezvous with the *Sergeant Jelal* again. As they started down the corridor toward the ambassador's office, Akira said, "I'll be in my quarters awhile, if that's all right with the both of you."

Chanda started to speak but looked at Galt first. The new ambassador nodded. Chanda said, "We'll let you know when we need you."

Akira didn't say anything more, just headed down an intersecting corridor toward her quarters.

Galt said, "She's going to be right back on the comm to talk to Irene."

"I know," Chanda said. "Uh, listen, I'll vacate the office soon as I get some rest — by the end of the day, I promise."

"You're still going to have work to do. You gotta work somewhere."

"Except that anyone looking for the ambassador is going to go there first. No, I'll clear out, but thank you."

"I'm sorry, Chanda."

"You don't have to keep saying that. I believe you. Should we schedule, I don't know, a meeting or something to figure out what to do next?"

"Schedule a meeting? That would be a first for you, wouldn't it?"

"Of course it would. But you strike me as a meeting kind of guy. We might as well get it over with."

"How about oh-eight-hundred in the ambassador's office?"

"Sure," Chanda said.

Galt continued: "And make sure Akira has the shuttle *Bashi* prepped and ready to go by then."

"Huh? Uh . . . sure."

"Called your bluff, didn't I? Screw the meeting, Chanda. I'm making the rounds, just as you always did. Tomorrow, I want to go visit Indirogar's tribe."

"Technically, it's Roraten's now. But I have a hard time thinking of it that way, too."

"Either way, I have to know what the people who live on this planet expect from Humanity. And how they may be able to help us protect them. After Indirogar, I want to meet with Dijirar and then the sweepers."

"Sounds reasonable," Chanda said. "See you in the morning." She turned away from the corridor that passed the ambassador's office to take a longer than normal route around to her quarters. *I'm not quite ready even to set eyes on that office yet*, she thought. *At least I can still call my quarters my own.*

Hours later, Chanda sat on her bed next to the half-dozen boxes of her belongings salvaged from her former office. *They don't amount to much*, she thought. She picked up a holo of her standing next to a Cetronen ambassador. *What was his name — oh, yeah, Nalingor. The agreement that was supposed to lead to joint exploratory missions among Humans and Cetronen.* Her and the paired symbiont's image stood staring straight ahead, then, on an unseen cue, turned and Chanda shook the tiny hand of the Cetronen "minor" who was sitting on a hump on the much larger "major's" belly. Hold for a second, and the sequence repeated. *Damn, that was fifteen years ago. And the first such mission only got started about two and a half years ago — the same mission to Moruteb that Govanek took part in, after the Sobre-nians forced their way onto it.*

She placed the holo back into the box, slid that box away and pulled another closer to her. Picked up an egg-shaped Arol emoting sculpture, a gift from her father.

Much of the sculpture's effect had degraded over the years; where it once radiated an almost indescribable joy, now it emitted only a vague sense of well-being. *And sometimes that's enough,* Chanda thought.

She recalled her eighth birthday party (which was actually ten years after she'd been born, thanks to being in stasis a couple of years as her parents roamed several star systems). It was 2087, and they'd traveled to Tranquility City on the Moon.

One of the reasons they'd gone to the Moon was so Chanda could fly! She was amazed that her father had done so countless times, and she'd never felt closer to him than the afternoon in which he gave her a series of lessons on how to launch herself, steer, and land safely. When her father took her to the top of the concrete dome that enclosed the lunar city, she wasn't even afraid. *Not as afraid as I am after the fact, thinking about it decades later,* she thought.

When she reached the wide ledge at the top of the dome provided for lunar fliers, Chanda didn't hesitate, but spread her artificial wings wide and took that first long step. Her exhilaration at the stomach-dropping feeling of knowing that no matter how gravity might tug at you, hoping to smash you into the broad green park below, that you were its master, and at the rushing of the wind against her goggled face, couldn't compare with the security she felt knowing that her father flew just to one side. *I knew that no matter how I screwed up, he'd save me,* Chanda thought.

I wish I had someone like that now.

CHAPTER 25

Old habits die hard, Chanda thought as Akira guided the *Bashi* to a soft landing just outside what she still thought of as Indirogar's village. She found herself still expecting the old highlander to rush outside and greet the shuttle, still found herself anticipating one of his familiar bone-crushing hugs.

Instead, it was Roraten who was Elder of the tribe now, who was walking toward the shuttle with a much more confident — younger! — gait than Indirogar could've mustered these days.

Another difference — two of Roraten's tribemates flanked him, each of them quite large, each carrying spears at the ready. *I have to wonder*, Chanda thought, *whether they're here because of rivals within his own tribe — or because of his suspicions of us — Humans.*

Either way, it's not a very positive sign.

Akira started going through the landing checklist. She would stay here with the shuttle as Chanda and Galt made the pilgrimage into Roraten's village. Chanda held back from the airlock as she paused to close her parka around her more tightly and lifted her hood, allowing Galt to be the first to step down from the shuttle.

A sudden sharp breeze swept across Chanda's face, and she

pulled the parka's hood even closer around her face. Powdery snow blew against her cheeks and into her eyes. She blinked as the snow particles melted, then froze into a thin film against her skin. Chanda wiped it away.

Roraten approached Galt and reached out his furred, thick-fingered hands to grasp Galt's gloved ones. "Congratulations, Senator Galt," the highlander said. "It seems we have new leadership among both Humans and highlanders. Let's hope it brings new ideas to this village and our world, especially as we search for ways for high-landers to return to their old ways of living."

"Thank you. I hope we can do just that."

Roraten nodded toward Chanda. "We also honor former Ambassador Kasmira's dedication over the years."

"Thank you," Chanda said. *In other words*, she thought, *I should sit down and shut up now.*

At a sign from Roraten, one of the bodyguards led the way toward the stone huts of the village, Roraten and Galt right behind him. Chanda trudged through the snow after them, the other bodyguard bringing up the rear.

As they entered the village, Chanda noticed several villagers staring at her and Galt as they went about their work of scraping carcasses and salting hides. She spotted more than one taking side-long glances at them from behind furs hanging between huts. *They know something's changed*, Chanda thought, *but aren't sure what it is or what it means.*

Chanda noted that Roraten was leading them to the same hut that Indirogar had inhabited when he was still Elder. *That must mean Indirogar has gone into the caves to live*, Chanda thought.

Traditionally, when the tribe's Elder ascended to the position of Eldest, he went to live in a series of caves on the north side of the village. The village's Elder was expected to make regular pilgrimages there to solicit his counsel. That the Eldest's advice was often ignored didn't negate the necessity of listening to it, thereby showing the proper respect for age and experience.

I have to find a way to talk to Indirogar in person, Chanda thought. *I could get hold of him on his datalink in an instant, but it wouldn't be the same.*

The lead bodyguard positioned himself outside Roraten's stone hut. Roraten held aside the thick furs hanging over the doorway as Galt and Chanda entered. As Roraten stepped inside, the bodyguard bringing up the rear followed them and stepped into one corner, standing impassively. The relative warmth of the hut was a comfort, but Chanda decided she wouldn't take off her parka just yet.

"Please, friends, sit," Roraten said. Chanda and Galt did so, on the same wide mats and stuffed pillows that had been here when this was Indirogar's home. Chanda noticed, though, that the wall that had been decorated with Indirogar's metal spears was now empty.

Roraten's eyes within their recessed sockets stared at Chanda. "I see you've noticed Indirogar's spears are gone," the highlander said.

"I have. But that's as I expected. This is your hut now."

"Yet I haven't replaced them with spears of my own."

Chanda gave as sincere a smile as she could. "That's certainly your right."

"But it's the *reason* that's important," Roraten said. "It's because I want to emphasize my peaceful ways. Certainly I'm a skilled hunter — one must eat. And that often makes one a skilled fighter, as well. And I am. But I prefer not to use my spears against my follow tribemates."

Which Indirogar never did, Chanda thought, *unless he was forced to.*

Roraten continued: "Indirogar has, however reluctantly, taken up his proper position as Eldest in the caves, as is proper."

There to provide his sage wisdom, Chanda thought, *and mostly to be ignored.*

Galt said, "I wanted to make sure to re-introduce myself to you, Roraten."

"I am glad you have. As I said just as you came off the shuttle, I believe we can bring new ideas to bear."

Galt said, "Humanity's main concern is still saving Splendor from the gas nebula."

Roraten examined his left arm as he smoothed its fur. "A problem which will outlive me."

Chanda said, "But a problem all the same. People do worry about what might happen to their children and grandchildren."

"As the Buruden might say, that is a truth. But this is a problem not of any grandchildren I may have one day, but of their grandchildren. Is it not?"

"Yes," Chanda admitted.

"I cannot speak to the grandchildren of my grandchildren. I cannot tell them to trust Humanity — or not to trust them. I don't even know if Humanity will be here."

Galt said, "We intend to be here as long as it takes to find a solution to that problem. Not to mention the more immediate problem of a possible Sobrenian attack."

Roraten said, "Another possible problem. We will deal with it as we may."

Chanda said, "You can't defend yourself without Human help."

Roraten leaned back and told Galt in a calm voice, "What if the day comes when we no longer wish for Humanity's help?"

Chanda felt the blood rush to her head and she wanted to jump up and scream at Roraten. Instead, she clasped her knees with hands she could barely keep from trembling and said, "On that day, you'll have made sure that all life on Splendor will one day die."

Roraten spread his arms wide. "All of us die, Chanda! Sometimes we can delay death, but we can never defeat it."

"We can — when others live on after us."

"Those others will deal with Splendor's future in their own way. I deal with the present — with reality."

Chanda forced herself toward a greater calm. She folded her hands in her lap and stared at them. *There's nothing more for me to say to Roraten*, she thought. *He'll guide the rest of his tribe into an acceptance of his attitudes. And his tribe is influential enough that it'll begin to change the attitudes of other highlander tribes.*

Roraten continued: "It must be frustrating for you that you have so few responsibilities compared to your former position."

Galt said, "Now wait just a minute. I won't have you speaking so disrespectfully — "

"You don't have to take up for me," Chanda told Galt. To Roraten, she said, "I have to wonder why, if I have so few responsibilities, you've been directing your attention almost entirely to me." She indicated Galt. "Here's your Unity ambassador. Tell him what you want from Humanity."

Roraten regarded Galt. "What we want is to be left alone to live our lives in peace." He lifted his left arm and pulled its brown fur back to display a long scar that ran most of its length. "You see here what I received for my faith in Humanity — this is only one of my scars. Others cover my other arm and my chest."

Galt said, "I'm sorry that happened — "

"We were placed on a forced journey to a strange world called Socrates — a Human name — that held no valley dwellers within it, no one to make our spears and other tools. None of our familiar animals — no quicksleep or burrowers. We hunted nothing, we ate tasteless rations created by the Unity."

Galt said, "It was early in the process. Things would've gotten better."

Chanda said, "We were going to import Splendorian animals that could live on Socrates."

Roraten said, "But our most important companions could not live there — the valley dwellers."

"That's true. We couldn't find another world like Splendor — one in which both highlanders and valley dwellers could live close to one another."

"And so your experiment failed."

Chanda bowed her head, exhaled a long breath, and closed her eyes. Roraten said, "Tell me I am wrong."

Chanda could only mutter, "I can't."

Roraten stood. "We have nothing more to say to one another."

Chanda and Galt stood. When Roraten made no move toward the doorway, Galt turned on one heel and headed outside, Chanda right behind.

Both of the highlanders Chanda had thought of as Roraten's bodyguards accompanied them as they started across the village. A glance back, and Chanda saw two more take their place in front of Roraten's doorway.

Once again, Chanda felt the stares of the highlanders at work all around them. The smell of hides being boiled seemed particularly harsh. *Roraten's already begun to turn his people against Humanity*, Chanda thought. *During Indirogar's time as Elder, we were greeted with smiles, sometimes cheers. Now I'm wondering whether these guards are here to protect their tribemates from us or us from them.*

They were only a few steps beyond Roraten's hut when a commotion arose behind them, sudden shouts, a clash of spears. "Get out of my way, or I'll have you run through!"

Indirogar!

He confronted the two guards standing with Chanda and Galt. They faced their Eldest, pointing their spears at him. *He seems much more vital, even younger than the last time I saw him*, Chanda thought.

Indirogar paused just a few meters away from the tips of the highlanders' spears. He looked at Chanda. "I cannot call you 'Ambassador' anymore."

"It doesn't matter, Indirogar," Chanda said. "That's not the most important thing between us."

"Roraten is betraying his own people — who should still be *my* people."

A flash of movement beyond Indirogar, and Chanda saw Roraten pulling aside the furs covering the doorway to his hut. "Dammit," she said under her breath. "Here we go." She started to pull her stunner, but Galt's hand covered hers and she hesitated. "Not yet," Galt told her.

Indirogar turned to face Roraten, who spread his arms wide and said, "My Eldest. I was just complementing you on your willingness to accept your traditional role."

"To accept your foot pushing down on my neck, you mean."

The two highlander guards in front of Chanda and Galt took a step toward Indirogar.

Galt put his hand on his stunner. Chanda gripped hers tighter. *But if we let ourselves defend Indirogar, we're taking sides in internal highlander politics. Try explaining that to the Unity.*

Roraten said, "You test the limits of our traditions."

"Not as much as you. How many times have you come to the caves to seek my counsel?"

Roraten said, "As many times as I've felt necessary."

"Yes, *none!*"

The two guards took another step toward Indirogar, who stood with his spear at the ready.

Chanda said, "Indirogar!"

The guards halted. Indirogar's eyes never left them, but he addressed Chanda: "I've been wanting to speak to you in person, but Roraten insisted I stay away."

Roraten said, "You see how much power I have over my Eldest."

"Indirogar," Chanda said. "Stand down for now. I'll come see you soon. We can speak by datalink in the meantime."

Indirogar looked all around him — at Roraten, the guards to either side, then back to Chanda. "Very well. It's not the same as looking into your face as you speak — I've always perceived your honesty there. But I'll return to my hole, for now."

Galt asked Roraten, "Do you promise Indirogar safe passage back to the caves?"

"Of course," Roraten said. "That is his proper place."

Indirogar lowered his spear. Without another word, he turned and headed back the way he had come. Roraten watched impassively for a moment, then gestured to the guards closest to him. They fell into place outside Roraten's hut as he entered it.

"Let's get the hell out of here," Galt said.

"Couldn't agree more," Chanda said, as she and Galt continued through the village, the two highlander guards falling in behind them to escort them back to the shuttle *Bashi*.

As Akira landed the *Bashi* back at the embassy, Chanda saw that another craft had arrived ahead of them — the personnel shuttle *Judith*, from the archeological ship *George Allenby*. As Chanda stepped down from the *Bashi*, Govanek left the embassy and headed toward *Judith*. She carried only one small bag that contained her few belongings.

"Govanek," Chanda said as snow swirled around them. "I'm so glad I got to see you before you left."

The Sobrenian clasped her parka around her and said, "I'm eager to go to the archeological site. Splendor is a fascinating place — three known species of intelligent life. And I may be able to help discover yet another!"

"I know it's more difficult for you to cope with the cold than it is for Humans. We wear the parkas for short trips and so we don't seem so strange to native Splendorians, but don't be ashamed to keep your lifesuit on if you have to. A lot of people at the site do just that."

"I'm grateful for the lifesuit implant. I wish I'd had one back on the Buruden homeworld!"

Galt came up to them and clapped his hand on Govanek's shoulder. "It didn't help me that much, but I know what you mean."

Govanek said, "I'll report back to you whenever we find anything interesting — who knows, perhaps we'll learn something that can help us with the threats from the gas nebula or my fellow Sobrenians."

Chanda smiled. "They've been up there for several months, and haven't found anything like that — but we can always hope for the best."

Galt said, "Keep in mind we may have to recall you if the Sobrenians act up — we'll need your insights."

"I'll return whenever you need me," Govanek said, and started toward the shuttle *Judith*, which quickly lifted.

Galt told Chanda, "I think she's the only person on the planet I know who's having fun."

Chanda shrugged. "Maybe someday it'll be our turn," she said, and went into the embassy.

———

Chanda entered her quarters, shook off her parka, and fell onto a couch. She wasn't as much physically exhausted as mentally. Without conscious thought, her gaze fell upon her "homespace," the small table in one corner containing the three baskets that reminded her of her mother. Her heart still filled with love at the thought of her even though she repeatedly forced Chanda into extended periods in stasis — *stashed me away,* she sometimes thought of it.

Then came the one time she awoke and neither she nor her father was there to greet her.

Abstract images of stars and planets decorated those baskets. *And now I live among the stars, and I've visited more planets than my parents ever dreamed of.*

And I have one chore I can take care of right now.

———

Chanda went down to what was once the engineering section of the Unity starcraft *Nivara*, empty now except for the stasis shell where she'd slept away all of two weeks. She carried a small nanotech controller in her right hand.

Just staring at the stasis shell made her mouth feel dry. *Seeing it the first time after Akira and Irene finished it was a powerful symbol for me. Escape. Freedom.*

Chanda examined the various instrumentation attached to the shell — temperature regulators, energy conduits, all of it designed to protect her for the many decades she would've slept, only to awaken to that idealized, transformed planet Splendor.

All of Splendor's problems solved, and therefore all of mine.

All of it bullshit.

She lifted the controller, made sure it was attuned to the various materials that made up the shell and its related equipment. Activated it.

The dome covering the shell dissolved first, then the platform where she would've spent her long sleep, and finally all the support equipment.

All of it became dust.

In a way, it really is as if I've come awake from decades of sleep. I've had my eyes opened, Chanda thought. *I'm wide awake and intend to stay that way.*

A final moment staring at what might have been, and Chanda turned and left.

CHAPTER 26

The next morning, Chanda rushed to the ambassador's office, but paused for a moment before the door. *I didn't want to find myself coming here this soon — but Galt said Captain Bram's information was urgent.*

She took that final step toward the door and it slid open. Her former assistant, Ken Westbrook, looked up at her from his desk in the outer room, mouth agape, as if she were the last person he expected to see. "Goddam," Chanda said. "I didn't *die.*"

"Sorry . . . uh, Chanda." He indicated the doorway to the ambassador's office. "They're waiting for you."

Chanda went into the next room, to find Galt and Bram examining a holo in the middle of the main room that depicted the entire Splendorian system — Splendor's image hovered at the far end of the room, a tiny but recognizable dot. But the focus of the holo was much farther out, beyond the orbits of the system's two Jovians and single sub-Jovian.

"Glad you could make it," Ambassador Galt said. He indicated a cluster of blurry dots beyond the sub-Jovian's orbit. "Those are Sobrenian ships. They're apparently looking in on Splendor just as the Buruden have been looking in on the Sobrenians. And all these ships are manned."

Chanda said, "I wonder if we see Tiernan's hand behind this."

"Do we think he's that influential among the Sobrenians?"

"Just look at the effect here — the symmetry with the Buruden's probes, just the idea of 'tweaking' us, and generally being a pest."

Bram said, "Although it also fits in with a common Sobrenian pattern — the bluster, as you like to say, without actually getting to the point of firing a shot."

"I'm not sure we can count on that anymore," Galt said.

Chanda said, "The Sobrenians, whether or not Tiernan is helping to guide them, are trying to provoke us, like someone yelling at you and poking their finger in your chest. If they succeed, and you shoot first, they've won."

"Yeah. 'Look what you made me do.'"

Bram said, "The question is, how do we respond? I can take *Nivara 2* out there, or have Hamadi take the *Jelal*, but I can't risk taking both. The whole thing might be a decoy to draw us away from the planet. Even if we did send both, they couldn't fight all those ships on their own."

"But if we don't respond," Chanda said, "we look weak."

Galt folded his arms. Rubbed his chin. Chanda thought, *This is actually where he can make a much more informed decision than I can. I don't have the military experience.*

Galt said, "Immediate response — unmanned probes." He looked at Bram. "Can you take care of that from *Nivara 2*?"

"Yes, I can."

"Then do so."

Bram hesitated, made a quick glance toward Chanda, then told Galt, "Officially, sir, you're not in the chain of command. You have to *request* an action, then I have to agree to the request."

Galt's lips pursed, and Chanda saw the muscles in his jaw work. He said, "Of course. Forgive me, I lapsed into command mode. I'd like to request that you launch those probes."

"I agree with that plan of action," Captain Bram said, his chin held high. "I'll make sure that's carried out right away. We can launch within an hour or so, and one good jump should take them within a few hundred thousand K."

"Another question, one I should know the answer to, quite honestly — where are *Azure Dragon* and *Black Tortoise?*"

Bram said, "*Dragon's* headed toward Socrates to pick up more highlanders and bring them back. It's five days out. *Tortoise* is coming in from Kardashev with valley dwellers. Two days away."

A wry smile from Galt. "Another request, then."

"Certainly, Ambassador."

"I'd like to have *Tortoise* drop out of stardrive behind those Sobrenians, at whatever distance you deem safe."

"That could put a lot of valley dwellers at risk, Ambassador."

"Rules of engagement would be to rabbit at the first sign of trouble. That crew needs to be ready to jump back into stardrive as quickly as possible."

Bram said, "I have every confidence in that crew. It sounds like a good plan, Ambassador. I'll head back up to *Nivara 2* to make arrangements." Bram left them.

Now Chanda felt as if she were just cooling her heels. "What can I do for you, Ambassador?" she asked.

Galt said, "I wish I could ask for a prayer from you."

"No one hears an atheist's prayer, Ambassador."

"I suppose not. Oh, I had some of our tech people check out my lifesuit. They figured out how Sedra de-activated it. And as usual, it all goes back to Tiernan."

"How so?" Chanda asked.

"Remember during those awful negotiations on the Buruden homeworld, when the Sobrenians were still bitching about their accommodations?"

"How can I forget? Though they *were* bad, if they were anything like ours. Still — an excuse for them to delay things even more."

"When that session broke up for the day, Tiernan went around and shook everyone's hand. He said something about having patience, that he was still educating the other Sobrenians in the ways of Humans. Remember?"

"How could I forget? It seemed creepy somehow."

"Creepy isn't half of it. The techs gave my lifesuit a deep scan. They discovered a 'Trojan horse' protocol in it — something transmitted through Tiernan's skin, into ours, that implanted itself into my lifesuit tech."

"He shook all our hands that day — went right down the line to me and Irene and Akira."

"He sure did," Galt said. "All three of you better get your lifesuits checked out."

"The bastard," Chanda said. "He or Sedra could've killed all of us anytime after that."

"The question is, why didn't he? Believe me, Ambassador, I'm glad none of you had to go through what I did — but what held Sedra back?"

"Like you say, it always comes back to Tiernan. Irene and Akira were sprawled in the middle of the street and weren't a threat. Sedra knew Tiernan has plans for me. He's obsessed with me."

"Because you defeated him four years ago."

"That, and he's shown a tendency to focus on a particular woman that, in his weird way, he tries to win over. The first time he came to Splendor, he was interested in a Unity Marine sergeant assigned to the *Nivara 2* — Catarina Avery."

Galt blinked. "And by 'interested,' you mean romantically?"

"On the surface. In reality, his desire is for power, not sex. Nowadays, of course, having turned Sobrenian, I guess that's a little more obvious."

"So he doesn't just want to win against you — "

"He wants to humiliate me. Just as he tried to do to Catarina. Who was one of the Marines who helped capture him, by the way. That part was nice."

"So the question before us is — how does Tiernan's weird obsession fit in with the Sobrenians' plans for Splendor?"

"I fear," Chanda said, "we may find out sooner than we'd wish."

Chanda was having a veggie sandwich and hot tea in the embassy's commons later that day. She wanted to remain visible to the embassy's staff, to show that her removal as ambassador hadn't caused her to sit and sulk in her quarters or become ashamed to be seen in public.

But maybe it wasn't such a good idea, she thought as one colleague after another passed her by with a polite nod or a nervous smile. *Maybe they're just giving me my privacy in this difficult time,* she thought. *Yeah, that's it.*

From her datalink: "Chanda — it's Irene. Can you talk?"

"Irene! I've been wanting to talk to you!"

"Me, too. But I was afraid of bothering you."

"You'd never be a bother," Chanda said, speaking in quiet tones so she wouldn't disturb any of the people who weren't sitting with her.

"Listen, I've gotten a lot better up here, but I want to come back down to Splendor."

"If it's about Akira, I was going to let her go back up there to see you pretty soon."

"Well, Akira's the main part of it, but the truth is I'm damn bored up here. And I miss everyone else, too. Especially you. Working with you, that is."

"OK . . . " *The last thing I need is Irene down here pining away for me. I wish Akira had never said anything.* "Uh . . . what do the docs say?"

A different voice chimed in: "Chanda, it's Ben."

Oh, crap, Chanda thought. *The other "last thing I need" is him pining away over me, too.*

Then another realization: *They're conspiring against me! Irene knows she can't have me, so she's going to live vicariously through Ben.* "Uh . . . hi, Ben. How's Irene doing?"

"I've cleared her to leave the *Jelal.* But she still has some recuperating to do. I'd like to come down with her to install some monitors and make sure Akira will be around to look after her awhile."

Definitely a conspiracy. "Can do. What's your ETA?"

"Sometime tomorrow afternoon your time, after I do one last exam up here."

Irene's voice came in: "I'm looking forward to it, Chanda. I know it'll take some time, but I'm eager to get back to work."

"Sounds great," Chanda said. "I'll look forward to seeing you again. And . . . you, too, Ben. Uh, Chanda out." She touched behind her ear to break the connection, grateful she couldn't see either Irene or Ben's reactions.

Chanda was approaching her quarters when she received a datalink message from Indirogar: "Chanda, I am doing something, and feel I must tell you about it." The highlander's voice was shaky, as if he'd been exerting himself.

The door to Chanda's quarters slid aside as she said, "What is it? Nothing's wrong, I hope."

"Nothing at all. In fact, I believe things may be better for me than they have been in many years."

"You sound out of breath. Are you sure you're OK?"

"I am leading a band of highlanders away from what is now Roraten's village. We are making a new life for ourselves."

"What? Where are you headed?"

"To build a new village at the foot of the Heavenlock Mountains."

Chanda said, "Indirogar, that's hundreds of kilometers. You might never make it. How many people do you have with you?"

"Forty-five. Most of them are males, a few of them a bit younger than myself. And I admit, most of our females are beyond their birthing years. But we will make do."

"You should've — "

"Should have what, Chanda? You are concerned with what is happening in the far stars, not what highlanders are doing."

"That's not fair, Indirogar."

"I am not complaining. I am simply stating a fact. I knew you could not help me in this journey, so I started it on my own."

"And Roraten didn't try to stop you?"

"He was glad to see me go. Friend Chanda, I wish we had gotten to speak more to one another during your visit without Roraten's thugs keeping us apart. This translated voice tells me the words you say, and I always believe them. But I'm reassured when I see your face speaking those words."

"You realize we had to restrain ourselves. We could've taken those guards out pretty easily."

"So, it's true," the highlander said. "All these years you restrained yourself from interfering with me because of your Unity restrictions."

"Why, yes, of course."

"I'd hoped it was actually because you knew I was in the right — that I was doing what was best for my people."

Chanda settled into her couch. "That just made it easier to do."

"So when you refused to support me over Roraten. . . . "

"Nothing had changed, Indirogar. I'm not allowed to interfere, whether it's in your favor or not."

Chanda wondered whether the silence that followed was a thoughtful one — or *because he's pissed*, she thought. "Indirogar?"

"Is not your mere presence on Splendor — and the attempt to evacuate us — itself interference?"

"It is. But it's allowed because otherwise all your people would die when the gas nebula comes."

"Some of my people are beginning to doubt the existence of your gas nebula."

"It's not *mine*," Chanda said. "In fact, I'd like to get rid of it."

"You've told me many times that isn't possible."

"And I've seen nothing that tells me any different. Indirogar, I know I've been busy with other things. But if you run into trouble — "

"I promise to ask for your help if I need it. Can you promise to provide it?"

"I . . . well, it depends upon — "

"Upon what happens among the stars. I truly understand, Chanda. This is how we lived before Humanity arrived. We made a decision, convinced others to follow that decision, then succeeded or failed."

A pause, and for once Chanda was unsure what to say to fill it. It was Indirogar who continued: "I know you have more worlds than this one to concern you. Take care."

"Take — " Chanda began. But the connection was broken.

Chanda touched behind her ear. "Captain Bram — this is Chanda."

"Go ahead, Chanda."

"Indirogar's headed toward the Heavenlock Mountains with some of his people to try to start a new village. Can we keep an eye on them?"

"Intermittently, here from the *Nivara* 2 and some of our other ships. If it's important enough, we can sprinkle some nanite uplinks all along their path and keep track of them that way."

"Please do. I'm pretty worried about them."

"I'll get on that. But with this Sobrenian threat ahead of us . . . who knows whether we'll even be able to help them at a particular moment."

"We do the best we can. Chanda out."

She thought, *Indirogar, you've been a dear friend. But this isn't what I needed just now.*

———

"It is good to see you again," Dijirar told Chanda as she and Galt entered the valley dweller's hut. Dijirar's lightly scaled hands could barely wrap themselves around Chanda's right hand.

"I wish we'd have happier reasons sometime to see one another," Chanda said.

Dijirar took Galt's hands and told him, "I understand congratulations are in order." She looked at Chanda. "And perhaps, in a way, for you as well."

"The jury's still out on that one."

"Failure to translate."

"Sorry — it means I don't know if it's good or not. We'll see."

Dijirar indicated wicker chairs. "Please — sit. Root tea?"

"Please."

"Yes, thank you," Galt said.

As Dijirar poured the tea, Chanda sat in the unaccustomed warmth of the hut and listened to the sounds of the valley dweller village all around them. Unlike the last time she'd been here, when everyone had abandoned their work temporarily to greet Dijirar, the noise of a busy village surrounded them: villagers pounding cakes of glowing iron into spears or tools, calls for a bellows to work even faster, shouts toward a couple wayward males who weren't bright enough to stay away from a searing-hot forge.

Once she served her Human guests, Dijirar said, "I have wonderful news for you. My males are carrying several children."

Thank goodness, was Chanda's first thought. *At least we don't have to sit here and watch them sexing with her.* "Then the congratulations go to you," she said.

Galt told her, "That's wonderful to hear. I know it's one reason you came back to Splendor."

Dijirar held her metal cup tightly. "Another reason is that I wished to help my fellow valley dwellers lead their own lives again. And *want* them to live their lives — we've had too many suicides among my people."

Chanda said, "I've been heartsick over that. I don't like that we had to end the evacuation effort — but maybe getting all the valley dwellers home will help."

"My people have been too concerned with the loss of the highlanders after going to Kardashev. People need to be able to look beyond themselves. But the evacuation effort made them look too far ahead."

"You sound like Roraten," Chanda said. "He said he was concerned with the lives of his children and grandchildren, and not much beyond."

"What can we do?" Dijirar said. "Especially since so many of my people believe Humanity will come up with a way to destroy the nebula."

Galt asked, "How can they believe that?"

"With respect, Humanity's own actions have brought about those beliefs. Many valley dwellers believe you have magical powers."

Chanda said, "After so many years around us, they should know better."

"Some of us do," Dijirar said. "Especially those of us who have worked directly with you. We know your abilities are not supernatural — that you simply know more things than we do, as an experienced spear-maker knows more than a novice."

Galt said, "But I imagine others just look at a shuttle coming in to land or see us using some other kind of tech and think it's magical."

"Many of my people still believe in gods who live within the frozen lands — places we have never been able to get to even wearing the highlanders' furs. They are too far away, and every group who has made the attempt has turned around without success — or died."

Chanda said, "I know contact with Humanity has led some of your people to lose those beliefs. I'm sorry that happened."

Dijirar stared at Chanda. "But you don't believe in gods, either."

"We changed your culture. Humans are supposed to avoid doing that."

"You made us smarter — some of us, anyway. Don't wish us to hold onto something you wouldn't want for yourself."

"Yeah. Sorry. Again."

"Tell me about the Sobrenians."

Galt said, "Their negotiators tried to kill several of us the last time we saw them. That told me the negotiations failed."

"So an attack could come."

"That's right," Chanda said. "And so far we haven't gotten the Unity to commit to a full defense of the planet."

Dijirar said, "You may have to abandon us."

"That's not quite fair," Galt said.

Chanda almost spoke up, but decided to wait this one out.

Dijirar said, "Fair or not, isn't it true?"

Galt said, "Abandon is a harsh word."

"The truth is often harsh."

"Fine, then. We may have to abandon Splendor. But that's not my choice."

"I wasn't looking for someone to blame," the valley dweller said. "I was just asking for the truth."

Galt said, "You're right, of course. I apologize."

"I've received many apologies this morning," Dijirar said. "Let's make that the last one. What can valley dwellers do to help against the Sobrenians?"

"You saw what they can do, when they used this world for target practice," Chanda said. "There's little you *can* do."

"As much as we have cooperated with Humanity, we will resist the Sobrenians — they will stop us only by killing us."

"Which they may not hesitate to do," Galt said. "They consider valley dwellers and highlanders and sweepers 'pre-sentients,' the same as they do Humans."

"Then that is a designation we will consider to be a matter of pride." Dijirar stood, and Chanda and Galt did the same. "I'm glad to see each of you again. Let me know if there is any way we can help resist the Sobrenians."

Chanda said, "We'll let you know. In the meantime, I guess we Humans will have to see if we can come up with some sort of magic."

CHAPTER 27

As Chanda and Galt left Dijirar's village and approached the shuttle *Bashi*, they noticed the craft was already powered up and ready to lift. Akira appeared in the outer airlock doorway and waved them on. "Com'on!" she told them.

Chanda and Galt exchanged glances, shrugged, and trotted the rest of the way. "What is it?" Galt asked as they approached. "Some sort of emergency?"

"Not if something good can be an emergency," Akira said. "Irene's on her way down." She moved into the pilot's position.

"Sounds good to me," Chanda said as she settled into the co-pilot's seat, with Galt in position behind them.

Akira favored Chanda with the widest grin she'd ever seen. "I guess Ambassador Galt doesn't know of my reputation as a 'hot-dogging' pilot, does he?"

"Maybe not," Chanda said, "but —"

Akira touched a control in front of her. "The effect is best if you back off the compensators a little bit." The whine of the shuttle's gravitic drive soared, and Chanda was pressed down into her seat as the *Bashi* leaped into the air.

Akira didn't bring the craft up more than sixty meters off the deck, guiding it smoothly among jutting cliffs and rolling mountain peaks alike. "How's that feel?" Akira asked. "Exhilarating?"

"Sorta," Chanda said, as her hands gripped the arms of her seat. "But maybe I've had enough exhilaration for now."

Akira tilted her head in amusement and flicked the inertial compensators back to full power. "How about you, Ambassador?"

Galt said, "It's a good thing you weren't a shuttle pilot for me when I commanded the *Jelal*. I'd have had you grounded in an instant."

"Oh," Akira said. "Ambassador, I'm sorry. I — "

Galt reached forward and clapped Akira on the shoulder, flashing her a big grin. "How'd you like that? Exhilarating?"

Chanda couldn't help grinning at Akira's gobsmacked expression. "I guess pilots have one kind of humor," she said. "Commanders — even former commanders — have another."

Akira guided *Bashi* in for a landing at one end of the embassy even as the shuttle *Rico* was setting down at the opposite end. Chanda told Akira, "Go on — I'll do the post-flight."

"Thank you!" Akira said, and was through the airlock and headed across the frozen landscape in an instant.

Galt, watching her, said, "That's great to see."

Chanda began the shuttle's post-flight checks. "I suppose I might be looking for a new pilot for a while."

"Irene's supposed to be making great strides. You'll have both of them back sooner than you think."

Irene and Ben appeared at *Rico*'s outer airlock. Ben was holding Irene's arm, and Akira held out her own arm as Irene made her way down to Splendor's surface. Once Irene set foot on solid ground, she reached out to Akira for a quick hug and kiss. Akira said something to

Irene, who looked toward *Bashi* and waved. Chanda and Galt waved back.

Akira and Ben each took one of Irene's arms, and they headed into the embassy.

"All done," Chanda said as she checked the final system on the shuttle. She looked at Galt, who was staring at her, Cheshire cat-like. "What?"

"Nothing."

"You want to ask me about Ben, don't you?" She wagged a finger at him. "Well, you just mind your own business, especially about my personal life. When you first came down here, you asked me a million questions, including whether I had any lovers. Well, I haven't in quite a while, and that's been my choice. All my energies have been focused on Splendor, and I haven't had the . . . the emotional energy for any kind of closeness. I haven't . . . "

"Chanda . . . ?"

"I haven't . . . you know . . . "

"Chanda."

"Yes?"

"I was only watching you watch Irene and Akira. It was great seeing you so happy for them."

"Oh. Well . . . thanks. I guess."

"Nothing to thank me for. They're more than colleagues to you. They're great friends. That's valuable to have."

"Yeah. You're right. And you . . . really weren't going to ask about . . . you know?"

"He has a name. Ben."

"Yeah. I guess I ended up saying more about myself than about him."

"That's not for me to say." Galt raised himself from his seat and went toward the airlock. "Why don't you go in and see them?"

"You don't think Akira and Irene want their privacy?"

"No time for privacy yet — Ben's supposed to be helping Irene settle in — and who knows how long he'll be here?"

A whine of gravitics from the opposite end of the embassy, and the *Rico* lifted. Its pilot wasn't as much of a "hot-dogger" as Akira, but the shuttle quickly became a dot against gray Splendorian skies, then a speck, then was gone.

Chanda said, "I guess he'll be here a little while, after all."

"Huh!" Galt said. "Nice to see he's so committed to Irene's health."

Chanda looked at Galt through narrowed eyes as she followed him through the airlock. "It's bad enough I'm starting to get paranoid. But I can't figure out which person -- or *how many* -- to be paranoid *about*."

The door to Akira and Irene's quarters stood open as Chanda approached. She knocked lightly at the doorframe, and heard Irene's voice from around the corner: "Com'on in!"

As Chanda came into their bedroom, she saw Irene lying in her and Akira's bed. Ben was giving her an injection as Akira stood to one side watching. "These are auxiliary nanomeds," he told her as Akira listened intently. "They supplement your usual biotech. It keeps an eye on any lasting effects from that concussion and your neck injury." To Akira, he said, "And *you* — did I see you flying that shuttle just now?"

"Uh . . . yeah," Akira said.

Ben turned toward Chanda. "What were you thinking *letting* her fly that shuttle?"

Chanda said, "I thought she was supposed to be OK?" To Akira, she said, "Aren't you supposed to be OK?"

Ben said, "She's a pilot, Chanda. Pilots lie if it gets them back into the air or into orbit. She can convince you a collapsed lung and broken arm and leg don't mean anything — and in a strict medical sense right now Akira is perfectly healed and qualified to fly. But those stresses still take a toll. My off-the-record advice was to take it easy."

Chanda gave Akira a good stare. "Forgive me, Akira." She turned to Ben. "She not only flew the shuttle, she turned down the inertials to give us a bit of a thrill along the way."

Ben looked at Akira as he placed his hand on Irene's shoulder. "And you're supposed to be taking care of her? You can't even take care of yourself!" He looked at Chanda. "Can you ground her?"

Chanda saw Akira's eyes go wide. "I sure can," Chanda said. She told Akira, "Sorry, sweetie — but until Ben gives me the word that you're OK to fly, I have only one assignment for you — take care of Irene."

Akira's dismayed expression switched immediately to relief, and she leaned over and gave Irene a gentle embrace. "The only assignment I'd like better than flying," she said.

Ben told Chanda, "They're not paying any more attention to us. How about we get outta here?"

As Ben closed the door to Irene and Akira's quarters behind them, he said, "I, uh . . . was going to stick around for a day or so to make sure Irene's OK."

"That's quite a commitment to one patient," Chanda told him.

"Well . . . I wanted the chance to come down here to Splendor, as well."

"Oh — because. . . . "

"You know, check out your medical facilities — maybe see some of the planet. I arranged for quarters down here. It's not good to be stuck up there on that starcraft all the time."

"I see," Chanda said.

"Maybe we could . . . have a cup of coffee, or tea. You like tea, don't you?"

"I like tea just fine. But I'm pretty busy right now."

"Oh," Ben said. "Some mission here on the planet?"

"Yeah. Uh, the sweepers. Ambassador Galt's been making the rounds. We've talked with Roraten and Indirogar, the highlanders. And the valley dweller, Dijirar."

"So it's the sweepers' turn."

"Yes, that's it."

"Well, best of luck with that mission. Hope to see you when you get back."

"I'm sure you will."

Ben gave a perfunctory wave as he headed down the corridor, presumably bound for his quarters.

Chanda headed toward the ambassador's office, thinking, *Now I just have to sell Galt on the idea of talking to the sweepers.*

Chanda was barely halfway to the ambassador's office when a voice came over her datalink. "Chanda? It's Govanek."

Chanda paused and stood to one side of the corridor. "Great to hear from you," she said. "How's everything going out there?"

Govanek's voice came in with the ambient sounds of many people speaking all at once behind her, along with plenty of scraping and brushing sounds. "Chanda! It's wonderful to work here with your fellow Humans. They're so eager and curious. Quite unlike most Sobrenians, and very much like me."

"It sounds busy out there."

"Quite busy, but I wanted to tell you, very quickly, that we may have some exciting news from here soon — a great discovery about the nature of life here on Splendor. But I feel I cannot reveal anything until we are certain of our findings."

Just as well, Chanda thought. *No time for exploration for most of us - we're too wrapped up in practical matters. But the* George Allenby *crew better make their discoveries pretty quickly. They may not have much more time left here.*

I'd better not say any of that just yet. "Great to hear. Let me know as soon as you have something solid, OK?"

"I will," Govanek said, and signed off.

Chanda continued toward the ambassador's quarters.

Chanda still felt self-conscious around Galt as the *Bashi*, piloted now by Irene's occasional backup Julian Rice, headed toward the contact point they'd established earlier with the sweepers.

Galt had also insisted upon getting some flying time — or at least co-piloting time — and was sitting up front on this journey, relegating Chanda to one of the rear seats. *Which may be just as well,* she thought. *This way I can't feel his eyes staring into my back.*

"So, Chanda," Galt said, and despite herself she started a bit. "This mission seemed awfully abrupt. Is it really that urgent?"

"Well, we haven't heard from them in a while. And what I'm afraid of, is that the sweepers will learn that we've been talking to the highlanders and the valley dwellers, and feel left out — and you said you wanted to meet with them."

"Well, you're probably right to insist upon it. They didn't care much for Humanity the last time we spoke with them."

As they approached the ridge where they'd last mad contact with the sweepers, Julian pointed just offshore and said, "It looks like they got the word somehow." The familiar kilometers-wide mass of a sweeper was lying about a half-K offshore, just as they'd seen before.

"Damn," Chanda said. "What kinda grapevine do they have out in the ocean?"

Julian brought the *Bashi* around and landed on top of the ridge. Chanda told him, "Why don't you stay here and be ready to lift? I'm not sure I trust these guys."

"Will do," Julian said.

"Good idea," Galt said as he and Chanda exited the airlock, their feet crunching down onto the thin layer of snow. They made their way down past a muddy area to the familiar pebbled beach and stood next to the barrel-shaped relay transmitter designed to send on any communication from the sweepers. Galt called up a diagnostic report on the transmitter. "Everything's working properly. But we haven't heard from the sweepers lately?"

"Not at all." Chanda pointed toward the choppy seas. "There are the messenger fish." The red and white striped fish performed their usual station-keeping duties, massed just offshore by the hundreds.

Galt touched behind his left ear. "This is Ambassador Gabriel Galt of the Earth Unity. I'd like to speak to the sweeper just offshore."

Chanda looked toward the dark mass of the sweeper who hovered just beneath the water, stretching for kilometers to either side. "No response," she said.

Galt said, "Doesn't make any sense." He lifted his left arm and worked the embedded sensor cluster. "I'm not reading anything that should interfere with our signal or theirs."

"Maybe they just don't want to talk."

"You try," Galt said. "Maybe they just don't like me."

Chanda said, "This is Chanda Kasmira speaking to any sweeper. Please respond."

Waves crashed against a nearby rock formation. Winds blew spray into Chanda's face — moisture on her cheeks, salt smell. "Same thing," she said. "No response."

Galt said, "Definitely the least satisfying of our meetings with Splendorian intelligences."

"I hope this isn't a permanent withdrawal from contact with Humans."

"They *are* the only ones who still want off the planet. Maybe they're just too pissed to talk."

Chanda said, "I have to admit to that particular failure — I wanted the sweepers on our side. But I could never convince them that we could give them anything they wanted."

"That's because we *can't* give them what they want. We can't keep the gas nebula from striking the planet. And the sweepers are too big to evacuate."

"I just thought of something — do we know how long sweepers live?"

"No clue," Galt said. "I guess I've assumed they live quite a while, given their size." He snapped his fingers. "You don't think —"

"I do — what if they live for a century or more? That makes the threat from the gas nebula pretty personal."

"Which could also explain why they're so pissed." Galt addressed the faraway sweeper. "Is that it? You're not just worried about your children or grandchildren's lives — you're afraid *you'll* die when the gas nebula arrives."

The messenger fish were still floating between the sweeper and the shoreline, but they relayed nothing.

"This is damn frustrating," Chanda said.

Galt said, "Somehow the sweepers' silence has me about as worried as any threats the Sobrenians might make."

Chanda started back up the slope. "Let 'em stew awhile, I guess," she said. "When they're ready to talk, they'll talk."

They were almost to the shuttle *Bashi* when Galt asked Chanda, "You said that last part with your datalink still open, didn't you?"

"Yeah."

"Thought ignoring them and walking away might get them even more pissed — enough to say something?"

"Yeah. Didn't work. Maybe next time. Though I'm not sure how many next times we'll have."

Even as Julian was landing the *Bashi* back at the embassy, Trenton Bram's voice came over her datalink: "Chanda — Ambassador Galt — we've detected a Sobrenian starcraft that's just come out of stardrive — only two hundred thousand K out."

Chanda turned in her seat and looked back at Galt. "That's *damn* close."

"Too close to be safe, normally," Galt said.

Julian settled the *Bashi* down to a soft landing, and looked at Chanda with a quizzical expression — clearly, Bram hadn't included him in the conversation. "Thanks," was all Chanda told him as she and Galt exited the shuttle.

As Chanda followed Galt into the embassy, she asked Bram over the link, "This is just the one ship?"

"Just the one — sensors going full intensity. I'm trying to get *Nivara 2* to bear on it, but it's headed opposite Splendor's spin — orbital mechanics are working against us."

"Keep us in the loop," Galt said as they neared the ambassador's office. "I want — I'd *like to* be informed of every move it makes."

"We'll let you know. Captain Bram out."

They breezed past a startled Ken Westbrook and entered the ambassador's inner office. Galt stood over his desk and activated a holo. An image of Splendor appeared, with the disposition of all the Unity's ships in orbit indicated, as well. Farther out, the Sobrenian craft was on a trajectory clearly designed to provide a close approach to the planet.

Chanda indicated the image of the *Nivara 2*. "It's turning hard, but it'll never make it to that Sobrenian in time. We just have to hope it's not on an attack run."

"I'd doubt it," Galt said. "They'd want to be a lot more stealthy if that were the case. This ship's got active sensors going in every direction — it might as well be shouting at us, 'Look here!'"

The Sobrenian craft neared Splendor itself now, actually passing closer than the Unity's ships orbited, though in the opposite direction. Galt said, "At least we're getting some good intel on their ship — *Nivara 2, George Allenby, Erasmus* are all in position to do some good scans."

Captain Bram's voice came over the datalink: "Ambassador Galt, Chanda, if I do a stardrive microburst, I may be able to intercept this Sobrenian."

Chanda saw Galt consider that, but only for a moment before saying, "No, Captain. I don't know what kind of capability this Sobrenian has, but I know it's quite a risk for your ship. And I'm worried that it could be a decoy."

"Thank you, Ambassador. We'll follow as closely as we can until they jump again."

The image of the Sobrenian ship flared within the holo. "And there it goes," Chanda said.

Bram said, "I'm going to head toward the site of that stardrive jump and see if we can read anything from the residual radiation there. *Nivara 2* should be back in Splendorian orbit within an hour or so. Captain Bram out."

Chanda asked, "Do you think that ship was one of those Sobrenians we saw at the edge of the system?"

Galt adjusted the holo. "Good question. Let's trace its trajectory back as far as we can. Looks like . . . I don't think so. Different direction entirely, and most likely with a head start from outside the system. The *Tortoise* should be about to make a pass by those ships — I want to know what they're up to."

"So that Sobrenian ship jumps into the system only two hundred thousand kilometers out from Splendor — and being that close to a planetary mass doesn't seem to bother it."

"Nope. Neither does jumping out again."

"Not a capability we want them to have," Chanda said.

Galt turned off the holo and sat behind his desk. "Especially if those jumps were a proof of performance for the rest of the Sobrenian fleet."

Chanda fell into a chair next to Galt's desk. "Damn. I suppose we can't hope for reinforcements from the Unity."

"Not if that could get us in the middle of a war with the Sobrenians."

"So Splendor gets sacrificed."

"I'm not saying I agree with it," Galt said. "I'm just telling you the truth. I've called in every contact, every favor I have. The Unity's not willing to go to its citizens and say it's willing to sacrifice their daughters and sons, even for the sake of three sentient species on a single planet."

Chanda sat staring into nothingness for a long moment. Then she said, "I suppose I can't blame them."

"You have to face facts, Chanda. Maybe we've done all we can for Splendor."

Chanda stood and faced Galt. "Not while I'm still breathing. Not while there's that one more thing to try." She left Galt behind, breezed past Ken Westbrook again, and headed out the door, meaning to make a beeline for her quarters . . .

CHAPTER 28

A nd ran head-on into Ben Farrington. "Oops!" he said, grasping her shoulders to steady her, then lifting his hands to show he wasn't trying to touch her inappropriately. "Sorry about that!"

"No," Chanda said. "I wasn't looking where I was going."

"I coulda kept a better eye out, too. Hey, about that — " Ben's voice trailed off for a moment, then he said, "What's wrong? I didn't mean — "

Chanda grasped Ben's arm. "Oh, no, it's nothing to do with you. It's just . . . things are looking pretty bad right now."

Ben said, "This is more than Irene's recovery, isn't it? A lot more."

Chanda gave Ben a hard look. "Do you really want to know?"

"I've come here pretty late in the game. But I want to be as much a part of it as I can."

"Then let's have that tea."

They found a quiet corner in the embassy's commons to sit across a small table from one another and sip their hot tea. Ben looked expectantly at Chanda.

She put down her cup and said, "I have no idea where to start. In fact, I don't even know what we're here to talk about — Splendor, or me."

Ben's spoke softly. "Which do you want to talk about?"

"Don't do that."

"I'm sorry — do what?"

"The psychological approach. Feed everything I say right back at me."

Ben said, "I didn't do it on purpose."

"I'm sure you didn't. Listen, I'm sorry, maybe this wasn't a good idea."

"You're concerned about Splendor."

Chanda smiled. "That's good. Make it about both me *and* Splendor."

Ben shrugged. "Sorry. Psychological approach again?"

"It's all right. I suppose for the past few years, you talk about one, you talk about the other."

"You should be proud."

"Hah! Senator — now Ambassador Galt — comes down here, and *he's* really the one with the psychological approach. Asking me about the time I spent in stasis over the years, my parents dying, what he called my 'failed marriage,' and eventually my hobbies and sex life."

"That's interesting," Ben said. "So — tell me about your hobbies."

Chanda, caught off guard, laughed so hard she nearly spilled her tea. "That's great. It really is." She placed her hand over Ben's, and he grasped hers in return. "The thing I've *not* been talking about this entire time is how reluctant I am to become involved with someone romantically or even sexually. I can go all 'girly,' which I hate. I can't control my emotions."

"Uh, first of all, I find that hard to believe. Secondly, you seem to be making quite a leap from having a cup of tea to, uh. . . ."

"Romance or sex?"

"Well . . . yeah. Though we do seem to be holding hands."

Chanda pulled her hand away. "I guess it's not your fault. It's just that everyone seems to be pushing me toward you. Anyone tries to push me one way, I try to go the other."

Ben tilted his head and his eyebrows narrowed. "Wait a minute — who's been pushing you toward me?"

Chanda made a dismissive gesture. "Who hasn't? Irene, Akira, even Ambassador Galt."

"Well, Chanda, I'm sorry about that — although I don't know why I'm apologizing for something other people are doing. I had no idea about any of that." He pushed back his chair and stood. "And I'm going to go to them right now and tell them what I think."

Chanda got up and touched Ben on the arm. "Please don't — they thought they were doing me a favor."

"I don't want you thinking I'd be a part of something like that."

"It's mostly Irene and Akira — they have something so great that they want everyone else to have the same thing."

Ben nodded, grinning. "They're so cute together."

"Don't let *them* hear that word."

"Which word? Oh, 'cute?'"

"Say it where they can hear it, you might have 'cute' stuffed up your —"

Over her datalink, Ambassador Galt's voice interrupted her: "Chanda, please come to the ambassador's office. We have a new development."

Ben stood watching Chanda as she said, "I'll be right there." She told Ben, "I have to go."

"I understand."

Chanda gave Ben a wide smile as she told him, "I think you do. This was good."

"Com'on, Chanda. Admit it. It wasn't just good. It was better than you thought it would be."

"Not much of a distinction."

"You thought it was going to be that bad?"

"Worse."

Ben said, "You sure *you're* not taking the psychological approach?"

Chanda took his hand in hers and squeezed, just for a moment. Then she headed for the ambassador's office.

When Chanda arrived, Galt was already standing before the holographic display. A pea-sized sphere in one corner represented Splendor. Even at such a tiny size, it was still much larger than it would have been had the display been to scale. "I just heard from *Black Tortoise*," Galt said. "Its crew saw dozens of Sobrenian ships massed on the edge of the system." Galt indicated several formations of tiny green indicators on the opposite side of the room.

Chanda asked, "Does it look as if they're massing for an attack?"

"It looks like they're keeping their options open. They've got several different kinds of ships there — battle cruisers, surveillance craft, troop carriers. And look at this from just a few minutes ago — " Galt touched a control on his desk and the image turned flat and unsteady — a close shot of one of the Sobrenian starcraft. Its design was typical, roughly the shape of a sideways water drop, the bow being the sharp-tipped end. Its otherwise smooth surface, however, sported countless blisters and projections.

"Kind of unusual for a Sobrenian ship," Chanda said. "Looks like a lot more sensors than weapons."

"*Tortoise* believes it's one of the surveillance craft. Still has a lot of firepower, but not enough to take us on all alone."

The image of the Sobrenian ship wavered, then shot forward and was visible only for an instant as a blurred image, then was gone. Galt said, "This was the last image we received before *Tortoise* fell into stardrive and started back here. Thanks to light delay, the Sobrenians couldn't have spotted them before they were gone."

Chanda asked, "Do we know where the Sobrenian was headed?"

"Its trajectory could take it right here to Splendor, just like that previous ship. I've got all the Unity starcraft in orbit here on alert. If that Sobrenian's coming this way, it'll arrive in about an hour. I'm hesitant to keep letting these ships make close passes."

"But if we shoot first, then we give the Sobrenians an excuse to start shooting, too. And that fleet of ships can overpower our forces easily."

"I know. I'm afraid we'll have to let it pass again unless it shoots first."

"We should talk again to Govanek," Chanda said. "Maybe she has some ideas about what's going on."

"An excellent idea," Galt said. "Let's do more than just talk to her. Let's bring her back here — right now."

Knowing it would be the better part of an hour before Govanek arrived, Chanda went to the embassy's Command Center. She asked a technician there, Tim Benningfield, "Can you get a reading on Indirogar and the highlanders he's got with him?"

Benningfield said, "We've been following him as best we can. I think we've got some nanite uplinks that have gotten some readings of them." He worked some controls, and said, finally, "Here you go. I've even got a decent holo from a few hours ago."

The image that appeared before them was from a distance, but clearly showed a long line of highlanders trudging along beneath iron skies and an icy landscape. And there was Indirogar, leading them! *I'd know that walk anywhere,* Chanda thought. *Old as he is, tired as he must be, every step is strong and determined.*

"It doesn't look like they're making good time," Benningfield said.

"I'm afraid you're right." *Part of me hopes we don't end up having to rescue them,* Chanda thought. *Indirogar would be crushed if he failed to create his new village. But another part of me just wants to see him safe and warm.*

"Thanks," she told Benningfield. "You'll let me know if something changes with them?"

"That order already came down, Ma'am. From Captain Bram himself."

Shoulda known, Chanda thought, and left to wait for Govanek's arrival.

Chanda stood outside the embassy, shielding her eyes against wind-blown snow as the shuttle *Judith* landed. Govanek stepped immediately out of the airlock, and the *Judith*, which hadn't even powered down, lifted in the next instant.

"What was that about?" Chanda asked Govanek.

The Sobrenian said, "The archeological team was not happy about my being recalled, especially the Human in charge, Dr. Warden."

Chanda walked with Govanek into the embassy. "Well, I'm sorry about that, but we have more important matters to discuss. Although you did say you thought you were near a big discovery."

"Again, something I feel I should not discuss in detail until we know more. We have been unable to discover the nature of the life-signs we've discovered. But it appears to be a fourth Splendorian species."

"Damn, that's quite a bombshell — and I say that as someone who helped discover the third species we learned about, the sweepers."

"It is, as you say, quite interesting. And we've contacted a consultant to help us interpret our findings. We hope to know more soon."

"Well, then," Chanda said, "to the issue at hand — " Chanda detailed the massing of Sobrenian starcraft, the close pass one such ship had already made, and the stardrive boost of the second surveillance craft, which was expected to arrive near Splendor at any moment.

"I'm not aware of any specific plans my former colleagues had for an attack," Govanek said. "That could, of course, be that they didn't trust me with such information."

"I thought as much," Chanda said. "But keep trying to think of anything else you might have heard."

"I will."

Chanda and Govanek entered the ambassador's office, where the holo display now showed a close shot of Splendor, with the positions of the various Unity craft orbiting the planet indicated as well. Galt told Govanek, "Good to see you again, though I wish the circumstances were different."

"I understand the feeling," Govanek said. "I wish to return to my work at the archeological site as quickly as possible."

Chanda asked, "How soon do we expect this next Sobrenian ship?"

"Could be within seconds — there it is!"

The green image of the Sobrenian starcraft appeared more closely to the planet than Chanda expected. She peered at the readout of stats next to that image and drew in a sharp breath. "Only 50 thousand K from the planet's surface! How does it make a jump that close?"

"I don't like this," Galt said. "If they can jump an entire fleet into our space that close — we'll have too little time to react effectively."

Govanek pointed at the image of the Sobrenian craft. "Look! It's breaking up!"

The holographic image of the ship shattered into several pieces, which continued on parallel trajectories as they passed Splendor by and headed into open space. "They've been pushing their limits," Chanda said. "And it looks like they found them."

"I'm glad we didn't shoot now," Galt said. "The Sobrenians can't claim we destroyed their ship." He told Govanek, "This is exactly why I had you brought back here. I want you and Chanda to take the *Jelal* out to what's left of that ship and see what you can find out about it."

By the time Chanda and Govanek shuttled up to the *Jelal*, and it broke orbit and reached the shattered remnants of the Sobrenian ship, several hours had passed. Chanda and Govanek stood on either side of Captain Hamadi's command chair on the bridge of the *Jelal*. On the main viewscreen before them was the image of the major pieces of the Sobrenian craft, still tumbling in parallel trajectories. Many were large chunks of mangled metal, but others still formed recognizable sections of the ship. "There's a big part of the engineering section," Hamadi said, indicating the viewscreen. "That other one looks as if contains a lot of the command center, including the bridge."

Chanda said, "Those pieces are tumbling pretty well."

"We'll take care of that," Hamadi said. He turned to a technician on his right. "Let's get a couple enticement beams on those two main pieces — settle them down a bit."

"Will do, Captain," the man said, and leaned over his console to begin work. The beams, invisible in the vacuum of space close to the *Jelal*, appeared as bright bolts of energy within the dust and debris surrounding the two sections of the Sobrenian craft. Chanda could see the tumbling of those two sections begin to slow right away.

Hamadi said, "By the time you get over there, we'll have them stabilized. I wish we could bring them aboard, but they're just too big."

"A wise move, Captain, in any case," Govanek said. "There could still be volatiles or even hidden snares designed to kill intruders, even with the ship itself destroyed."

Chanda said, "Well, Captain, I guess we'll be on our way."

Hamadi said, "I'll go with you down to the hangar deck."

Once there, pilot Lt. Mura waited to take them aboard the shuttle *Dubois*. Chanda reached out to shake Hamadi's hand. "Well, Captain, I guess we'll see you later — "

Hamadi, though, didn't take her hand. "You'll continue seeing me right now," he said. "I'm going with you."

"Captain, that's not necessary."

"I think it is, Chanda. You've been mostly planetbound for some time."

"You don't have to be insulting."

"Says the woman who mutters 'explorer' like it's a dirty word."

"Does *everyone* know *everything* about me?"

"A lot of us know just enough, it seems. Just as I know Govanek's an experienced spacer and explorer. But she doesn't know Human systems and protocols that well. And I have the engineering expertise. I hate to put it this way, but that makes you the junior partner on this trip."

Govanek said, "I understand your decision. But for the captain to make such a trip — "

"That's right. The captain. My ship, my decision."

Chanda said, "You coulda said something a little sooner."

"And have this argument all the way out here? No thanks."

Chanda bowed to the inevitable and sat in the rear of the shuttle's cockpit next to Govanek. Mura sat in the pilot's seat while Hamadi settled into the right-hand position. Soon the wide hangar bay doors opened and *Dubois* glided out toward what remained of the shattered Sobrenian ship.

As Lt. Mura guided the shuttle closer to the section of the Sobrenian ship containing its engineering module, Hamadi said, "First thing to establish, I'm in command on this little trip. That should be obvious to you both, but I want to hear both of you acknowledge it."

Chanda felt ashamed that she was tempted to give Hamadi a mock salute. *Admit it Chanda*, she thought. *Your ego's screaming at you to tell Hamadi to back off. But he has a point — experience in diplomacy, frontier or otherwise, doesn't have much to do with this mission.* She told Hamadi, "I certainly acknowledge that."

"As do I," Govanek said.

"Great," Hamadi said. "You move when I say move, don't go near something unless I say it's OK, and when I say to back off from something or get the hell out of somewhere, you go."

"Understood," Chanda said.

"Very well. Lifesuits on — let's get to the airlock."

Mura eased the shuttle next to the open area of the section of the Sobrenian ship. Through the airlock window, Chanda saw jagged metal, long narrow corridors, and larger spaces filled with what remained of the usual equipment that created new-space before a starcraft, kept the transition from regular space to stardrive stable, and held the ship's energies in check, allowing a stardrive jump while keeping the ship's structure intact.

One of those systems apparently didn't do its job quite right, Chanda thought as she followed Hamadi and Govanek out of the airlock. A control pad in her left palm allowed her to operate thrusters, leaving her right hand free to aim a light attached to her right wrist or to operate sensors or grab something of interest.

As they approached the stricken ship, Chanda made sure to turn and catch a glimpse of Splendor — she was struck as always by its beauty, which was apparent even in the narrow blue and white crescent which was slowly receding behind them. The system's primary, Pinpoint, cast sharp reflections upon Splendor's Great Sea.

"Be careful as we head into this thing," Hamadi said, bringing Chanda's thoughts back to the purpose at hand. "One wrong move at the right speed, and even a lifesuit can be punctured for an instant before it 'heals' itself. You could find yourself cut up or have a body part flash-frozen."

Chanda glided into the Sobrenian ship's engineering section, keeping a close eye on her and her companions' beams of light as they swept back and forth. They advanced through a cloud of tiny particles of debris that gave the disconcerting impression of a horizontal snowstorm.

Govanek gave a gasp and Chanda shone her light in her direction. "What is it?" Chanda asked, as she guided herself closer to the Sobrenian.

Govanek indicated an uncertain form centered in her light. "There!"

Chanda moved closer and saw the mangled body of a Sobrenian crewmember. Its legs and one arm had been severed and were nowhere to be seen. Its eyes stared blindly. "You don't have to keep looking at it," Chanda told Govanek.

"I know," the Sobrenian said. "But I must face this — as I did the *koraht*."

"As much as I appreciate your emotional epiphany here, I have to remind you we have a job to do."

"Chanda's right," Captain Hamadi said. "Let's keep focused."

Govanek turned away from the floating body and faced one of the ship's larger systems, a cylindrical unit just over nine meters tall. "Very well, then," she said. "In looking at this phase transition module, it looks as if it has tech attached to it that I'm a bit familiar with. I believe they are scaled up versions of devices the missiles launched at Splendor years ago used."

Chanda said, "And those missiles pretty much came out of nowhere."

Hamadi aimed thrusters and brought himself closer to the side of the giant unit. Chanda followed. Hamadi ran his hand over several dead readouts on the side of the module, then along the burnt and scarred metal of several smaller modules attached to the main one. "I guess we won't be getting any information directly out of this thing," he said.

"Doubtful," Govanek said. "But we can extrapolate further."

"Me first," Hamadi said. "What was this ship's purpose? To see how closely a starcraft can come out of stardrive into a planet's gravitational field."

Chanda said, "The closer to the planet, the greater the element of surprise."

"Exactly. And for all their 'bluster,' as you like to put it, Chanda —
"

"*Again* with knowing everything about me!"

" — Later! For all that bluster, Sobrenians, with all respect, Govanek, don't actually shoot first that often."

Govanek said, "I certainly agree, Captain. It's one of our redeeming qualities."

"Given that, if they were finally going to start a shooting war, they'd want it over with quickly."

"That shouldn't be much of a problem," Chanda said, "given how small a presence the Unity has here."

Govanek said, "From what I know of Sedra and Tiernan, they'll want to take every precaution. They're not interested in a fight — only in winning."

CHAPTER 29

C aptain Hamadi insisted that they travel over to the other large piece of the Sobrenian craft. "I want to see if there's any chance of finding any records in that command center. Here's where you become particularly important, Govanek."

The Sobrenian said, "I'm eager to help — I don't want to see Splendor attacked."

Chanda followed Hamadi's lead as he eased himself past the jagged metal of the engineering section once again and launched himself toward the command center.

As she and Hamadi and Govanek approached the remnants of the bridge, Chanda couldn't help thinking that she was accustomed to what a Sobrenian starcraft bridge usually looked like — so brightly lit that a Human sometimes had to shield her eyes against the light, with holos and displays everywhere. But this ship's bridge had been torn in half, the oval console that was the centerpiece of most such bridges shattered, the holos and flat readouts blank. *It's going to be difficult to learn much here*, Chanda thought.

Govanek rushed past her, swiftly enough that Hamadi placed himself in front of her to keep her from colliding with a wall. "Careful, my friend," he told her. "You don't know what surprises this place could still hold."

"Precisely why I am so eager to get to this particular module," Govanek said. "I'm familiar with these kind of storage capabilities. I believe I can learn more of this ship's capabilities and its mission."

"Then feel free," Hamadi said, easing himself out of the Sobrenian's way.

Govanek worked the sensor controls of her lifesuit so efficiently that Chanda couldn't believe she'd only had one for a few days. After taking several readings from different consoles, Govanek started working controls on her suit that Chanda couldn't recognize. *She's not only mastered what we've given her*, Chanda thought, *she's come up with her own tech!*

One of the bridge's flat readouts lit up for a instant, then another, and another. Govanek clearly was trying to get some of the holo displays to work, as well, but without success. Finally she stopped and stared at the dark readouts and Chanda heard a low sigh that didn't require translation. She asked, "So, what have you learned?"

"Very little so far," Govanek said. "I've downloaded a lot of raw data. I know that this is the starcraft *Aurator*. It's primarily a reconnaissance craft. And it looks as if that unusual tech back in the engineering section is additional shielding against gravitational stresses."

"Doesn't look like it worked," Chanda said.

"From what I know of Sedra, she would want to push the technology as far as possible."

Hamadi asked, "Would that include the possibility of sacrificing an entire crew?"

"Sedra would think of it as insisting that a crew would solve problems on the spot that automation could not."

"What are the odds," Chanda wondered, "that the crew would have no idea just how dangerous their mission was — that it could even be considered a suicide mission?"

"They would be given a choice — certain death upon refusing the mission or a chance to save themselves if something went wrong during the mission."

"Either way," Hamadi said, "it doesn't seem to have worked out very well for them. What else can you tell us?"

"Very little. But once we get back to Splendor, I can continue to analyze this information."

Hamadi said, "Then let's get you back there."

It was several hours later when Chanda and Govanek arrived back at the Unity embassy on Splendor; they'd been up for the better part of a day, and it was the middle of the night when the shuttle *Rico* deposited them back onto Splendor's surface and they walked through the former starcraft's main entrance. But with Chanda's first step inside, Ambassador Galt's voice came over her datalink: "Chanda, can you come see me in my office?"

"My" office, Chanda thought. *Up until now it's been the "ambassador's office," whether out of respect for me or not quite believing it himself, I don't know.*

But I don't have time for petty thoughts. "I'll be right there," Chanda said. She turned to Govanek. "Go ahead and get some sleep if you want. But afterwards, I need you to stay here and work on all that information you got from the Sobrenian ship."

"I will do that," Govanek said. "First the sleep, that is — then the work." Chanda headed toward the ambassador's office.

Ken Westbrook wasn't there when Chanda went through the outer office, which was only dimly lit. Galt's office, in fact, was lit mostly by the glow of the usual holo display, which was showing the massed Sobrenian ships at the edge of the system again. Galt stood there, either unaware of her presence or ignoring her for now, eyes seemingly focused somewhere past the display, one arm folded across his chest, the other cupping his chin.

Another moment passed, and Galt's eyes seemed to focus more

closely. He blinked a couple times, then his arms dropped to his sides. Without turning toward Chanda, he asked, "Do you still resent me for becoming the ambassador?"

"Resent you? I . . . no. I can't."

"I wouldn't blame you. Dealing with all this, I don't know how you did it. The Sobrenians. Valley dwellers. Highlanders. Sweepers. Buruden. And never mind the Unity politics."

Chanda stepped closer. "Just looking at you right now — I can see how everything's weighing on you."

"If you did have any feelings against me, Chanda, this would be your revenge — my having this job."

"I suppose you're the only person who might understand what I've been coping with these past few years. But you've been in combat. You've had lives in your hands before."

"Not a whole planet's worth — not three entire species. I haven't slept in three days, you know that? Stims only take you so far. I'm about to hit the wall." Galt took a couple of steps back and slumped into a chair. "Viewer off," he said, and the holo display disappeared. The subdued lighting that remained revealed deeply etched lines in Galt's face; his features stood out in sharp relief. *He looks old just days after taking the job*, Chanda thought. *What the hell must I look like?*

Galt asked, "I got your preliminary report, of course. Has Govanek figured out anything else from that raw data?"

"She's getting some sleep — then she'll keep working on finding out as much as she can."

"I envy her the sleep. Not anything else."

"Stop the stims. Get about twelve hours sleep. You'll be better for it."

"You're right, of course. I've been going against all my training. What if a Sobrenian attack came right now? I'd be almost useless. But these continued incursions into Splendorian space — and this massing of forces out there — I hate to say this, Chanda. But I need you to coordinate another kind of evacuation effort for us — one that takes all Unity personnel off this planet."

Chanda felt the blood pulsing in her neck. She squeezed her eyes shut and rubbed her temples. When she looked up at Galt, she said, "Goddam, that's not what I ever expected to hear from you. From some Unity puke who's never been off Earth, maybe never been outside Brussels, maybe, but not from you. You've commanded a star-craft, you've gotten yourself elected to the Unity Senate. You've *done* things, *seen* things."

Galt placed his elbows on his desk and looked at Chanda across folded hands. "That's exactly why I'm insisting upon this. I've seen women and men die right in front of me. And not always from a nice clean disruptor blast — how about from the concussion and fire when your ship takes a good hit from an energy bolt? Body parts everywhere?"

"I've been under fire," Chanda said, but her voice didn't carry the weight she'd intended it would.

"I know you have. But I've seen more, and worse. I'm not in denial."

"How am I in denial?"

"You don't really believe the Sobrenians will attack this world. Or if it looks like they're about to, you think you can talk them out of it, or pull something out of a hat at the last minute, the way you did when you established this embassy even as the Sobrenian missiles were bearing down on you."

"I wasn't thinking of myself as particularly clever then. Just desperate."

Galt said, "This is what desperate looks like when it has a chance to plan ahead. I'm asking you to get together with Captain Bram tomorrow morning and work out a plan to get every last Human off of Splendor. And I mean yourself, too. No heroics. Can you do that?"

Chanda took a deep breath and placed a hand against her chest. She could feel the rapid beat of her heart. *My mother leaned over and spoke softly into my right ear. "We do a lot of things for love, Chanda. One day you'll understand."*

Galt leaned forward, almost got out of his chair. "Chanda, are you all right?"

"Yeah. Fine. I'll . . . make sure to get together with Bram on that."

Chanda went to her quarters, stood in her small kitchen, started to fix herself some tea, then stopped in mid-motion. *I thought I'd feel more emotion,* she thought. *I knew this time was likely to come — when I'd be told I'd be leaving Splendor.*

No, not just leaving it. Abandoning *it — to the Sobrenians, to the gas nebula, to the problems the highlanders and valley dwellers are having as they try to recreate their former societies since the evacuation effort failed.*

Since I failed.

Chanda poured her drink into the sink.

She left her quarters and walked with determined strides toward visitors' quarters, hoping she could arrive at her destination before she lost her nerve.

She didn't touch the buzzer at Ben's door. A soft knock seemed more appropriate, as if assuming that Ben might still be up, that she wouldn't really be disturbing him.

No response, though — Chanda knocked a bit louder.

And louder still, just a little bit.

A muted, sleepy voice, from inside: "Who's there? Is it important?"

"It's Chanda. And . . . I think it's important."

Ben's voice was louder, more engaged: "Lemme get something on." A rustling of clothing from within, and Ben's door slid open. The room was only dimly lit; he wore a tightly belted robe. "What's wrong? Irene's biotech should've alerted me if she was having a problem."

"It's not about Irene," Chanda said. "Can I come in?"

"Of course," Ben said, and stepped aside. Chanda felt he was looking at her in a new way, with a new seriousness. "Would you like something to drink?" he asked.

"I was about to make some tea. But I didn't. Or . . . I did, but I poured it out. I don't know why."

"Then let me make you some more. Go ahead, sit down."

"Maybe in a minute," Chanda said. She found herself looking around her, to see whether Ben had his own idea of a "homespace." She saw no evidence for one. *But then, he's headed back up to* Sergeant Jelal *anytime now*, she thought. *Of course he's not made himself at home. I'm not thinking right.*

Ben handed her the cup of tea. "Watch out," he told her. "It's hot."

Chanda took the cup gingerly by its handle, didn't take a sip. Ben picked up his own cup, looked at her. "Chanda — what can I do for you?"

She gave him a tentative smile. "Sometimes just tea's enough."

"Then won't you sit?"

"Yeah." She settled into a chair, and Ben sat across from her. Chanda didn't meet his eyes again, but she could feel his gaze on her. He leaned forward, expectantly. Chanda brought her steaming cup to her lips, took a careful sip. "You're right. It is hot."

Ben leaned back in his chair. Chanda looked at him, and her smile lingered longer this time. "I guess you've decided to wait me out," Chanda said.

Ben said, "You wouldn't be here if it wasn't important. I can figure out the Sobrenians haven't invaded or anything like that because you'd be right in the middle of it. So it's not that kind of emergency."

"You think I'm here because of some kind of emergency?"

"I think you're here because this is where you need to be."

Chanda took a longer sip. "You sound rather sure of yourself."

"You're the one who came here. I just opened the door."

"Huh. That may've been your mistake. You open a door, you gotta take whatever comes through it."

Ben leaned forward again. "Chanda — this back and forth is all very cute. But I'm sincere. I haven't known you very long, or very well, but I can tell you don't do anything casually. Like you said, I can 'wait you out.'"

"I have to come up with another evacuation plan. This time, one that has Humans leaving Splendor forever."

"Things are that bad."

"The Sobrenians could attack at any time."

"What do they want here?"

"Splendor's placed right between their homeworld and the Buruden's. It would make a great way station for them — a place to rearm or refuel or repair their starcraft. It's a comfortable planet for them. They could use it to train ground troops."

"Or for target practice."

"Yeah. Lived through that."

"And Humanity's just in the way."

"Not to mention three intelligent Splendorian species. Four, if Govanek and the *George Allenby* crew's found something."

"It's sad, Chanda. That we aren't here just to explore rather than have to defend this planet."

"Yeah. I have my own issues with explorers, sometimes."

"What's wrong with being an explorer?"

"Nothing as such. It just that sometimes they can't see that there are values and necessities other than their own obsession."

"Hmm. I see."

Chanda shook her head. "Again with the psychological approach." Ben held his hands wide and looked all around the room as if the "psychological approach" was hiding close by. "What?" Chanda asked.

"You might not like it."

"Ben, my whole career is either hearing things I don't like or saying things other people don't like."

"I was just thinking you're not the person to be criticizing other people for their obsessions."

Chanda's teacup was warm enough to grasp with both hands; its warmth comforted her. "Well . . . that might be fair enough. But I think my obsessions are more important."

Ben licked his lips, swallowed, and made a quiet cough. "I can't think of anything to say to that won't be another supposed psychological observation."

A couple short breaths, and Chanda said, "I guess I did place you into a corner. I wasn't trying to. It's just . . . I've always tried to look forward. You talk about supposed obsessions, and it starts sounding like I have unfinished business from my past."

"We all do," Ben said. "And I don't know all of your past," Ben said. "But it seems. . . . "

"Unusual at best. In stasis much of my childhood. Parents dead at an early age. Married to an Arol for a time."

"Really? To a non-Human? An . . . "

"You can say it. An asexual being. Yes."

"That must have been . . . unusual."

"Most people would say love is more important than sex. I just put that into action." She smiled mischievously at Ben. "Sorry if that's disappointing."

Ben's return smile was undercut by the concern Chanda could read in his eyes. "We're still just talking, Chanda. Though we did hold hands for a moment once. So . . . it didn't work out?"

"I was . . . unfaithful to him. To my husband, Pordo."

"I don't understand. If you — "

"I had an affair with a doctor in the town near our home. But Pordo got me back."

Ben said, "So he was unfaithful, too?"

"I was unfaithful sexually — I know, to someone who doesn't even have sex. But he was unfaithful emotionally. With another Human woman. He sat with her in her home. Talked. Shared himself."

Ben said, "I'm not sure what to say. Except I'm sorry it didn't work out."

"No, you're not," Chanda said. "I wouldn't be here talking with you otherwise."

"I'll concede that point."

"I'm just . . . sorry I've brought you into the middle of all my problems — past and present."

Ben leaned close to Chanda and took both her hands. "It shows you trust me, Chanda — though we barely know each other. I take that as a compliment."

Chanda found her hands shaking as she slid them up Ben's arms and took him into a tight embrace. She didn't quantify how long they embraced one another. Eventually she broke the embrace and kissed Ben on the cheek as they returned to their previous position holding hands.

Over Chanda's datalink: "Chanda — this is Govanek. I hope I'm not disturbing you."

Ben was about to speak again, but she held up a hand to him as she spoke to Govanek: "It's all right, Govanek. Did you manage to get some sleep?"

"I found I could not. I've been working instead. And I'd like you to see what I've discovered."

Chanda told Govanek, "I'll be right there." She cut the link to the Sobrenian and told Ben, "I'm sorry. I've got to go."

Ben leaned forward for a quick kiss, then said, "I wish I could go with you. But I was about to get up, anyway. They're sending the *Rico* down to get me. And I'd better help get the infirmary ready if there could be an attack."

"Which doesn't say much for our diplomatic efforts."

"I don't think the Sobrenians are much for diplomacy."

"They pretend to be when it suits their purposes."

Ben leaned over and gave Chanda a lingering kiss. Afterwards, he said, "I was tired of talking."

"It's all I do," Chanda said.

"We'll see each other soon. When this is all over."

If we're both still alive, Chanda thought but didn't dare say. She pulled Ben down and kissed him again. "It's never over," she said. "Even if we survive the Sobrenians, the gas nebula's still on the way."

"That's decades away. Somewhere in there you can find some time for yourself."

"I'm not sure what else to say. Maybe I need to stick to the big picture. You know, negotiating with other Galactic species, saving worlds, that kind of thing."

Ben looked at her. "You've neglected yourself. Shut yourself off emotionally."

"I never meant to."

"Yeah." Chanda pulled away from Ben but held onto his hand for another moment. "See ya soon."

"I'll be waiting."

Chanda was supposed to be headed to Govanek's quarters, but she made a detour to her own rooms, sat on her bed, shut her eyes tight, and wondered why tears wouldn't come.

After a few moments, she got up and continued on her way to see Govanek.

CHAPTER 30

The Sobrenian's quarters were smaller than Ben's, but Chanda knew Govanek preferred it that way, that sometimes she felt overwhelmed in larger Human living spaces.

Chanda barely had a chance to sit down before Govanek told her, "Either this is an amazing coincidence or we've found connections between Splendor and another Galactic species we never dreamed of."

Chanda was even more intrigued now. "Which species?"

"The Buruden."

"But the Buruden only came here originally by accident — when one of the Sobrenians's ships was destroyed and its crew tried to take over a Buruden ship."

"Which ended up crashing here — yes, I know. But the Sobrenian starcraft we just examined — the *Aurator* — had several possible scenarios in its memory banks involving Buruden attacks on their forces here at Splendor, and various responses to those attacks."

Chanda asked, "But why would the Buruden attack the Sobrenians here? They've been trying to keep conflict away from here."

"There could be many reasons. Perhaps the Buruden have

decided, however, reluctantly, that they would prefer such violence take place here at Splendor rather than on their homeworld."

"Which isn't really their homeworld, of course."

"That is true, Chanda. But it is as close to one as they have for now. All sentient Galactic species have a strong sense of self-preservation. Otherwise they wouldn't have survived to travel into space."

Chanda said, "Could this have been a plant?"

"Failure to translate. Unless you are speaking of the local flora."

"I'm not. Could this have been information the Sobrenians placed on the *Aurator* hoping we'd find it?"

"I'm willing to believe my former colleagues would place a ship and its crew in severe danger, and would not tell them of the severity of that danger. I'm not yet willing to concede that they would send a crew on a certain suicide mission simply to provide us with false information. And how would they know we would go after that ship once it broke apart?"

"I have to agree with you about the latter. Though not necessarily the former."

"Chanda, I think it more likely that their arrogance told them the ship would never be destroyed and that we would never find any secrets it contained."

"I suspect you're right, there."

"Which brings me to the other possible connection between Splendor and the Buruden. I hesitate to tell you about this. None of this is confirmed."

"Govanek — anything you know could be important. If I don't know what you've found, I have no way of evaluating it."

"Very well. It has to do with the investigation at the anthropological site. We believe we've found evidence of Buruden genetic material there."

"The hell? You mean, genetic material as in something that originated on this planet?"

"We believe so, yes."

"Govanek, you gotta understand what that means. If the Buruden originated here — "

"Yes. Then Splendor is the Buruden homeworld."

"Do the Buruden even know that?"

"Apparently they never suspected it. But they should be arriving soon."

"What? Who? The Buruden?"

"Yes," Govanek said. "You may recall I said a consultant was to arrive soon to interpret our findings of a fourth Splendorian species? A Buruden ship should be arriving soon with that consultant."

"Holy shit," Chanda said. "You should've told me, or told Galt about this."

"About which item?"

"*All* of it — Splendor being the Buruden homeworld — "

"Not yet proven, Chanda."

" — A Buruden ship coming here when Sobrenians may be looking for any excuse to attack us — "

"The Buruden ship is only expected to be an exploratory craft."

"The Sobrenians don't know that!"

"Oh, dear," Govanek said. "I fear I may not have the proper diplomatic or military mindset."

"When do you expect the Buruden ship to arrive?"

"Any moment."

"Any *moment*?" Chanda touched behind her ear. "Chanda to Captain Bram."

His response was immediate; Chanda wondered whether he was already awake: "Bram here. What can I do for you?"

Chanda explained to Bram why a Buruden starcraft might be entering Splendorian space any minute, concluding, "Ambassador Galt wanted us to come up with an evacuation plan for all the Humans on Splendor. But it may be too late for that."

"I've had people right here on *Nivara* 2 working on that, Chanda," Bram said. "The plan's not complete, it's not perfect, but we'll have a chance to get pretty much everybody off the planet given just a little notice."

"'Just about' everybody?"

"There's hundreds of us, Chanda — and some people were just dropped off by ships that moved on. It's going to be a tight fit just to squeeze everyone aboard the ships we have."

"All right — I'd better go see the ambassador — he needs to know about all of this."

"In the meantime — " Bram began, then fell silent as Chanda heard a commotion in the background. After a moment, Bram, speaking to someone on the *Nivara 2*'s bridge, said, "Very well. Keep me posted." To Chanda, he said, "You've got an update for the ambassador and you haven't even talked to him yet. The Buruden ship just arrived in orbit."

Bram cut the connection. Chanda couldn't move, couldn't speak for a moment. Then she told Govanek, "They're here. Let's go see Galt, and get ready to receive them."

"We have to make a trip of our own," Govanek said. "They're not going to land at the embassy."

Chanda stopped in mid-step. "Where the hell are they landing, then?"

Govanek told her.

Moments later, Chanda was back at Ben's door, leaning on the call bell. When he opened his door, his mouth split into a wide grin. "I know you said 'see ya soon,' but this is redic — "

"Ben, sorry, no time. I need a pilot and I'd like to take Irene or Akira. Can you clear either one of them?"

Ben took a deep breath. "If you need them that badly, then yes."

Chanda leaned forward and gave Ben a quick peck on the mouth. "Thanks!" And she headed fast as she could down the corridor, grinning to herself as she imagined the look on Ben's face as he stared after her.

Irene and Akira's quarters were the next stop. She explained the situation as they yawned and rubbed their eyes. Then she asked them, "Who wants to be my pilot? Govanek and I are headed for the archeological site."

The women traded looks, apparently came to a wordless decision. Irene said, "Looks like you're sitting in the back, Chanda."

One final stop. Ambassador Galt was still in his office, as she knew he would be. At Chanda's assertion that Splendor was the Buruden homeworld, he said, "Chanda, that seems pretty far-fetched to me. But I can't afford to ignore the possibility. I take it you're going to check it out?"

"Unless you have some objection."

"Never. Information's our most valuable commodity. Let me know if you find anything that can help us. It's started looking even more desperate just in the last few minutes."

Galt activated the holo of the Splendorian system and indicated the area at its edge where the Sobrenian ships had gathered earlier. "There's more of them now." He pointed upward. "A lot of them are gathered here, too — out of the plane of the ecliptic."

"If they can come out of stardrive so close to Splendor, why are they coming together where we can see them? Why not just jump directly from their homeworld?"

"It looks as if those stardrive jumps have some pretty severe limitations — they can't jump that closely to a planet from outside the system. Given what happened to the *Aurator*, it looks like they're already pushing those limitations."

Chanda said, "So we'll know their overall strength before they get here. But this makes things even more complicated."

"Technology is only a single factor in any conflict, and perhaps not as important as how your enemy reacts — how he uses it."

"I'd think superior tech would make a big difference."

CHANDA'S AWAKENING   333

"Only if it's used properly. A determined guerrilla force can make a particular campaign too costly to win."

"Ambassador — with all this talk of military capabilities and advantages in a fight, does that mean I don't need to come up with an evacuation plan anymore?"

"Any evacuation we do will be on a much smaller scale — mostly getting Dr. Warden and his colleagues off the planet, and any other civilians. That's probably not more than a hundred people. We can arrange that in an hour or so if we have to."

"So you think the Unity will approve of our military forces sticking here?"

Galt's eyebrows raised. "Chanda, as far as the Unity's going to be concerned, the Sobrenians are just continuing to bluster, as you put it, and this whole business with the Buruden mobilizing to protect their homeworld is just a rumor."

"Because that's what you're going to tell them."

"Well . . . that may be the gist of my next report."

"Then I'll be goddamned," Chanda said. "Now you see how easy it is to get involved in 'frontier diplomacy.'"

"Huh. Either way, I've bought us some time apart from Unity interference."

"Good deal," Chanda said as she headed for the door. "Time is the one thing we can't make more of."

———

As Chanda reached the main entrance of the embassy, she heard the whine of a shuttle's gravitics, a piercing sound that ramped up quickly. Chanda gathered her parka around her and hurried outside. The shuttle *Rico* was ascending toward overcast skies, and Chanda knew Ben was one of its passengers.

Within seconds, *Rico* disappeared into the cloud cover, and Chanda listened as the sound of the unseen shuttle's gravitics faded.

A hand slapped down on Chanda's shoulder. Irene said, "Don't worry, Chanda, he'll be back soon enough."

"Uh . . . yeah."

Irene looked at her with tilted head and raised eyebrows. "Really? That's all you've got to say? I know you've always been happy about what Akira and I have. Let us be happy for you."

Govanek joined them and they started walking toward the *Bashi*, which Akira was already aboard and prepping. Chanda said, "To be honest, I'm not quite sure what I have."

"I wasn't sure with Akira for a while. Didn't know how good I had it. Now . . . well, I just don't think of being with anyone else."

Any subtext there? Chanda wondered as they headed toward the *Bashi. Is Irene trying to tell me she's over any infatuation she had with me?*

Damn. Now I almost feel spurned. Good thing I've got Ben. Sort of got him.

As Irene was bringing the *Bashi* down about a hundred meters away from the excavation site, she told Chanda, "You don't know how happy I am to be flying again." Akira's wide grin punctuated that statement.

"I'm glad to have the both of you back," Chanda told them. "Right now, you'll excuse me if I leave you both here. Keep the shuttle warmed up and ready to go. The Buruden could be coming down here any minute now."

Chanda was still zipping up her parka as she exited the shuttle and headed toward the archeological site with Govanek right behind her. She squinted against a blast of cold air that blew snow and dust into her eyes. *I'd be tempted to activate my lifesuit,* she thought, *but I'd rather suffer than be looked down upon as weak by a group of groundhugger explorers.*

Never mind that some spacers might consider me *a* "*groundhugger.*"

Chanda and Govanek topped a ridge and looked down at the excavation, which was about sixty meters wide and ninety long. It had been dug down to a depth of about six meters. About two dozen people were present; several were in the pit while others stood to one side, operating insectile-limbed 'bots that made as little contact with the ice, snow, and dirt as possible as they brushed artifacts clean or carefully drilled into the earth. Other workers were checking readouts on portable sensor units.

Govanek said, "I find this so exciting. This is where we might figure out how to save the planet."

"Don't overstate things," Chanda said. "The Buruden aren't here yet. We don't know the details of what they're about to see, or how they'll react to it."

As they approached the excavation site, Captain Bram's voice came over Chanda's datalink. "Chanda, we've got a potential problem with Indirogar's people."

Chanda asked, "What's wrong with them?"

"It looks like all of them except Indirogar himself have turned back."

"They've given up?"

"Looks like it," Bram said. "As much as our sensors can make out, they're all undernourished and worn out. They didn't even make it halfway to the Heavenlock Mountains — which must make a return to Roraten's village look pretty appealing. They should make it back just fine."

"But Indirogar's continuing on."

"That's right. And this happened about half a day ago, apparently. We never noticed because they took a different path than we anticipated — away from the nanite uplinks, a bit closer to the Great Sea. The orbits didn't work out for any of our ships to keep an eye on them until just a few minutes ago."

"Do we have anyone that can help him out?"

"No one but you — I've got everyone else on combat readiness."

"OK — I've got this meeting with the Buruden about the archeological site, then we'll see what we can do."

"Bram out."

Govanek asked, "Do we need to help Indirogar?"

"We will in just a minute," Chanda said.

"For now, I will introduce you to the head of the archeological effort." She led them down to the edge of the excavation. A curly-haired man in his forties stood, apparently oblivious to their approach, concentrating on one of the portable sensors. He was rubbing his full beard and though his parka stood open and he wore no hat or hood, the cold didn't seem to affect him.

"Dr. Warden," Govanek said.

Warden looked up at Chanda and the others as if they'd just dropped from the sky. "Govanek — I'm so glad to have you back! But — who is your . . . uh . . . friend?"

Is it strange that he doesn't recognize me? Chanda wondered. *Or is that just my own ego talking?* "I'm Chanda Kasmira, Doctor The former ambassador. It's good to meet you, especially since you're doing such important work here."

Warden accepted Chanda's hand, but perfunctorily, without a sense of social obligation. His words were more enthusiastic: "At last someone is recognizing the work we're doing here. I have to admit, Ambassador — "

"Just Chanda, please — Senator Galt is now the ambassador."

"Oh . . . sorry. I have to admit, we've been disappointed that you've never visited our site."

"Dr. Warden — I'm afraid you might not realize why I've finally come here."

Warden finally focused on Chanda, and she could see the worry in his features. "It's not the love of discovery, is it? Of knowledge for its own sake?"

"I'm afraid not. But it seems you know something that the Buruden should."

"I should've realized — it's more of this political bullshit that's kept us from getting the resources we need."

Chanda said, "Listen, I know something about 'political bullshit.' I've seen more than my share of it. But that's not what we're dealing with now. We're talking about preventing this planet from being caught up in a war."

Some of the other workers were staring at them now, and Warden held up his hands as if in surrender. "All right, I understand. Humans aren't the only species that has to mark its territory or show everyone its strength. I know how these social patterns work."

Govanek said, "Please, Dr. Warden. This Human is my friend, every bit as much as you. She's only trying to help."

Warden abruptly seemed to feel the cold. He zipped his parka and thrust his hands into his pockets. "Then how can I help you?"

Chanda asked, "Is Splendor the Buruden homeworld?"

Warden looked from Chanda to Govanek in turn. "*That's* it? That's all you want to know?"

"That's *all*?" Chanda exclaimed. She took a step toward Warden, who actually pulled his hands from his pockets and held them up as if to defend himself from an expected blow.

"Sorry," he said. "I didn't know how important it was to you."

"Don't you realize what that might mean to everyone on this planet? That includes you, by the way. The Buruden might just want to help us defend Splendor against a Sobrenian attack."

Warden gave them a quizzical look. "That's a real possibility? I thought it was just so the diplomats and the military could keep control over us."

Chanda waved that idea away. "Jesus Christ, man, you think if I don't know about your discoveries here, maybe that means I'm not as curious as I should be. Which might actually be true. But if you don't know what the diplomats and soldiers are taking on, you could wake up dead one morning and not even know why!"

Warden could only manage, "Uh, uh . . . "

"So tell us," Chanda said. "Is this the Buruden homeworld?"

"Well — *yes*," Warden said. "We believe it is. So what do you think the Buruden will make of that?"

Chanda pointed toward the western sky. "We'll know soon enough. There's the Buruden shuttle."

The long cylindrical craft sported the usual Buruden markings of yellow, maroon, and gold. It touched down soundlessly next to the *Bashi* and a dozen linked Buruden rushed out of the craft.

"Dr. Warden," Chanda said, "do you have a way to protect your excavation from being trampled on?"

"Yes — energy shields. They're designed to keep quicksleep or burrowers or whatever from just wandering in."

"I'd suggest you activate them."

Warden started to say, "What do you — " Then he took a good look at the approaching Buruden. "They wouldn't — "

Chanda said, "They won't mean to, but they'll trample everything in sight in their enthusiasm."

Warden turned to his colleagues. "Everyone, out of the pit — and turn on the energy shields!"

The workers who were in the pit scrambled out of it, the last person jumping clear just as a technician activated the shields with the Buruden less than five meters from the edge. Chanda feared they would all pile up against the barely visible wall of energy, but they managed a reasonably dignified halt.

As one, the dozen Buruden turned toward Chanda. "We are the ambassador."

Chanda found herself smiling as if she was greeting a long-lost friend, though she had no way of knowing whether this version of the Buruden ambassador even consisted of any individuals she'd encountered before. "I'm sorry we had to prevent you from entering the pit. But what's being uncovered there is very sensitive and could be damaged easily."

"Forgive our enthusiasm," the ambassador said. "May we detach two of ourselves to inspect the pit?"

Chanda looked toward Dr. Warden, hoping her expression

made it clear that the diplomatic value of such an inspection was worth the risk of damage to his precious excavation. But to her surprise, Warden seemed thrilled with the idea: "Certainly you may! I'd be pleased to hear any insights you may be able to contribute!"

Two of the Buruden detached themselves, and at a nod from Warden, a Human technician de-activated the energy shield. One of the Buruden explored around the edge of the pit while the other moved gingerly toward the center.

"Look at that!" Chanda said. "Their legs are perfect for the job." The Buruden's spiny legs, much like those of the 'bots, barely disturbed the ground beneath them.

Govanek went to the ten remaining linked Buruden. "I'm sure Dr. Warden would be pleased to show you some of the findings we've made here."

Chanda was grateful that for once Warden was quick on the uptake — he wheeled over one of the portable sensor units and tilted its screen down so the Buruden could view it. He touched a couple controls, and a succession of images appeared, mostly bone fragments, but a few fossils and even a series of rocks. Warden said, "We've been looking for anything that might tell us about the origins of life here on Splendor. Discovering three sentient species — the highlanders, valley dwellers, and sweepers — is unprecedented. We've never found another world like it."

Chanda said, "Forgive a layman's ignorance, Doctor — but what about whales and dolphins on Earth? We communicate with them easily with datalinks."

"Communicate, yes. But their mentality is mostly devoted to music and philosophy, respectively. They don't shape the world around them. Mostly that's due to their aquatic origins, which they've never transcended."

"I get it," Chanda said. "Whereas a sweeper can knock a shuttle out of the sky if it wants to. But I still suspect sentience is located along a continuum, and not just on one side of a dividing line."

Warden didn't take his eyes off the Buruden as he said, "On that, I'm sure we can agree."

The two Buruden who had detached from the rest left the excavation and rejoined the group. After a pause, the Buruden ambassador said, "We have confirmed your theory. It seems we originated here on Splendor."

Chanda said, "So — a *fourth* intelligent Splendorian species!"

"In a sense," the Buruden said. "Somehow rather than developing a single sentient species, life split from our original Buruden form into several others — those you know as the highlanders, valley dwellers, and sweepers. And each developed sentience as a primary survival tool."

Dr. Warden spoke up: "Do you have any theories as to how your species developed here? Splendor has a slow pace for evolution, and the nature of the highlanders, valley dwellers, and sweepers reflect that. But the Buruden evolve very quickly."

The Buruden ambassador said, "We can only speculate — our species has lived many years on other worlds. We did not develop starflight ourselves. Perhaps we adapted to those other worlds with a faster evolutionary rate. We can, in fact, guide our own evolution."

Dr. Warden asked, "What species gave you starflight?"

"That is information lost within our deepest history."

"This is all very interesting," Chanda said, "but what does this mean for the Buruden and Splendor?"

"It means that we must preserve this planet against the Sobrenians — and against the gas nebula. This is a truth."

A truth expressed in singular terms, not as one of four, Chanda thought. *So they mean it.* "Can you help us militarily?"

The Buruden ambassador said, "We've already summoned one of our fleets, while being careful not to leave our current 'homeworld' unprotected. The message should arrive within hours, and the fleet can be here within a day or so. We can only hope it arrives in time — more Sobrenian starcraft are leaving their homeworld, and we believe they are heading toward Splendor."

Warden said, "I'm ready to help you. And, I apologize for my attitude earlier. I realize now what's at stake."

"Quite honestly, the best thing you can do now is just continue with your work and cooperate with the Buruden the best you can." Chanda slapped Warden on the shoulder, sending him stumbling to one side. "Help us save the planet, and I'll make sure the Unity sends everything you need to dig out every secret this planet is hiding."

Warden held out his hand for Chanda to shake. "You can count on me."

Chanda told Govanek, "I'll be grateful for any insights into the Sobrenians you might be able to give us."

Govanek said, "Chanda — I must remind you — though I've pledged myself to help Humanity, I do not consider myself a traitor to my own people. I hesitate to provide information that will allow you to kill them more effectively."

Chanda reached down and placed her gloved hands on Govanek's shoulders. "I'm so sorry. I didn't mean to imply you were a traitor. I'll leave it up to you. Whatever help your conscience tells you to provide, do so. Anything else — we'll cope on our own."

Govanek looked up at Chanda. "Do you have any idea how loyal that makes me want to be to you?"

"I really don't think of it in those terms, Govanek."

"I know."

Bram's voice came back, this time a shout over the datalink: "Sobrenian warcraft out of stardrive at the edge of the atmosphere! It's firing on your position!"

CHAPTER 31

A touch to Chanda's ear, and she said, "Irene, Akira, be ready to lift!" To Dr. Warden, she said, "Get your people ready to evacuate."

Warden said, "But our work — our equipment. . . . "

"Goddam it, man, we're under fire!" And Chanda had only the briefest glimpse of an energy bolt splitting the sky, and a massive explosion in the direction of the *Bashi*.

The ground rocked Chanda to one side, and she nearly fell. She looked toward the shuttle, but smoke and dust and debris obscured it. "Shit!" She started running toward the shuttle, but about two steps into the cloud of dust, she nearly ran head-on into Irene, who was supporting Akira on one arm.

"Are you hurt?" Chanda asked Akira.

"The shuttle got knocked over," Akira said, "but the gravitics kicked in and saved us. I only hurt my leg trying to jump out of the damn thing."

Another explosion, this time closer to the excavation site. Chanda saw Warden guiding his people toward the shuttle *Judith*. She turned to Govanek — you go, too. They're who you should be with now."

"I prefer to stay with you."

"Govanek — the shooting war has started. We're past the point where you can help. *Go.*" Govanek went.

"They're really packing them in there," Irene said. "I think it took a couple of trips to get everyone down here in the first place."

Another energy bolt, another explosion, this time between Chanda and the *Judith*. As the dust cleared, Chanda saw Govanek dive into the shuttle. She gestured for Warden to lift off. "Get everyone out of here! Go!"

Warden, at the outer airlock door, turned to his pilot and gave a "thumbs up" motion. *Judith* lifted, its pilot sending the craft skimming the ground until it was about a kilometer distant, then sending it higher on a direct trajectory toward the Unity Embassy. "I'm glad Govanek's gone," she said. "I feel responsible for her."

The linked Buruden came up to Chanda. "We can take you in our shuttle."

"You're sure?" Chanda asked. "It might be pretty cramped for us. And the atmosphere — "

"Your lifesuits will protect you from our atmosphere. That you will die here is a potential truth. Severe injury is a likely truth. That you — "

"All right, all right," Chanda said. "Let's go."

Wonder of wonders, the Buruden actually abandoned their litany of fours, unlinked, then skittered toward their shuttle. A ramp in back allowed the Buruden to rush into their craft quickly. An energy field that living beings could pass through easily held in the Buruden atmosphere.

With that first step aboard, though, Chanda's knees threatened to buckle even as her lifesuit snapped on. "Dammit, I forgot about the grav." The Buruden's accustomed 2.3 G was asserting itself within the shuttle.

It didn't help that Akira was still hampered by her injured leg as she hopped along, with Irene helping her with one hand and the other grasping a medkit.

Chanda went ahead to reconnoiter. She peered into the depths of the Buruden shuttle and told Irene and Akira as they caught up to her, "It looks like there's a corridor we can take here. We'll have to keep bent over, though."

An explosion nearby rocked the shuttle. Irene said, "It's a lot better than the alternative."

As Chanda, Irene, and Akira hunkered down and made their way down the narrow corridor, the ramp behind them closed. Irene said, "Can you tell if we're lifting off?"

"Their gravitics are pretty quiet," Akira said.

Chanda peered ahead of them, seeing only more narrow corridor that took a turn to the right just ahead. "Let's keep moving," she said. "Best if we find a place to settle in and just stay out of everyone's way."

"At least the ceiling's smooth," Akira said. "Otherwise we'd keep braining ourselves."

"I've got these old bones, though," Chanda said. "I'm not sure how much longer I can walk along doubled over like this, in this kind of grav."

"Bullshit," Irene said. "You're just, what . . . 48? That's late youth."

"Subjectively, yes. It's also 72 objective. Which shouldn't make a difference, as much time as I've spent in stasis, but sometimes I think it's catching up with me."

They rounded the corner and stopped. The corridor split into six diverging pathways, none of them tall enough for a Human to fit through. "Dammit," Chanda said. "I guess we're waiting right here." She and Irene helped Akira sit on the smooth, unblemished floor.

Chanda turned her hand palm-up and activated her wrist sensor. "The leg's not broken," she said. "Just some nasty bruising and some pretty good abrasions."

Akira said, "We took the full force of the blast. Damn lifesuit came on, but an instant too late."

Irene sat next to Akira and opened the medkit. She pulled out a dermal mender, activated it, and passed it over Akira's injured leg. "I don't know how much this'll help," Irene said. "Mostly it'll ease the pain."

"Even that much will be a *big* help," Akira said. She asked Chanda, "Can you see anything down those passageways?"

Chanda sat down at one of the entrances, leaned forward, shielded her eyes with one hand, and squinted. "All I can see is darkness. Oh — wait a minute. There's — "

A squat form came rushing down the narrow corridor, quickly enough that Chanda had to scoot back to keep from being run down. A single Buruden exited the passageway and, without slowing down, went down the slightly wider corridor they'd used to enter the Buruden shuttle.

"I wonder what's happening," Irene said.

Chanda said, "Maybe it's getting us ready to dock."

"That would be a pretty fast trip upstairs," Akira said.

"Buruden tech is ahead of ours in some ways," Chanda said. "I just wish I knew what was going on. A viewscreen or port would be nice."

Akira indicated the six corridors in front of them. "There's probably plenty up there somewhere. We're just too darn big to get there."

Chanda touched behind her ear. Then again. "Nothing. I was hoping to raise Captain Bram or Ambassador Galt. And, shit, I just remembered about Indirogar. Who knows what's happening with him."

Irene asked, "Could the Sobrenians be jamming our signals?"

"Maybe — or even the Buruden, for that matter. It may be localized to this shuttle, to keep it from being detected."

The shuttle shook hard enough that Chanda was thrown into Irene and Akira. "Damn," Chanda said as she sat up again. "A hit that could affect the inertials like that — "

"Must be a pretty damn big hit," Irene said.

It was about ten minutes later that the Buruden craft shuddered again, this time not nearly as violently as the previous instance. "That may have been part of a docking maneuver," Chanda said.

Irene said, "Listen! Here they come!"

The rest of the Buruden arrived, one or two at a time down the six offshoot passageways. They hurried down the main corridor toward the rear ramp.

Chanda got up. "Let's go — Akira, how's your leg?"

"Much better," Akira said, as she stood without any help, even in the higher grav. She bumped her head against the low ceiling. "Ready to get out of here, though."

Chanda led the way. As they rounded the corner in the opposite direction from which they'd come, a bright spear of light pierced the area of the ramp. She could hear the chittering sounds of many Buruden beyond the ramp, so many voices at once that none of them translated.

From behind her, Akira asked, "What the hell's going on?"

"I don't know," Chanda said. "But I don't think we can stay in this shuttle."

The ramp led them into a corridor that was a bit wider than what they'd seen aboard the shuttle, not quite six meters across. Chanda said, "This corridor's wide enough to let them pass one another, which is pretty wide for a Buruden ship."

"And a good thing, too," Irene said. Scores of Buruden were rushing in opposite directions, enough of them moving quickly enough that Chanda and the others didn't dare step into the corridor themselves. "Though I wish it was tall enough for us to stand upright."

"I don't get it," Akira said. "A lot of the Buruden are essentially interchangeable. Why would they be running around in both directions?"

Chanda said, "We can't worry about that right now. We've got to find out where in this ship we are and what the hell's happening."

Irene indicated the constant flow of Buruden. "How do we do that?"

Chanda said, "Maybe just one step at a time." Still bent over, she took that first step into the flow of Buruden. Without acknowledging her, the individual Buruden sidestepped just enough that they didn't run into her. Another step, and Buruden on both sides of the corridor squeezed together as they passed just enough to let the Humans move alongside them.

"They've never barreled us over before when they've swarmed toward us. I hoped they wouldn't now."

Akira said, "I'm still pretty eager to get somewhere that isn't quite so closed in."

"I just want to find a port or a viewscreen," Chanda said, as she led the way down the cramped corridor, which featured the usual yellow, maroon, and gold markings on walls, floor, and ceiling.

They were just starting to make progress when the flow of Buruden stopped. Chanda, Irene, and Akira found themselves all alone. "This almost seems roomy," Akira said.

"If we weren't all still bent over like our backs were aching," Chanda said. "Actually, my back *is* starting to ache."

"Hold up," Irene said. "Listen!"

Chanda stopped and listened. "Sounds like some activity just ahead. Can't tell what it is." She tried her datalink again. "Still nothing. Let's head that way."

The corridor led to a circular room about eight meters across where several dozen Buruden were operating equipment set into the floor — not having a sense of "forward" or "backward," each Buruden could balance on any two of their four legs while standing over clusters of sensor, navigation, or weapons units. Which two legs balanced while the other two worked could change with blinding speed.

Irene asked, "Have we found the bridge?"

"Depends on how big this ship is," Chanda said. "If this is a big battle cruiser, I'd say this is an auxiliary control room, perhaps taking some of the load off the main bridge."

"There doesn't seem to be anybody in charge," Akira said.

Chanda said, "These Buruden are all singletons, so they'd be performing functions where they don't need to be supervised."

Irene asked, "So what do we do now?"

"These Buruden won't be able to tell us anything. We'd better keep moving, see if the ambassador or some equivalent is aboard."

The starcraft shook, and Chanda stumbled again. "Dammit, I can't imagine a force that strong that didn't destroy us outright!"

All the Buruden around them abandoned their posts and ran for an adjoining corridor on the far side of the room. Three of the Buruden stopped in front of Chanda and the others, and Chanda heard over her datalink, "Come this way. We need your help."

"Need our help?" Chanda said. "What does that mean?" But the Buruden had unlinked and couldn't respond.

"What do we do?" Irene asked.

"What *can* we do?" Chanda said. "We follow them."

The ceiling of the far corridor was even lower than the others they'd traversed. "We'll be crawling soon at this rate," Chanda said.

The unlinked Buruden led them several dozen meters down that corridor. Chanda started the first time the lights went out, only to return seconds later. She could hear Irene mutter, "It's like going through a haunted house."

"I hate haunted houses," Chanda said.

They rounded a corner, and found themselves in a room Chanda recognized. "Lifepods," she said. "That's both good and bad, I guess." Several rows, amounting to fifty or more lifepods, all of them a dark blue, stood before them.

Akira said, "If this ship took that bad a hit, it's probably good we're getting the hell off of it."

"Except who knows what new hell we might be flying into. And unless the Buruden have come up with bigger lifepods since the last time I was in one, get ready to be even more cramped than we have been."

Irene said, "They do look kinda small."

"It also means we'll be heading down to the planet separately.

Let's hope our datalinks will start working again once we're off this ship."

More Buruden poured into the room. One would open a pod at one end, and it and seven more would squeeze inside. Chanda was impressed at how they jammed themselves in, and how they could withstand being in such close quarters.

Three Buruden linked themselves together. Chanda had no way of knowing if they were the same ones who had spoken to them before. "Please enter the lifepods," she heard. "We believe only one of you can fit inside a single pod."

"You're correct," Chanda began, but the Buruden had already unlinked and were entering an adjacent lifepod.

She turned to Irene and Akira. "You heard them — pick a pod." Which is what Chanda did, and indicated a control on one side of the hatch. Be careful," she said. "They open and close pretty quickly." A touch, and the hatch of Chanda's pod seemed to vanish. "There's a similar control inside." All around them, Buruden were still entering pods, but she saw that most of them were filled.

Chanda started to pull herself into one of the pods. She couldn't help but notice that what had been a tight fit when she'd been escaping from that Buruden hospital ship four years earlier was an even tighter fit now. *Got to adjust the biotech a little bit*, she thought. *Never mind "old bones" — there's more of me wrapped around them. At least there's a port here at the other end — I can see a little something.*

Chanda got herself into the pod, then hit the interior control. The hatch reappeared, and as she'd been aboard the Buruden hospital ship three years earlier, was grateful she didn't have a leg or arm in the way.

Now comes the wait, Chanda thought. But she didn't have to wait long, as a dull sound of metal against metal was transmitted through her pod. *They're about to launch us*, Chanda thought, and squeezed herself around to peer out the port in front of her. *Looks like all these pods are lining up to launch all at once. There's about a dozen in front of me. And there's the main hatch — I can see stars!*

Her next thought — *That previous lifepod didn't activate inertial compensators, but we were just bobbing up to the surface of the Great Sea. I wonder if —*

The lifepod at the front of the line shot out into space — then the next, and the next, until —

The interior of the Buruden craft was swept away, and Chanda found herself free and clear, a myriad of stars her only companion, all of them shining steady and eternal. Adrenaline rushed as she had a brief sense of falling, but thankfully the pod did have inertials, and she was soon able to look through the port almost as if it were a holo rather than something real.

Where's the planet? she wondered. *This pod better turn itself around toward Splendor pretty quickly.*

Out of the corner of her eye — a starcraft whipped past. *Damn,* she thought. *I couldn't even see whose ship that was. That's the problem with space battles — everything's too big -- the velocities, the distances.*

Except for that Sobrenian ship that just came into view. She instantly recognized the green water drop shape. *It's, what, just half a click away? And getting closer.*

Check that — I'm seeing it from behind — which means I'm getting closer to it!

Chanda looked all around for anything resembling navigation controls, all in vain. *Goddam, why the hell would the Buruden shoot me toward a Sobrenian ship? Or have the Sobrenians gotten an enticement beam on me?*

She touched behind her ear. "This is Chanda to Irene and Akira. Do you copy?"

No response. *I have to hope this is some kind of glitch and they're headed toward Splendor like they're supposed to be.*

Just ahead of her, though, Chanda suddenly spotted another

Buruden lifepod — and another. *They must be the ones that shot out ahead of me*, she thought.

What the hell is going on?

Chanda found herself easing back involuntarily from the port as the Sobrenian starcraft grew larger and larger. In the last instant before the expected deadly impact, she groaned, shut her eyes tightly, and turned her head away from the port.

CHAPTER 32

A loud metallic clang! And Chanda was surprised to find herself still alive. She peered out of the port again, and realized the pod had attached itself to the side of the Sobrenian ship. *If it was the Sobrenians themselves who drew me in,* she wondered, *why wouldn't they have brought the pod onto a hangar deck?*

A flash of light and a sharp-edged sound erupted from one side of the lifepod — as Chanda shielded her eyes, an inrush of air brought sounds of Buruden chittering and loud Sobrenian speech from too many sources to translate.

Chanda uncovered her eyes and saw that one side of the lifepod had dissolved, revealing a corridor of the Sobrenian ship. Beneath lighting much brighter than aboard a Human vessel, Chanda saw Buruden individuals swarming over Sobrenians who fired pulse pistols in return. Within moments, the pulse pistols were silenced, the Sobrenians all dead or disabled.

Chanda tumbled onto the floor, grateful for a ship's grav that was just four-fifths Earth's. She looked back at the remnants of the pod and realized it hadn't just attached itself to the outside of the

Sobrenian ship, it had *bored into* it, sealing the hole it made as it went along.

I wasn't in a lifepod, Chanda realized. *It was an attack pod.*

The Buruden continued to advance down the corridor of the Sobrenian starcraft. Several Sobrenians armed with energy pistols tried a counterattack from a cross-corridor and gunned down four or five Buruden, but were quickly overwhelmed by the sheer numbers of Buruden individuals. *It's the Sobrenians' biggest nightmare,* Chanda thought. *Massive numbers of Buruden advancing toward them in swarm mode.*

A stray energy bolt struck just above Chanda's head, sending sparks flying. *I've got to keep my head down,* she thought. *My lifesuit can only protect against so much. I've got to find Irene and Akira — assuming they ended up here, too — and we've got to figure out how the hell to get out of here.*

Seeing the continued skirmishes down the corridor in front of her, Chanda rose and went the other way. *I've got to hope the Buruden have secured part of this ship,* she thought. *At least the Sobrenians are closer to Human height — I can easily touch the ceiling, but at least I don't have to walk around all hunched over.*

Chanda activated her datalink: "Irene — Akira — do you copy?" *Dammit, still no response. Probably the Sobrenians jamming anything that's not their own tech.*

She drew her stunner, walked at a determined pace down the corridor. Every few steps, she had to make her way around bodies, both Buruden and Sobrenian. Most of the Buruden had clearly died of the effects of energy bolts that had passed cleanly through their bodies; the Sobrenians had just as clearly been crushed or torn apart by the combined mass of countless Buruden.

Just ahead — another Buruden attack pod embedded in the skin of the ship. She saw no sign of whether Irene or Akira had occupied it, or the usual eight Buruden. Chanda peered around a corner when she reached a cross-corridor that formed a "T" intersection. The lighting had failed in the cross-corridor, making it a path into darkness. *I'm sure as hell not going down that way*, she thought, and took a step to continue down the main corridor.

A series of energy bolts erupted from down that corridor, and Chanda jumped back behind the corner. After a moment, the firing ceased, and she heard the familiar chittering sound of running Buruden, risked a peek around the corner, and saw a couple dozen Buruden headed her way.

Nine of the Buruden individuals went to Chanda and linked together. Over her datalink, she heard, "We are most of the ambassador. We require your help."

"You mean — you brought me here *on purpose?*"

"This is the Sobrenian flagship *Merusta*. Destroy it and the effort to attack Splendor may be crippled."

"How the hell can I help with that?"

The Buruden said, "You may help by striving to understand how Tiernan may react."

"He's on this ship?"

"We have confirmed that."

"Why board it? Why not just blast this ship out of the sky?"

"We are trying. We thought it best to employ two methods to achieve the goal of neutralizing this warcraft."

Oh, crap, Chanda thought. *To the Buruden, losing a few individuals is like having some dry skin peel off. It definitely means more than that to me.* She asked, "Have you seen the Humans Irene Radford or Akira Kuroda?"

"We have not seen Akira Kuroda. Irene Radford is, however, in contact with another group of Buruden."

"I need to see her immediately."

"We'll have her brought to you." The Buruden detached from one another and scattered, some back down the darkened side corridor, the rest in either direction down the main corridor. Within moments, she stood alone, the only sounds those of various ship's systems. She wasn't about to venture down that darkened corridor.

Dammit, she thought, *how far away is Irene? How big is this goddamned ship, anyway?*

From behind her: "Chanda!" Irene approached with about half a dozen linked Buruden following her.

Irene gave Chanda a quick embrace, then asked, "Have you seen Akira?"

"I haven't, and neither have the Buruden. Turns out we're here to help them figure out how Tiernan might act. Never mind that their fleet's also trying to destroy this ship."

"And us along with it!"

"That's called 'collateral damage,' I think."

"It's called insane!"

"Either way," Chanda said, "our best bet to get the hell off this ship is to find Tiernan and help the Buruden take it over." She turned to the linked Buruden next to them. "Do you know where to find the Human turned Sobrenian called Tiernan?"

The Buruden said, "We believe he is in a forward area of this warcraft. We will take you there." The linked individuals started back down the corridor the way they'd come. Chanda and Irene followed, and had to adopt a brisk pace to keep up with the determined Buruden, who never seemed to tire.

The Sobrenian ship shook violently, and Irene grasped Chanda's arm so hard it was painful. "That had to be a helluva hit for us to feel it," Chanda said.

"We've *got* to find Akira," Irene said.

The Buruden in front of them slowed as they neared a new section of the ship; Chanda took the opportunity to stop and face Irene. "Listen," she said, "We're in a war — and any one of us could become a casualty. We have to accept that. I bet Akira understands that even better than we do."

Irene's eyes flared in anger. "You don't know what I've been through. And you've been in some firefights, but you've never been in a war, so don't talk to me like that."

Chanda was taken aback by Irene's vehemence: *She's never used such a tone with me before,* she thought.

But I guess I deserved it. "I'm sorry," Chanda said.

A lighter touch on Chanda's arm this time. "I'm sorry. I'm just . . . "

"It's all right."

Just ahead, Sobrenian energy bolts burst in all directions, and Chanda could hear the mass movement of Buruden, no doubt trying to swarm over the Sobrenians.

A group of Buruden, only six of them this time, linked up in front of Chanda and Akira. "We are all that remains of the ambassador," the Buruden said. "Please speak plainly — understanding could be difficult."

Damn, Chanda thought. *This mission is taking a toll. No doubt the ambassador can be re-formed elsewhere sometime, but this will make things tough.* "Have you found the former Human Tiernan?"

"He is ahead — attempting to reach a shuttle bay. We do not understand. He cannot defeat us from there."

"He's saving himself," Chanda said. "Humans aren't collective beings like Buruden are. He has value to himself as an individual."

"As much as we believe we understand such a thing, its meaning often escapes us."

Irene said, "A Human individual's consciousness is as fully formed as the Sobrenian collective consciousness."

"We cannot believe that is possible. However, we can believe that individual Humans can act as if that is possible."

Like the Sobrenians can grudgingly acknowledge that Humans will act "as if" we're sentient, Chanda thought. "Just realize that Tiernan will work as desperately to save himself as masses of Buruden would to save their species."

"We should kill him," the Buruden said. "Do you object to this treatment of a former Human?"

"*Hell,* no," Chanda said. "If he's in the way of saving this planet, blow him straight to hell."

"We will increase the number of warcraft attempting to destroy this ship."

Irene said, "Then you've got to help us find Akira and get us the hell off this thing!"

"We apologize," the Buruden said. "It did not occur to us that, as Humans, you share this desire to preserve yourselves as individuals."

Chanda said, "You know, this would be a lovely philosophical conversation to have sometime. But right now I'd rather find another lifepod and get the hell off this ship."

"Our values coincide, then. Tiernan has reached the shuttle bay, which is just ahead. We are attempting to swarm over his Sobrenian protectors."

"Let's get up there, then."

"Be sure to protect yourselves," the Buruden said. "We would hate for the equivalent of our entire species to perish." The six Buruden unlinked and moved forward.

Chanda looked at Irene. "Have you ever heard sarcasm from a Buruden before?"

"I didn't think they were capable of it," Irene said. "Until now."

They moved forward cautiously, heads down, and Chanda marveled once again at how the Buruden simply threw a mass of individuals toward a particular target, in this case a line of Sobrenians guarding the entrance to the hangar bay. The bay's doors had been twisted and broken, but Chanda couldn't tell how. *That's not something they did by swarming*, she thought. Several water drop-shaped Sobrenian shuttles stood within the bay. Beyond them, Chanda saw the hangar doors were opening, with an energy field maintaining the bay's atmosphere.

Dozens of Buruden were being maimed, blown apart, or disintegrated beneath persistent Sobrenian fire, but they just kept coming.

Within the bay, one of the shuttles was powering up. "Look!" Chanda said. "There's Tiernan!" Chanda spotted the Human-turned-Sobrenian at the controls of the shuttle.

Irene said, "We've got to stop the son-of-a-bitch!"

"Do you know how to pilot a Sobrenian shuttle?"

"I . . . of course I don't. I'd be lying if I said I'd have the first clue."

The Sobrenian shuttle with Tiernan aboard eased through the energy field. Beyond it, Chanda caught a glimpse of Buruden ships firing upon the *Merusta*, but so far to little effect as their energy bolts were deflected and disruptor beams harmlessly absorbed.

Four linked Buruden came up to Chanda and Irene. Over her datalink, Chanda heard, "One of us can fly a Sobrenian shuttle."

"How the hell — " Chanda began, then said. "Never mind. With so many of you on board here, I'm sure someone has a specialty for about anything we'd ask."

Irene's voice was unsteady. "Chanda — what about Akira?"

Chanda asked the linked Buruden, "Have you seen the Human, Akira?"

"We have not," the Buruden said.

Chanda started to speak: "Irene — "

"I *know*. Akira's tough. She can take care of herself. And she'd never forgive me if I let Tiernan get away."

"Let's go, then." Chanda headed toward one of the Sobrenian shuttles, which was another of the typical green water drop shaped craft. She paused at the short ladder, all of two rungs, made for short Sobrenian legs, that led to its entrance. The Buruden clambered up those rungs and stood as tall as it could on two of its four legs. *I'd think of it as on 'tippy-toes' if it had toes*, Chanda thought. It touched a control at the side of the shuttle's airlock and the outer hatch opened.

Once through the inner hatch, Chanda tried to take the measure of the shuttle's interior and controls. First step in, though, she bumped her head. "Great," she said. "It's like being back in the damn — "

Irene interrupted: "Don't say it, Chanda." She indicated the Buruden, which was climbing up into the pilot's position.

"Don't worry. It's not intelligent enough to understand what we're saying, though it might be able to take some simple commands. It'll be flying purely by rote learning."

"I'm not sure that reassures me very much," Irene said.

"Neither of us can do any better," Chanda said. "Though maybe now's when we could've used Govanek." Chanda tried to squeeze herself into a Sobrenian seat that wasn't designed for Human bottoms. "Aren't there any fat Sobrenians?"

"Guess not," Irene said as she attempted a similar landing into the seat next to the Buruden, who was balancing itself on two legs, reaching forward with its other two legs, and starting systems up and operating controls. Visual readouts before them and to each side were much brighter than on a Human vessel, making Chanda want to shield her eyes.

The shuttle's gravitics powered up. More quickly than Chanda would have thought, the craft eased itself off the hangar deck and headed out. It passed through the energy field and was flying in open space, down toward Splendor.

Chanda touched behind her ear. "This is Chanda Kasmira to any Earth Unity starcraft. Irene Radford and I are in a Sobrenian shuttle in pursuit of Lewis Tiernan. Please do not fire upon us!"

Chanda held her breath as she caught the occasional glimpse of a starcraft making a rapid passage across the face of the planet. Then Trenton Bram's voice responded: "Chanda! We saw the destruction of the archeological site. How the hell did you get into orbit?"

"Much too long a story. Can you help us with Tiernan?"

"I'm aboard *Nivara II*, and we're on the other side of the planet. Most other Unity ships are being kept pretty busy. I'll see whether anyone can divert your way."

"All right. Be careful. Chanda out."

Irene said, "So we may be on our own."

"Looks like it. At least our own people won't shoot us out of the sky. I'm assuming our Buruden friend here has notified his people. And we have to hope the Sobrenians don't know we're not really one of them."

"So we just have to catch up to Tiernan."

"Can you make heads or tails of the controls or readouts?"

Irene pointed out a display between her and the Buruden. "This one looks to be purely visual — I think it's showing our location and trajectory in relation to Splendor. A lot of these others that are text-based, I'm lost. And I wouldn't know which control to touch, anyway."

"Either way," Chanda said, "we're going where Tiernan's going. Of course, that's probably toward another Sobrenian ship."

"Which means we've got to catch up to him before he can get there."

Chanda asked the Buruden pilot, "Do you understand what we have to do? Catch up to that other Sobrenian shuttle?"

The Buruden didn't speak, probably couldn't, but instead pointed toward one of the readout graphics. Irene pointed to a small moving dot on the screen that appeared to be traversing the face of a stylized representation of Splendor. "Well, that's easy enough. That's Tiernan's ship." Another dot was right behind it, slowing gaining. "That's us."

"So we're gaining on him. Wish we had a purely visual readout."

Irene pointed out the front viewscreen. "We don't need one — there he is!"

Their shuttle was zeroing in on Tiernan's craft rapidly enough that Chanda closed her eyes and ducked. Then they were past Tiernan's craft and their own shuttle rocked from the impact of an energy bolt from behind them.

Chanda said, "I wanted to find Tiernan, but I didn't want to get into a shootout with him!"

CHAPTER 33

The Buruden pilot began a series of evasive maneuvers, and Chanda saw the plasma trails of several energy bolts pass by, much too closely.

And the shuttle rocked again!

"Dammit," Chanda said. "He's too good of a shot!"

The Buruden pilot's legs and eyes seemed to go into overdrive, as it worked to take aim at Tiernan's craft while dodging another series of energy bolts.

A series of purple lights went on in various readouts. "Uh, oh," Irene said.

Chanda told her, "You know I never like 'uh, oh.' What's happening?"

"I think we just lost a bunch of systems."

"How bad?"

Irene indicated out the forward viewscreen. "Look ahead of us — doesn't the planet look to be getting closer?"

"All too close. Can we land near the embassy?"

"It's just going over the horizon," Irene said. She shook her head. "No other Unity outposts within reach."

Chanda said, "Hey, wait a minute — Indirogar's supposed to be right at the edge of the Great Sea. Look down there where the cloud cover's just broken."

Irene pointed to the graphic display of Splendor they'd looked at before. She asked the Buruden, "Here? Can you put us down here?"

The Buruden didn't say a word, but Chanda could tell it had adjusted the shuttle's course slightly. "I think we're headed there," she said. She contacted Bram again: "We're headed toward Indirogar's location. Once we set down, either we can help rescue him or he can rescue us — help us survive in the wilderness until help comes."

Bram's response was quick: "It may be a while." He signed off immediately, as well.

"He sounded busy," Chanda said.

Irene looked at all the readouts before them in turn, and said, "I've lost Tiernan. I don't have a way of telling if our Buruden friend here got a good shot off."

"If we're lucky," Chanda said, "he's in a bad a shape as we are."

"Preferably worse. But just eyeballing things, it looks like we're coming in pretty hot."

"Then we gotta hope this is the Buruden equivalent of Akira."

"Hah! The hot-dogger?" Irene fell silent.

Chanda reached forward and touched Irene's arm. "Akira's OK. I know it. She's better than either of us. If we made it out. . . . "

"Yeah. She made it out, too, and in style. She's probably back at the embassy right now wondering where the hell we are." Irene looked at the various readouts. "We're out of cloud cover — and we *are* coming in awfully hot."

"If not for the inertials," Chanda said, "we'd feel like we were taking a ride on the world's tallest roller coaster."

The shuttle was making nearly a vertical drop, and Chanda could see more detail of their destination by the moment — there a wind-blown cliff, there an icy plain that was surely where they would find Indirogar. Which reminded her: "This is Chanda to Indirogar — do you copy?"

No response for a moment, and Chanda was just about to speak again when she finally heard Indirogar's voice: "Chanda . . . I tried to call you earlier."

I've never heard his voice sound so weak, Chanda thought. "We've been . . . kinda busy. How are you doing?"

"Not as well as usual. The others have all turned back. I do not like asking for help. But I must. Can you pick me up?"

"Actually, Irene and I may need your help. We're headed your way, but it's in a crippled Sobrenian shuttle."

"I'm sure there is an excellent story leading up to that."

"Which you'll hear as soon as we land. It looks like you're in a nice smooth area."

"I shall watch the skies, and begin preparing a shelter."

"Thanks, Indirogar. Chanda out."

Irene said, "We're leveling out. Should be touching down in just a few — what the hell?" All the shuttle's systems went to purple on the readouts, the craft began to shake, and the inertials went out. The Buruden pilot kept trying to work the shuttle's systems, but nothing worked.

Chanda and Irene's lifesuits failed as well. "Now I've got that roller coaster feeling," Chanda said, trying to keep her voice steady and hold off panic. "And I don't like it."

"I don't understand," Irene said. "I didn't think the damage was that severe." All the purple indicators on the readouts went black. "And why would our lifesuits fail, too?"

"It's just like . . . when the goddam sweepers took over the controls of the *Bashi*. *That's* what's happened! Either way, here we come — hot as hell!"

Just a few dozen meters from the ground, the landscape didn't look "nice and smooth" as it had from altitude — the sun glinted off sharp outcroppings of ice, and what had appeared to be a softly rolling snowscape looked to have plenty of rough edges now.

The Sobrenian shuttle glanced off one of those ice outcroppings, and Chanda felt herself go flying. The world seemed to spin around her, and her head struck the interior of their stricken craft a couple of times.

Finally the shuttle spun to a halt. Battered and bruised, Chanda opened her eyes. It took her a moment to realize the shuttle was on its side. The Buruden pilot was hanging by its spiny legs from the side of the shuttle that had become the ceiling, and seemed none the worse for wear.

It doesn't seem like the shuttle's skin has been breached, Chanda thought. *That's good. We can keep warm awhile.*

But where's Irene?

Then she heard her voice — from *beneath* her. "Chanda — you're not that heavy, but still — "

"Oh!" Chanda managed to lift herself up and step to one side. "Sorry." She grabbed Irene's arm and helped her up. It was only now that she noticed the sweet smell of the craft's Sobrenian atmosphere. "We can only hope we came down close enough to Indirogar that he saw us, and can get to us pretty quickly."

"I think we came down just to his west. If we're lucky, he should be able to get to us within an hour — maybe just a few minutes."

"Even wearing our parkas, with no lifesuits, I think we'll stay inside the shuttle — preserve its warmth as long as we can."

The Buruden pilot let go of the side of the craft and landed next to Chanda. She said, "I wish I could talk directly to you, little buddy — you did a great job!"

"And god*dam* those sweepers," Irene said. "I thought they were supposed to be on our side if the Sobrenians attacked."

"I don't understand that, either. I can't believe that they didn't get the word — "

Irene clasped Chanda's shoulder. "Wait — hear that?"

"Sounds like . . . a gravitic drive."

"Not just that — a *Sobrenian* gravitic drive."

"It couldn't be," Chanda said. "But the sweepers — why aren't they affecting that ship? Wait, try to start something up in here — it doesn't matter what!"

Irene tried to activate several different systems, pressing her hand in places she'd seen the Buruden use. "Nothing," she said.

"Never mind preserving warmth," Chanda said. "If we don't get out of this thing, it could be our coffin."

The shuttle's airlock was straight up now. Chanda reached toward it, but wasn't quite tall enough to touch it. "Hold on," Irene said, and reached past Chanda to work the lock's manual controls. A turn of a lever, one good push straight up on the inner door, and it opened. "Lemme boost you up," Irene said, then cupped her hands for Chanda to step into. A high step, then the boost from Irene's arms, and Chanda was in the lock. Irene grabbed the Buruden bodily and handed him up to Chanda.

The outer lock was within Chanda's reach, and she opened it as Irene pulled herself up into the lock. Chanda got the hatch open and sharp winds stung her face as a dull, endless roar assaulted her ears.

The hood of her parka blew back as she pulled herself up from the hatch, balancing herself carefully on the Sobrenian shuttle's smooth, rounded surface. Even as she reached down to accept the Buruden's round form as Irene handed it up, she looked into Splendorian skies for the source of the sound of gravitics.

And there it was! Another Sobrenian shuttle, the same blue water drop shape as their own — and with the scars of battle damage apparent all over its skin. As Irene pulled herself up through the hatch of their own craft, she said, "You don't think that's Tiernan, do you?"

"Either way, the sweepers aren't doing their job right — at least when it comes to that ship."

The other craft came in for a landing about thirty meters away, the sound of its gravitics quickly fading. Beyond it, Chanda saw the wide expanse of the Great Sea, and the dark presence of a sweeper that stretched nearly to the horizon.

She slid down the side of their own shuttle — it was a height of only about two and a half meters, but Chanda was also very aware of

Splendor's gravity, one-third higher than Earth's. She flexed her knees and also broke her fall with her hands.

Irene dropped down beside her, followed by their Buruden pilot. There was no movement from the other shuttle. Chanda pulled her stunner. Seeing Irene's questioning glance, she said, "Just making sure." She aimed the stunner at the ground and squeezed its trigger.

Nothing. "No more than I expected. I suppose I could try to throw it at his head." She advanced toward the other shuttle. "I don't intend to just stand here like a sitting duck. Maybe we can grab him as he comes out."

Irene followed, but said, "He's sure to be armed."

"He's also too damn sure of himself much of the time. I'm counting on that."

Chanda positioned herself to the left of the shuttle's outer airlock hatch. Irene took position on the right side, with the Buruden right behind her.

Still no response from within the shuttle. Chanda asked Irene, "Should we try to go inside? Maybe our Buruden friend can open this hatch for us."

"It might be worth a shot," Irene said. "If we — "

A heavy blow to Chanda's body, and she was flying through the air and landing hard on her back. She shook her head to clear it and found she'd been thrown several meters away from the Sobrenian shuttle.

Its hatch was opening —

— Revealing Tiernan!

Even with the man wearing a Sobrenian spacesuit complete with bubble helmet, Chanda could tell Tiernan had no vestige of Human features remaining — his torso was three times as thick as a Human's, his snout fully-formed. *He's gone all the way over,* Chanda thought as she struggled to her feet. *He's even got those goddammed eyes that can swivel in different directions!*

Chanda caught a glimpse of Irene, who was still lying on the ground and just now seemed to be coming to her senses. She shook her head, then put a hand to her temple. The Buruden pilot was lying on its back, all four legs up in the air.

Tiernan stood next to his shuttle. He pulled a disruptor pistol from his spacesuit, which was standard issue for Sobrenians — static matter, not nanotech-based or implanted within his body. As he spoke, Chanda heard him over her datalink. "I'm glad my expanding force-shield didn't harm you very much, Chanda. I so much wanted to have this conversation with you."

Chanda took a tentative step toward this Human-turned-Sobrenian. "I may have a few choice words for you, as well, Tiernan."

"Don't call me that Human name any longer. As a fully reborn Sobrenian, I've adopted the name Direg."

Chanda took a couple more steps. *I've got to wait for Irene to get her act together,* she thought. *Then if I can try to get close enough to Tiernan — Direg — whoever — to jump him. Even if he cuts me down maybe Irene has a chance to take him out.*

Tiernan raised the disruptor. "Don't even think about it, Chanda."

"I was just getting closer. You know, so you won't have to shout."

"I already wasn't shouting."

"All the same — " In her peripheral vision, Chanda saw Irene raising herself from the ground.

"Your damn Buruden friends destroyed our fleet."

"That's what friends are for."

"I see your point, Chanda. But I still have a few friends left. The sweepers, for instance."

"I thought that's who grounded us." A glance, and Irene was making her way, however slowly, toward them. The Buruden was in the process of flipping itself over from its turtle-like inverted position.

Tiernan/Direg said, "Gather as many of your friends as you like, it won't help you."

Chanda held out her hand. "Just go ahead and give me the weapon," she said. "Help will be coming any minute."

"Not while the sweepers can control what tech works and what doesn't."

Time to stall, Chanda thought. "What do you hope to gain?"

"We want this world, Chanda. It's our buffer between the Sobrenian homeworld and the Buruden." Direg gestured toward the Buruden pilot, who was standing to one side. "You saw how they can board a starcraft and swarm over anything and anyone in sight. They're vermin!" Direg fired his disruptor at the Buruden pilot, whose body disintegrated, leaving behind only a fine ash that blew away in the chill wind.

"You son-of-a-bitch," Chanda said. She started toward Direg, but Irene grabbed her from behind and held her tightly.

"Not yet," Irene whispered in Chanda's ear, her breath misting in front of her, her voice shaky from shivering.

Chanda quit struggling against Irene's grip. Irene let her go. "Why are you here on Splendor, Chanda? All these years? You'll never see the results of your work."

"I want to save lives."

"Even lives of generations you'll never see. Because you take the long view. It's why I admire you."

"I don't want your admiration."

"I give it to you anyway. We Sobrenians also take the long view, which most of Humanity does not. It's why we're better."

"Cut the crap, Tiernan. What do you want?"

"It's Direg. And what I want, Chanda, is *you*. If I can turn you, you can help make the Unity's support for Splendor waver — just enough that we can declare an all-out war here."

Chanda waved her arms. "Oh, just shoot me and get it over with! You know that'll never happen."

"Let's do an experiment. Either you accept the offer I'm about to give you, or all of you die."

Chanda said, "What could you possibly offer us?"

"How about a way to save Splendor from the gas nebula?"

From behind Chanda, Irene said, "Bullshit!"

Direg pointed behind his left ear. "All the details are right here in my datalink. We can destroy the gas nebula itself. No more need to consider evacuating the Splendorians."

"Your species has shown no love for the Splendorians. Weapons tests — attacking their world — what comes next?"

"What comes next, Chanda, is I guarantee the safety of all the planet's natives."

"If I join you."

"It's just that simple. And if you're thinking of some kind of betrayal, you should know that if I'm killed, the datalink erases itself."

Out of the corner of her eye, Chanda glimpsed a shadowy figure to one side of Direg's shuttle — it took an extreme mental effort for her not to look in that direction.

About four meters separated her and Direg. *That ought to be just about right*, Chanda thought. She started walking toward him, knowing his attention would be focused utterly on her. "Nothing's that simple, Direg. Why don't you — "

The shadowy figure jumped from behind the shuttle — Indirogar, brandishing a valley dweller-made spear! He cast it at Direg with the strength and accuracy made of a lifetime keeping his tribe safe and fed.

The spear struck Direg in the side, but his spacesuit lessened much of the blow and it barely pierced his skin. He fell to the ground, and Chanda charged him, Irene right behind her. Indirogar was closer by about two steps and pushed both Chanda and Irene aside, falling on Direg and pulling out the spear so he could stab the Human-Sobrenian with it again.

Direg, on his back, raised his disruptor and fired, the beam striking Indirogar's body point-blank.

CHAPTER 34

Indirogar didn't even have a chance to cry out — the wind whisked away the ashen remnants of his body in an instant.

Direg brought the disruptor to bear on Chanda — she grabbed his arm and banged it against the side of the shuttle — then again!

The disruptor fell from his hand. Chanda snatched it up and aimed it squarely at Direg's midsection as Irene came up behind her.

"Kill me," he said, "and you'll never learn how to destroy the gas nebula."

"Fine," Chanda said. "Let's see who blinks first. Irene — gimme Indirogar's spear."

Irene picked up the spear, and Chanda took it as she handed Irene the disruptor.

Direg asked, "What are you going to do?"

"Dig the datalink out of you, my friend."

"What?" Direg said. "You can't!"

"Actually, I will," Chanda said. To Irene, she said, "If he gives me any problems, start with the left foot." She grabbed the top of Direg's head and turned him toward her. Direg tried to grab Chanda's hand.

Irene aimed the disruptor at his left foot and fired. That foot disintegrated, and Direg fell to the ground, screaming in pain. He wasn't bleeding; the energy beam had cauterized the end of his leg.

"You've got another foot left, and a couple hands," Chanda told him. "Now *sit still*."

Chanda kneeled, balanced the weight of the spear on her leg, and applied its sharp tip to the left side of Direg's head and started digging. More screams from him as she probed for the datalink, and blood that wasn't quite as red as a Human's began to flow. "I was lying!" Direg screamed. "There's nothing on the link!"

"Too late for that," Chanda said. "I'm taking you at your original word. Hmm . . . it's kinda hard to find. Not quite where it is in a Human. Or former Human."

Chanda continued to dig into Direg's flesh with the spear and her free hand. Finally: "Got it!" She stood as Direg's hand clutched the side of his head.

"You *bitches*!" Direg screamed as he stood, blood flowing down the side of his head. "You're everything that's wrong with Humanity."

"You're not one of us anymore," Chanda said, sticking the wet and sticky datalink into a pocket of her parka. "You don't get to criticize."

Direg braced himself against the outer skin of his shuttle, then launched himself at Chanda. She brought up Indirogar's spear and thrust it as hard as she could into Direg's chest. But even the sharp highlander spearpoint could barely pierce his spacesuit, and Direg grabbed the spear to try to pull it away from his body.

Irene shouted, "Chanda, move! I can't shoot!"

Chanda, enraged, ignored Irene and brought all her strength to bear as she pushed Direg back against the skin of the shuttle. Finally the spacesuit's material parted, and Chanda felt the spearpoint tear through skin, organs, and the back of his spacesuit until it stopped cold at surface of the shuttle.

Blood spurted from Direg's chest as Chanda held her position. More blood began to pour from his mouth, and his eyes rolled in opposite directions. He slumped against the spear, his weight pulling him down abruptly enough that Chanda lost her grip. Direg's body fell to the ground and the spear, still embedded in his chest, wobbled back and forth a couple of times.

Chanda could only stand there looking down at his body. After a moment, she started to shiver again.

Irene said, "I couldn't shoot. You were in the way."

"It's all right," Chanda said, indicating Direg's body. "He probably thought it a more romantic death."

"You did what you had to do."

"Mostly I was just tired of fucking with him."

"But -- poor Indirogar."

"He saved us," Chanda said. "Probably would've preferred dying for us than all alone in the wilderness."

"Now who's thinking of a romantic death?"

"I know. He's still dead."

Irene said, "We oughta go into Tiernan's — excuse me, Direg's — shuttle. It still has power."

"Yeah. At least we won't freeze to death."

Chanda jumped as her lifesuit activated, complete with bubble helmet. Irene stared down at her own body, also encased in a lifesuit.

Chanda looked toward the Great Sea. She said over her datalink, "Is this the sweeper?"

The response came in loud and clear, without any of the static of previous transmissions. Chanda could just make out the presence of messenger fish close to shore. "It is. And we apologize."

"For helping Tiernan?"

"Yes. Tiernan. Direg. He deceived us. He promised us things we now realize he could not deliver. Space flight for us. A world without interference by other beings."

"You're right, there. The Sobrenians *love* to interfere with other species."

"A fact their attempted invasion of Splendor and Direg's attempt to convert you have shown us. We will no longer interfere with Humanity. We ask that you forgive us."

Chanda said, "We're all better off if we can work together."

"We wish only peace for you, Chanda and Irene. We hope that when we speak to you again, it is in better circumstances."

Chanda looked across the Great Sea, where the messenger fish broke contact with her and turned as one to head toward the sweeper. The gigantic being's dark presence was slowly backing away.

Chanda imagined Indirogar's ashes, along with those of the hapless Buruden who'd brought them safely back to Splendor, wafting across the Great Sea in the sweeper's wake, and put her head in her hands and began to sob. Irene embraced her.

A Unity shuttle emerged from the clouds, passed through the airspace in which Indirogar's remains had dispersed, and landed next to the shuttle where Direg's body was lying, and it was Akira who leapt from the shuttle and embraced both lover and friend and helped them cry their hearts out in relief.

CHAPTER 35

It was the better part of a day before Chanda could arrange passage up to the *Sergeant Jelal*. The entire time, she resisted the temptation to contact Ben, to give him a heads-up that she was on her way to see him. *I don't want to say, even to myself, that he's the first person I wanted to see when it was clear I'd live.*

But after boarding the *Jelal*, Chanda headed right toward Ben's quarters. *I can still turn around at any moment*, she told herself. *Sure, people know I came here — they have to know I'm here to see Ben, they'll be sure to ask why I was here. But if I turn around and leave, it's actually none of their goddam business, is it?*

But I have to settle things between us. One way or the other.

If I can figure out how. Men — the aliens among us!

Chanda arrived at the door to Ben's quarters, took a deep breath, and buzzed for him. When he opened the door, his face beamed and he took her into a strong embrace. As the door slid shut behind her, Chanda put her hand behind his neck and pulled him in for a long kiss.

"Well," Ben said afterwards, "that's a better reception than I feared."

"I — what do you mean?"

"I hadn't heard from you since the fighting ended. I knew you'd survived. I thought maybe . . . you were done with me."

"What? No, not at all. I just . . . "

"Splendor comes first. I understand."

"It doesn't have to be that way forever."

"Listen, Chanda, I get it. You've accomplished a lot here. I respect that probably more than you can know. But either you're going to keep working here at Splendor or you're headed out to some new diplomatic adventure in some other system. Whichever happens. . . . "

"You think I'm just going to set you aside!"

Chanda saw an unexpected flash of anger in Ben's eyes. "I'm just looking at the evidence. I know you had it tough growing up — placed in stasis, your parents growing old more quickly than they should've right before your eyes — dying early. I see how you've coped. Married an asexual being. Poured yourself into your work. I just want to know how I fit in there."

Chanda looked into Ben's eyes and asked, "Will you trust me?"

"Well . . . to do what?"

She took both his hands and squeezed. "*Will* you?"

Ben squeezed her hands. "Of course."

Chanda pulled Ben toward the bedroom. "Then don't ask questions. Don't wonder why I'm doing this. Just . . . go along."

Once in the bedroom, Chanda stood in front of Ben and began to undress. He reached for her, but she told him, "No. Not yet." Once she was naked, she started undressing Ben. Again he reached for her, and again she said, "Uh, uh. I'm in charge here."

Once they were both naked, Chanda pulled Ben closer, and she let him touch her, tentatively at first, then with more urgency. Chanda guided him onto the bed without even pulling the covers over them; the room was warm, and she didn't care about covering up for modesty's sake. She sensed neither of them wanted to wait an instant longer.

Ben's fingertips caressed Chanda's cheekbone, then slid between her breasts, then lower. Chanda's breathing quickened. She allowed his explorations for about a dozen quick breaths, then pulled his hand away. She pressed gently on his shoulders until he was lying on his back. She kissed him, light pecks on his lips this time, then slid her thigh over his. She smiled at Ben's immediate response. She kissed his nearly hairless chest, then moved down his body.

Ben lasted maybe six or seven of his own rushed breaths, then pulled her forward. Chanda straddled him and began to move. Soon rational thought, responsibility, and consequences were part of a foreign realm.

Her time arrived within moments, as she was seldom capable of, and she closed her eyes tightly as that other realm receded and reality flowed back into her consciousness. Still joined to Ben, she brought her upper body down onto his and whispered. "I'm sorry, I know it hasn't happened for you yet."

The catch in Ben's voice surprised her. "It's all right."

"I'm not usually so . . . well, *sexual*."

"That's . . . OK."

"I'm not much for typical notions of romance, as you can imagine. That's what I've been missing in my love life, I suppose. Romance. You know, someday I want to make love on the beach, or in a cottage next to an ocean."

"What made you think of that?"

"Just that I've never done it. We originated in the sea. Sexuality brings us back there. Perspiration. Lubrication. Ejaculation."

"A gift from the sea, then," Ben said.

"I think so."

"Maybe you're more romantic than you think. You had your gift. I . . . think I'm ready for mine."

Chanda rose up on her hands and moved to help him find it.

———

For Chanda, the best part was the cuddling afterwards, her back to his front. It was different with a Human; Ben wasn't as bony as her former Arol husband Pordo; his skin was much smoother, softer than she'd remembered a Human male's skin being. She fit into his arms more easily, as if nature had measured them and molded their forms into the optimum shape for such closeness.

And Ben *smelled* right. She'd forgotten how much she enjoyed that post-coital Human scent. Perhaps because she'd enjoyed such couplings too few times before.

An instinct born of years spent on Splendor tried to kick in now — *What's next?* she wondered. *Do I keep cuddling awhile, do I get up and we talk things out, do I just slip out of bed and slink back to my own room?*

But her mind couldn't muster the energy needed to make the decision, and her exhausted body took over and guided her, unknowing, toward sleep.

Chanda was disoriented when the first stirrings of wakefulness came upon her, before she opened her eyes or her mind formed words. She was lying on her left side and, besides feeling the usual pressure to pee, she felt an unaccustomed warmth against her back. Her left arm was tingling in a way that told her she may have been lying on it all night. Her legs ached as if she'd run a marathon the day before.

And beneath the sheet and blanket covering her, she wasn't wearing a nightgown, or anything else, for that matter.

Her eyes blinked open and she opened her eyes wide to try to take in details of her surroundings.

Ben's bedroom. Of course. The warm presence behind her.

Remembering their activities of the night before explained the aching in her legs, and . . . elsewhere. She'd used muscles that weren't used to such exertions.

She eased out from beneath the bed coverings, and gasped at the relative chill of the air contrasted with the warmth of the bed.

Chanda made her way toward the bathroom. Before closing the door, she looked back at the bed, as Ben stirred and absently embraced Chanda's pillow.

I'm confused, Chanda thought, *and don't even know why. I don't regret anything Ben and I didn't last night. In fact, I'm a lot warmer than I should be in this chilly room just thinking about what we did, and how many times we did it. I'm pretty sure four's a personal best. Not to mention an impressive show of vigor from Ben.*

As she left the bathroom, Chanda crossed the bedroom and slid beneath the covers to wake Ben with kisses. He smiled and pulled her to him without even opening his eyes.

When he finally did look at Chanda, Ben's grin grew wider. Chanda asked, "What?"

"We've left so much unsaid between us the last few days . . . I'm just surprised."

Chanda tapped a finger against Ben's chest. "We didn't say a whole lot to each other last night."

Ben's expression turned serious. "Maybe we should have."

"What do you mean? I'm not ashamed about anything we did."

Ben ran the tips of his fingers from Chanda's brow down to her chin. "Neither am I. It was a pleasant surprise, in fact. I had no idea you were so . . . passionate."

Chanda's shoulders were cold and she pulled the covers up to her neck. "I'm not, usually."

"I consider that a compliment. So . . . you're saying we have nothing to worry about?"

Chanda rolled her eyes. "You're exasperating! The first time in months, maybe years, I've thought about something other than being an ambassador, or whatever I am these days, the best night of sex I've had in my life, and you're worried about *us*? I think *we're* doing great."

"I have to ask, Chanda. Whatever's next for you — is it *us* doing it?"

"I'd like that . . . if you want."

"How about we make a deal? From now on, it's OK to assume

each of us wants to be where the other is, each of us is willing to sacrifice something of ourselves for the other. Because if we are, it isn't really a sacrifice."

Chanda held out her hand. "Deal."

They shook hands. Then pulled one another closer.

CHAPTER 36

Chanda listened as Indirogar was memorialized by those gathered in the *Nivara 2*'s viewing room. Curtains covered the twelve-meter-wide viewport that normally brought people there. Chanda sat near the front of the room with Ben, Irene, and Akira on her right, and Ambassador Galt and Captain Bram on her left. Around them were many others who had known Indirogar personally, or at least by reputation — the valley dweller Dijirar, his friend and former trading partner, his rival and eventual successor Roraten, the Sobrenian Govanek, and standing linked together off to one side, the twelve individuals making up the Buruden ambassador.

Chanda listened to others' words as they recalled Indirogar's bravery, his skill with his spear, his determination to protect his people from the danger Humans had convinced him would arrive in a few decades.

When Chanda's turn to speak arrived, she stood before those gathered and realized she'd barely given a thought to what she might say. *Which is disrespectful to him,* Chanda thought. *I'm not being a good friend.*

Just start talking, she thought. *You'll find the words.*

"Indirogar encompassed the best of his people," she said. "Others have spoken of his bravery and skill. I'll best remember him for his compassion. It may not have been the first quality you thought of when you saw him aiming his spear or arguing the fine points of high-lander politics. But I believe it's what drove him to sacrifice so much for his people."

Chanda felt the tears began to flow and didn't try to stop them or wipe them away. "I believe it's what drove him to throw that spear at Tiernan — yes, to hell with his adopted name. Irene and I owe our lives to Indirogar. If I can live the rest of that life he gave me with half the commitment and compassion he had, I would consider it a success."

Then the ceremony was over, but most of those gathered remained to speak with one another and perhaps share a drink. Chanda and Ben wandered over to one side of the room and Chanda poured them both a cup of hot tea. They found themselves next to Captain Bram and Ambassador Galt.

The curtains covering the viewport withdrew. The planet Splendor dominated the view to the left, all clouds and water and ice. The view to their right was of a heavily damaged Sobrenian warcraft, its usual water drop shape shattered and mangled.

"That's the *Merusta*," Captain Bram told Chanda. "The Sobrenian flagship. You're a bit familiar with it, of course."

Chanda said, "It looks like Irene and I got away just in time."

"The Sobrenians look down upon the Buruden, sometimes consider them comical. But they know how to fight. They took the brunt of the battle. We didn't lose any Unity ships. Very few casual-ties, no fatalities on our part."

"It's horrible to watch the Buruden in battle, though — sending troops onto enemy ships even as their own warcraft try to destroy them. They take a lot of casualties, many of them at the hands of their own people."

Ambassador Galt said, "It's not the same for them, of course. Individuals don't mean much to them. But I agree — it would be awful to watch."

"I can't help thinking of the Buruden individual that took Irene and me down to Splendor. I don't even have a name to call it, of course, and I can't even say it was brave — it was working entirely on instinct and training."

Chanda looked out at Splendor. The view was almost directly above the Strait of Ancestors, a narrow channel less than a kilometer across that separated two great land masses. Many valley dwellers could only reach their highlander trading partners by crossing the strait, which they accomplished by hopping across ice floes.

"Such a beautiful world," Chanda said.

Galt said, "You say that as if you're going to be missing it soon."

Chanda smiled. "That's a nice way of asking what I've decided."

"You might as well give up," Ben said. "She won't tell me, either."

"Not won't, *can't*. The truth is, I don't know." *How can I decide?* Chanda wondered. *Splendor has meant so much to me — it's become my home, and everyone from Irene and Akira to Indirogar and Dijirar are my family.*

Galt said, "The Unity's going to be reducing its presence here, with the evacuation effort cancelled, and with the Buruden moving in. There may not be that much for you to do here."

"Think about what Humanity has done to this world since Mike Christopher first came here twelve years ago. We've disrupted their societies, shown them tech that seems like magic to them. They can't go back. They'll want more."

Captain Bram said, "We did more than that. Our research showed this was the original Buruden homeworld. We helped the Buruden stave off the Sobrenian attack."

"But what will the Buruden — " Chanda shut up as a dozen linked Buruden approached. "We are the ambassador," Chanda heard.

Ambassador Galt said, "On behalf of the Earth Unity, I thank you for what you've done to save this planet."

"It's our home," the Buruden said. "It's what we had to do. A truth."

Chanda asked, "What do you intend to do now?"

"We are dismantling our city on our former homeworld. We are building more starcraft and will resettle our species here on Splendor."

"What about the species already here — the valley dwellers, highlanders, sweepers?"

"They are part of us. Our flesh, as surely as any of us standing before you."

"But they think so differently from you. Their individuals have a much more determined sense of self."

"Just as Humans do. We will use our experiences dealing with Humans in our relations with them. Above all, we will be patient, and hope they can be, as well."

Ben asked, "But what about the gas nebula? Should you really be moving your entire species to a planet where all life could be destroyed in a few decades?"

"We will eliminate the gas nebula."

"What!" Chanda exclaimed. "How's that possible?"

"Any number of ways — if we can launch several sweepers into space, they can create a stardrive jump field wide enough to envelop a Splendor-sized area of the nebula. We send a mass of the nebula elsewhere and create a hole that Splendor will simply pass through at the proper moment."

"You're talking — some kind of super-science here. Real Arthur Clarke advanced-technology-looking-like-magic stuff."

"Not all of that translated, but we understand the concept. If that would not work, perhaps we can station moon-sized objects close enough to the nebula to steer it away from Splendor. Or perhaps we can develop other techniques."

"You say that so calmly."

"We have many decades ahead of us to consider the matter. But we would be interested in the method Direg mentioned — the one on his datalink."

Chanda sighed. "He was lying, just as he admitted there at the end. There was nothing on his datalink about a way to eliminate the gas nebula."

Galt told the Buruden, "If there's anything we can do to help you — anything at all — let us know."

"You can promise such assistance?"

"Well, I . . . I can promise to make your case to the Unity in the strongest terms possible."

"Such are the promises of individualistic species. We Buruden decide what we want and move forward without hesitation."

"I see," Galt said.

"We appreciate Humanity's help, and approve of your continued presence on Splendor. You may maintain your embassy at its current location. You may travel wherever you wish, explore as you wish."

"Thank you," Chanda said. "That's very generous."

"Know, however, this truth. For some time Humanity has, in a way, been in charge of Splendor's fate. That stops now."

Galt said, "We never intended to — "

"Intention does not matter," the Buruden said. "Splendor belongs to the Buruden and its descendants again. The valley dwellers and highlanders did not know the nature of star systems and higher technology when you contacted them. They could not challenge your plans. Their very cultures have been altered. The sweepers are more advanced, but limited due to their large size. Their challenges to Human authority had only mixed success."

Chanda said, "We were trying to *save* the sweepers, and everyone else!"

"Please understand, we know that Humanity did its best, and did much good work. We thank you. But we accept the responsibility for Splendor's future now."

Chanda could tell from Galt's pursed lips and the way he folded his hands in front of him that he was pissed. But his voice was neutral as he said, "Very well, then. We appreciate the opportunity to remain and perform research."

Without another word, the Buruden unlinked and left the viewing room in single file.

"Well," Galt said, "I suppose that settles that."

Chanda asked Galt, "Are you going to stay?"

"A few weeks, until someone else is assigned."

Chanda turned to Captain Bram. "What about you?"

"Most likely *Nivara 2*'s going to be taking the ambassador here back to Earth. Any Unity presence at Splendor will most likely just be exploratory ships from here on out. Chanda — if I don't get the chance later, I just wanted to tell you it's been a pleasure and an honor serving with you all these years." He held out his hand and Chanda took it, then pulled him into a brief embrace.

As they broke the embrace, Bram cleared his throat. "I have some inspections to make." He nodded to Chanda and Galt and left as Govanek approached.

"I could not help but overhear," the Sobrenian said. "I, too, must say goodbye to you, Chanda."

"I thought you'd stay here and continue your research with the Buruden."

"It has been a fascinating time. But I wish to explore many other worlds, as well. I'll also be on the *Nivara 2* as it heads toward Earth. I'm to be a crewmember aboard the *Asaph Hall* with my friend Mike Christopher."

"Well, if that isn't something," Chanda said. "You know I'm sometimes cynical around explorers. But I could never be cynical about you, Govanek. I admire your enthusiasm. I appreciate what you had to sacrifice to help us."

"I thank you for that. Now I must go prepare for my new life." Govanek turned briskly and headed for the door.

Ben said, "Sort of the anti-Tiernan, isn't he? I think we got the better deal."

"Yeah." Chanda turned to Galt: "So back to Earth for you."

"I have to get home while my grandchildren are still little enough to bounce on my knee. What are you going to do? You haven't been home in quite a while."

"Home for you is Earth. But I grew up on the New Lancaster Habitat. I spent much of my youth just wanting to get away from it. I won't be going back to Earth system anytime soon."

"So maybe you'll stay on Splendor after all?"

"There's still work to do," Chanda said. She noticed, off to one side, Dijirar and Roraten speaking to one another. "I don't think the Buruden give us enough credit for what we did. But they're right — we changed the valley dwellers' and highlanders' cultures. Whether it's for the better or not, I don't know. But if I could help them get through those changes . . . it would be worthwhile."

Galt said, "You saved the planet when you landed the first *Nivara* here and created an instant embassy. You saved the Buruden aboard their hospital ship that crashed here. You were invaluable during the negotiations on the Sobrenian homeworld and the planet the Buruden are about to evacuate. You supported the archeological project that led to the discovery that this is the real Buruden home-world. You've done more than anybody to help this planet."

"I . . . thanks. Your acknowledging that means more than I can say."

"Chanda, when I first came to Splendor, I had my doubts about you. So did the Unity — that's why it sent me here. But it shouldn't have worried. You always had the best interests of this planet and its people at heart."

"Maybe to the exclusion of the Unity's interests at times. That could be the real reason they sent you."

"I know better. You're an overachiever, Chanda. You've been serving two masters all these years — the Unity *and* Splendor. You wanted everyone to win."

"Yeah. I suppose I did."

"Soon after I met you, I was talking about all the time you spent in stasis, your parents dying, your marriage to Pordo."

Chanda looked away from Galt. "You did." She made herself turn back toward him and look him in the eye. "You were kinda rude about it, actually."

"I realize that, now. I'm sorry. You've been through a lot in your life. I think it gave you a respect for what other people go through. I think you've sacrificed a lot to help others. But it's time you thought more of yourself for awhile. And I don't think you can do that while you're still on this planet. You need fresh surroundings, different responsibilities — or no responsibilities for awhile."

Chanda said, "I've come to respect you, too, you know. I didn't know whether I should at first. But I've learned there's more to you than I realized."

"I appreciate that, Chanda. But you're not responding to what I just told you."

Ben said, "She does that a lot."

Galt told Chanda, "Indecision's never been a problem with you before. I'll be eager to hear what's next for you."

"And what about you?"

"Back to Earth. Grandchildren, you know. What about you?"

"Still deciding. The Unity says I could stay on here. Be the ambassador again. But I've got some other options, too."

"My only advice -- make sure you're making the best decision for yourself. You deserve it." Galt left.

The *Nivara 2*'s orbit had left the Strait of Ancestors behind and brought Skyreach Mountain into view. Its peak extended from low-hanging clouds, but just to the east the clouds cleared and Chanda could make out the extended mountain range called the Heavenlock Mountains, and the glacier flow that extended to its east. The icy surface of the glacier had remained smooth during much of its slow descent down one of the mountain, but turned rocky and disordered as it came to a halt.

Dijirar and Roraten approached. Dijirar said, "Roraten and I have been talking, mostly of re-establishing trade now that most of the valley dwellers and highlanders are back home. But of other things, as well. We understand the Unity will withdraw much of its presence here."

"Which I, to be blunt, approve of," Roraten said.

Dijirar gave the highlander a sideways glance. "I, however, shall miss our Human friends. We hope some of you are staying. Especially our friend Chanda, who has done so much for us."

Chanda said, "I haven't decided yet."

Irene and Akira came up to them. Irene said, "That's all we've heard from her."

Dijirar said, "The last time we spoke, Chanda, you told us of harsh truths — that the Unity might abandon Splendor. But it did not. My people will remember that."

"My own people," Roraten said, "will remember how the Human presence has changed them forever. We will see if it has been for better or worse." Roraten headed for the door, not looking to see whether Dijirar followed.

My life is more than my work here on Splendor. Making the break with my adoptive family, marrying Pordo — not everything has worked out the way I'd hoped, but I've become stronger, more sure of myself every time I've taken a chance.

Dijirar, for her part, said, "New friendships are often trying, are they not?" She left, as well.

Akira asked, "So what's it going to be, Chanda? We can't just stand here waiting for you forever."

Perhaps those times are over. Perhaps the way I'll grow stronger now is to hold fast, stay on Splendor, know it and its people more deeply, maintain my commitment. She asked, "What are you and Irene going to do next?"

Irene said, "Go wherever you do — if you'll have us."

"That might mean staying right here on Splendor."

"If that's what you want," Ben said.

"Or maybe Ambassador Galt's right — maybe fresh surroundings would be good."

Irene said, "We'll all go there with you, Chanda."

"Or wildest idea of all — a vacation!"

Akira spoke up. "I'd like that!"

Either way, that's how I have to decide — not just by looking at Splendor and what it means to me, but at my entire life. Time to leave emotional stasis. Time to wake up for good.

With that realization, Chanda's decision became clear.

Ben was looking at her with a knowing smile. "You've decided, haven't you?"

"I have."

"Then tell us!"

She did.

ABOUT THE AUTHOR

Dave Creek is the author of the novels *Some Distant Shore*, novellas *Tranquility* and *The Silent Sentinels*, and short story collections *A Glimpse of Splendor* and *The Human Equations*.

He's also published the Great Human War trilogy, including *A Crowd of Stars* (2016 Imadjinn Award winner), *The Fallen Sun*, and *The Unmoving Stars*.

His short stories have appeared in ANALOG SCIENCE FICTION AND FACT and APEX magazines, and the anthologies *Far Orbit Apogee*, *Touching the Face of the Cosmos*, and *Dystopian Express*.

Keep in touch with Dave Creek:
www.davecreek.com
Dave@davecreek.com

www.ingramcontent.com/pod-product-compliance
Lightning Source LLC
Chambersburg PA
CBHW070723280626

47159CB00023B/2372